BLACK MAGIC

Raising his arms and closing his eyes, he began to chant silently, invoking the forces of evil. Then he reached with one hand for a shallow pottery bowl on the altar, pulling it closer. The long, dark fingers of his other hand disappeared in the folds of his robe, and, a moment later, produced two cardboard rectangles.

He stared at them for a long moment. Finally, with a flourish, he dropped them so that they fluttered into the shallow bowl, landing face up.

Identical pairs of eyes stared at him from the photographs—black, almond-shaped, exotic eyes.

One pair belonged to Megan McKenna.

The other pair of eyes were Candra Bowen's, captured in a shot he had snapped surreptitiously on the street just the other day.

He met their unsuspecting, frozen stares with a narrowed gaze and reached for a small vial on the altar. He poured the few ounces of liquid it contained into the bowl. Now the familiar faces watched him from beneath the watery surface.

A long black candle burned beside him, and he carefully removed it from its holder. In one swift movement, he passed the flame over the bowl, then watched as the contents ignited.

He had only one last fleeting glimpse of the faces before both photographs were obliterated to ashes in the furious orang

A sinister s

BOOKS BY WENDY MORGAN

OBSESSION

POSSESSION

Published by Pinnacle Books

WENDY
MORGAN
POSSESSION

PINNACLE BOOKS
Kensington Publishing Corp.
http://www.kensingtonbooks.com

One

Elmont Avenue was the broad main drag in what had once been a colorful section of Spring City. Years ago, the neighborhood had been home to jazz bars, night-clubs, and restaurants that had drawn the wealthy New Yorkers who summered in Westchester County and Connecticut. Now many of those places had been turned into sleazy bars or X-rated video stores, and some of them were boarded up or falling down. Bums lay in doorways, and the occasional hooker paraded down the street or loitered on the corner. Shady char-acters congregated here and there, and shifty-eyed kids roamed around looking for trouble.

Amidst the seedy atmosphere there was a conclave of immigrants from the Caribbean region. Many of them worked for the wealthy families in nearby Crawford Cor-ners or Greenwich.

As a result of their presence, new businesses had begun to crop up on the Elmont strip. Small fruit and vegetable markets sold plantains and papayas and man-gos. Secondhand stores featured bright-colored clothing and beaded jewelry. And a few dimly lit occult shops sold herbs and incense and special powders, among other things.

It was in front of one of these shops that Candra Bowen parked her twin sister Meg's Honda. She stepped out, set the alarm, and looked around again to make sure Meg's boyfriend Shea's car wasn't lurking somewhere nearby. She hadn't seen it behind her as she drove here, though she felt vaguely aware of a lingering sense of danger.

Still, the car was nowhere to be seen. She must be imagining things.

Candra walked briskly toward the shop. She pushed the door open and was greeted by the sound of reggae music and a pungent, spicy aroma that instantly carried her back to Jamaica.

Caught off guard by an unexpected wave of homesickness, she hesitated in the doorway.

"Good mornin', my lady, can I help you today?" a voice said in a familiar, lilting dialect.

Candra turned and saw an enormous woman sitting in the corner, beside a counter. Her skin was so black that her eyes and teeth looked stark in contrast, and her round body was clad in a garish turquoise and orange caftan.

"Yeah, *mon*, I need to buy a few things." As soon as the words had left her lips, Candra realized she'd forgotten to use the American accent that had started to become second nature to her. Now her accent was as pronounced as the shopkeeper's Jamaican *patois*.

She shifted uncomfortably and looked hard at the woman, who didn't seem fazed.

She merely nodded, and, with a grunt, hoisted her enormous heft out of the chair. She lumbered over to stand behind the long glass counter that lined one wall of the shop. On a shelf behind the counter was a portable tape player and a stack of tapes. She reached up and turned down the volume, then turned back to Candra.

"And what items would you be needin' today, my

lady?" the woman asked, motioning around. "I have everything here. Everything. You see?"

Candra stepped over and glanced at the objects that were arranged inside the counter on a tattered length of black velvet. There were pentacles, chalices, and ritual knives with carved handles. There were cords of different materials and colors, and bowls and incense burners. On a wide tray at one end was an arrangement of wands, some of them crystal, some made of wood or silver.

"You need something in this case, *mon*?" prodded the woman. "What do you need? Let me take something out and show you."

"No, nothing that's in there," Candra said, and turned around. "I need . . ."

She trailed off. Against the opposite wall was a wide network of shelves that were lined with stacks of vials and jars and candles and paper-wrapped packages.

That was more like it. She moved over and started to inspect the contents of the shelves.

"You browse, my lady," the woman said as the reggae song ended. "I'm going to change this cassette tape. Maybe we hear some Bob Marley, eh?"

Candra nodded, scanning a row of small jars. *There.* She reached up and selected one that contained a rust-colored powder. One ingredient down, two to go.

She moved over to a display of vials that held different oils. It didn't take her long to locate the one she needed.

Behind her, the reggae music had started on the tape player again, and the woman asked, "You finding what you want, *mon*?"

"Mmm hmm."

Now for the last item. Candra examined a neat stack

of paper-wrapped parcels, each marked with the name of a different root. She found the one she needed and pulled it off the shelf, then walked back over to the woman.

She set the items on the counter and said, "That's it."

The woman nodded and turned to the cash register. As she rang in the last item, she looked up at Candra. "These three things together will cast a powerful spell, my lady."

Candra nodded. She met the woman's scrutiny with a level gaze of her own.

After a moment, the woman shook her head and muttered, "That's your business."

"That's right," Candra agreed, reaching for Meg's wallet. "How much do I owe you?"

Shea looked at his watch as the waitress walked away after taking his and Mirabelle's order.

"What's wrong?" Mirabelle asked, though she knew. Shea wasn't the type of boy who would take cutting school lightly. But she knew he was desperate to make sure Meg was all right. "You're going to miss another class?"

He nodded, then said, "It's okay. This is more important." He leaned forward, propped his elbow, rested his chin on his open hand, and looked at her. "Tell me what's going on."

Mirabelle took a deep breath. "I don't know where to start."

"The beginning is always a good place," Shea prompted.

So she started there. She told him how, the first time

she had met Meg, at Zoe's party, she had sensed that Meg had powers.

"Powers?" Shea repeated incredulously. "What are you talking about?"

And so Mirabelle had to backtrack even further, and tell him about Cecile, her family's maid back in New Orleans, and her own voodoo powers. She could see the doubt building in Shea's expression as she talked, and finally, she broke off and said, "You don't believe me."

"You're right," he told her as the waitress came back to their booth with a tray. "I don't."

Mirabelle waited until the woman had set down a steaming cup of coffee in front of her and a foamy, whipped-cream-topped hot chocolate in front of Shea, then walked away again.

Then she said, "I know it's not something that seems plausible at first, Shea, but you've got to believe me."

"You're trying to tell me Meg McKenna—my *girlfriend*—is a witch?" he asked, and shook his head. "Impossible."

"That's not what I'm trying to tell you at all. You're missing the point. I'm saying that Meg has a certain—energy—that, should she choose to develop it, could allow her to have control over different aspects of her life, and other people's lives."

"Uh-huh, right." Shea sipped his cocoa.

Frustrated, Mirabelle dumped creamer into her coffee, stirred it, then set the spoon down and said, "Look, whether or not you believe this is beside the point. The real issue here is that Meg's gotten involved in something that's way over her head."

"What do you mean?"

Mirabelle told him everything she knew then—about the box Mirabelle had found in her grandmother's attic, and about the mystery surrounding her birth, and about Dalila Parker, the enigmatic woman who had mistaken her for someone else. Someone who looked just like Meg.

Shea listened and asked an occasional question. She could tell that though he found some of this surprising, he didn't seem to doubt any of it.

She concluded with how, on Monday afternoon, Meg had gone over to Dalila's apartment to meet the twin sister she had never known. And how, ever since then, she'd been distant and—well, different.

"You're right about that," Shea said. "We broke up Monday night. I went over to her house, just like I'd told her I would. We were going to get back together— we'd talked about it at school that afternoon, and she'd told me she would explain everything that night. I guess she was going to tell me all the stuff you just did."

"Probably."

"But she didn't. When I got there that night, she was acting really strange."

"Strange, how?"

"I don't know . . . not like herself. What do you think happened, Mirabelle?"

She hesitated. If she told him what she suspected, would he think she was out of her mind?

There was only one way to find out.

She sipped her coffee, put her cup down, and cleared her throat. "I think that the reason Meg's not acting like Meg is because she's *not*."

"She's not what?"

"Not *Meg*." Mirabelle looked Shea in the eye and said, "Meg's gone, Shea. The person you and I just saw driving her car was Candra."

* * *

Out on the avenue again, Candra tucked the small brown paper bag into Meg's leather purse and decided to walk the few blocks to Dalila Parker's apartment over Rivera's Newsstand.

As she moved down the sidewalk she attracted whistles and catcalls from men on the street, and honks from those who passed by in cars.

She couldn't help being pleased at the attention.

She was still wearing the plaid school uniform, but it was short enough to show off her long, lean legs. She swung her hair as she moved down the street, feeling momentarily carefree.

Then, as she waited to cross a busy side street, she felt a prickle of awareness coming over her again.

Startled, she looked around, half-expecting to see Shea's car behind her.

It wasn't there.

But the sensation grew steadily stronger.

Someone was nearby.

Who?

The light changed and Candra moved across the street. When she reached the opposite curb, she looked over her shoulder again, then scanned the sidewalk and street ahead. She didn't see anything out of the ordinary. Cars and buses moved along, and here and there, people loitered or walked or sat on steps, all of them strangers.

Puzzled, Candra picked up her pace.

Again, she glanced over her shoulder.

Behind her on the sidewalk she saw an older white woman dressed in shabby clothes and carrying shopping bags, and, farther back, a young-looking black man who was walking along with his head down.

She'd never seen either of them before.

And yet . . .

She couldn't shake the eerie feeling that she was being shadowed.

She crossed another street. This was the last block before Dalila's. She walked quickly, as though that would allow her to escape whatever, or whoever, was making her anxious.

But the feeling grew more intense.

She looked back again. The woman who'd been there was gone.

Now only the young black man remained. He wore black pants and a black coat, Candra noted vaguely. He was too far behind her for her to make out his features, but he raised his head, and Candra could feel him staring at her.

He's just some neighborhood guy—probably one of the ones who whistled at me before, she told herself.

But she wasn't reassured.

There was something about him—something that made her uneasy.

Candra turned her head again and kept walking, fighting back the sense of panic that was building inside her.

A few more steps, and she had reached Rivera's Newsstand. She stopped in front of the door that led to Dalila's apartment above, then looked over her shoulder one more time.

The man was gone.

But she knew that he was still nearby. He might not be watching her, but he was in tune with her on a deeper, *darker* level.

The realization made her tremble.

She hesitated, wondering what to do.

But what *could* she do? The man was a stranger. He'd done nothing but walk down the street.

Get hold of yourself, Candra, she thought, and took a deep breath, let it out slowly.

Could it be that all the stress she had been through lately was causing her mind to play tricks on her?

Was she imagining danger where there was none?

That had to be it, she concluded. Just her imagination.

It *had* to be.

Mirabelle looked at Shea as they walked out of the diner, leaving behind their unfinished beverages and a few dollars they'd tossed on the table to cover the bill.

"Are you all right?" she asked again.

"Fine," he repeated. "Really."

But he didn't look fine at all. His handsome face was pale and she could see his hands trembling as he fumbled in his pocket for the car keys.

He unlocked the passenger's side door and opened it for her, then went around to the other side and climbed in. As he put the keys into the ignition, Mirabelle reached out and touched his sleeve.

"Wait," she said. "Shea, I know you need to get back to class, but—"

"No," he interrupted. "I'm not going back to school today. I just . . . I can't."

"What about—I mean, won't you get into trouble?"

He shrugged.

Mirabelle hesitated, then said, "Look, Shea, I know you're pretty shocked right now. I feel the same way, believe me. But we've both got to get past that and concentrate on what's important."

"Meg," he said in a voice that was barely audible.

She nodded. "We've got to find her."

"We've got to go to the police."

"We can't," Mirabelle said immediately.

"Why not?"

"What would we tell them? That Meg is missing, even though she's not? That Meg isn't Meg, even though she looks just like her? They'll think we're nuts."

"Not if we explain the whole story."

"We can't. There's no proof of anything. And besides, we don't *know* the whole story. There's way more to this than you can imagine."

"What do you mean by that?"

"I mean, it's just like I told you before. Meg is mixed up in something very . . . dark. Something the police have no control over."

"Yeah, right. Meg's a witch."

Frustrated by his mocking tone, Mirabelle folded her arms and looked out the window.

After a moment of silence, Shea cleared his throat and said, "I'm sorry, Mirabelle. It's just that I have a hard time believing that my girlfriend, who is the most normal person in the world, has some kind of magical powers, or whatever."

She looked at him. "I told you, she wasn't even aware of them."

"I know what you told me." He sighed. "Aside from that, what are we talking about here?"

"Voodoo. Black Magic. Whatever you want to call it— that's what's happening, on some level. And we have to be extremely careful, Shea. This isn't something you handle lightly."

He was staring at her in disbelief. "Voodoo. Black magic," he echoed, then slapped the steering wheel and shook his head. "Mirabelle, no offense, but I don't buy it."

"Why not?"

"There's no such thing as magic."

"Maybe not in your world—at least, not that you know of. But where I come from, it's real, Shea, and you don't mess with it. You have to believe me when I tell you that Meg stumbled into something that's way over her head, and there's no easy way out."

"How do you know?"

She paused. She couldn't tell him about the strange, dark-skinned man she'd seen outside Meg's house, and again on the street near campus. It didn't necessarily mean anything—at least, it wouldn't to Shea. But the more Mirabelle thought about the man, the more certain she was that he was part of something powerful—and sinister.

"Mirabelle? How do you know all this?" Shea asked again.

"Intuition," she said simply.

She waited for him to scoff again.

But he didn't. He was just quiet for a long time.

Mirabelle looked out the window. Outside, the day that had started off sunny and unseasonably warm had become gray and chilly. When she got back to campus, she'd have to go back to her room for a jacket before going to class.

For some reason, she thought of Ben Schacter, then promptly tried to push the image of him out of her head.

It wouldn't budge.

She saw his face again, felt his reassuring grasp on her hand. . . .

With Ben, she had felt safe. She'd been removed from this whole crazy Meg thing in those fleeting moments they'd spent together. Ben was so solid, so levelheaded . . .

How would he react if he knew what Mirabelle was tangled up in? Would he think she was out of her mind? Or would he somehow be able to help?

Of course he couldn't help, she told herself. *Don't even think of dragging him into this. Don't even think of having anything to do with him, period. You already made up your mind to steer clear of guys like Ben. Remember what happened with Alex?*

Shea's voice startled her. "So if we don't go to the police," he said abruptly, "what do you suggest we do?"

It took a moment for Mirabelle to focus again. When she did, she realized that until now, she'd had no idea what they should do. All she knew was that they had to find out where Meg was.

But as she thought about it, she realized that there was one person who might be able to help.

"Dalila Parker," she said resolutely.

Shea blinked. *"What?"*

"Dalila Parker. She's the woman I told you about, the one who was supposed to introduce Meg to Candra."

"What about her? You think she knows where Meg is?"

Mirabelle hesitated. "I don't know. If she *does* . . . then I guess it would mean she's involved somehow. Although I doubt that. I didn't get that kind of feeling about her."

"You don't think she'd hurt Meg?"

"I don't think she would. But . . ." Mirabelle shook her head. She'd been so distracted lately, could she really trust her own perception of Dalila?

She sat up straight and looked at Shea.

"Mirabelle? Now what?"

"If you're not going back to school, let's go over there

and see what we can find out," she said, motioning at
the keys in the ignition. "Come on."

"Where is 'there'?"

"Elmont Avenue in Spring City."

"Elmont Avenue! Do you know what kind of neighborhood that is?"

"Yeah, it's pretty bad. But that's where Dalila lives.
And it's not that big a deal—we'll be fine. Come on,
Shea. Let's go." Suddenly, she felt an urgent need to get
to Dalila's.

He shrugged and, looking reluctant, started the engine.

Don't worry, Meg, Mirabelle thought as Shea pulled
out onto the highway. *We're going to find you and get you
out of this mess. Just hang in there, wherever you are.*

Two

"Candra? What are you doing here, *mon*?" Dalila Parker asked in her thick Jamaican accent. She stood in the doorway of her apartment wearing a flowered housedress and an orange turban wrapped around her head. Vibrant beaded earrings dangled against her cheeks, and on both wrists she wore stacks of brightly colored bangles.

"How have you been, *mon*?" Candra asked, shedding her American accent once again.

She stepped past the woman into the familiar apartment. The splashy color scheme was a stark contrast, not just to the cloudy day outside, but to the seedy neighborhood itself, and to the dingy stairway that led up to Dalila's door. Crossing the threshold was like walking into a Caribbean beach scene.

Candra glanced at the tropical fabric that covered the couch and chairs, the jungle of plants, the aquarium filled with exotic fish, and the parakeets in their bird-cages near the window. On the clean white walls were framed posters in coral and turquoise and yellow and purple, island-style art that depicted simply drawn stick people and animals.

"What do you want, *mon*?" Dalila asked again in her lilting *patois*.

Again, just as she had been earlier in the store, Candra was being swept by a wave of homesickness.

She forced it away.

It was bad enough that she'd been distracted by her wild imagination out on the street, when she'd convinced herself that that man was following her. She needed to gather her wits about her now.

She shot the woman a level look and forced her voice to sound businesslike. "I just wanted to see how things are going. You know, with . . ." She trailed off and gestured at the closed door that led to Dalila's bedroom.

Behind that door, she knew, Megan McKenna lay prone on the long dresser top, looking for all the world like she was merely asleep.

"It's fine, *mon*," Dalila said. "Why wouldn't it be?"

"Of course it's fine." Candra shrugged. Out of the corner of her eye, she spotted Dalila's cat, Erzulie, lying on a throw rug nearby.

Good, she thought. *This might work.*

"I also wanted to thank you, Dalila," she continued, reaching out and taking the woman's ebony-skinned hand in hers. She squeezed Dalila's fingers and injected a note of warmth into her tone. "I don't know what I would have done without you. You're the only one who's ever understood me. You cared enough about me to help me make my most precious dream come true, and I hope you know how much it means to me."

She raised her eyes and glanced at Dalila's face. The woman was studying her intently, and Candra could tell she wasn't entirely buying this sudden heap of gratitude.

No, Dalila was wary. And she should be.

But Candra was going to get past that.

"So? Did you meet your mother, like you wanted to?" Dalila asked, pulling her hand out of Candra's grasp.

"I'll tell you all about everything. Why don't we sit down and have a cup of tea?" Candra suggested.

Dalila tilted her head and shrugged. "Why not," she agreed. "I'll go put the water on. Come on into the kitchen with me."

"All right, but first I need to use your bathroom."

"Over there," Dalila said, jerking a thumb at a door on the opposite wall.

"Thanks." Candra made her way over. Inside the bathroom, she locked the door behind her and turned on the water in case Dalila was listening on the other side.

She unzipped her purse and, trying not to rattle the bag, took out the items she'd bought at the store down the street. She spread a tissue on the edge of the sink and swiftly sprinkled the powder and the herb into the center of it. She carefully folded the tissue, tucked it into her pocket, then opened the package containing the root. She removed a gnarled stalk half the length of a pencil and put that into her pocket, too.

Then she stashed the bag back in her purse, zipped it, and flushed the toilet. As she reached for the doorknob, she willed the room on the other side to be empty.

It was, except for the snoozing cat on the rug.

She could hear Dalila moving around in the kitchen.

Moving with combined stealth and speed, Candra slipped over to the door that led out to the hall. She opened it cautiously, just a crack. Then she approached Erzulie, who was still asleep a few feet away.

In one quick motion, she swooped down over the cat, picked her up, and deposited her in the hallway outside the door. She closed it with a quiet click, muffling the cat's startled *meow*.

Then she strolled into the kitchen, patting her pocket casually to make sure the tissue packet and the root were both still there.

"What kind of tea do you like?" Dalila asked, busy at the counter. She had taken two mugs out of the cupboard and was peering into a glass canister.

"What do you have?"

"Regular, camomile, rose hip . . ."

"Regular's fine."

"No problem, *mon*."

Candra watched as Dalila took out two tea bags and put one in each mug just as the kettle on the stove started rattling. Dalila quickly took it off the burner before the low-pitched whistle could build and poured steaming water into the cups.

"Have a seat," she said, gesturing at the small table in a corner of the tiny kitchen.

"Why don't we go into the living room?" Candra suggested quickly, then added, "My back is bothering me and I'll be more comfortable on the couch."

Dalila shrugged, picked up both mugs, and headed for the other room.

Candra followed, making a point of rubbing her shoulders as though they were aching. She settled back into the couch and said, "That feels good."

Dalila frowned. "What happened to your back, *mon*?"

"I don't know—I guess I pulled it out somehow." She watched as the woman set both mugs down on the coffee table in front of the couch. She was about to sit in a nearby chair when Candra looked around and said, "Where's Erzulie? Don't you have her anymore?"

"Of course I have her. She's right—" Dalila turned and started to gesture at the spot on the rug near the door where the cat had been snoozing. "She was right there. Where is she?"

"I haven't seen her." Candra leaned forward and pulled one of the mugs toward her. The other one was within easy reach. "I hope she didn't get out when you opened the door to let me in, Dalila."

"She does that sometimes, but I didn't think she— Erzulie, here kitty, kitty," the woman said, walking around the room and making kissing sounds. "Erzulie?"

"What was that?" Candra asked.

"What?" Dalila stopped and listened.

"I don't know, I just thought I heard a meowing sound coming from somewhere. Maybe out in the hall?"

Dalila frowned and crossed to the door.

Candra immediately reached into her pocket and withdrew the small tissue packet and the root.

As Dalila undid the locks and opened the door, Candra emptied the mixture of powder and herb into the mug that was farthest from her.

"Erzulie?" Dalila called stepping out into the hall. "Are you out here? Come on, kitty. . . ."

Candra swiftly stuck the root into the tea and stirred it around, chanting silently.

"There you are, you sneaky, naughty girl. What are you doing out here?" Dalila bent and scooped the cat into her arms, then closed and locked the door again and turned back to Candra. "I didn't even see her slip past me when I let you in," she said, shaking her head. "I must be getting old."

Candra tried to be casual about tucking the wet piece of root and crumpled tissue back into her pocket. "You're not getting old. I didn't see her do it either."

Dalila set the cat down and shook her head, coming

back over to the chair. She sat down and reached for her mug of tea. "Now tell me about your mother."

"Well, actually, she isn't around. She and Meg's step-father are out of the country."

"Out of the country? Where?" Dalila paused with the cup half-raised to her lips.

"In Fiji. On vacation. They won't be back for a few more days." She tried not to stare as the woman sipped her tea at last. To focus on something else, she averted her gaze and caught sight of Erzulie. The cat was a few feet away, sitting perfectly still. Her feline eyes were fixed intently on Candra, as if to say, *I know what you're up to.*

"Well," Dalila said, lowering the mug again, "If your mother's out of town, you're out of luck."

"What do you mean?"

"You only had one week to see her. In a few days, I take the spell off your twin in there."

"That's what I wanted to talk to you about."

"No, *mon.*"

"No, what?"

"No, I'm not going to extend the spell," Dalila said firmly. "We had a deal. It's a shame you didn't get to spend time with your mother, but that's not my fault. I can't be involved any longer than I agreed to be. I don't like this. I need to get your sister out of here."

"I didn't say she wouldn't be out of here." Candra sipped her own steaming tea and willed Dalila to drink more of hers.

As if spurred by the silent command, the woman raised her cup and downed some more. When she'd finished swallowing, she said, "What do you mean, *mon?* You want me to keep the spell on her and move her someplace else?"

A smile curved Candra's lips. "Exactly."

"No way, *mon*."

Drink some more tea, Dalila. Go ahead. Drink it down.

Candra said, "You don't even know what I want you to do."

Dalila seemed as though she was about to protest again, but instead she hesitated, then said, "Okay, what is it?"

Candra cleared her throat, leaned forward, and lowered her voice to a near-whisper. "I want you to take Meg out into the middle of nowhere, to the spot I picked out, and I want you to dig a hole, and I want you to put her in it. Do you understand what I'm saying?"

Dalila's eyes widened in dismay, but Candra noticed with satisfaction that they were beginning to look a little glassy. The spell was starting to work.

"You're talking about murder," Dalila protested, but her voice sounded almost flat. She set down her mug on the table.

Candra said nothing, just looked at her.

"I can't kill someone, Candra. I can't do that."

"Not even," Candra took a dainty sip of her own tea, "for a lot of money?"

"How much money?" Dalila asked, then in the next breath shook her head and said again, "No, *mon*. I can't kill someone."

"A hundred thousand dollars." Candra had planned to offer her more—as much as it took. But maybe it wouldn't take much. The woman was under a powerful spell.

"A hundred thousand dollars?" Dalila made a scoffing sound and picked up the mug again. "Where are you going to get that kind of money? You have nothing."

Candra tilted her head. "Don't be so sure, Dalila. I'm not Candra this week, remember? I'm Meg."

The woman stared at her.

"And as Meg," Candra continued, "I have everything Meg has. Everything I *should* have had all along. It's only right, Dalila. *It's my turn!*"

Her voice rose on the last three words and she clamped her mouth shut, struggling to remain calm.

"I see what you're saying, Candra," Dalila said. A tiny frown settled between her dark eyebrows. "But I can't do it."

"Why not? Think about the money. Think about *me*, Dalila. I've had nothing my whole life, because *she* stole it all from me." She jerked a hand in the direction of the closed bedroom door. "She had everything, the house, the clothes, the fancy school, the car—a family. She had a family. I had no one. She had our mother. As far as they were concerned, I didn't even exist!"

Candra stood up and her angry words blazed through the quiet room.

"You don't have to help me, Dalila. And I don't expect you to understand. But this past week, for the first time in my life, I've felt like I was *someone.* People have treated me differently. They've noticed me. They've respected me."

But it wasn't you, an inner voice intruded. *You were pretending to be someone else.*

She sank into the couch again and rubbed her temples. Suddenly, she was exhausted. She didn't want to try, any longer, to convince this woman to help her, and she didn't want to think about how miserable her life had been before she'd stepped into Meg's world.

She just wished everything would go away—Meg, Dalila, her mother . . .

And what about Landon Keller?

Just thinking about his all-American good looks, about the way he had kissed her, made Candra tingle.

And what about the money?

You know you don't want the money to go away. Landon either. You can have it all, and you will if you can just hold on a little longer. Don't give up on it now—not when you're so close . . .

She moved her hands from her face and looked up at Dalila.

The woman was sitting absolutely still, clutching her mug between her palms and staring off into space.

"Dalila?" Candra prodded.

As if she was coming out of a trance, Dalila blinked and focused on her. "Yeah, *mon*, I understand."

"What?"

"I understand what you're saying. I'll do it."

"Do what?"

"Whatever you say."

Candra felt a pinprick of guilt. *This isn't Dalila talking. It's the spell. She has no control over her own mind, her own actions, and she's sitting here agreeing to murder. Look what you've done.*

But Candra forced those thoughts away and focused on what was important.

"You'll help me?" she asked, just to be sure.

Dalila nodded. "Yeah, *mon*. For a hundred thousand dollars, I'll do it."

Power. What an exhilarating sense of power, knowing that her wish was this woman's command.

Money and magic—what a combination!

There's nothing you can't do, Candra told herself, feeling a delicious prickle of excitement. *There's nothing that can't be yours now.*

She fought the urge to hug herself in anticipation, instead folding her hands in her lap and focusing intently on Dalila's willing face.

"I'm glad you see things my way," she said smoothly. "Now here's you need to do . . ."

"Turn right! You can park right over there," Mirabelle said, pointing to a spot on a side street off of Elmont.

Shea automatically made the turn, but protested, "I can't leave the car on the street around here, Mirabelle. I mean . . . *look.*"

She glanced out the window and saw a group of scuzzy-looking teenage boys eyeing them from the steps of a run-down house nearby. "It'll be fine, Shea. It's broad daylight. No one's going to do anything."

"Yeah, right." Still, he pulled into the spot she'd indicated, between a twenty-year-old Buick that was missing its hubcaps and a rattletrap pickup truck with plastic sheeting fixed over the spot where the side window should have been. He put the car in Park and hesitated with his hand on the key, again looking nervously at the group of kids.

"Think of Meg," Mirabelle said, as a bum teetered along the sidewalk, sipping from a bottle in a paperbag.

"I *am* thinking of Meg. It makes me sick that she's been hanging around in this neighborhood, for God knows what reason. Do you know what kind of lowlifes there are around here? Do you know what they can do to innocent girls like Meg?"

Mirabelle just nodded. Now wasn't the time to remind him that Meg was apparently involved with people who were far more threatening than the vagrants and street kids on Elmont.

"Come on, Shea," she said, putting her hand on the door handle. "Let's go. This shouldn't take long. We just have to find out if Dalila knows anything."

He nodded and got out of the car. He shot a wary look at the kids on the steps as he locked the doors.

"Don't *worry*," Mirabelle said, grabbing his arm and pulling him across the street. "It's only a car."

"I know. But if something happens to it, my dad'll have a fit. He'll want to know what the hell I was doing in this section of town. He'll probably think I'm on drugs—he's always asking me about that."

"Your dad thinks you're on drugs?"

Shea shrugged as they walked around the corner onto Elmont. "It's because he used to be pretty messed up himself, before he went through rehab—which was after he left me and my mom. Now he's a model husband and father to his new family. And he keeps telling me to stay out of trouble. As if I'd want to get *into* trouble, after growing up watching what drugs and booze did to him."

"Mmm hmm." Mirabelle had stopped entirely listening to Shea. She looked over her shoulder as they headed down Elmont, then scanned the sidewalk ahead. Something wasn't right. She was getting bad vibes.

"Mirabelle?"

"Yeah?" She darted a glance at Shea, then checked over her shoulder again.

"I said, is everything all right?"

"Yeah." She picked up her pace. "Come on, let's get to Dalila's. It's a block away."

"You seem like something's wrong."

"Nothing's wrong." *Not that I can see. But there's something, somewhere . . .*

The block before Rivera's Newsstand was long and lined with several porn video stores, a run-down mom and pop market, and a few occult shops. The shops, most of which didn't have signs, were identifiable by the odd assortments of items displayed in the windows. Back in New Orleans, Mirabelle had been no stranger to places like these. But here she hadn't yet ventured into one—there had been no need. Yet.

Now, as she passed the last occult shop before the corner, she felt an almost magnetic tug. She turned, looked in the window, and gasped.

"What?" Shea asked, touching her sleeve as she stopped on the sidewalk. "What happened?"

She blinked and peered at the storefront.

"Mirabelle?"

"I just . . . it's . . . it's nothing," she said faintly, staring.

"Then why are you looking at that store like that?" Shea followed her line of vision. "Is that a *skull* in the window?"

Mirabelle nodded vaguely.

"No wonder you're freaked out."

"It's not a real one," she said, trying to focus on what he was saying. "It's carved, you know, like—a decoration."

"Nice," Shea said, shaking his head.

"Yeah, well, come on." She started walking again. "Dalila lives right over that newsstand across the street."

As they stood waiting for the light to change, Mirabelle threw one last look over her shoulder. She half-expected to see him standing there on the sidewalk, staring at her.

But he wasn't there.

No, and she was sure she had only imagined seeing the familiar glittering black eyes of the dark-skinned man watching her from inside that store.

"Do you understand everything?" Candra asked Dalila one more time.

"Yeah, *mon.*" She nodded, and Candra tried not to be bothered by the detached look in her eyes or the mechanical sound of her voice.

"Good. And you're sure you can do it?"

Dalila lifted a shoulder, as if to say, *Why not?* "No problem, *mon,*" she said in an offhand manner. As the spell had taken a more solid hold on her over the past hour, she had been entirely agreeable, not at all fazed by the details of Candra's plan.

It was Candra who was having a hard time with it. Even as she laid it out neatly, step-by-step, for Dalila, she found herself balking mentally, emotionally. It was all she could do to keep from telling Dalila to forget it, that she'd changed her mind, that she couldn't do something so drastic—at least, not just yet.

But then she kept reminding herself that *she* didn't have to do anything. It was Dalila who would handle the whole thing.

All Candra had to do was give orders . . . then leave, and never look back.

Now she set down her mug—the tea had long since grown cold—and rose from the couch, shaking her long hair back from her face. "I'm going to go now," she told Dalila. "I have a few details to take care of. But I need you to make sure that you—"

She broke off and stood absolutely still, listening, suddenly wary.

"What is it?" Dalila asked after a minute, watching Candra from her chair. "Did you hear something?"

"No, it's not that, I just . . ."

I felt something.

It was an all-too-familiar, keen awareness of something—or someone—threatening.

Whatever—*whoever*—it was, they were nearby.

Her thoughts flew to the dark-skinned man she'd glimpsed on the street earlier.

But no, it wasn't him. She was certain of that.

This sensation was different than the chill that had overtaken her as she'd walked to Dalila's. That had been stark, irrational fear.

This was more like a vague anxiety, the same thing she had felt when she'd been driving away from the school earlier. . . .

Could Shea and that strange Southern girl have followed her here? Were they lurking somewhere nearby?

She discarded the possibility, even as she acknowledged that she seemed to be sensing their presence again. It was impossible. She hadn't seen them behind her. She was positive of that.

But then . . .

"Somebody's here," Dalila said, as a door suddenly creaked somewhere downstairs.

Candra heard footsteps—two pairs of them—coming up the stairs. And though she didn't hear their voices, she was instantly certain that her instincts had been right. It was Meg's boyfriend and that nosy girl—she was sure of it. They had found her somehow.

She fixed Dalila with a grim, warning gaze and held a finger to her lips, motioning for the woman to be quiet.

Dalila nodded. At her feet, Erzulie kept her suspicious feline eyes leveled at Candra, but she, too, seemed tuned in to the approaching visitors. Her back arched and her tail stood upright.

There was a knock on the apartment door.

Nobody moved.

Another knock.

After another long pause, Candra faintly heard a voice and strained her ears.

"She's here," said the Southern-accented whisper.

"How do you know?" That voice belonged to Shea Alcott, Candra knew.

"Shhh . . ." The girl murmured something else to him, but Candra couldn't catch it.

After a moment, the footsteps retreated down the stairs, and the door at the bottom opened to allow a brief interlude of street noise to float upward before it was slammed closed again.

Out on the street again, Shea said to Mirabelle, "What did you mean, she was in there? How did you know?"

"I just *felt* her," she said, distracted. She didn't like the vibrations she was getting around here. First, she'd thought she'd seen that guy watching her from the window of the occult store, and now she had the unsettling feeling that Dalila had been on the other side of the door, listening, not answering. Why?

"What do we do now?" asked Shea as they crossed the street again and started toward the car.

"We wait . . ."

"For what?"

"For me to come up with another idea."

He muttered something, and Mirabelle looked sharply at him.

"What did you say?"

"Nothing," he said, then added, "just that we should stop screwing around and go to the police."

"That's what I thought. We can't go to the police, Shea—I thought I explained all that to you."

"Look, Mirabelle, I know what you said, but I can't stop thinking that Meg might be in trouble somewhere, and we're just sitting here wasting time."

"We aren't wasting time! I have a plan already—just give me until tomorrow, and I promise things will be all right."

"Why until tomorrow? What's the plan?"

She couldn't tell him. She couldn't say that she was going to astral project herself tonight, no matter what. No distractions. No more delays. She had to do it. She had to find Meg, before it was too late . . .

Too late for what?

She had no idea why she felt as though time was running out, she only knew that she was beginning to feel a growing sense of urgency. Meg was in danger—she was as sure of that as she was that the girl driving the Honda this morning had been Candra.

"There's that skull again," Shea said, pointing as they passed the store again.

Mirabelle looked closely at the plate-glass window, but she knew she wasn't going to see what she'd seen before. The aura of darkness was gone. If the man had actually been there earlier, he was nowhere near her now. She would have sensed it.

She and Shea walked the remaining blocks in silence. When they turned the corner onto the street where they'd left the car, Shea stopped in his tracks and cursed under his breath.

Startled, Mirabelle looked up at him, then followed his gaze to the car.

The driver's side window was smashed.

"Oh, Shea . . ." She didn't know what to say, only hurried to catch up with him as he stalked toward the car. There was no sign of the gang of kids who had been hanging around at the house nearby.

"The stereo's gone," he informed her flatly. "And the portable CD player. And my case of CDs."

"I'm really sorry."

She half-expected him to blame her—after all, she'd assured him that everything would be fine despite the seedy neighborhood. What had she said? *It's only a car.* She cringed at the memory of her impatience with his cautious attitude. She'd deserve it if he wanted to be angry now.

But Shea only nodded grimly and kicked a piece of glass with his foot.

"Y'all have to report this. I'll go call the police from the pay phone on the corner," Mirabelle offered.

He could have made a sarcastic comment about her willingness to go to the police now. But instead he nodded again and muttered, "Thanks."

As Mirabelle walked away, she glanced over her shoulder. She saw Shea leaning on the hood of the car, everything about him bleak and miserable.

Shaking her head, she hurried toward the pay phone.

"Who was that girl?" Candra demanded, turning to Dalila as soon as she was sure the visitors weren't going to come back.

"Mirabelle Moreau," the woman said, fiddling with a ring on her hand.

"Who?" Candra repeated, even though she thought she'd heard the name. The woman was mumbling, and it irritated her.

"That was Mirabelle Moreau. A friend of Meg's. She was here with Meg one day last week, *mon.* I don't know who the other person was—some guy."

"Meg's boyfriend, Shea," Candra told her. "I thought they'd followed me here, but if Mirabelle has been here before with Meg, maybe it's just a coincidence."

Dalila shrugged. "I don't like hiding, *mon.* They knew I was in here. I heard her say it. Do you think they know about . . ." She trailed off and jerked a hand in the direction of the bedroom door.

"No," Candra assured Dalila, though she wasn't at all sure Shea and Mirabelle weren't somehow aware of Meg's presence here.

"I don't like this," Dalila said again. "I tell you what, *mon.* I don't want to wait to get rid of her. Let me do it tonight, before—"

"No!" Candra said sharply. "Don't do it tonight. Wait, just like I told you."

"All right, *mon,* all right."

Candra ignored the little voice inside her brain that said Dalila was probably right—that it would be wiser to get rid of Meg as soon as possible. For some reason, she didn't want that.

I'm not ready, she told herself, before she realized again that *she* wasn't the one who had to do the deed.

Dalila would handle it.

So what wasn't Candra ready for? Annoyed with herself, she searched her mind for an answer.

She didn't like the one she found.

I'm not ready to let go of her just yet, she realized with a pang, and then shoved the thought away as urgently as it had come. "Don't do anything until I tell you," she warned Dalila again. "I mean it."

"I won't." The woman looked at her. "Are you sure this is what you want, *mon*? You're not going to change your mind?"

"Of course I'm sure," she said, scowling. "Just not yet, okay?"

"Okay, *mon*, no problem. Not yet."

Candra hardened her expression, the muscles in her face aching with the effort.

If only she could easily do the same thing to her heart.

Three

By the time Candra got home from Dalila's, the sky had darkened ominously and it was pouring out.

She parked her car as close to the door as she could, then dashed through the rain with her sweater over her head. It wasn't until she had opened the front door and stepped into the warm, quiet foyer that she realized Sophie was here. And the housekeeper was sure to notice the fact that she—well, Meg—was still supposed to be in school at this time of day.

Sure enough, she'd no sooner taken the sweater from over her head and shaken the moisture out of her hair than she heard footsteps coming in from the kitchen. "Meg? Is that you?"

"Hi, Sophie."

"What are you doing home? Are you all right?"

"I'm fine. I just . . . I forgot something I need for an afternoon class, so I ran home on my lunch hour."

"I hope you were careful driving. It looks nasty out there. I hate weather like this."

"I was careful." Candra started up the stairs.

"Meg?"

"Yeah?"

"I want you and Carrie to keep the doors locked at night until your parents get back from this trip."

Candra paused and turned around to look at the woman. "Of course we keep the doors locked," she said, though that wasn't necessarily the case. "Why? Is something wrong?"

"No, everything's fine," Sophie said, then wrung her dustcloth in her hands and added, "I just thought I saw someone hanging around here when I pulled up early this morning, that's all."

"What do you mean? Where?"

"Now, Meg, don't get all worried. I told you, I'm not even sure I saw it. Lord knows with these old eyes of mine, I can barely see to do my counted cross-stitch anymore."

"Sophie," Candra said in a low voice. "*What did you see?*"

For a moment the woman looked startled at her tone. She frowned and seemed about to admonish Candra. But instead she simply shrugged and said, "It looked like a man—a dark-skinned man, and I thought I saw him hiding in the bushes in front of the house as I pulled into the driveway. But when I looked again, I didn't see anyone. So it was probably just my imagination."

"Probably," Candra agreed, nodding. But her heart had started pounding, and she thought of the man she'd thought was following her on Elmont earlier. He'd been dark skinned.

"So anyway, I just wanted to warn you to keep the doors locked. You know how your mother likes to tell the whole town all about her business. Everyone in Crawford Corners probably knows she and Lester are away for the week, and that you and your sister are here alone overnight—not that you should worry," she tacked on hastily.

"I'm not worried," Candra assured her, and continued on up the stairs.

She walked down the hall to Meg's rose-bordered bedroom and closed the door behind her. Then, still standing in the same spot, she looked around carefully, making sure everything was as she'd left it this morning.

It was, and this time she didn't feel what she had when she'd come home late last night—that eerie sensation that someone had been here.

Last night it had been easy to chalk the feeling up to stress and her imagination. Now, given what had happened over on Elmont Avenue, and what Sophie had just told her, Candra wasn't so sure.

But if someone really had been here, who was it? And if the dark-skinned man on Elmont really had been following her, then again, who was he? Candra had never seen him before in her life—at least, she didn't think she had.

Don't make yourself crazy, she told herself, sitting down at Meg's desk and reaching for the phone.

You have other things to worry about. And now, thanks to that nosy housekeeper, you have only a few minutes before you have to leave again and pretend you're going back to school.

Which, of course, she wasn't about to do.

No, there was no way she was going to risk having to face Meg's friends Chasey Norman and Zoe Cunningham again, or that obnoxious teacher Mr. Pfeiffer, or Meg's boyfriend, Shea. No, she would just have to lay low until tomorrow, and then it would all be over.

She dialed the phone and then waited until a pleasant voice said, "Good afternoon, The Lawson School."

"Good afternoon. I need to speak to one of your students," she said briskly and in a flawless American accent. "His name is Landon Keller."

The voice on the other end started to protest, just as Candra had expected.

She narrowed her eyes and concentrated, focusing her energy on controlling the woman on the other end of the line. After a moment, she smoothly interrupted and said, "I understand your policy during class hours, but I'm afraid this is an emergency. I'm Landon's mother, and it really is urgent that I speak to him right away."

"Oh, I'm sorry, Mrs. Keller," came the swift response. "Can you hold for a moment, please?"

"Certainly."

But it took more than a moment. As Candra sat there clutching the phone to her hear, she listened to the rain thumping on the roof of the big old house, and to the sound of Sophie vacuuming somewhere downstairs. She tapped her fingers on the desk and, as she waited, wondered where she was going to go now that she had to leave the house again.

Back to school was out of the question, and she certainly couldn't go back to Dalila's now that Meg's boyfriend and that girl, Mirabelle, were sniffing around there. . . .

For some reason, she suddenly thought about Rosamund.

Why had *she* popped into Candra's head?

You hate her, remember? Don't even think of having anything to do with her ever again. She lied to you; she was a fraud.

But still, Candra found herself picturing the woman's familiar face and wondering how she was. How had she reacted when she'd found the note Candra had left, telling her she was going back to Jamaica and not to look for her or report her missing? Had she been at all upset? Did she miss Candra even slightly?

Of course not. She was a cold, uncaring person. She never showed you any warmth, never kissed you or hugged you or acted like family.

And why should she have? Candra asked herself bitterly.

Rosamund *wasn't* family. And yet, she'd raised Candra and had led her to believe she was her grandmother.

And Candra had actually believed it.

That was part of what hurt so much. She had never suspected that Rosamund was lying to her. She had instinctively trusted the woman, had even, on some level, loved her.

After all, Rosamund was the only family Candra had ever known. They had spent every day of their lives together until Candra had left the Drayer household early this week and become Meg. It was only natural that she should wonder about Rosamund now.

But she wasn't going to do anything about it.

No, she certainly wasn't going to give it another thought. Not now, when she was on the verge of getting what she'd always wanted. Not when she was about to put all this behind her and start over.

There was a click in her ear, and then Landon's voice came on the line. He sounded worried. "Mom?"

She heard typing in the background and realized he was on the phone in the secretary's office. "Landon, don't give it away—it's me, Candra."

There was a pause, and then he said hesitantly, "Uh, is everything all right?"

"Yes, everything's fine. I was just calling to say that I'll pick you up tomorrow night outside the main gate of the school."

"Why?"

"Because I want us to be together, Landon. I have a surprise for you."

"All right, that will be fine," he said stiffly. "I'll see you then, Mom."

She smiled. "I'll see you then. And Landon?"

"Yes?"

"Be sure you pack a bag."

There was another startled pause, and then he said, "Okay, I will. Thanks. Bye."

"Good-bye."

She replaced the phone in the cradle and sighed. He hadn't given her any argument. She hadn't expected him to. He was under a powerful spell—just like Dalila was.

Landon would do whatever she asked.

Just as Dalila would do whatever she asked.

For the first time in her life, Candra was tasting power, real power.

She settled back in Meg's desk chair and waited for a feeling of satisfaction to come over her.

But all she felt was a sharp twinge of doubt.

And as hard as she tried, this time, she couldn't make it go away.

By the time the police were through writing up their report, Mirabelle realized that she would have to hurry if she was going to make it back to campus in time for Philosophy class.

She and Shea got back into the car wordlessly. He started the engine and pulled out onto the street.

It was raining out now, and Mirabelle knew he had to be getting soaked through the broken driver's side window, but he didn't mention it.

"Where to?" was all he said after he'd made a circle back around to Elmont Avenue.

"Would you mind dropping me on campus?"

"Wainwright? It's not far from here, is it?"

"Nope. Go up there to that next light and take a left, and that should put you back on the road that leads to

I-95. Then all you have to do is stay on for two exits, and we'll be there." She tried to inject an upbeat note into her voice.

Shea only nodded and followed her instructions. The windshield wipers beat a glum rhythm in time with the rain on the car roof.

"Wow, this is lousy weather, huh?" Mirabelle said to break the silence as they waited for another light to turn.

"Yeah, and I guess it's only going to get worse," Shea said, flipping the defog lever to high. "That hurricane that hit the Caribbean and Florida the other day is supposed to be headed up the coast."

"A *hurricane*?"

"Yeah, only now it's just a tropical storm, supposedly. But we're supposed to get rain and high winds by tomorrow night."

"I hope we've found Meg by then," Mirabelle said without thinking. She glanced at Shea belatedly and saw his jaw tighten.

"We'll find her," he said firmly. "We have to. You said you have another plan, right?"

"Yeah, but . . ."

"What is it?"

"You're not going to believe it." Still, Mirabelle decided to bite the bullet and tell him about the astral projection. The worst he could do was laugh at her.

He didn't do that. Instead, he just listened carefully, tilted his head when she was finished, and said, "You know what, Mirabelle? I believe you."

"You do?"

He shrugged. "What choice do I have? Is it really any stranger than everything else that's happened?"

Mirabelle's lips curved in a tiny smile. There was

more to Shea Alcott than she'd first suspected. He kept
surprising her. She hoped Meg knew how lucky she was.

They reached the campus a few minutes later, and
Mirabelle directed Shea to the building where her Philosophy class was held.

"Perfect timing," she said as he pulled up to the curb
out front. "I thought I was going to be late."

"Don't you need your books or anything?"

"It's okay, I'll share with someone." She leaned across
the seat and spontaneously gave him a tight squeeze.
"You've been great, Shea. Don't worry, everything is
going to be all right. I promise."

"Are you sure? Are you saying that because you can
see the future?"

She hesitated, seeing in his eyes how much he
needed to be reassured. But she couldn't give him false
hope. "No," she said after a moment. "I'm saying it because it's what I need to believe—that Meg will be fine."

He nodded.

Mirabelle opened the door and stepped out into the
rain, waving as Shea pulled away. She turned and had
taken two steps toward the building when she saw him.

Ben.

He was standing a few feet in front of her holding an
umbrella, merely watching her, and she knew from the
look on his face that he had seen her get out of the car.
She knew, too, what he was thinking.

"Hi, Ben, what's up?" she asked, trying to sound casual. She expected him to hold the umbrella out, to
shelter her from the rain, but he didn't move it.

"Who was that?" he asked flatly.

"Who was who?"

"That guy you were hugging in the car."

"Oh, him." She stood there with rain pouring down

over her, streaming through her hair and over her face. "Nobody you know."

He nodded, then without a word, turned and walked toward the building.

Mirabelle had no choice but to follow him to class.

There was nothing she could say. She couldn't tell Ben who Shea was, because that would mean telling him about Meg, and there was no way she was going to go into that with him.

It's better this way, she told herself as she slid into her seat and wrung the water from her hair.

You wanted Ben to leave you alone. That's exactly what he's going to do now. You'll be able to concentrate on Meg.

After all, Ben certainly wasn't distracting her now. He sat in front of her and kept his back turned. Mirabelle could feel the chill radiating from him.

For a moment, she again considered trying to explain. But what could she say? And what would it matter in the long run? She had no intention of getting involved with him again.

But still, she thought of last night, how he'd kissed her out in front of the dorm, and she couldn't help feeling wistful.

Candra drove slowly down Soundview Avenue toward the huge white house where the Drayers—and Rosamund—lived. She didn't know what she was doing here, only that the car had seemed to head in this direction of its own accord.

She checked the rearview mirror and saw that there was no one behind her. Good. She slowed as she approached the familiar house, unsure of what she expected—or wanted—to see there, but again unable to help herself.

She saw that Monica Drayer's black Mercedes was parked in the circular driveway. Jonas's Ranger Rover was missing, and so was Craig's BMW, which would be with him at The Lawson School.

As Candra passed the house, she couldn't help wondering what Rosamund was doing right this second. Probably down in the basement, folding laundry, or maybe dusting the upstairs bedrooms. She thought of how Rosamund had always worked with silent efficiency, her hands flying from task to task and her mouth set in concentration.

It was hard to believe she would never see the woman again.

The realization brought a sudden and unwelcome lump to Candra's throat.

She pressed her foot on the accelerator and left the big white house behind abruptly, not looking back.

You should be glad you're leaving her behind—her, and all the rest of it.

She thought of Crawford Corners High School, of Mrs. Birch, her kindly gray-haired homeroom teacher, of Kim Williams, the Jamaican girl who had tried to befriend her.

And she thought of how uncomfortable she'd been there from the very first day, of how she hadn't fit in—not that she'd tried. Funny—the kids at Crawford Corners had looked down on her even as Candra had secretly looked down on them, knowing that she was destined for something better.

Now here she was driving a sleek black car, wearing a private school uniform, living on Meadowview Terrace. . . .

As someone else.

So what? It's your birthright, she reminded herself, turning off Soundview without thinking. *You deserve this just as much as Meg ever did. More, because she's already had eighteen years of it. It's your turn now.*

Candra drove blindly, trying to convince herself that she was doing the right thing—that all of this was the right thing. Not just what she'd done so far, but what she planned to do.

But murder . . . how can that be the right thing? How can Meg deserve that?

"Stop it!" Candra said into the empty car, as though the sharp sound of her own voice could stop the thoughts from intruding and threatening to ruin everything.

There could be no turning back now.

And if the guilt was going to come, let it come later, when she could deal with it. Right now, it was all she could do to hang on until tomorrow.

The light ahead turned red and Candra made another turn at the corner, driving aimlessly along the leaf-strewn streets that were shiny and wet.

The rain had stopped, Candra noted vaguely, but the sky still looked ominously gray, as though it could open up again at any second.

Her thoughts wandered back to Meg, and then, because she didn't want to dwell on that, found their way to Rosamund again.

And more guilt.

What's wrong with you? You can't do this to yourself!

She clenched her jaw and turned another corner, then realized, with a start, where she was.

On the street that led to Crawford Corners High. And, she realized, looking at the dashboard clock, classes had just ended for the day. She saw a trickle of students on the sidewalks around the school.

There was nothing to do but keep going, past the yellow-brick building.

She found herself searching the faces of the kids she passed, looking for someone familiar. But they were all strangers. She hadn't been there long enough, really, to recognize many people, or, luckily, to *be* recognized. The last thing she would need now was for someone to spot her driving by.

She wondered what her grandmother—no, Rosamund—had told the school when she'd disappeared. That she'd run away? That was doubtful. Probably just that she'd gone back to Jamaica . . .

She slowed for another light that was just turning red, at the corner just past the school. A group of students waited to cross on the opposite sidewalk. Candra braked and glanced idly at them as they started across the street.

Her heart did an abrupt flip-flop in her chest.

Kim Williams.

As though she suddenly sensed Candra's presence, the girl turned her head and looked right at her through the windshield of the car. Her ebony eyes widened in recognition.

Candra? her mouth said silently, and she broke away from the group of kids and hurried to the driver's side window, tapping on the glass.

Reluctantly, Candra rolled it down. "Hi, Kim," she said.

"Hey, *mon.* What are you doing here? I thought you had left town."

"Oh, really?" She looked up at the light. *Come on, change, so I can get out of here.*

"Yeah, your grandmother told Mrs. Birch that you'd gone back to Jamaica."

Just as she'd thought. She nodded. "I am going back, I just haven't left yet."

"I wish I had known that, *mon*. Some guy was asking me about you the other day, but I told him you'd left the country."

A warning bell went off somewhere in the back of Candra's mind. "Some guy? Who was he?"

Kim shrugged. "He was young, about eighteen. And he was black—had a heavy Jamaican accent. And he was *very* good-looking."

"What did he ask you?"

"Only whether you—"

Kim was interrupted by an angry honk from the car behind Candra.

The light had turned green.

"Pull over, *mon*, so we can talk—over there," Kim said, gesturing at a parking lot up ahead.

"No, I can't," Candra said automatically. "I have an appointment in a few minutes."

"Well then, give me a call tonight. I'll be home. Do you still have my number?"

"Yeah, I have it . . . bye." Candra pulled away, through the light, and looked in her rearview mirror.

Kim had run to the opposite curb and was standing there, watching her drive away.

You probably should have stopped and talked to her, Candra told herself, biting her bottom lip. But she hadn't been willing to risk the prying questions Kim would be sure to ask.

Still, she needed to know more about this person who had been asking about her. Again, she thought of the man she'd seen on Elmont this morning.

He had been in his late teens, she thought, remembering. And he'd been black, and he'd been hanging around a neighborhood that was full of Caribbean immigrants.

But Candra had never seen him before in her life.

So how could he have been asking about her, if he was the one?

And if he wasn't the one, who had it been?

The whole thing was a puzzle.

There was only one thing she knew for sure—something suspicious was going on, something that made her distinctly uneasy.

And for the first time in a long time, Candra felt helpless.

Four

The first thing Mirabelle did when she got back to the dorm was take a long, steamy shower. She felt chilled to the bone, and not just from getting soaked in the rain.

She kept thinking about how cold Ben had turned in a matter of seconds, how he'd walked out of Philosophy when class was over without giving her a backward glance.

It's just as well—she'd repeated that to herself so many times it was like a mantra. But she couldn't seem to forget about him.

And she had to, because she needed to concentrate on finding Meg. Astral projection was hard enough when you knew where you needed to go. This time, she would be striking out blindly, feeling her way along the astral plane until she found her friend, wherever she was.

She felt better after her shower. Wrapped in a warm terry-cloth robe, she made her way back along the corridor to her room. The dorm was quiet at this time of day—most people had gone to the dining hall for dinner.

Mirabelle realized now that she hadn't eaten a thing all day, and she felt hollow inside. But there was no time to go to dinner. Char would be leaving any second now, and she was counting on using the time while her roommate was gone.

When she opened the door to her room, she found

Char sitting cross-legged on her bed, talking on the phone.

Make that crying into the phone. Again.

Mirabelle sighed inwardly and tried to ignore her roommate's tearful conversation as she got dressed in sweats and an old flannel shirt.

"I know, Mom, I'm trying," Char said, sniffling. "But it's just not working . . . . I know, but—I am. . . ."

Mirabelle towel-dried her hair in the mirror above her bed, then sat down with a magazine to wait. She turned the pages idly and wished Char would get off the phone and go to dinner.

Finally, she heard her say, "All right, Mom, I will . . . I know, and I'm really going to try and do that . . . Okay, I love you, too. Good-bye."

There was a click, and Mirabelle looked up to see her roommate putting the receiver back into the cradle.

"That was my mother," Char said, meeting her gaze.

As if I didn't know. "How is she?" Mirabelle asked aloud.

"She's fine. But—" Char's voice broke.

"Char? You okay?" Mirabelle got up and walked over to her roommate, laying a hand on her shoulder.

"No," Char said, crying again. Suddenly, she looked and sounded like a lost little girl, and Mirabelle's heart wrenched. "I'm not okay at all. I'm miserable here, Mirabelle. I just want to go home."

Mirabelle patted her shoulder and tried to think of something reassuring to say.

Char's tears grew more bitter, and she buried her face in her hands. "I *hate* it here. I want to go home," she wailed again.

"Well, look, Char, you're going for Thanksgiving, right? That's not so far away."

"It's almost two whole months! That's *forever*!"

Wrong thing to say, Mirabelle realized. She hesitated, not wanting to do what she knew she should. She had other things to worry about; she couldn't spend the night hand-holding this girl who was still practically a stranger.

But as she listened to Char's sobbing, she knew she didn't have much choice. Finally, she patted the girl's shoulder again and said, "Listen, I know what will make you feel better."

"What?"

"A big burger from Radish's. And some french fries. They always make me feel better when I'm miserable. Come on, I'll treat you."

Char looked up, and her round, pitiful, tear-drenched face brightened a little. "Yeah?"

"Yeah. Come on, stop crying, before y'all end up with a big headache and swollen eyes."

Char actually smiled and sniffled. "I've had headaches and swollen eyes from crying ever since I got here."

Mirabelle grinned and nodded. Wasn't that the truth!

Char stood up and wiped her eyes on her sleeve. "Thanks, Mirabelle. Going to Radish's would be nice. Just let me run to the bathroom and wash my face, and then we can go." She grabbed a towel and dashed out of the room.

There goes your chance to try and find Meg, Mirabelle told herself. Now she'd have to wait until later—much later.

But what else could she have done? Poor Char really needed a friend right now.

Mirabelle just wished she'd suggested going someplace other than Radish's.

It had been the first thing to pop into her head, but going there would only remind her of Ben. Again.

Candra was in Meg's room, packing, when she heard a door slam downstairs.

She froze, instantly remembering Sophie's warning, and listened intently, then relaxed.

It was only Carrie—even after these few days, she already recognized the pounding footsteps on the stairs. She knew what Carrie was going to do, too—go into her room, slam the door, and blast rap music on the stereo.

Oh, well. This was the last night Candra would have to put up with her.

She turned back to Meg's closet and was reaching for a pair of burgundy Italian leather boots when she heard the bedroom door open suddenly behind her. Startled, she turned and saw Carrie framed in the doorway.

"Hey, what are you doing?" the girl demanded, her bloodshot green eyes going from Candra to the open suitcase on the bed.

Candra hesitated, then realized a denial would be ridiculous, since it was obvious what she was doing. "Packing," she said shortly, and turned back to the closet.

"Why? Where are you going?"

"I'm visiting someone overnight tomorrow."

"Who?"

"A friend."

"Which friend?"

"None of your business." Out of the corner of her eye, she saw Carrie walking over to the bed. Candra moved to stop her before she could look inside the suitcase, but it was too late.

"How come you need all this stuff for one night?" Carrie asked, as Candra zoomed in and closed the top of the bag beneath her nosy scrutiny.

"None of your business," Candra repeated.

Carrie shrugged. "Whatever."

Surprised, Candra looked up at her.

"I mean, I don't blame you if you're skipping town," Carrie told her, and Candra saw an amused smile forming on her lips.

"What do you mean by that?"

"Didn't you hear? It's all over school."

"*What's* all over school?" Candra realized her voice was starting to sound shrill, and she struggled to calm down.

"That you stole Chasey Norman's mother's diamond earrings."

"*Stole* her mother's—? I did not! That's ridiculous."

"Oh, yeah? Well Chasey and Zoe both think you did. And I heard that they're going to go to the police to file a report on you."

Candra's stomach turned over, but she fought to remain blase. For all she knew, Carrie was making this up.

"Why would they go to the police? That's the stupidest thing I ever heard. I haven't done anything."

"*Except* steal the earrings. And you know what's weird about that?" Carrie went on, casually folding her arms across her skinny body and looking Candra in the eye. "That you'd rip off your best friend the day before you get your million-dollar inheritance from Gram."

Carrie's suspicious, Candra realized, feeling a twinge of panic as she stared at the tiny blonde. *She's suspicious . . . but what is she thinking? She can't possibly know who I am . . . can she?*

She turned back to the closet and said evenly, "Would you please get out of my room now? I have a lot to do."

"I'll just bet you do."

Candra's hands shook. What was that supposed to mean?

She doesn't know. She can't know, she reassured herself. But as she felt Carrie's eyes probing into her back, she couldn't be entirely positive.

After a moment, she heard the girl walk out of the room, closing the door hard behind her. Seconds later, another door slammed down the hall, and rap music blasted from the stereo.

Candra let out a shaky breath.

Things were getting too weird, too fast.

All you have to do is hang in there until you meet Meg's grandmother for the trip to the city, she reminded herself.

But suddenly, tomorrow morning seemed a long way off.

The phone was ringing as Mirabelle and Char unlocked the door to their room.

"I'll get it!" Char bounced across the room and snatched up the receiver.

Mirabelle noticed that her roommate looked a hundred percent better than she had before. Dinner had actually been fun. They'd run into a bunch of other people from the dorm at the diner, and had spent a pleasant couple of hours laughing and talking over burgers and fries.

Mirabelle had found herself keeping an eye on the door, hoping that Ben wouldn't show up . . . or was she hoping that he would?

In any case, he hadn't, and she'd resolved to put him firmly out of her mind—again.

"Mirabelle?" Char said, holding out the telephone receiver. "It's for you. *A guy,*" she added in a stage whisper.

Ben, Mirabelle thought as she accepted the phone and sat on her bed.

What was she going to say to him?

You don't owe him any explanations, she reminded herself firmly.

"Hello?" she said curtly, as Char opened her closet across the room and took out a long flannel nightgown.

"Mirabelle?"

She frowned. "Who's this?"

"It's me . . . Shea."

"Oh, Shea—hi."

"I've been waiting for you to call, and finally I just couldn't stand it anymore. Sorry to—"

"No, it's okay. I just hadn't called because, um . . ." She eyed Char, who was humming to herself and pulling the nightgown over her head. "I haven't been able to find anything out yet."

"Oh." He sighed. "Well, I'll tell you one thing. You were right about Meg not being . . . Meg. I'm positive now that Candra's switched places with her."

"What do you mean?"

"Zoe just called me. She said Meg stole a pair of diamond earrings from Chasey Norman. Meg would never do a thing like that in a million years."

"No, she wouldn't," Mirabelle agreed. "What else did Zoe say?"

"That the earrings actually belonged to Chasey's mother, and that if Chasey told her, she knew they'd have to go to the police and report it."

Mirabelle shook her head. "That's not good."

"It sure isn't. What if they arrest Meg? I mean, Candra? It'll be a huge scandal around here, Mirabelle. Crawford Corners is a small town. People don't forget things like that. Meg's reputation will be shot. I think . . . I mean, I know you don't want to do it, but I think we should go to the police now. Before they go to Meg—I mean, Candra," he corrected again.

Mirabelle sighed. The last thing she wanted to do was go through this whole thing once more. "Go to the police, and tell them what?" she asked Shea, trying to be patient.

"That Meg is missing."

"But she isn't. They'll take one look at Candra and haul *us* off for psychiatric testing."

"Well, there must be some way to prove that she's an imposter."

"Shea, trust me. There isn't. Not yet. What we have to do is worry about finding Meg, before . . ." She hesitated, then decided to tell him the truth. "Before it's too late. She's in danger, Shea. I can feel it. Something really dark is closing in on her, wherever she is."

There was silence on the other end of the line.

"Just let me try this my way, Shea," Mirabelle said. "Give me until tomorrow. And if I haven't found Meg, then we'll talk about an alternative plan. Please, Shea."

"Okay," he said in a voice so soft she could barely hear him.

"I'll call you first thing in the morning. I promise."

"Okay. G'night." He hung up before she could say another word.

Slowly, she replaced the phone in its cradle.

"What was that all about?"

She looked up to see Char watching her curiously,

and realized she'd forgotten all about her roommate. She must have overheard every word.

"Nothing," Mirabelle said shortly.

"But didn't you say something about the police? What's going on?"

She wanted to snap, *It's none of your business,* but caught herself. She wasn't in the mood to deal with Char's wounded feelings, especially after she'd spent the last few hours trying to cheer her up.

So she just shrugged and said, "A friend of mine is missing, that's all. That was her boyfriend. He's worried about her."

"But what was that about her being in danger, and something dark . . ."

"I just have a hunch she's in trouble, that's all."

That answer seemed to satisfy Char, who merely shrugged and said, "Oh. Hey, want to go watch TV in the lounge for a while? I heard that Nina and those guys rented *How to Lose a Guy in 10 Days.*"

"Again?"

Char shrugged. "They love that movie. So do I. Kate Hudson is so excellent in it. Come on, let's go."

"No thanks," Mirabelle said. "I've seen it a zillion times. But you go ahead." *Please. Get out of here so that I can do what I have to do.*

Char hesitated. "I don't know. I've seen it a zillion times, too. Maybe I'll just stay here and finish that letter to my mom and dad."

"Char, go on," Mirabelle urged, trying not to sound too forceful. "You'll have fun. I'm just really exhausted. I think I'll try to get some sleep." She yawned loudly.

"Okay," Char said after another moment, and pulled her fluffy pink bathrobe on. "But if anyone calls for me, will you come and get me?"

"Definitely," Mirabelle promised.

"Don't lock the door. I'm not bringing my key."

"Okay."

She watched as her roommate walked out the door. As soon as it had closed behind her, Mirabelle got undressed and threw a pair of pajamas on. Then she climbed into bed, turned off the light, squeezed her eyes closed, and began her relaxation exercises.

Candra waited until Carrie had left the house, apparently on her way to some party with Eddie. Then she slipped down the hall to Lester's study.

She hadn't forgotten what she'd sensed that first night she'd been here—that Meg's stepfather wasn't what he appeared to be.

This was her last chance to find out what was in those locked drawers and cabinets in his office. After tomorrow, she'd be gone.

So it shouldn't matter, she told herself, hesitating with her hand on the doorknob. *You're leaving all of this behind. Why would you care what Lester's up to?*

The truth was, she wasn't sure why, but she wanted to know. Maybe because the more time she spent in Meg's world, the more she felt like she actually *was* Meg. Or at least, the more she felt linked to her twin sister.

Not that any link could be strong enough to stop Candra from what she had to do, she reminded herself hastily.

But it couldn't hurt to do a little investigating, as long as she had a whole night to kill here, and nothing else to do.

She pushed the study door open and saw that everything was exactly the same as it had been the other night.

The blinds were still drawn, the few items on the desktop were undisturbed, and the drawers were still locked.

Candra reached into her pocket and took out the bobby pin she'd found in Meg's bathroom. She sat in the desk chair and surveyed the row of drawers thoughtfully, rolling the bobby pin back and forth between her forefinger and thumb.

As she tried to concentrate, she began to feel a prickly sensation on the back of her neck, as though she was being watched. Though she knew it was ridiculous, she turned anyway and saw that only a window was behind her. It looked out over the backyard, and she was on the second story, so no one could possibly be peering in at her.

Still, she stared at the glass, feeling anxious.

The room and her own face were mirrored there, and she could vaguely make out the outline of tree branches beyond the reflection.

If she lowered the blinds, she could be certain no one could see her. But that was silly.

There's no one there, she told herself, shaking her head and turning back to the desk. She forced herself to ignore the irrational eerie feeling and to concentrate.

After a moment, she zeroed in on the bottom drawer and said aloud, "That's the one."

Whatever she was looking for would be in there—she sensed that. Now all she had to do was get it open.

She knelt on the plush forest green carpet and got to work.

It was working!

Mirabelle turned and looked over her shoulder. There, on the bed beneath her, was her body. The other

Mirabelle was merely a physical shell, now that she had separated her astral body from it and willed her consciousness into it.

And there, shimmering in the dim light of the room, was the silver cord that connected her astral self to her other self. The cord would stretch indefinitely, allowing her to travel through the night to Meg's side, and then back again before anyone realized she'd been gone.

Turning away from the bed, Mirabelle again focused her concentration on Meg.

Within moments, she had left the dorm room behind, and was soaring rapidly along the astral plane in search of her friend.

Must find her . . . I must find her . . .

Fleeting images rushed past—houses that spilled yellow lamplight from their windows, city streets dotted with passing headlights, dark patches of woodland where small animals scampered in the undergrowth.

And then the blur of scenes became one vivid impression, and she was drifting through it, and recognition settled over her.

Elmont Avenue stretched before her, alive with neon signs and prowling hustlers and the mingling rhythms of rap and reggae music.

Mirabelle moved more slowly but with a growing sense of purpose toward Rivera's Newsstand. It had long since closed for the night, metal gates locked over the windows and door.

As Mirabelle floated toward Dalila's apartment, she realized somehow that the woman wasn't there, that she'd gone out for the evening.

And yet, the apartment wasn't empty.

Her senses seemed to grow sharper, intensifying everything around her. She could hear the ticking clock on the living room wall even before she entered the room, and beyond that, a dripping faucet in the kitchen and the quiet breathing of Erzulie, who was asleep on the floor.

As she moved toward the bedroom as though guided by some unseen force, she heard something else. A rhythmic sound.

A heartbeat.

It seemed to be beckoning her. Mirabelle drifted over to the closed door, and then through it.

And there, on the long, low, dresser beneath the window, was Meg.

At last, Candra heard a faint click and felt the lock give.

It had taken longer to pick this thing than she'd expected. As she'd worked, she'd tried to focus on the task instead of on the vague uneasiness that wouldn't seem to leave her. But she kept glancing over her shoulder at the window, expecting to see something suspicious.

You're just jittery because you're snooping, she told herself.

And she couldn't imagine what she might find in Lester's desk, or what she was even looking for. She only knew that some inexplicable force had drawn her here, and she didn't question it. Too many times in her life, intuition had been her guide. She didn't doubt that there was some reason it had led her here.

Now, as she slid the drawer carefully out toward her, she eagerly looked inside, half-expecting the answer to jump out at her immediately.

But all she saw was a neat row of labeled hanging files. Lester Hudson was obviously a meticulous, organized person. The labels were typed and each folder was precisely aligned with the one before.

She thumbed quickly through the clear plastic tabs and saw that there was nothing out of the ordinary—*Insurance, Mortgage, Taxes* . . .

This was ridiculous. She didn't even know what she was looking for. She should just forget the whole thing. But . . .

No. Keep searching. It's here, a voice whispered in the back of Candra's mind.

It was the same voice that had guided her to Meg, even before Candra had been aware that she had a sister somewhere.

And so she settled more comfortably in front of the drawer and went through the labeled file folders again, this time more carefully.

And five minutes later, as her fingers grazed a file whose label read simply, *Merriweather,* she knew, inexplicably, that she had stumbled upon whatever it was that had drawn her here.

She drew the folder out and leaned back against the wall. Just as she opened it on her lap, a sound from the doorway startled her.

She gasped and looked up, expecting to see . . .

What?

Lester Hudson standing there, pointing a finger and saying, *A-ha! I've caught you red-handed*?

"Oh, it's just you," she said, exhaling and shaking her head at Meg's cat, who trotted into the room.

The animal stopped in front of her and looked at her. Its fixed green eyes were unnerving, and Candra frowned and said, "Go on, get out of here."

The cat didn't flinch, didn't move.

After a moment, Candra shrugged and said, "Fine, then, stay. You're just a stupid animal anyway."

She went back to the folder. The first thing she saw was a pale pink invoice.

It was from Merriweather Investigation Services, located in Spring City, Connecticut, and it was addressed to Lester Hudson.

So Lester had hired a private detective agency. Why?

Obviously, to find something. But what?

Frowning, Candra glanced over the bill. It wasn't itemized, and there was nothing to see but the five-figure total and the red stamp that marked it Paid.

Beneath the bill was a sheet of yellow legal pad paper. On it, someone had scrawled a telephone number.

As soon as Candra saw the area code, her heart did a startled flip-flop.

809.

The area code was all too familiar.

Jamaica.

Whatever—or whoever—Lester sought had something to do with the island.

Beneath the yellow sheet was a white folder marked *Confidential Report.*

This was it, Candra realized. Somewhere in this report was the answer.

But as she reached for it, the front doorbell shattered the silence.

Mirabelle stared at Meg, who lay perfectly still on the dresser top, except for the barely visibly rise and fall of her chest. She was dressed in a pair of shabby jeans and a navy New York Yankees T-shirt, and her dark hair fanned out beneath her head. Around her neck was the familiar jade baby ring on its slender gold chain. Her eyes were closed, her lips slightly parted, and she looked as though she were sleeping.

But she wasn't.

She was under some spell, Mirabelle realized, moving closer. Just as she reached out to touch her, she heard something.

The sound was coming from the distance—from her dorm room miles away. It grew louder, more insistent, and Mirabelle turned away from Meg, looking back over the astral plane.

"Mirabelle!" someone shouted. "My God, come on, Mirabelle, wake up! Wake up!"

The voice was frantic, and it belonged to Ben.

Instantly, Mirabelle understood what had happened.

She had to get back there immediately.

As soon as she'd made the decision, she found herself hurtling back along the plane toward her physical body.

Even as she went, she was aware that it was happening too fast. The energy was too powerful . . .

It was dangerous to be jerked back into her body this way . . . she had to slow down, before . . .

Too late—it was too late.

Mirabelle saw a blurred image of her other self rushing up to meet her, and then there was nothing but blackness.

"Hi, Meg," Zoe said unsteadily, standing on the front porch with Chasey, who looked equally nervous.

Candra eyed the two of them, then nodded and said, "Hi."

They looked at each other, and Candra saw Zoe give Chasey a little nudge.

"We just, um, wanted to talk to you," Chasey said, not meeting Candra's gaze. "We thought it was better than—well, you know."

Candra shook her head. "Better than what?" Her mind was still on the report she'd found in the file upstairs. She had to get this confrontation with Meg's friends over with and get back to Lester's study before . . .

Before what?

You have all night, she reminded herself, even as her sense of urgency grew.

When Chasey didn't respond, Zoe took over. "We thought coming to see you was better than going to the police," she said, trying to sound matter-of-fact but not quite succeeding.

Candra made her voice sound alarmed. "The *police?*"

"We don't want to do that," Zoe said hastily. "After all, Meg, the three of us have been friends for a long time, and—look, can we come in?"

Candra shrugged and stepped back, holding the door open.

Zoe and Chasey walked into the foyer, then stopped and looked at each other, and then at her. They seemed to be waiting for something.

Candra realized she was supposed to play hostess. Glancing up the stairs, thinking again of the detective's report that lay waiting for her, she said, "Come on into the living room."

The two of them were obviously familiar with the house, because they led the way and flopped down on the floral print couch, side by side.

Candra perched on the edge of a Windsor chair across from them, and waited.

"Meg, I don't want to believe that you would do something like this," Chasey blurted.

"Something like what?"

"Stealing my mom's earrings. I mean, *why* would you do it?"

"I didn't—"

"We figured you didn't *steal* them," Zoe interrupted. "That's why we came over."

"Well, it's about time," Candra said, folding her arms across her chest.

There was a moment of silence. Candra glanced over her shoulder into the foyer. Had she just heard a sound coming from upstairs—like a creaking floorboard?

No, it must have been her imagination.

"You lost them, didn't you, Meg?" Chasey said.

"We figured that must have been what happened— you lost them and then panicked," Zoe chimed in quickly. "And if that's what happened, it's okay, just— admit it."

Suddenly, Candra resented both of these girls, with their expensive clothes and Connecticut accents and uncomplicated lives. How dare they come here and demand that she confess to them, as though she were some lowlife criminal and they were—

"What was that?" Chasey asked abruptly, looking toward the stairway in the next room.

"What was what?" Candra asked, following her gaze.

"I just thought I heard something coming from upstairs."

"So did I," Zoe agreed. "It sounded like a footstep."

"A footstep?"

"Aren't you alone?" Chasey asked. "Is Carrie here?"

"No, she's out." Candra tried to ignore a renewed twinge of trepidation. "There's no one here but me . . . and the cat," she suddenly remembered with relief. "It must have been the cat."

Of course that's it, Candra told herself. The animal had been in the study with her when she came downstairs. Thank goodness. For a second there, she had thought—

What?

Why did she keep catching herself having these irrational, paranoid thoughts?

"Well, anyway . . ." Zoe said, leaning forward and clasping her hands over her knees. "Did you lose the earrings, Meg?"

Reluctantly, Candra turned her attention back to the two girls on the couch. What was she supposed to say? If she continued to deny ever getting the earrings, they might go to the police. The last thing Candra wanted was to get them involved.

If she admitted she'd lost the earrings, she'd be off the hook—at least where the law was concerned. All she'd be guilty of was lying. Besides, who cared? As of tomorrow, she—and Megan McKenna—would vanish forever.

"You're right," she said abruptly, looking from Zoe to Chasey. "I lost one of them. I was really upset, and I didn't know what to do, so I . . . I lied. I'm really sorry, you guys."

She couldn't tell if they looked relieved or disappointed.

Chasey cleared her throat and said, "I'm really glad it wasn't . . . something else. You know, that you didn't . . ."

"Steal them?" Candra offered helpfully, suddenly feeling as though a weight had been lifted from her shoulders.

"Yeah," Chasey said.

"We knew you hadn't been yourself lately, Meg, with the breakup and everything," Zoe told her. "We kind of thought there had to be a reasonable explanation."

"I guess I just panicked when I couldn't find that earring," Candra said. "But don't worry, Chasey, I'll pay you back. Tell your mother I'll replace the one that was lost."

"I don't think you'll be able to do that," Chasey said. "They're one of a kind earrings. You'll probably have to buy her a whole new pair. It's going to cost a fortune."

"Oh, well," Candra said lightly with a shrug. "As of tomorrow, I'll *have* a fortune. It's my birthday, and my grandmother's giving me my inheritance."

"Oh, yeah, it's your birthday," Zoe said, slapping her forehead. "How could we have forgotten?"

"Don't worry about it," Candra told her.

"Well, we have to celebrate. We'll take you out tomorrow night, right?" Zoe said, looking at Chasey.

"Yeah," Chasey said, although Candra could tell she wasn't entirely enthusiastic.

"You guys don't have to do that."

"Don't be ridiculous. We always celebrate each other's birthdays." Zoe stood up. "We'll talk about the plans in school tomorrow."

"I won't be there," Candra told her, getting to her feet. "I'm going into the city with my grandmother."

"Well, then, we'll pick you up at eight. Okay?" Zoe offered.

"Fine," Candra said, smiling. She was thinking, *By that time, I'll be long gone.*

She led the two of them back into the foyer and opened the front door, anxious to get rid of them.

Finally, after a few minutes of small talk, they left, heading down to the shiny BMW parked behind Meg's car.

Candra waved and called good-bye, then closed and locked the door. "Good riddance," she muttered, and headed up the stairs again.

She quickly walked down the hall to Lester's study. The door was still ajar, just as she'd left it. The cat had left the room, she noticed as she walked back toward the desk.

She bent to retrieve the file, which she'd left on the floor where she'd been sitting.

It was empty.

Candra gasped, tossed it to the floor, and looked around, quickly scanning the desk, the chair, the tops of the file cabinets.

There was no sign of the pink invoice, the yellow legal paper, or the confidential report.

And she knew she'd left them in the folder, carefully tucking them inside before she went down to answer the door.

Panic built inside of her as she picked up the folder again. It was empty. No doubt about that.

She thought again of the creak she had thought she'd heard coming from upstairs, and of Zoe saying, "It sounded like a footstep."

Somehow, someone had gotten into this office and stolen the contents of the file.

But who?

And why?

And *how*?

"She's coming around! Mirabelle?"

It was Char's voice, traveling to her as though across a vast distance. Mirabelle tried to turn her head toward it, but it felt like it was weighed down by a boulder. Her eyelids, too, were heavy—too heavy to lift, though she struggled to do it.

"Mirabelle?" another voice said. "Come on, please? Open your eyes, Mirabelle."

That was Ben. And she realized, then, that it must be his fingers that were stroking her hand, which was lying across her stomach like another lead weight. Ben's touch was gentle and warm and so reassuring that she needed desperately to see him.

Focusing every drop of strength she could muster, she managed to raise her eyelids slightly, enough to see what was going on around her.

The first thing she noticed was Ben's face, above her, and the broad grin that spread over his features as his eyes collided with hers.

"She's awake," he said to someone over his shoulder, then turned back to her. "Mirabelle, stay with us now. Don't slip away again."

She tried desperately to find her voice, to reassure him that she wasn't going anywhere. But the effort was too draining, and she couldn't speak, couldn't even keep her eyes open again.

Before she allowed them to drift shut, she noticed that she wasn't in her bed in the dorm. The walls around her were stark white, not pale yellow, and the light in the ceiling beyond Ben's head had been the square, fluorescent kind.

"She's going out again," she heard Char say worriedly.

"Mirabelle," another voice said, "if you can hear me, open your eyes again."

Who was that? She had no idea.

She labored to raise her eyelids, to let them know she heard them, but it was impossible. Her strength was zapped.

The last thing she heard, before she drifted away

again, was Ben saying, "Is she going to be all right, Doctor?"

Doctor, she realized groggily. *There's a doctor with me. I'll be just fine . . .*

And then, once again, there was nothing at all.

Five

At exactly seven o'clock on Friday morning, a gleaming silver Cadillac turned into the driveway of 41 Meadowview Terrace.

Candra had been standing in the foyer, peering out the window, waiting. She'd been up since five—well, actually, she'd been awake all night, but had forced herself to stay in bed until then. Now, as she slipped into Meg's dark blue Burberry raincoat and headed for the door, she felt the bone-numbing ache of exhaustion.

Maybe you can take a nap when you get back from the city, she told herself, picking up Meg's leather purse from the table near the door.

But she knew that a nap was out of the question. Even if she *did* have time for one, she couldn't imagine actually sleeping. Not in this house. Not after what had happened last night.

The fact that the contents of the Merriweather file had disappeared had left her so shaken she'd thought of little else in the hours since. It wasn't so much that she was frustrated at having it snatched out from under her . . .

No, it was more that she detected a growing aura of darkness around her. Whoever had taken the file was the same person whose presence she had sensed in her room that night, and on the street yesterday near Dalila's.

Was it the young black man she'd imagined was following her?

It didn't make any sense—she'd never seen him before in her life, so why would he have been following her? And what did he have to do with any of this, if he *had* been?

A horn tooted outside, and Candra sighed and unlocked the heavy front door. It was pouring, and a steady, chilly wind had blown in off the water sometime during the night. Now it pushed against the door as Candra struggled to pull it closed, and drove the rain against her as though it were being tossed from buckets as she ran down the steps and opened the passenger's door of the car.

It wasn't until she was actually climbing into the front seat that it struck her: she was about to meet her grandmother. Her *real* grandmother, unlike Rosamund.

Suddenly, her hands were trembling, and to calm herself, she concentrated momentarily on pulling the heavy car door shut against the gusting wind. Only when it had slammed abruptly, closing her into the plush maroon interior, did she turn to look at the stranger on the seat beside her.

"Meg," the woman said warmly, and reached for her. "Happy birthday, sweetheart."

Candra allowed herself to be folded into a hug that was surprisingly fragile. She closed her eyes, overcome with unexpected emotion, and breathed the scent of expensive, powdery perfume.

"Hi, Grandma," she nearly whispered when she managed to speak around the lump that had risen in her throat.

The woman released her and stroked her hair briefly. "You're soaked. It's so awful out there."

Candra nodded, not trusting her voice.

She studied her grandmother. She was built like Carrie, small and slender. Her hair was the same blond color as Carrie's, and as Giselle's had been in the photographs Candra had seen, and her eyes were an identical light green color. But this woman's expression lacked the saucy glint Candra had seen in every picture of Giselle.

If anything, her gaze was the opposite—introverted and worn and troubled.

And when she spoke again, Candra's heart plummeted.

"Meg," she said worriedly, "they're saying that hurricane might be headed in our direction. I don't think it's such a good idea to go into the city today."

"Hurricane?" Candra forced herself to say lightly, and laughed. "This is no hurricane, Grandma. Just a little rain. We'll be fine."

"But on the weather report last night, they said—"

"Those reports are never right," Candra interrupted. "Besides, I heard that the storm is most likely going to veer off course and go out into the ocean later today." That was actually true—she'd been listening to the radio reports on Meg's stereo as she was getting dressed. Well, it was *mostly* true—the meteorologist had said the unpredictable storm *might* veer off course—it was still too soon to tell.

The woman looked doubtful. "I don't know . . ."

"Come on, Grandma," Candra cajoled, trying not to come across as frantic as she felt.

You can't back out now! She screamed silently. Not when the million dollars was so close.

"It'll be fun to spend the day together," she added hopefully, "Just the two of us."

"We can always go Monday . . ." Her grandmother bit

her thin lower lip, which was carefully lined with plum lipstick.

"But Monday isn't my birthday," Candra pointed out, making sure her voice came out sounding wistful.

That seemed to do the trick.

Though she still seemed reluctant, the woman nodded and said, "You're right. Today is your special day, and I did promise. Besides, we'll be home before the weather gets any worse."

"Of course we will."

"Well, then, we'd better get going before we're late for our train." Her grandmother shifted the car into drive and pulled out onto the street.

Candra settled back against the seat and smiled.

"Mirabelle?"

Again, the voice intruded on the dark, silent place where she was drifting.

"Mirabelle, it's me, Ben. Wake up, please?"

She felt the quiet urgency of his words drawing her slowly out of oblivion, and struggled to remember where she was, what was happening.

It came back to her in a rush, and her eyes snapped open.

"Hey—you're awake!"

She saw Ben standing over her, wearing a rumpled blue plaid shirt and looking startled. She blinked and glanced beyond him, again seeing the stark white walls and rectangular fluorescent lights she'd glimpsed before . . . was it last night?

"You're in the infirmary," Ben informed her, as if he sensed her confusion.

She frowned and searched for her voice. "How . . . ?" she managed to croak.

"Shhh, don't try to talk. I found you unconscious in your room. I stopped by to—well, to say I was sorry for jumping to conclusions when I saw you with that guy yesterday afternoon. I thought you were asleep when I saw you in bed, but when I tried to wake you up, you didn't respond. It was like you were . . ." He trailed off and shuddered.

Mirabelle remembered hearing him calling her when she was in Dalila's apartment, how his voice had jerked her astral body violently across the astral plane, back to her physical self.

Cecile had warned her that something like that could be deadly, if the sudden pressure on the silver cord caused it to sever.

Thank God that hadn't happened, Mirabelle realized now. She'd survived.

But the trauma had obviously left her in bad shape. She felt feeble and listless and sore all over, and it was all she could do to muster the strength to speak again.

"When . . . what . . . day . . . is . . . it?" she asked Ben, and found herself exhausted by the mere effort to communicate.

She felt a squeeze on her fingers and realized he was holding her hand, that he had been even before she'd come to. How long had he been here?

"It's Friday," he told her. "Friday morning."

Friday? Mirabelle fought to concentrate. That meant she had only been out overnight. Grateful that more time hadn't elapsed, Mirabelle suddenly thought of Meg.

Alarm shot through her as she recalled what she had seen in Dalila's apartment.

She had to get back to Meg, had to help her before it was too late.

I have to get out of here! she hollered at Ben.

When he didn't respond, she realized, with trepidation, that she hadn't made a sound. Her mouth seemed to be moving but nothing was coming out.

"Shhh," Ben soothed, and stroked the back of her hand. "Don't try to talk, Mirabelle. You need to rest now. Go back to sleep."

She attempted to speak again, but now her lips wouldn't even budge. She was utterly drained of what little physical energy she'd recovered, and mentally, she was fading fast.

To her horror, she felt her eyelids fluttering closed again.

She tried to fight the wave of drowsiness that was overtaking her.

It was futile.

No . . . she thought weakly, even as the darkness rushed in to claim her again.

Can't . . . must get to Meg before . . .

"Grand Central Station—last stop on this train. Grand Central Station," the conductor's voice boomed over the loudspeaker.

Candra, who was sitting beside her grandmother, in the window seat, watched eagerly through the rain-spattered glass as they pulled out of the black tunnel they'd entered somewhere up in Harlem.

She wasn't sure what she expected to greet her on this, her first real visit to Manhattan, but she couldn't help being disappointed. The train creaked and groaned and slowed to a painstaking halt beside a dingy-looking platform, its concrete columns and walls lit by bare yellow bulbs.

Candra glanced at the woman beside her, who offered a tight smile. "Here we are," she said, as around them, commuters gathered their belongings and headed for the doors.

Candra nodded. Her grandmother hadn't spoken much during the trip. She'd seemed nervous, and spent most of the time with her head back and her eyes closed, though she jumped and gave a little gasp every time they hit a bump or another train rushed past them.

Now Candra followed her out of the row and down the aisle, noting the bustle that was taking place around them. The people who rode the train into Manhattan from the Connecticut suburbs appeared to be a well-to-do and sophisticated bunch. No one seemed fazed by the grungy-looking platform or by the way they were forced to stand crowded together as they inched up the stairway toward the station itself.

Candra felt her grandmother clutch her arm as they joined the throng. "Stay with me," she said. "Don't get lost."

"I won't."

Within a few minutes, they were emerging into the main terminal, and Candra tried not to look around in awe. This was more like it! Grand Central Station was an impressive, cavernous structure that belied the shabbiness of the tracks below. Candra glanced from the rows of ticket windows and shops to the sweeping staircases to the trio of musicians who were entertaining a crowd of commuters at one end.

This is New York, Candra told herself. *At last.*

This was the place where the most wealthy, powerful, glamorous people in the world lived and worked. And she was among them, about to come into her own fortune after so many difficult years. She felt dizzy with anticipation, and she wanted desperately to stand still and savor the moment that had been so long in coming.

But her grandmother tugged her sleeve and pulled her along toward a long corridor. "Come on, this way, Meg."

Moments later, they were stepping through wooden-paned doors. While her grandmother stopped and put up an enormous black umbrella, Candra glanced around and saw a sign that read, "Vanderbilt Avenue."

Vanderbilt, she thought—wasn't that the name of an American tycoon?

Someday, she wondered dreamily, would there be an avenue named after her?

"The bank is around that corner, on Park Avenue," her grandmother said, pointing, and holding the umbrella over both their heads as the rain poured down around them.

Candra could only nod again, not trusting her voice to conceal her excitement. Park Avenue! Everyone knew that was the stomping grounds of the richest of New York's rich. She thought back to the days, not so long ago, of living in the Drayers' servant quarters and wearing secondhand clothes, and wanted to pinch herself. Could this be real? Was she, Candra Bowen, actually here at last?

Too soon, they had been swept a few blocks along the sidewalk among fast-paced walkers, and her grandmother was saying, "This is it."

Candra wished she could protest, wanting only to keep walking along the vibrant city streets, feeling like a part of the city's rhythm. But then she looked up at the large stone bank building, and was instantly reminded of the reason for this trip.

The money.

Jittery excitement pulsed through her veins as she followed her grandmother up the steps and into the vast lobby. "Wait right here, Meg," the woman said, pointing to a row of chairs.

"Okay." Candra took a seat and watched as her grandmother approached a woman seated behind a lamp-lit desk.

The two of them conferred for a moment, and then her grandmother turned and beckoned to her.

Five minutes later, they were both seated across from a short, balding man in a well-cut gray suit, who introduced himself as Mr. Warner.

"And how do you like school this year, Miss McKenna?" he asked jovially, forming a steeple with his fingers on the polished desk in front of him.

"It's fine, thank you."

"And let's see, today you're turning eighteen, is that right? Happy birthday!"

"Thank you," Candra said again, trying not to sound impatient.

He turned to her grandmother. "It's always good to see you, Hope."

Hope? So that was her name. Candra had been wondering.

"It's good to see you, too, Mortimer," her grandmother said, fiddling with the raspberry-colored chiffon scarf around her neck.

"I do miss Harry. We always used to have a good laugh when he came in to take care of business, didn't we?"

Candra noticed that her grandmother had stiffened at his words. Harry had been her husband—Meg's grandfather.

And mine, Candra reminded herself.

"It seems like only yesterday that I last saw him—hard

to believe it's been two years," Mr. Warner—Mortimer—
went on.

He chatted for another few moments about what a
terrific guy Harry had been, apparently oblivious to
Hope's increasingly strained expression.

Candra wanted to reach out and shake him, to tell
him to shut up. Couldn't he see he was upsetting her
grandmother? Feeling a sudden and surprisingly fierce
protective instinct, she laid a hand over her grandmother's frail, blue-veined one that clutched the arm of
her chair.

Hope looked up gratefully, and Candra smiled at her,
feeling a disturbing sense of warmth toward the woman.

And guilt—she felt guilty, again, at the thought of
what she was about to do.

Take the money and run.

Well, so what? Didn't she deserve it as much as Meg
would have? She was Harry McKenna's granddaughter,
too. And the money wouldn't make up for all the lonely
years she'd spent in Jamaica, unaware that she had a
family somewhere—a family that had given her up without looking back.

So, when Mortimer reached for a file at last and took
out a stack of paperwork to begin the financial trans-
action, Candra pushed the nagging guilt aside.

This was her birthright, and nothing was going to
stop her from claiming it.

Mirabelle opened her eyes abruptly.

She was still in the same white-walled, fluorescent-lit
room, but Ben was gone.

At first she thought she was alone. She managed to
turn her head slightly, then, and realized that someone

was sitting in the chair beside her bed. It was a male someone, and his dark head was buried in his hands.

"Shea . . ." she whispered.

His head jerked up and he stared at her. "You're awake!"

She could only nod, and barely managed that. She was still so weak.

Shea jumped out of his chair and stood over her. "Are you all right?" he asked tentatively, and looked over his shoulder. "Do you want me to call someone? The nurse is right—"

"No!" she forced out, through lips that felt parched and stiff.

"Okay, okay, don't worry—I won't." He sat down again, but leaned forward so that his face was close to hers.

"What time . . . ?" she began.

"Almost noon," he told her quickly. "I didn't go to school today."

"How did you . . . ?"

As though he were reading her mind, Shea said, "Your roommate, Char. She told me you were here—I called the dorm this morning, looking for you. Mirabelle, they're saying you must have a severe case of the flu, because they can't find any other explanation for your symptoms. But you seemed fine yesterday. What happened?"

She lifted her shoulders in a weak shrug, and the effort drained her. There was no way she could go into the whole story without risking losing consciousness again. She had to conserve her strength.

"Shea," she said raggedly, "we have to . . ."

She stopped as a wave of numbing exhaustion swept over her, closing her eyes briefly as she fought it off.

When she opened them again, she saw that he'd bent
closer still, and was watching her worriedly.

"What is it, Mirabelle?" he asked. "Are you all right?"

"Call . . ." she began, and her voice faded into a
hoarse croak. She struggled to get it back, to stay awake.

She did, but only long enough to utter three more
words. "Call the police."

"Would you like more tea, ladies?" the waiter asked,
discreetly appearing at the table again.

"No, thank you," Hope told him. "Meg?"

Candra shook her head, and watched as he slipped
away, his jacket as starkly white and impeccably pressed
as the linen napkins and cloth on the small round table.

Never in her life had Candra been to a restaurant as
elegant as this one was. Never had she been treated so
well, her every whim catered to by the attentive staff
and by her grandmother, who kept telling her to order
whatever she wanted.

After all, you are the birthday girl, Hope had said more
than once, and every time she did, Candra was reminded of Meg—her twin—who shared this day with
her. Eighteen years ago today, the two of them had
come into the world together.

Tonight, only one of them would leave it.

Candra wanted to be able to enjoy the rich, crumbly
pastry and succulent light souffle that sat in front of her,
but all of it was sodden in her mouth.

Meg. Her twin sister. Her own flesh and blood. How
could she knowingly send her to her death in only a few
more hours? Especially on this day, of all days?

"Meg, you haven't touched your fruit," her grandmother said, pointing at the crystal bowl in front of her.

"Yes, I have," Candra protested, and speared a plump red strawberry with her fork so that its juices spilled out. She put it into her mouth and chewed mechanically.

"You seem awfully quiet today, though. Is everything all right?" Hope asked, watching her.

"Everything's fine."

"You aren't disappointed that we're having breakfast in the city instead of lunch? I just didn't want to risk getting back to Crawford Corners any later, with the weather and everything . . ."

"It's fine, Grandma," Candra assured her, lifting the gold-rimmed porcelain cup and taking a sip of her still-hot tea.

"After all, we still have to get to the bank back home," Hope went on, toying with her own teacup. "You need to deposit your check."

Candra nodded, and again felt the back of her chair to make sure that Meg's purse was still there. Inside, folded safely into the leather wallet, was a cashier's check for one million dollars, made out to Megan McKenna.

All she had to do was put it into Meg's bank account this afternoon, and then withdraw the money later using Meg's photo driver's license and credit cards as identification.

It was so simple.

And yet . . .

Sitting here, in this quiet, refined Manhattan restaurant with her grandmother, Candra couldn't help feeling wistful. Maybe even . . . doubtful?

Would it be so bad to keep things the way they were— to keep posing as Meg, and forget about running away, and about . . . the rest of her plan?

Life would be pretty wonderful if she lived it as Megan

McKenna. She could continue to live in the comfortable house on Meadowview Terrace, and go to private school, and wear designer clothes, and have a loving grandmother, not to mention a mother, at last. . . .

But what about Landon?

She couldn't give him up. He was the piece that made her picture puzzle complete.

No, she had to proceed with the plan, she thought reluctantly, as she smiled reassuringly at the woman across the table from her.

She would take the money and leave town with Landon.

But first, she would give Dalila her orders to get rid of Meg.

It was the only way.

Six

This time, when Mirabelle came to again, she saw a whole group of people standing around her bed, conferring quietly.

Shea . . .

And Ben . . .

And a man in a white lab coat . . .

And a uniformed police officer.

"Mirabelle?" The man in the coat was at her side a moment after she opened her eyes. He was young and handsome, and looked almost like he could have been a student on campus. But he said, "I'm Doctor Rapaport. How are you feeling?"

Horrible was how she was feeling, but she wasn't about to tell him that.

"Fine," she said, and was surprised to find that her voice was much stronger than it had been before.

"Fine enough to speak with Officer Garrety, here?" the doctor asked, gesturing over his shoulder at the police officer.

Mirabelle nodded.

The doctor stepped back, whispered something to the officer, and then they both moved out of Mirabelle's line of vision.

She caught Ben's eye, and then Shea's. Both of them looked worried—and relieved.

"What time is it?" she asked, and they both looked at their watches.

"Four-thirty," they said in unison, then glanced at each other and laughed nervously.

Mirabelle frowned. "Four-thirty? The day is almost gone."

"You went out again while I was here earlier," Shea told her, and glanced at Ben, who nodded. "I did what you told me to do, though. I called the police. The officer has been waiting for you to come to so he can ask you some questions."

Mirabelle directed her attention to Ben. "Do you know . . . ?" she asked him.

"Yeah. Shea told me what happened."

"What did he tell you?"

"That his girlfriend is missing, but her twin sister is in her place, impersonating her."

"That's all you told him?" Mirabelle asked Shea, who nodded.

Ben frowned. "What else is there?"

Mirabelle shrugged and opened her mouth to tell him she'd explain the rest later.

She was interrupted by Officer Garrety, who appeared by the bed again.

"Hello, Miss Moreau," he said in a deep voice. He was tall and blond and broad shouldered, and had a pleasant face that was touched with concern. "I'm going to make this quick so you can get your rest. Doctor's orders. Your friend here"—he motioned toward Shea—"says you have something to tell me."

She nodded. "Can I . . . would someone please get me a drink of water before I start talking?" she asked, not trusting her voice to hold up without it. Her throat felt raw and dry, and she couldn't risk fading again.

"I'll get it," Ben said. He reached down to squeeze her hand quickly before he walked away.

"Thanks," Mirabelle whispered, and turned back to the policeman. "Okay. I don't know if you're going to believe this, but I hope you'll hear me out, Officer . . ."

"Dalila?" Candra said into the phone. "It's me."

"Yeah, *mon*," said the voice with its familiar island accent. "I've been waiting for you to call. It's raining like crazy outside, and it's almost four-thirty."

"I know," she said dully, fidgeting with a corner of the comforter on Meg's bed. "I just got back from the bank."

"You have the money for me?"

"Yes," Candra lied. "I'll give it to you tomorrow morning."

The woman started to protest, but Candra interrupted her.

"Dalila, you said you would help me. Now listen carefully."

There was silence on the other end of the line.

Candra started talking, giving her directions to Rocky Forest State Park, and to the spot she'd picked out the other night on the way back from Landon's school.

And she told Dalila exactly what she expected her to do, keeping her voice methodical and her emotions detached.

When she was finished, she said simply, "Did you get that?"

"Yeah, *mon*, I got it."

"Okay, then. Go."

"When?"

"Now," Candra said sharply. "There's no time to waste, Dalila. The sooner you get rid of her, the better."

"Okay, no problem, *mon*. But the money—"

"I said I'll give it to you!"

"Okay, okay . . ."

There was a pause, and when the woman said nothing else, Candra barked, "So go on, get busy, Dalila."

"I will, *mon*. I will. Don't you worry about a thing. Dalila will take care of everything for you."

There was a click, and then Candra heard the dial tone.

Still, she sat frozen, clutching the receiver against her ear, staring off into space.

Then the tears started.

They caught her off guard, huge, heaving sobs that consumed her so that she could barely catch her breath between them.

She huddled there in Meg's shadowy bedroom, rocking back and forth and wailing her sister's name over and over as darkness fell outside and the wind and rain howled around the house.

"You don't believe me, do you," Mirabelle said flatly, watching Officer Garrety.

He shrugged and patted her arm. "I believe that you're truly worried about your friend, Mirabelle, but what you're saying is pretty outrageous."

"But it's true, Officer!" Shea protested. "You've got to believe us. Meg isn't *Meg* anymore, she's Candra, just like Mirabelle said. And Meg is in trouble."

"You want me to believe that your friend is lying there, under a spell, in this woman's apartment?" the policeman said incredulously. "And that the reason you know this is that the spirit of Mirabelle, here, flew over to that apartment last night while her body was in bed in the dorm?"

"It wasn't my *spirit* that went, it was my astral body!" Mirabelle looked from Officer Garrety's doubtful expression to Ben's, then settled her gaze on Shea. "I told you no one would believe us, especially the police," she said bitterly. The burst of energy she'd felt after drinking some water was starting to dribble away. It was no use.

Shea grabbed the officer's arm. "Look, can't you at least check it out? Send someone over to the apartment on Elmont to make sure Meg really isn't there?"

"I'd like to help you kids," Officer Garrety said, "but I don't even have a missing person's report on this girl. As far as I'm concerned, there's no problem."

"Okay, then, how do I file a missing person's report?" Shea asked, his voice rising in anger.

"You can't, unless someone's missing."

"She *is* missing!" Shea exclaimed, then looked at Mirabelle for help.

"Listen, Officer Garrety," she said, desperate to get through to him. "I know how this whole thing must sound to y'all. I mean, we're talking about astral projection and ESP and all this stuff you probably don't believe in the first place. But I swear to you that it's real, and that we wouldn't have come to you if this wasn't a case of life or death."

"I'm sorry, Mirabelle. But there's nothing I can do." The officer picked up his hat from the foot of the bed and took a step backward, toward the door.

"Wait!" Ben said sharply, startling everyone else. "Wait just a second. Remember that kidnapping case in Spring City a few weeks back? A little girl was taken from a park?"

The officer frowned. "What does that have to do with

anything? I suppose you're going to tell me now that Meg McKenna was kidnapped."

"I am not," Ben said, looking insulted. "I'm going to tell you to think about how the cops managed to solve the case."

"How?" Shea asked, and Mirabelle echoed him.

"They used a psychic," Ben said triumphantly.

Officer Garrety shrugged.

"You have to admit that if the police were willing to listen to a psychic in that case, the least you could do is listen to one in this case."

Mirabelle shot a grateful glance at Ben. So he didn't think she was strange, after all, despite everything she'd said about magical powers and astral projection. She never would have expected him to not only take it in stride, but jump to her defense where the police were concerned.

If only Officer Garrety were as easy to win over. But he just stood there, clutching his navy cap and wearing the same expression of skepticism.

Then it dawned on Mirabelle. She knew exactly how to convince the man that she was telling the truth.

"Would you mind giving me your hat?" she asked him abruptly, propping herself up on her elbows.

He looked startled. "My hat?"

"Yes. Just for a few seconds. I want to try something."

He hesitated.

"Please," Mirabelle said, and finally he shrugged and handed it to her.

She closed her eyes and stroked it, concentrating.

It wasn't easy. She was still so weak, and she hadn't done this in a long time. But she had to . . .

Do it for Meg, a voice whispered somewhere in her mind, and she struggled to focus.

After a moment, images began to come to her.

She studied them intently, and the room was silent around her.

Finally, satisfied that she'd seen enough, she opened her eyes and looked at the policeman.

"You can have your hat back," she told him, and handed it over.

"What was that all about?" he asked, examining it suspiciously before settling it on his blond head.

Ben and Shea looked at each other, and then at her.

Mirabelle shrugged. "I wanted to find out more about you, Officer. And I did."

"What do you mean?"

"Well, I know that you grew up in the Midwest—right outside of Chicago, right?"

He raised his eyebrows but said nothing.

"And that you loved your father very much," Mirabelle continued. "He was a police officer. But he died when you were ten."

"I was eleven—I'd just turned eleven," Officer Garrety said quietly, a faraway look coming over his face momentarily, then being replaced with a frown. "Who told you about my father? And where I grew up?"

"No one told me. I picked up on it from holding your hat."

The officer made a noise that was a cross between a snort and a laugh. "That's impossible." He started toward the door again.

"But what about the tree?" Mirabelle called after him.

He stopped in his tracks. "What tree?" he asked, still facing the door.

"I'm not sure where it is, but there's a tree that meant a lot to you and to your dad."

The police officer turned slowly back to look at her,

and the expression on his face was haunted. "How did you know about that?" he asked in a voice that was nearly a whisper.

"I told you . . ."

"She's psychic," Ben said, beside her.

"No one knows about the tree. It was in the woods behind our house, and it was ours, mine and dad's. He was going to build me a treehouse in it that summer. Then he was killed during that robbery . . . I used to climb the tree and talk to him after he was gone. I was sure he could hear me," Officer Garrety said, shaking his head and staring off into space.

Mirabelle watched him and waited.

Finally, he met her eyes. "I'll see what I can do about checking out that address on Elmont."

Candra tossed the last bag in the backseat of Meg's car. As she reached out to shut the door, the wind picked it up and carried it out of her grasp, slamming it closed.

Candra ran back through the pouring rain to the house. She slipped into the foyer and shook the water out of her hair.

No one was home, and only the ticking of the antique grandfather clock in the next room disturbed the silence. She looked around, remembering how she'd felt the first time she'd stepped into this house.

Had it really only been days ago? It felt like months.

Well, it didn't matter. It was over. She'd never set foot in this place again.

Never meet her mother after all. She felt a pang at the realization, then pushed it away. Meeting Giselle wouldn't have been worthwhile, anyway. After all, she'd just think Candra was Meg, the daughter she'd raised. She'd never know she'd met her other child—the one she'd abandoned.

A sound from above startled Candra, and she glanced up to see the cat watching her from the second-floor balcony.

"What are you looking at?" she snapped.

The animal just stared at her.

Candra stared back, but couldn't help feeling uncomfortable. The cat had never liked her. She was the only one who had guessed that Candra was an imposter.

Good thing you can't talk, Candra told the animal silently.

On second thought, maybe it was too bad the cat couldn't speak. After all, she might be able to tell Candra who had been in Meg's bedroom before she got home the other night, when she'd sensed that presence. And the cat had been in Lester's study when Candra had found the file—and probably when it had been stolen.

What had the animal witnessed?

"You know what?" Candra said aloud to the cat. "It doesn't even matter. You know why, *mon*? Because I'm out of here for good. See you."

It wasn't until she'd walked out the front door that she realized she'd reverted back to her Jamaican accent without thinking. She cringed. She wouldn't let that happen again.

Now that she was starting her new life—a life of privilege—she was cutting all ties to the old one. In no time, she'd forget that she'd ever lived in poverty in Jamaica, that she'd ever wanted for anything.

She would be a wealthy American, and that was that.

She reached into her pocket and took out the note

she'd written earlier, then propped it on the hall table near the door.

Then, smiling, she splashed back through the downpour, got into the car, and started the engine.

She didn't allow herself a backward glance in the rearview mirror as she drove away. She was afraid that if she looked, she'd feel regret, and she didn't want to feel that.

She didn't want to feel *anything*, she reminded herself firmly. Steeling herself against emotion was the only way she'd be able to get through this night, knowing what Dalila was up to.

Mirabelle sat propped against a pile of pillows, brooding. In chairs on either side of the bed, Shea and Ben slouched, both staring off into space.

They were waiting for Officer Garrety to come back. He'd left to make arrangements for someone to check out Dalila's apartment on Elmont, as well as Meg's house in Crawford Corners.

Mirabelle closed her eyes, then opened them again.

"It's too late," she said abruptly, shaking her head.

"What?" Shea asked, sitting up straighter.

Ben did the same. "What do you mean, it's too late?"

"Meg's gone."

"Gone?" Shea echoed.

Mirabelle nodded. "I'm getting this feeling that they're not going to find her in that apartment. She's been moved."

"Moved where?" Ben asked.

"I don't know. I'm still not feeling a hundred percent like myself. Everything I'm getting on Meg seems fuzzy, but . . ." She shrugged. "I just know she's not on Elmont anymore."

Shea stood and started pacing, raking a hand through his dark hair.

Ben looked at him, then at Mirabelle. "Do you want me to go find Officer Garrety?"

"Would you?"

"Sure."

She looked into his eyes. "Ben, thank you so much for . . . everything."

He flashed a brief smile and reached out to squeeze her hand. "No problem. I'm glad you're all right . . . and glad I know the truth about what's going on with you."

"I should have told you all along. I don't know why I didn't trust you. I *wanted* to."

"You didn't want me to get involved," Ben said simply.

"I was an idiot," she told him, then looked over her shoulder at Shea, who had stopped in front of the window and was watching the dreary, stormy dusk settle in.

"I'll be right back," Ben said, standing and starting for the door.

Before he got any farther, Officer Garrety appeared.

"I was just coming to find you," Ben told him.

"Well, here I am . . . I must be psychic," the policeman said, and cracked a grin. Then he became serious again. "I just spoke to the officers in Spring City, and they went over to that address on Elmont. No one was there."

Shea groaned. "Mirabelle just told us Meg had been moved."

The officer raised an eyebrow in her direction, but said only, "There's something else." He looked around at the three of them. "A source in the vicinity of the Parker woman's apartment revealed that a short time ago, she hired two men to move a heavy cabinet or chest out of her apartment and into a rented vehicle."

"Oh my God," Mirabelle said quietly. "Meg."

"We have someone in Crawford Corners checking out that address on Meadowview Terrace," the officer went on, not meeting her eyes. He turned and headed for the door again. "I'll be back when I know what they've found."

"They're not going to find Meg there!" Shea said, looking disgusted. "She's been abducted!"

"Unfortunately, there's been no indication of that up until this time. We've been trying to track her parents down in Fiji, but so far we've had no luck. And her sister, Carrie Hudson, hasn't shown up either. So, until someone in her family can confirm that she's missing we can't be sure of anything." Officer Garrety said. "However . . ."

"What?"

"We checked with the Adamson-Swift School. Megan McKenna was absent today, without an excuse."

"Would that make her a missing person?"

"Not until she's been unaccounted for after twenty-four hours. Unfortunately, she's eighteen years old as of today. If she were a minor, we wouldn't have to wait the twenty-four hours."

"That's ridiculous!" Shea exclaimed.

"Look, I know you're upset, and I'm doing what I can to help you," the policeman said. He left the room again, calling over his shoulder, "I'll be back. Just sit tight."

Traffic on I-95 was horrendous because of the weather. There were accidents all over the place, and according to the meteorologist's report on the radio, the worst was yet to come. The storm had been down-graded from a hurricane, but it was still headed for the New England coast, bringing a promise of stronger winds and heavier rain yet.

By the time Candra reached the exit for The Lawson School, her hands ached from clenching the wheel and her nerves were shot. The only positive thing about the horrible driving conditions was that they forced her to concentrate on the road. She couldn't let her attention shift to the disturbing thoughts that flitted on the fringes of her mind.

Thoughts about Meg.

As she turned onto the private drive that led to the school, she spotted a figure huddled outside the main gate up ahead. An enormous black umbrella shielded the top of his body from her, but she knew it was Landon even before she drew closer.

She saw that a large duffel bag was slung over his shoulder, and relaxed. Until now, she hadn't realized she'd been subconsciously worried that he wasn't going to show, or that if he did, he wouldn't want to go away with her.

But he's here, waiting, she told herself as she pulled to a stop beside the gate. *Everything's going to be fine now. You'll see.*

He waved and opened the back door, tossing his duffel bag onto the seat beside her luggage. Then he got into the front and turned to her.

"Candra!" he exclaimed, pulling her into his arms. He was damp and his cheek against hers was icy, but she burrowed against him anyway.

"I was worried about you," he told her, pulling back to look at her face in the dim interior of the car.

"Worried about me? Why?"

"Driving alone in this weather. I would have called to tell you not to come if I'd had a number where I could reach you."

"You didn't want to see me?" she asked, narrowing her eyes at him.

"Of course I wanted to see you. But I didn't think it was safe for you to make the trip."

"Oh." Relieved, she gave him what she hoped was a sunny smile. "Well, here I am, safe and sound."

"Thank God." He settled back in the seat and said, "Mind if I turn up the heat? I'm chilled through."

"Go ahead." She put the car into Drive and pulled out into the road to turn around.

"So where are we going?" Landon asked, after he'd adjusted the temperature control on the dashboard.

"Away," she said lightly, casting a sideways glance at him.

"I know that, but where?"

"Does it matter?"

He hesitated, then shrugged. "No. As long as I'm with you, I don't care where we go." He reached out and trailed a finger along her cheek.

His touch sent shivers of pleasure through her—and something else. She pushed her misgivings aside and said simply, "I'm glad you feel that way, Landon."

She turned her attention to the road ahead. The windshield wipers were on at top speed, but still it was difficult to see through the downpour. She would have to really concentrate on driving.

But as the school fell into the distance in the rearview mirror, and her eyes got used to the darkness and rain and wipers again, she couldn't help letting her mind stray back to yet another thought she wanted to avoid.

It's only the spell.

The spell she'd cast on Landon—that was the reason he was going along with her so willingly. How would he feel about her if his feelings were under his own control?

She would never know.

Just be glad he's with you, she told herself. *This way, he's not going to put up any fight when he realizes we're leaving for good.*

Yet again, she felt a pang of regret. She had what she wanted—but not the *way* she wanted it. She hadn't realized it would matter to her whether Landon was with her of his own free will, or not.

Well, there could be no backing out now. There was nothing to do but move forward with the plan.

"I've never seen anything like it," Dr. Rapaport said, sitting back and putting his stethoscope aside. His brown eyes were focused intently on Mirabelle.

"I *told* you I feel fine."

"Your temperature and blood pressure are back to normal, all your vitals are good, the color's back in your face—basically, you've made the speediest recovery I've ever seen," he told her, and shook his head.

"So I can leave the infirmary, right?"

He hesitated. "Well, you look a little tired. Maybe—"

"No, I feel great. Really."

A nurse stuck her head in the door. "Doctor Rapaport? You have a phone call."

"Tell them I'll call back."

"It's your wife. It's kind of urgent. She said a tree branch came down on the roof and now there's water coming in the baby's room."

"Oh, great," he muttered, glancing at the window.

Darkness had fallen outside, and the rain and wind seemed to have grown more violent.

He stood and looked at Mirabelle, distracted, as though he'd forgotten she was there.

She silently thanked his wife and the fallen branch.

"You're free, if you want to go," he said quickly, and on the way out the door, added, "Just take good care of yourself over the next few days, okay? Nothing too strenuous. Promise?"

"I promise."

As soon as he closed the door, she got out of bed. For a moment, she had to grasp the back of the chair for support. Her legs were wobbly and she felt lightheaded.

But after a moment, she felt better, and swiftly got dressed in the clothes Ben had picked up from Char. As soon as she was ready, she opened the door and found Shea, Ben, and Officer Garrety waiting for her, looking anxious.

Something had happened. She could tell.

"What? What is it?" she asked, looking from one to the others.

"We're going down to the station," Officer Garrety told her. "Right away."

"Why?"

"We just linked Meg with a report that came in at Crawford Corners—"

"One of Candra's friends saw her driving Meg's car yesterday afternoon!" Shea cut in. "This girl—Kim something—thought it was suspicious, since Candra had supposedly gone back to Jamaica earlier this week. She said she acted strange when she realized she'd been recognized, and drove off in a hurry."

"And this girl called the police?"

"Yes, this afternoon," Officer Garrety told Mirabelle. "She noted the license plate of the car, figuring Candra may have stolen it, and it's been traced to Meg. The only thing is, we have no real proof that it wasn't Meg driving the car—"

"Except that this girl, Kim, didn't know Meg existed," Ben pointed out. "She swears it was Candra."

"The Crawford Corners police are in the process of questioning Kim Williams—that's the girl who called in the report—and investigating this Candra person right now," the officer said. "No one's home at the McKenna place. They want to talk to you and Shea."

"Well then, let's go," Mirabelle said, and started down the hall.

She'd only taken a few steps when a surge of dizziness came over her. She blinked and reached out to steady herself against the wall.

Ben was at her side in an instant, putting his arm around her. "Mirabelle, are you sure you're all right?"

Behind her, she heard Shea and Officer Garrety echoing his concern.

"I'm fine," she murmured, taking a deep breath and closing her eyes for a moment, then forcing them open again. "Come on. We've got to hurry."

She started walking again, and Ben kept a steadying grip across her shoulders as they made their way to the police car parked out front.

Seven

"Do you want me to drive for a while?"

Landon's voice startled Candra out of her faraway thoughts, and she shook her head. "No . . . No, I'm fine," she muttered, and forced her full attention back to the Interstate ahead. Traffic was crawling and she'd been in the right lane, following the same set of headlights, for over an hour now.

"How far is it?" Landon asked.

"How far is what?"

"The place where we're spending the weekend."

"Oh, that." She hesitated.

Was now the time to tell him that they weren't just spending the weekend together? That they were running off to start a new life, someplace out west? Candra had no idea where . . . she hadn't gotten that far in her plan.

All she knew was that they had to get rid of the car and buy a couple of plane tickets first thing in the morning. And as for tonight . . . well, she'd just assumed they'd stop at some hotel later, near the airport.

Before, she'd been electrified at the thought of being alone, overnight, in a hotel room with Landon. Now, she felt only dread over the evening ahead.

Why can't you forget about why he's with you, and just enjoy the fact that he is? she berated herself.

But she couldn't.

And it wasn't just that.

How could she concentrate on being alone with Landon when she knew that Meg was out there somewhere in the storm, dying?

Being murdered, she corrected herself bluntly.

Because of you, your sister is going to die. And for what? For being the one our mother chose.

But Meg couldn't help that, any more than Candra had been able to help being left behind.

Tears sprang to her eyes, blurring the road through the windshield even more. She reached up and hurriedly wiped at them, but not before Landon noticed.

"Hey, Candra . . . are you okay?" He reached out and touched her shoulder.

She flinched. "I'm fine."

"No, you're not. Your eyes . . . are you *crying?*"

"No. It's just . . . they're just strained, from driving."

"Pull over," he said firmly. "I'll take over."

"But you don't know where we're going."

"So you can give me directions. Come on, pull off."

It *would* be a relief to sit back and let him take over, she thought, noticing for the first time that her shoulders ached and her hands were sore from clenching the wheel so tightly.

She glanced at the side of the road, then at the steady line of headlights in the rearview mirror. "We can't just pull off to the side of the road, Landon. It's too dangerous . . . the weather's too bad. Someone could hit us."

"Well, fine. Get off the highway at the next exit, and we'll switch places there."

She nodded, then allowed herself to recognize something she'd been fighting to ignore.

They were approaching the area of the Rocky Forest State Park. The exit couldn't be more than a few miles ahead.

Right at this very minute, Dalila should be someplace nearby, either hiking to the spot Candra had described, or maybe even digging in the ground, which had to be pure mud at this point.

You can stop her, a voice whispered in Candra's mind. *There's still time, and you're close enough.*

Stop her? Why would I want to do that? If I stop her, and let Meg live, everything will be ruined.

She bit her lower lip.

If she didn't stop Dalila, Meg would be dead.

Meg.

Her twin sister.

Candra didn't realize she was pushing down on the accelerator until Landon shouted, "Hey, slow down!"

Startled, she saw that she was right on the tail of the car in front of them, and she lifted her foot from the pedal.

"What are you doing tailgating in this weather, Candra?" Landon asked. "It's dangerous. And anyway, what's your hurry? It's like you're suddenly in a race or something. Relax."

"Sorry," she muttered, not looking at him. What *was* she doing?

"I know you're tired, but don't get us into an accident trying to make it to the next exit. Look—we're almost there. See that green sign?"

She knew what it would say even before she glanced at it.

Rocky Forest State Park, Exit 1 Mile.

Mirabelle looked from Officer Garrety, who stood beside her, to the man seated behind the desk.

His name was Sergeant Scovall, and he was the grandfatherly type, with a fringe of white hair and bright blue eyes.

Mirabelle had liked him immediately, even more so when he didn't seem to doubt her story.

But now, she had to convince him to go a few steps further and do something about it. There was no time to waste.

"So you're saying"—he said thoughtfully, resting his chin on his hand—"that you want to track your friend down using ESP."

"It's the only way," she said again, glancing at Officer Garrety for backup. "She's in danger. I know she is."

Officer Garrety cleared his throat. "I think we have no choice but to listen to Miss Moreau, here, and follow up on this, Sergeant. Remember the case last month with the kidnapped child in Spring City? A psychic found her."

"I know, I know," Scovall said impatiently. "I'm not denying that. But until we get a solid lead on this Candra person, there's not much to go on. And the officers who went out to Jonas Drayer's house on Soundview found that no one was home."

Mirabelle glanced over her shoulder. Through the office's glass window, she could see Ben leaning on the wall in the corridor, while Shea paced anxiously. The poor guy was at his wits' end, frantic with worry over Meg.

Just as Mirabelle was.

She closed her eyes and bent her head, tuning out the voices of the two men, concentrating on Meg.

Where are you?

A series of images flashed before her so swiftly and sharply that she was caught off guard. She gasped and clutched the armrests of the chair.

"What is it?" Officer Garrety asked, grabbing her elbow. "Are you all right, Mirabelle?"

"I saw her!" she announced, her eyes snapping open. "I saw Meg. Her hands and feet are tied, and she's unconscious. She's in a blue van parked in the woods."

"A blue van?" Officer Garrety repeated, and looked at the sergeant. "I didn't tell her that."

"You didn't tell me what?"

"That the vehicle Dalila Parker had rented and had those men load the cabinet into was a blue van."

"I swear he didn't tell me!" Mirabelle turned to Sergeant Scovall. "I saw it. You've got to believe me. And it's still here in Connecticut—I'm sure of that, too. In the woods someplace. If you'll just give me a chance, I can figure out exactly where. *Please!*"

The sergeant studied her. "Wait right here," he said after a long moment, and stood up. He left the office, closing the door behind him.

"Where do you think he's going?" Mirabelle asked Officer Garrety.

Out of the corner of her eye, she saw Shea and Ben looking after the sergeant as he strode down the hall, then facing her expectantly through the office window.

"I have no idea," the policeman said. "But I wouldn't be surprised if you just got through to him. This is exactly what happened with that psychic who was used in the kidnapping case, from what I hear. She knew details that no one had been told."

"I've got to figure out the rest," Mirabelle said, closing her eyes again and concentrating.

After a moment, she murmured, "East. And south. I'm getting those directions clearly . . . Meg's southeast of here."

"In the woods?"

"In the woods. But—"

Just then the office door opened again. Sergeant Scovall stood there with several other uniformed men.

"All right, Miss Moreau," he said abruptly. "I'm convinced. Help us locate Megan McKenna."

The exit road was familiar. Candra followed its curve to a two-lane highway and a sign with an arrow.

Rocky Forest State Park, 2 Miles.

"Just pull off in that convenience store parking lot," Landon said, pointing.

Candra glanced at it. It was where she had bought the flashlight the other night. She eyed the gas pumps in front of the store, and said, "You know what? We need gas. Let's fill up while we're here."

Landon peered at the sign in front of the store. "Okay. It says that it's self-serve only. Figures. I'll get out and do it."

"Thanks." She drove over and pulled up in front of the pumps. Her hand was shaking badly as she reached for the button that released the tank panel. She heard it pop open.

Landon put up the leather collar on his blue Nautica jacket and reached for the door handle. "That sign says 'Pay before you Pump,'" he told Mirabelle. "Do you want anything from inside? Something to drink?"

"Uh, yeah. I'll have a bottle of iced tea," she said impulsively. "And a bag of potato chips. And one of those little fruit pies. Cherry."

"Thirsty *and* hungry, huh?" He grinned. "Me, too. Be right back."

She nodded and turned away from him, not wanting to watch him walk away.

Setting her face grimly, she took a deep breath and counted to ten.

Then, telling herself she was doing the right thing, she shifted the car into Drive and pulled out onto the highway.

She headed, as fast as she could drive on the wet, bumpy road, in the direction of the park.

Mirabelle opened her eyes, shook her head, and sat up on the couch. She turned and knocked on the glass partition above her head, and a moment later, the office door opened.

"It's no use," she told Sergeant Scovall, who poked his head in. He had been waiting outside with the other officers.

"What's the matter?" he asked.

"I can't do it this way. I keep getting the same images—Meg, the van, the trees—but I can't get past that enough to tell exactly where she is, let alone to project myself there."

"But you still say she's someplace southeast of here, right?"

She nodded. "You know what would work? If I could be driven in that general direction, my instincts might take over so that I could lead you right to the spot."

"The roads are a mess—weekend rush hour traffic is still going strong, and everything's backed up because of the weather. That would take forever. But let me see what I can do. Just sit tight for a minute, okay?"

"Sure." She sighed and leaned back as he disappeared, tailed by the officers who had been clustered outside the door.

Moments later, Ben asked from the doorway, "What's going on?"

"Nothing yet. It's not working. I can't seem to concentrate enough to figure out exactly where Meg is. If I could just get closer to her, I have a feeling I'd be able to tell a lot more."

"Where'd the sergeant run off to?"

She shook her head. "I have no idea. He said he's going to see what he can do."

Ben came over and perched on the arm of the couch, looking down into her face. "You're exhausted."

"I'm fine," she lied. She was starting to feel awful again, but she couldn't give in to that. Meg needed her.

"Where's Shea?" she asked, to change the subject.

"Still out in the hallway. He's really upset."

"I know." Frustrated, Mirabelle banged a fist on the cushion beside her and said, "If I could just get closer . . . Ben, I know I'm capable of finding her! She's still alive—"

"Are you sure?"

"Positive. But not for long. That woman is going to murder her, Ben." Saying the words aloud for the first time seemed to make it real, and Mirabelle felt a lump rise swiftly in her throat.

Ben patted her shoulder in silence.

There seemed to be nothing else to say.

After what seemed like hours, but was probably no more than ten minutes, Sergeant Scovall reappeared. "Mirabelle?"

"Yes?"

"I need you to come with me, please."

She jumped up.

So did Ben. "Where are you going?" he asked the sergeant.

"We're going to do what we did in the kidnapping case last month. That time, we flew the psychic over the area in a helicopter until she was able to pinpoint the site where the child was being held."

Mirabelle froze halfway to the door. "A helicopter?" she echoed weakly.

"Yes. I've lined it up. They're waiting for you."

She swallowed hard over the lump that had become solid fear.

Cecile's words echoed back at her.

I see danger for you if you fly, Mirabelle.

The maid's premonition of something terrible happening to her while she was flying was one Mirabelle had shared on more than one occasion. For years, it had kept her from taking plane trips.

Now, in the space of a few seconds, she had to decide whether to risk her life by boarding a helicopter tonight to look for Meg.

There might be nothing to this whole thing about me flying, she told herself, trying to be reasonable.

But she wasn't convinced. Too often, she'd had shattering visions of danger involving planes.

But this isn't a plane—it's a helicopter. That's different. Is it?

As she hesitated, barely aware of the puzzled looks she was getting from Scovall and Ben, she glimpsed Shea through the open door over the sergeant's shoulder. He was sitting on the floor in the corridor, his face buried in his hands, his shoulders quaking.

He was crying, Mirabelle realized.

She made her decision in that instant.

"Okay, let's go," she said, lifting her chin and clenching her hands into fists at her sides.

Candra slowed the car at the entrance to the park. The rain had let up a little, and in the murky glare of the headlights, she could make out a chain stretched across the road, beside the deserted gatehouse. It had been there the other night, along with the sign that said *Park Closed After Dark.*

Just as she had then, she jumped out of the car and unfastened the chain, moving it out of the way. After she'd driven through, she got out again and grabbed the chain fumbling clumsily until she got it hooked.

Getting back in the driver's seat, she clenched the wheel and pulled forward. Her fingers were stiff and her hands were icy, not as much from the raw weather as from the dread that was building in the pit of her stomach.

How much time did she have? It could be mere minutes.

But Meg was still alive. She was positive of that.

She knew it, she realized with sudden clarity, the way she would know the instant her twin died.

She's a part of me . . . my other half, she told herself bitterly. *How could I have done this to her? I need her.*

A sob escaped her throat as she drove forward, following the narrow, tree-sheltered road in the direction she had taken the other night. It was nearly underwater in spots, and as she approached the turnoff up ahead, the car hydroplaned. Candra fought to get it back under control, then forged ahead.

As soon as she'd turned onto the side road that led to the hiking trail she'd taken, she realized she was in trou-

ble. It wasn't paved, and the rain had turned it into a
marsh. There were deep ruts where a vehicle had recently passed.

Dalila had come this way with Meg, recently enough
for the tracks to still be evident.

Candra followed the tire marks as fast as she could,
but the road was mostly uphill and it was rough going.
Several times, she started to skid, but managed to stop.

Then it happened—she skidded, lost control, and
ended up veering off the road.

"No!" she screamed, not so much out of fear for herself, but because she couldn't get stuck now. She had to
get to Meg.

The car narrowly missed hitting a stand of trees, and
when she'd brought it to a stop, she surveyed her position. She might be able to steer out of here.

She put the car into reverse, but as soon as she put
her foot on the gas, the wheels spun noisily. She shifted
into Drive, but that was no better. After a few minutes of
shifting back and forth, she realized it was no use. The
tires were mired in dense mud, and there was no way
she was going to be able to move it.

Peering out into the darkness, she tried to figure out
how far she was from the trail. The other night, it had
taken her only moments to drive up this road and park.
Now that she'd been forced to go so slowly, there was no
way to tell where she was.

But there was no time to waste, and she had only one
option.

She'd have to start hiking from here, and pray that
she got there in time.

She opened the car door and stepped out.

Instantly, her foot, clad in Meg's Italian leather boot,

sank into slimy muck. She winced and silently promised to buy her sister another pair . . . if she saw her again.

No . . . not if . . . *when I see her again,* she corrected herself.

Then, her jaw set grimly, she began hiking as fast as she could through the black, rainy, windswept forest.

Mirabelle felt hot and sweaty despite the chill in the aircraft as the motors revved on the launch pad. She rubbed her forehead, willing the light-headed feeling that had increasingly come over her to go away.

She needed to stay alert if she was going to find Meg.

"All set?" the uniformed pilot called over the roar of the engines, turning to look at her.

She nodded and checked her seat belt again with trembling hands, then folded them in her lap so that the pilot and Sergeant Scovell, who sat beside her, wouldn't notice.

She wanted to ask whether it was safe to take off in rain and wind like this, but told herself not to be ridiculous. Of course it was safe, otherwise they wouldn't be doing it.

All you have to worry about is Meg, Mirabelle reminded herself. *Just concentrate on Meg.*

The whir of the engines grew louder, and the pilot said, "Here we go."

Mirabelle turned and looked out the window. In the dark, rainy mist, she saw Ben and Shea standing off to the side with Officer Garrety. The officer had a hand on Shea's shoulder and was saying something to him, probably reassuring him that Meg was going to be all right.

Ben was watching the copter, and his eyes locked with Mirabelle's through the window.

Good-bye, Ben, she told him silently, wishing she could touch him one last time. He'd given her a brief hug and told her to be careful before she'd boarded the helicopter, and his arms around her had been such a comfort. . . .

You'll feel them again, she promised herself as the aircraft gave a little lurch.

But as it lifted off the ground, buffeted by wind and water, Mirabelle wasn't so sure.

Cecile's warning, and her own terrifying premonitions, shot through her mind again.

She fixed her gaze on Ben, watching as he fell away below her, telling herself that this might be the last time she would ever see him.

Suddenly, she realized she'd been a fool to have resisted getting involved with him. Why had she fought her feelings for him? Life was too short.

When she did come back from this helicopter ride, she promised herself, the first thing she would do was throw her arms around Ben and tell him how much he meant to her.

If she came back.

Candra found an abandoned blue rental van about a quarter of a mile away from where she'd left Meg's car in the mud. As soon as she spotted the van, she ran toward it, briefly seized by the hope that Dalila might have abandoned Meg in it while she went up the trail to dig.

But even as she drew closer, Candra instinctively knew that the vehicle was empty. She peered in the windshield anyway, then pounded on the locked doors and metal sides of the van, calling her sister's name vainly.

After a moment, she got hold of herself and knew she had to press on.

Leaving the van behind without a backward glance, she continued to move through the dark forest. Finally, she turned off the road at the hiking trail she'd followed the other night, the one she'd instructed Dalila to take.

The woods were heavy with shadows and mist, and she plunged ahead with her arms stretched out in front of her, pushing away the branches and stalks that crowded the narrow trail. Every so often she stopped to listen, but the steadily moaning wind made it impossible to hear anything, even if there had been anything to hear.

What was she expecting?

Dalila's voice?

Or Meg's?

What she wouldn't give to hear Meg's voice, she thought, pressing on desperately. How could she have blamed her sister for her own misfortune? How could she have schemed to kill her own flesh and blood?

Tears rolled down Candra's cheeks, mingling with the raindrops.

She was beginning to lose hope that her sister was still alive. She hadn't yet felt the stab of knowledge she felt certain would come over her at the moment Meg died, but she knew time was running out. Even now, Dalila might be pushing Meg's limp body into the trench she'd dug in the clearing. . . .

Even now, the black, slimy mud might be smothering the life out of Meg. . . .

The going was becoming more and more difficult as the trail grew steeper. It was impossible to tell in the darkness how far she still had to go.

Suddenly, Candra slipped and fell onto her knees

and outstretched hands on the muddy ground, and for a moment, she wanted to just stay there, and sob, and sleep . . .

Escape this nightmare.

But as she lay trying to find the energy and will to move on, the wind died down momentarily.

In that lull, she heard something just ahead.

A voice . . .

Dalila's voice, chanting.

Candra scrambled to her feet and rushed forward, clawing her way to the top of the trail to rescue her sister.

"Nervous flier?" Sergeant Scovall asked above the roar of the engines, eyeing Mirabelle across the tiny cabin of the helicopter.

As he spoke, a gust of wind slammed into the aircraft. She merely nodded, her throat choked with fear.

"Me, too. Takeoffs are the worst," he told her. She noticed that he was clutching his armrests so hard that his knuckles were a mottled pinkish white. The sight did nothing to reassure her.

She nodded again, and turned away to look back out the window.

Behind her, the sergeant said, "Don't worry, you'll relax in a few minutes. I always do. Gordy's an excellent pilot."

That doesn't matter, Mirabelle wanted to tell him. If something was going to happen, it was going to happen despite Gordy's skill.

The copter lurched again, and Mirabelle bit down hard on her lower lip to keep from crying out.

Why had she ignored her own sense of foreboding and flown after all these years?

How could she have been so foolish?

She knew, with growing certainty, that they weren't going to come down safely tonight. Her premonitions were rarely wrong, and they wouldn't be this time.

"Miss Moreau? We're headed southeast," Gordy said over his shoulder.

"Go to it, Mirabelle," Sergeant Scovall said, reaching across to touch her arm.

She nodded, closed her eyes, and struggled to concentrate.

After a few moments, she opened them again. "We're getting closer to her, but we're still not in the right territory. There are too many buildings and roads."

"In a few minutes we'll be away from the urban area," Gordy told her. "We're about to move into a region of several large wooded expanses that stretches from here to the shore—whoops, that's some wind," he said, adjusting a control on the panel in front of him as the copter pitched again.

Grimly, Mirabelle nodded, squeezed her eyes closed again, and tried to tune out everything but the thought of Meg.

At the top of the trail, Candra moved stealthily through the undergrowth, creeping toward the small clearing at the edge of the ravine several hundred feet away.

She could no longer hear Dalila, but whether it was because she'd stopped chanting or because her voice was drowned out by the wind, Candra wasn't sure.

She saw marks on the ground now, where something heavy had been dragged recently. She knew that it had been her sister's unconscious body, probably concealed in the canvas tarp she herself had advised Dalila to use.

As she moved slowly closer to the spot she had chosen—had it only been days ago?—for Meg's execution, Candra became aware of something hovering nearby. It was nothing tangible, just an aura, and yet it was so real—so ominous and evil—that she had to fight for control over her instincts, forcing herself not to turn and flee.

Only the knowledge that her sister's life was hanging in the balance kept her moving toward it.

That, and the realization that she, herself, had conjured the dark power.

As she slipped toward the edge of the tangled undergrowth and braced herself for whatever it was that she was about to find, Candra fully acknowledged her responsibility for the first time.

If anyone was to die here tonight, it should—and *would*—be her.

"There," Mirabelle shouted across the roar of the helicopter engines, pointing, for Gordy, in the right direction. "Keep going . . . she's down in those woods somewhere. We're almost there."

She felt as though she couldn't breathe as the helicopter flew lower, toward the spot that was drawing her instincts like a magnet, and yet somehow repelling her at the same time.

The images of Meg that kept flitting through her mind were shrouded now in a haze of murky darkness. There was a negative energy emanating from that wooded spot that made Mirabelle shudder in its very intensity.

Evil.

Pure evil, and it was stalking helpless Meg.

"We're getting closer. Come on! We have to get to her before it's too late!" Mirabelle practically screamed at the pilot.

"It's all right, Mirabelle, don't worry. We'll make it." Sergeant Scovall's tone was soothing, but she couldn't let it comfort her.

The copter flew lower still, fighting the stormy weather, and Mirabelle's eyes were riveted out the window on the black woods below.

Just as she was about to announce to the pilot that they were closing in on the spot where Meg was, the aircraft rolled crazily, then careened out of control.

It all happened in a fraction of a second—the pilot's panicked curse as he grappled with the controls, Sergeant Scovall's terrified shout, and a horrible, high-pitched shriek that encompassed a single, futile word.

"Nooooooo!"

That's me—that ungodly scream is coming from me, was Mirabelle's last startled, conscious thought before the unforgiving ground abruptly rose to meet them.

Eight

Candra carefully started to part the dense leaves that shielded her view of the clearing, then froze.

Something had just reverberated through the woods.

Something distant, yet more violent than the storm, something she couldn't put her finger on.

Her hands kept moving the branches aside even as her brain tried to imagine what it had been, and she realized, with a start, that she was looking right at Dalila Parker, who stood less than ten feet away.

The woman was motionless, her head cocked to one side, as though she, too, had sensed whatever it was that had just startled Candra.

Candra saw that Dalila was wearing a long, hooded robe made of some inky fabric. The hood concealed her face from Candra, who forced her gaze to travel downward, to the long, lumpy bundle on the ground beside the trench the woman had dug a few yards from the edge of a steep ravine.

Inside that filthy canvas tarp was her twin sister.

Now Dalila shrugged and turned her attention back to Meg. She stooped and removed something from the folds of her robe. It glinted, and Candra realized, with numbing horror, what it was.

Dalila stooped over the bundle on the ground, and then, in one sudden, violent motion, swooped in with the blade before Candra could react.

The ropes . . . she's just cutting the ropes, Candra realized after a chilling instant, watching as the woman
sliced away at the cords that encircled the tarp.

She stood again and tossed the knife aside, then bent
and grabbed the edge of the canvas and pulled at it
roughly, causing the bundle on the ground to flip over.
Dalila tugged again, and unwrapped the tarp until Candra spotted a long strand of dark hair poking out from
beneath it, and then a waxen-looking hand.

Moments later, Dalila had pulled the rest of the
shroud away so that Meg's outstretched, unconscious
form was revealed on the ground.

For a moment, as Dalila pushed the sleeves back on
her robe and reached down again, Candra thought the
woman was going to simply nudge the body until it tumbled into the shallow grave she'd dug.

But then, in a blur, she spotted Dalila's hand closing
over the handle of the knife again, and she realized that
she was going to stab Meg, killing her before she buried
her.

Candra moved instinctively as Dalila raised the blade.

Leaping forward, out of the bushes that had concealed her, she cried out, "Dalila, no! Stop!"

"Candra?" the woman looked up, the knife poised
inches from Meg's stomach. "What are you doing here?"

Her voice was different, Candra realized—not her own.
It was more guttural, and her words were monotone.

"I came to stop you," Candra said, and stifled a gasp
as the woman raised her head farther, and the folds of
the hood revealed her face.

Dalila's eyes betrayed the diabolic powers that had
taken over her body, just as Candra had willed them to
when she'd cast her spell.

This isn't Dalila, Candra realized with a stab of utter terror. *This is my worst nightmare come to life.*

"Stop me?" the strange voice echoed, and then laughed. "Why would you want to stop me? You were the one who wanted this. You were the one who made this happen."

"Well, I've changed my mind. I don't want Meg to die."

"Oh, you've changed your mind." The words were mocking. "You don't want Meg to die. Well, it's too late for that. *I* want Meg to die. She's going to die." The hand that held the knife raised menacingly again, hovering over Meg's body.

"No, please . . . she's my sister," Candra said, her voice coming out a whimper.

She expected to see the blade flash downward, but it remained poised, and the figure before her spoke again. "That's true. She's your sister. Your other half. And in ordering her death, *mon,* you have committed the most heinous crime of all: the destruction of your own flesh and blood."

"I know." It came out a sob, and Candra pressed a trembling fist against her lips. "I can't let you do it. I was wrong."

"No. She's responsible for your misery. She has stolen everything you should have had—the wealth, the comforts . . . your mother."

The words were an echo of Candra's own, spoken only yesterday. But she no longer believed them. Maybe she never had . . . maybe she'd only been trying to convince herself all along.

Now she only knew that she desperately needed her sister. Meg was all she had left . . . all that really mattered, anyway.

Meg was what she had been missing all her life, not

the rest of it—not the wealthy lifestyle she'd thought could make her happy.

Dalila's eyes were fixed on Candra's, and in their depths she saw glittering hatred. It was as though that hatred, along with bitter resentment and vengeance, had been transferred there from Candra's very soul. And in purging herself of those vile emotions, she had been left with something stronger.

A feeling more intense than any she had ever known swept over Candra as she moved her gaze from Dalila's face down to the figure on the ground. She wanted to reach out and stroke Meg's bruised forehead, to brush her tangled, matted hair back from her face, to whisper that everything was going to be all right.

But with a strangled cry, Dalila suddenly brought the knife straight downward.

Without thinking, Candra reached out and caught the woman's wrist, fighting with every ounce of strength to keep her from jabbing Meg with the deadly blade.

She reached out with her foot and wrapped it around Dalila's ankle, sending the woman tumbling backward onto the marshy ground. Candra pounced on her as she scrambled toward Meg, still brandishing the knife.

She clawed at Dalila through the folds of the robe, grabbing for the blade as it went by in a blur. The fingers of her left hand grazed the edge of it and she vaguely realized she'd been cut.

But Dalila still had the knife, and she had to stop her.

Impulsively, as the sleeve of the woman's robe bared her forearm, Candra bent and swiftly sank her teeth into the smooth brown flesh.

Dalila let out a howl, and her grasp on the knife went slack. Candra seized the handle and, clutching it tightly, scrambled to her feet and stepped back.

She held it up threateningly as Dalila rolled onto her back and pushed herself to a standing position. She glanced down at Meg, who still lay unconscious behind Candra.

"Don't go near her," Candra warned. "If you do, I swear I'll kill you."

The woman laughed, an eerie sound that was barely human. "Go ahead," she taunted. "Even if you do kill me, you'll still be in danger. Both of you," she added, with a dark glance at Meg. "You'll never be safe."

"What do you mean?"

"Someone is after you. Someone who is far more powerful than either of you. Someone who will stop at nothing to get what he wants."

"What are you talking about?" Candra demanded. She waved the knife slightly and hoped her hand didn't appear to be trembling. She felt as though her entire body was shaking, on the verge of collapse. "Who's after me?"

"He's after you *and* your sister. And . . . never mind," Dalila said, taking a step backward and shrugging. "Why should I tell you?"

"Dalila, listen to me. . . . You're not yourself. You're under my spell. I can take it off of you, and you can help me. We can help each other. You have to tell me what you're talking about."

The response was another laugh and another step backward. But this time, Dalila lost her footing.

Candra realized, in the instant the woman stumbled toward the ground, that she was too close to the edge of the ravine.

She dropped the knife and sprang forward to grab Dalila, but she wasn't fast enough.

With a cry of terror—or was it rage?—the woman went tumbling backward down the steep, rocky cliff.

Candra could do nothing but stop at the edge and listen and watch until the terrible dull thuds had ceased and Dalila's body lay broken and limp far below.

> *Forces of goodness*
> *Powers of light*
> *work with me*
> *with all your might . . .*
> *To break the spell*
> *that has been cast*
> *so that she*
> *may rise at last.*

Kneeling on the wet ground beside Meg, Candra stopped chanting and, with her hands still outstretched across her sister's prone body, bowed her head.

The rain still poured down from the unforgiving skies, and she was drenched and chilled through, but that didn't matter. Nothing mattered but bringing her sister back.

But she couldn't help wondering, again, whether it was any use to keep on trying. She'd been at it for what felt like hours, and still Meg hadn't moved.

Stubbornly, she told herself that she couldn't give up. She owed it to Meg.

And to herself.

Come on, she silently begged her twin. *I need you so much . . .*

With a heavy sigh, Candra lifted her head and began the chant yet again, not knowing what else she could do.

Forces of goodness
Powers of light
work with—

She froze and stared down into Meg's face. Was it her imagination, or had her sister's eyelids just fluttered?

She waited, holding her breath, but nothing happened.

Grimly, she began again.

"Forces of good—"

Yes! This time, she was positive that Meg's eyelashes had moved slightly.

"Meg!" Candra called, grabbing her sister's shoulders and giving her a little shake. "Can you hear me? It's me, Candra . . . your twin. Meg, please come back. I need you so much. I—I love you, Meg. Please . . ."

Suddenly, with a shudder that racked her whole body, Meg moaned and opened her eyes.

Candra gasped.

For a moment, she couldn't speak, could do nothing but stare down into the face that was a mirror image of her own.

Then, with a sob, she reached up to smooth the tangled strands of wet dark hair off her rain-drenched face. "Oh, Meg," she whispered raggedly, shaking her head.

"Candra?"

Hearing her name slip past those parched lips was a wonder. She had been waiting so long, hoping against hope. . . .

Candra looked gratefully into her sister's bewildered eyes. "Yes, it's me," she told her, and added, "I'm your twin."

Meg nodded, and, wincing, lifted her head. Candra

slipped her arms beneath Meg's and helped prop her into a sitting position.

Her sister glanced around, appearing dazed. "Where am I?"

Candra hesitated.

"It's a long story," she finally said. "I'll tell you later. Right now, we've got to get out of here. It's kind of far. Do you think you can get up and walk?"

"If you help me," Meg said simply, looking at her with trusting dark eyes.

Candra had to swallow over a sudden lump in her throat before she could reply.

"Sure, I'll help you. Come on—we'll do it together," she promised, and, reaching out, she slipped her hand into her sister's at last.

The back room of the small occult shop on Elmont Avenue was tiny and overpowered with the scent of exotic herbs and powders, damp wooden floorboards, and age.

The lone occupant, a dark-skinned, strong-bodied young man, didn't notice the close, stale atmosphere or the violent sounds of the storm that raged outside in the night.

He stood, clad in a long black hooded robe, before the Obeah altar he had prepared on top of several stacked packing crates.

Flickering candlelight danced on the walls, casting eerie shadows and mingling occasionally with bright flashes of lightning that slashed through the one small window on the back wall.

He lit the incense burner on the altar, and a pungent wisp of smoke rose to blend with the already musty air.

Raising his arms and closing his eyes, he began to

chant silently, invoking the forces of evil. Then he reached with one hand for a shallow pottery bowl on the altar, pulling it closer, as the long, dark fingers of his other hand disappeared in the folds of his robe, and, a moment later, produced two cardboard rectangles.

He stared at them for a long moment, then shook his head as if to clear it. Holding the rectangles above his head in both hands, he began muttering a new chant, each phrase growing more feverish and punctuated by claps of thunder from above.

Finally, with a flourish, he dropped them so that they fluttered into the shallow bowl, landing face up.

Identical pairs of eyes stared at him from the photographs—black, almond-shaped, exotic eyes.

One pair belonged to Megan McKenna, and the formal school picture was one he had stolen from her own bedroom.

The other pair of eyes were Candra Bowen's, captured in a shot he had snapped surreptitiously on the street just the other day.

He met their unsuspecting, frozen stares with a narrowed gaze and reached for a small vial on the altar. He poured the few ounces of liquid it contained into the bowl. Now the familiar faces watched him from beneath the watery surface.

A long black candle burned beside him, and he carefully removed it from its holder. In one swift movement, he passed the flame over the bowl, then watched as the contents ignited.

He had only one last fleeting glimpse of the faces of the twin sisters before both photographs were obliterated to ashes in the furious orange and yellow inferno.

A sinister smile curled his lips.

Nine

"Just a little farther . . . can you make it?" Candra asked Meg, shouting to be heard above the wind and rain that swirled around them.

"I think so." Meg was clutching Candra's arm so hard that it hurt.

Her flesh was probably actually going to be bruised, Candra realized, as Meg stumbled a little and tightened her grasp even more.

Grimly, Candra looked straight ahead along the dark trail, thinking that she deserved the pain after what she had done. She deserved a far worse punishment.

Oh, Meg, how could I have done it?

She bit down on her lip to keep from saying the words aloud, instead telling her sister, "We're almost there."

"But where are we going?" Meg asked, stopping for a moment and pushing her long, soggy hair from her face. "We're in the middle of nowhere."

Candra stopped, too, and peered at her twin in the darkness.

It was still so startling to stare at a mirror image of her own features. Meg had the same large, almond-shaped dark eyes, the same full lips and exotic bone structure, the same olive-toned skin. She even wore her straight black hair the same, parted in the middle and hanging down her back.

"We're in Rocky Forest State Park," she told Meg patiently, as she shoved her own dripping tresses out of her eyes. "Remember? I told you that when you asked a few minutes ago."

"I know, but . . . why?"

Candra hesitated. She knew her sister didn't have any memory of how she'd gotten here. She couldn't know that Dalila Parker had driven her unconscious body in a rented blue van from her apartment in Spring City, Connecticut.

She couldn't know *anything* that had happened to her, in fact, from the moment Dalila had slipped the powerful potion into Meg's tea and cast a spell on her that afternoon almost a week ago.

As Candra locked into her sister's blank, confused expression, she knew what she *should* do.

She should tell Meg the truth.

That she, Candra, had been behind the whole scheme. That she had not only bribed Dalila to get Meg out of the way for a while so that Candra could step into her charmed world . . .

But that Candra, caught up in a frenzy of greed and fury, had also cast a spell on Dalila. She had beckoned the forces of evil to overpower Dalila so that she would agree to bring Meg to this desolate spot for one diabolical reason.

Candra had wanted Meg murdered.

But you changed your mind! she told herself, fighting to control the wave of near-hysteria that rose in her gut. *You're the one who saved her from Dalila. If you hadn't gotten here when you did, Meg wouldn't be alive.*

Instead, it was Dalila who had been killed, in a fall over the edge of a steep ravine a few miles up the trail.

And she's the only one who knew, Candra reminded herself. *With her out of the way, there's no way Meg can find out what you did—what you* almost *did.*

"Candra?" Meg asked, reaching out and taking her arm again. Her other hand clenched the stiff canvas tarp that Candra had wrapped around her, since Meg was wearing only a T-shirt and jeans.

Meanwhile, Candra was wearing Meg's clothes, just as she had been all week. If Meg had recognized the black jeans or storm coat, she hadn't said anything. And the Italian leather boots on Candra's feet were so coated in mud that they were well beyond easy identification.

"Candra?" Meg repeated. "Are you okay?"

"Yeah, *mon*," Candra said vaguely, automatically taking on the Jamaican dialect she had fought so hard to lose over the past several weeks.

Meg smiled faintly. "You have an island accent."

"No, I don't," Candra denied quickly, realizing what she had done and slipping back into the smooth Connecticut speech pattern that had become second nature while she was posing as Meg.

"I didn't mean it in a bad way," Meg said. "Actually, I think it sounds cool."

Candra said nothing, just looked away.

She couldn't bear that her sister was being so kind. After what she'd done—what she'd *tried* to do to Meg.

Tell her! her conscience demanded. *Tell her right now. Get it over with.*

But she couldn't bring herself to confess.

Instead, she said, "Come on, let's keep going. I think it's starting to rain harder."

Meg didn't protest, just grabbed Candra's sore arm again, causing her to wince slightly as they trudged on through the stormy woods.

Meg's mind was spinning.

Was she really hiking through the woods at night in the middle of a downpour . . . with her long-lost twin sister at her side?

The whole thing was surreal, and yet, somehow, she accepted it.

It was Candra's presence that reassured her. Though they were strangers, she felt an odd sense of comfort at finally coming face-to-face with her sister after a lifetime apart. It was as though, bewildering as it had been to regain consciousness in this bizarre setting, nothing seemed to matter for now but the fact that she had found her other half.

Eventually, Meg knew, Candra would tell her what was going on.

Until then, there was nothing to do but follow her sister over the narrow, uneven trail toward wherever it was that they were going.

She trusted Candra instinctively, in a way that she had never trusted another person in her life. With Candra, she knew she was safe.

How could it be otherwise? Candra was a part of her. They had been formed from the same cells, had been carried, intertwined, for nine months in the intimate confines of their mother's womb.

Until somehow, something had wrenched them apart.

Someone, Meg told herself, and thought of her mother. Giselle was weak—she'd always known that. But Meg had never doubted that her mother loved her. And she wondered, not for the first time, how the same woman who had raised her could have denied her twin.

How must Candra feel, knowing that their mother had given her up? Did Candra know why? Or was their past as much a mystery to her as it was to Meg?

Meg pushed away the endless questions that coursed through her mind, telling herself that soon, when they were warm and dry and back home, her sister would provide some answers.

Or if Candra knew nothing more than she did, at least they could unravel the secrets of their past, together.

And now that they'd found each other, they wouldn't let anything—*anyone* tear them apart again.

For now, Meg kept her mouth shut and her eyes focused on Candra's dark silhouette in front of her as they made their way out of the woods.

"There it is," Candra announced to Meg as they emerged from the trail at last onto the muddy road that wound through the park. She pointed to Meg's black Honda, which was mired where Candra had deserted it . . . could it have only been a short hour or two ago?

"My car . . . what's it doing there? I don't remember driving it here," Meg said, her voice a high-pitched protest that mingled with the rising wind.

"You didn't," Candra said simply. "I did."

"But how did *I* get here?"

"Dalila Parker drove you here in that van," Candra said, pointing at the second abandoned vehicle nearby. "You don't remember it, do you?"

"No." Meg shook her head slowly, frowning as though she was trying to come up with some recollection.

"Do you know who Dalila is?"

"She's the woman who lives over on Elmont Avenue . . . the one I met at that carnival with Zoe. The one who brought us back together . . . right?"

Candra turned her head so she wouldn't have to see Meg searching her face for answers.

"Right," she mumbled, and tugged Meg along the last few yards to the car.

"Let's get in and warm up for a few minutes," Candra said, her teeth suddenly chattering. She reached into her pocket for the keys and unlocked the driver's side door with shaking fingers.

Only when she'd pulled the door open did she realize that it was Meg, and not her, who belonged behind the wheel. This was Meg's car, not Candra's.

The masquerade was over. It was time for Candra to step back into her rightful place.

"Here, go ahead," she said, moving away from the door and motioning for Meg to get in.

Her sister shook her head. "You drive," she told Candra, and added, "I mean, if you don't mind. I still feel too out of it. And besides, I still have no idea where we are."

Without protest, Candra climbed behind the wheel and pressed the button to unlock the passenger's side door. Guiltily, she fingered Meg's silver Tiffany key ring before jabbing it into the ignition and turning on the engine. She busied herself pushing the heat control onto the highest setting as Meg got in beside her and closed her door, shutting out the roar of the wind.

"It takes a few minutes for the heat to get going," Meg

said, settling back against the seat with a sigh. "It'll kick in soon. It always does."

And again Candra was reminded that the car belonged to Meg, not to her.

Meg had no idea that Candra had been driving it for the past week, or that Candra had been living in her home, sleeping in her bed, inhabiting every part of her privileged world.

She had no way of even suspecting what had been going on.

No one knows the truth, except Dalila, Candra thought again, and lifted her gaze from the dashboard to look out through the rain-drenched windshield into the darkness that surrounded them.

And with Dalila gone, there's only one way Meg is going to find out what I've done.

I have to tell her.

I have to tell her now, before I change my mind.

And of course, Candra knew she couldn't change her mind. She couldn't lie to her sister about what had happened over the past week.

Could she?

Of course, she *could.*

It was *possible* that she could get away with what she had done.

But she *wouldn't* do something like that.

It was time to stop living a lie.

Time to do what was right.

Time to tell the truth and face the consequences.

"Candra," Meg said beside her, and reached across the seat to grasp Candra's cold, damp hand in her own.

A lump rose suddenly and violently in Candra's throat at the contact with her sister's bare skin.

"Please tell me," Meg said quietly. "What's going on?

Why are we here? Where did I get these clothes that I'm
wearing? I've never seen them before in my life. I feel
so strange . . . like I'm losing my mind, or something.
Why can't I remember anything?"

Something in Meg's voice reached down into Candra's
soul, and she felt herself quaking inside, too overcome
with emotion to speak right away. Meg sounded uncertain, and frightened, and yet there was an unsettling
intimacy in the way she had spoken to Candra.

It was as though she trusted Candra to make everything all right, the way she had blindly trusted Candra
to guide her out of the woods just now.

But how can she trust me after what I've done?

I have to tell her.

No more putting it off.

I have to confess . . .

"Candra, come on, you have to tell me what's going
on. I have to know. Please . . ."

Miserably, Candra turned to look at her sister.

Meg's eyes fastened immediately on her own, and
even in the shadowy interior of the car, Candra could
read the expression on her sister's face.

It was one of utter faith.

"I . . ."

Candra stopped, took a deep breath, and started
again. "Dalila . . ." she said, and forced herself to go on.
"Dalila brought you here to kill you, Meg."

Though her sister gasped at the words and her free
hand flew up to press against her mouth, Candra saw in
her eyes that she wasn't entirely shocked.

She paused, searching for the words to convey the
rest of the story.

Before she could go on, Meg said, "I knew there was
something about that woman . . . from the moment I

met her, she gave me the creeps, Candra. Thank God you saved me from her."

Wide-eyed, Candra asked, "But . . . how did you know that?"

"I just assumed . . . I mean, isn't that what happened? Didn't you save me?"

Slowly, Candra nodded.

She felt Meg's grasp tighten around her hand. Somehow, Meg's flesh was warm, and Candra vaguely willed her sister's body heat to banish the chill from her own icy hands.

"But why did Dalila want to kill me?" Meg asked. "I mean, she was odd, but she didn't seem evil. And she promised to introduce me to you. She brought us together, didn't she?"

Without waiting for a reply, Meg added, "But I can't even remember what happened after I went over to her apartment to meet you this afternoon."

"This after . . ." Candra echoed, staring at her sister. The rain-spattered windshield cast her face in an eerie polka-dot pattern. "Meg, that wasn't this afternoon."

"What do you mean?"

Candra couldn't reply. Her mind was racing.

"You mean," Meg said slowly, frowning, "that I've blanked out more than a few *hours?* Oh, God . . . What day is it?"

"It's Friday. Actually, not anymore," Candra said, glancing at the dashboard clock, which told her that it was well after midnight. "It's Saturday."

"Which . . . which Saturday? How much time has passed since that day at Dalila's?"

"Almost a week."

Meg nodded, looking too stunned to speak again.

Candra's thoughts tumbled over each other.

Not only didn't Meg realize what Candra had been up to, but she now seemed to think she was suffering from some form of amnesia.

Which was true, actually.

The spell Dalila had cast had rendered Meg into a state of suspended animation. For her, time had obviously stood still from the moment she'd lost consciousness after drinking that tea Monday afternoon.

She'll never know if you don't tell her, Candra thought again, staring out at the storm through the windshield.

"So," Meg said in a small, hollow-sounding voice, "I've been out of it for almost a week. What happened during that time?"

Candra found herself shrugging.

How could she tell Meg what had happened? How could she say, *You've been lying unconscious in Dalila's apartment since Monday?*

After another moment's hesitation, she lied, "I have no idea what you did during most of that time, Meg."

"But you do remember that we were supposed to meet in Dalila's apartment on Monday afternoon, right?" Meg asked. "Please tell me I didn't imagine that whole thing."

"No, you didn't imagine it."

"Thank God I'm not a total nut case." Meg smiled faintly. "So we met . . . I wish I could remember it. Ever since I found out you existed, I fantasized about what it would be like to come face to face with you. I can't believe that when it actually happened, I somehow zoned out."

"Maybe that's why," Candra found herself blurting. "Maybe it was too much for you, emotionally. Maybe you couldn't handle something like that—so you sort of . . . lost it for a while."

"You think?" Meg looked relieved.

Candra nodded, ignoring the protests of her conscience, which was warning her to confess. "I know what it was like for me, meeting you," she told Meg. "Intense."

At least that was the truth.

And Meg was bobbing her head up and down, like she understood. "When did you find out that I existed?" she asked Candra. "Did you know when you were living back in Jamaica?"

"No. I didn't find out until I came to Crawford Corners."

"But that's such an unbelievable coincidence, isn't it?" Meg asked. "That you would end up here, in Crawford Corners, out of all the towns in the whole country? Dalila said you were living on an estate with . . . your grandmother."

"Not my grandmother," Candra corrected swiftly, and bitterly. "Rosamund Bowen isn't related to me in any way. But yes, I did think she was my grandmother. She was a housekeeper for the Drayers . . . Jonas Drayer." She paused, and when Meg didn't say anything, went on. "He's an American. Gran—Rosamund worked for him in Jamaica, where he was a developer for SNE Real Estate. Then—"

"SNE?" Meg interrupted. "As in, Southern New England? My grandfather worked for them, too. The company is based here in Crawford Corners. I guess that explains the coincidence. His job was the reason my mother—sorry, *our* mother—was in Jamaica in the first place back when we were born."

"So obviously, she left me behind and brought you back here to the States with her," Candra said, unable to keep the chill out of her voice.

Meg looked troubled. "I guess," she said quietly, her eyebrows furrowing.

"Anyway"—Candra went on, shrugging as though it didn't bring fresh pain every time she acknowledged what Giselle had done—"when Jonas decided to move his family back home, he brought Rosamund and me with him. We've been living at the Drayers' place out on Soundview Road."

A flicker of recognition lit Meg's eyes. "I know where that is," she said, nodding. "Mom mentioned something about them being back in town, and one night, Shea and I turned around in the driveway of their house. A big white place with a curved driveway, right?"

"Right."

"Shea's my boyfriend—did you know that?" Meg asked, her expression clouding over again. She didn't wait for an answer. "At least, he *was*. We've been having trouble lately. I hope . . . I wonder what's going on with us now. It's so weird that I can't remember . . . Oh, God, Candra, you have to tell me everything you know."

"I will," Candra assured her, even as guilt stole over her again, stronger than ever. "Don't worry, Meg. I'll tell you everything."

You can't do this. You have to tell her the truth.

It's now or never.

You won't be able to live with yourself if you don't confess.

And she realized it was true.

She hated herself for what she had done.

She owed it to Meg, and to herself, to tell the truth.

There was only one way to pay the price for the sins she had committed against her sister. She had to own up to what she had done, and she had to do it now.

She opened her mouth and forced herself to speak. "Meg, there's something I have to—"

"What was that? Did you hear it?" Meg interrupted, and both sisters looked around, startled, as a blinding beam of light suddenly came out of nowhere and swept through the car.

"Oh, thank God. Look—it's the police." Meg squinted into the misty darkness and glimpsed two men in uniforms stepping out of the car that had pulled up behind the Honda.

There was a third person with them, she noted—another man. Or, rather, a guy about Meg's age, she revised as he drew closer. He was tall and broad shouldered. Meg sensed the hurry in his pace as he and the officers approached the car, but she saw one of the cops put a hand on his arm and caution him to stay behind them.

Frowning, she looked at Candra. "Who's that guy with them?"

Her sister was just staring out the back window of the car, a strange, unreadable expression on her face.

A moment later, there was a cop on each side of the car, opening both doors and jerking blinding flashlight beams into the interior.

"Candra Bowen?" the officer on Meg's side asked, peering at her.

And Meg heard the officer on Candra's side ask the same thing. *How strange,* she thought fleetingly, *that they don't know the difference. We could switch places and no one would ever know . . .*

"No, I'm Meg," she heard herself say, and the officer looked relieved.

"Megan McKenna?"

"Uh-huh."

"Are you all right, miss?" he asked, and she noticed

that he was young and baby-faced, probably not much older than his midtwenties.

"I'm fine." Obviously, they knew that she had been in danger. "My sister got to me in time," she added, and looked over to see that Candra was being helped—or pulled?—out of the car by the other officer, who was bigger and older and gruffer looking.

Meg heard him say, "You have a lot of explaining to do."

And then the young guy in the down jacket was there, too, pushing his way in and asking, "Candra, are you all right? I thought you'd been kidnapped when I came out of the store and—"

"Mr. Keller," the other officer cut in, "would you please step back and be quiet?"

"Sorry, Officer, I just—"

"It's okay, Landon," Candra interrupted. "I'm fine."

Bewildered, Meg turned to the policeman on her side of the car. "What happened?"

"We were hoping you'd be able to tell us," he said, leaning into the car so that his head was out of the downpour. He seemed to be waiting for her to reply.

"I . . . I can't," she admitted slowly. "I have no idea how I got here. All I know is that my sister saved me from that woman."

"What woman?"

"Dalila Parker."

The officer nodded, as though he recognized the name. "And where is she now?"

Meg jerked her head in the direction of the trail. "Up there, somewhere. She tripped and fell over the edge of the ravine. Candra said she's dead."

The officer's jaw stiffened and he lifted his head to call to his partner. "Hey, Chuck? Can I talk to you a minute?" He looked back at Meg and said sternly but not unkindly, "You stay put right in this car, okay?"

"Okay."

She watched as the two policemen walked around to the back of the car, one of them dragging Candra along by the arm. The guy she'd called Landon stood a few yards away, apparently focused intently on the conversation they were having.

Meg wished she could hear what was being said, but even with her door open, it was impossible with the storm raging around them. The cops were doing a lot of finger pointing and arm waving at Candra, and she seemed to be cooperating calmly, nodding or shaking her head or shrugging.

After what seemed like an eternity, the cop Meg had been talking to came back over to the car and bent to look at her again. She saw that his dark hair was now plastered to the sides of his wet face, and his uniform was soaked.

"Miss McKenna? I'd like to ask you a few questions," he said grimly.

It seemed like the younger officer had been in the car for hours, questioning Meg. Candra stood stiffly, watching, her arm—the same sore arm Meg had clung to earlier—imprisoned in the officer's iron grasp.

Relax, she told herself, not for the first time since the cops had approached the car. *They can't prove anything. As far as they know, as far as anyone knows, you did nothing wrong.*

She felt Landon's gaze on her, and deliberately kept her attention focused on the car. She didn't want to acknowledge the questions she'd seen when she'd looked into his eyes before.

He hadn't seemed accusing, like the policemen, but maybe the fact that he wasn't suspicious of her was even worse.

He'd looked at her with bewilderment and anxiety and, mostly, concern. But Candra knew why. His emotions weren't coming from his heart, they were coming from the spell she'd placed on him. The spell that made him want her, passionately and blindly.

It was the only reason he'd ever wanted to be with her, the only reason he'd agreed to go away with her tonight, no questions asked.

And obviously, he wasn't even daunted by the fact that she'd taken off and left him while he was paying for gasoline in that convenience store back on the highway. No, he'd actually thought she'd been kidnapped.

He'd called the police from a pay phone in front of the store, the officers had told her, and reported that his girlfriend had been abducted.

His *girlfriend*.

What Candra wouldn't have given, just a short time ago, to hear him call her that.

A guy like Landon Keller—with his all-American good looks, private school education, and easygoing popularity—a guy like him shouldn't have noticed someone like Candra Bowen. All right, most males *did* look twice at her, but once Landon realized that she was merely the Jamaican immigrant who lived in the servants' quarters at his friend Craig's home, he should have moved on.

She had made sure that wouldn't happen.

And now, knowing that what he felt for her wasn't real, she wished more than anything that she had simply left him alone in the first place. Indifference—or even Craig Drayer's brand of mocking sarcasm—would be better than magically manufactured care and concern.

"All right, Miss McKenna," the young officer finally said. "If you're sure you don't remember anything else, we'll have to give it up for tonight."

"I don't remember anything that happened after Monday afternoon," Meg insisted, feeling like a broken record.

"And I believe you, okay? Temporary amnesia is a typical response after trauma. We want to have you checked out by paramedics to make sure you're all right. And then we'll arrange to get you back to Crawford Corners so that—"

"And my sister, too," Meg cut in quickly, casting a glance at Candra, who still stood out in the pouring rain, flanked by the burly cop.

"I'm not sure what's going to happen to your sister," the policeman said, opening the car door. "We have to radio in for backup, and— look, we'll know more in a little while. You stay here."

"Can't I get out and talk to Candra for a second? I just want to make sure she's all right."

"I'm afraid not. And don't worry, she's fine."

"But she's getting soaked out in the rain."

The officer shrugged. With a brief wave, he was gone, leaving Meg alone in the dark again.

She twisted in her seat and watched him going back over to his partner. The two conferred briefly before the younger one apparently took over guarding Candra as the older one went to the police car.

Oh, Candra, what's going on? Meg wondered, and sighed. *Are you in some sort of trouble?*

But if her sister was in trouble, Meg vowed fiercely that she'd do everything she could to help.

After all, she and Candra were a team, and she wasn't about to let anything come between them ever again.

"I'm exhausted," Meg said, yawning and stretching as the police car left I-95 on the exit leading to Crawford Corners at dawn. She turned to Candra, who sat beside her on the backseat. "Aren't you beat?"

Candra nodded. It had been a few hours since she had been cleared of any wrongdoing, but she still felt edgy, especially since the two police officers in the front seat seemed to regard her with undercurrents of suspicion anyway.

But there was nothing they could pin on her. No one could prove that she had tried to harm Meg, especially with Meg vehemently insisting that if it weren't for Candra, Dalila Parker would have killed her.

All they could do was ask Candra to point the backup squad in the direction of Dalila's body.

Then an emergency rescue truck had arrived on the scene, and the paramedics had wrapped Candra and Meg in thick blankets and examined them both.

The whole time, Landon had hovered, looking worried and mostly staying silent. Luckily, it was hard for him to get close enough to speak to Candra, with Meg pretty much clinging to her side, and all the police officers and rescue workers bustling around.

Finally, the two original cops announced that they would be transporting Candra and Meg back to Crawford Corners, and that they had arranged for another officer to drive Landon back to The Lawson School. Meg's car, which was still mired in mud, would be left behind for now.

As the officers prepared to escort Meg and Candra to their car, Landon had touched Candra's shoulder gently and whispered, "Call me in the morning, okay?"

She'd simply nodded, and tore her gaze from his— though not before seeing the tender expression in them.

"It's Meadowview Terrace, the next one up." Meg's voice crashed into Candra's thoughts, and she realized they were almost home.

Home? It's not your home. Not anymore, though it was fun pretending for a while . . .

"Too bad Mom isn't here—but she'll be back from Fiji sometime tomorrow," Meg told Candra as the car made the turn onto the quiet, familiar street.

The houses here were large and upscale and set far back from the road, with well-tended, sweeping lawns. Candra remembered how satisfying it had been to pretend she belonged here during these last fleeting days.

"I can't wait until she finds out about you. She's going to—"

When Meg stopped short, Candra looked up and followed her gaze to number forty-one, a familiar red brick colonial. And she saw what had startled her sister. A police car was parked in the driveway.

"What are the cops doing at my house? What's going on?" Meg asked, sounding panicky and leaning toward the two cops in the front seat.

"I don't know," the younger one, Officer Hammond, said with a frown. He looked at his partner, who was behind the wheel. "What do you think, Chuck?"

The older officer shrugged and pulled the car to a stop at the curb.

"I hope it's not about my sister . . . I mean Carrie, my other sister," Meg added with a quick, almost apologetic glance at Candra before she opened the door and jumped out. She raced across the lawn as a cop got out of the car in the driveway.

Candra and the two officers followed, arriving just in time to see Meg burst into tears.

"What is it?" Candra asked, a sick feeling in her stomach.

"An accident," the uniformed officer said.

"Her sister?" Officer Hammond asked.

"No, it's my friend Mirabelle," Meg wailed. "Oh, God . . ."

Mirabelle.

Candra's gut twisted with recognition at the name.

Mirabelle Moreau was the girl who, along with Shea, had followed Candra when she'd been driving Meg's car the other day. It was Dalila Parker who had told her that Mirabelle was Meg's friend, and that she, too, had powers.

She forced her attention back on the situation at hand.

"I'm Officer Garrety," the cop was saying. Candra felt his eyes sweeping over her and sensed the same aura of suspicion she had gotten from the other two men.

She met his gaze head-on and straightened her shoulders. After a moment, she was pleased to see that he seemed uncomfortable and looked away, addressing the other two men.

"I heard you were on your way here and I was sent over to meet you. I've been working with Mirabelle and a few of Meg's other friends, who were concerned that she was in danger. You don't know how relieved we were when we got the call a few hours ago that she'd been located."

Officer Hammond nodded. "Did they tell you what had happened?"

"I know she had been kidnapped by the Parker woman, who then tried to kill her. That was what Mirabelle said. She knew the Parker woman's plans, though we still have no clear motive."

Again, Candra was aware of Officer Garrety flicking a distrustful glance in her direction.

"But how did Mirabelle find out what was going on?" Meg asked.

Officer Garrety hesitated, then said, mostly to the other two officers, "Uh, we don't normally use psychics to locate missing persons, but this girl knew what she was talking about."

Candra stiffened. So Mirabelle had figured out what Dalila was up to. What else had she known?

"Anyway," the officer continued, "she was up in a police chopper, leading the pilot and our sergeant to Rocky Forest, when it went down. Weather like this, they shouldn't have been flying," he added, shaking his head and gesturing at the sky, which was still gray-black and spilling torrents of rain.

"You said she was in critical condition. Is she going to pull through?" Meg asked, sniffling and calming down.

"I don't know. She's at Spring City General."

Candra caught her lower lip in her front teeth and pondered that. If Mirabelle lived, she might implicate Candra. And yet, what evidence could she possibly have that Candra had schemed to have Meg killed?

Beside her, she suddenly realized, Meg was shivering violently.

Candra instinctively put an arm around her twin's shoulder and said, both for her sister's benefit and for the officers', "We have to get inside. After everything she's been through, she needs to rest."

She flashed a brief smile at Meg's grateful, exhausted expression, then turned back to the three policemen.

"I'm sure you'll keep us posted on Mirabelle's condition," Candra informed Officer Garrety in a no-nonsense voice, then added to the other two men, "And thank you for driving us back here, and for everything else."

They nodded, all three of them.

Her arm still around Meg's shoulder, she started leading her sister up the walk to the front porch.

It wasn't until they were in the foyer, with the door closed and locked against the storm and the three pairs of suspicious eyes, that Candra realized she'd been holding her breath.

She let it out in a sigh of relief.

"Are you okay, Candra?" Meg asked.

"I'm fine." *Now that that's over,* she added silently.

And it *was* over.

Case closed.

"You know"—Meg said, looking closely at her in the bright overhead light—"you really do look exactly like me. I even have a coat like that."

"It's yours," Candra said truthfully, and impulsively added, "you loaned it to me the other day. Remember?"

"No." Meg's eyes were sleepy-looking, and she yawned. "I can't remember anything . . ."

"Come on," Candra told Meg, and gestured at the balcony above, where the bedrooms were. "You have to get upstairs."

"I don't know if I can walk another step," Meg said wearily. "I feel like I want to just drop right here and curl up on the floor."

"No, don't do that," Candra told her firmly.

Meg protested with a weary groan and really did look like she was going to collapse on the spot.

"Listen, Meg, I'll help you. Come on."

She was grateful when Meg allowed herself to be led across the foyer, with its polished honey-hued wooden floors, framed original watercolors, and delicate crystal chandelier that was suspended from the twenty-foot ceiling.

"You've been so great to me, Candra," Meg murmured.

"You're my sister," Candra said simply.

You're my sister, but I can't bring myself to tell you the truth. And now you think I'm your savior, instead of the person who tried to kill you.

But, she promised herself, as she and Meg started up the curved staircase, that starting this moment, she'd make it up to Meg.

She'd do whatever it took . . . as long as she didn't have to tell her the truth.

Ten

Saturday morning dawned gray and rainy on Elmont Avenue in Spring City, making the seedy neighborhood appear more dismal than ever. The storm had stalled just off the New England coast, and it wasn't expected to move out of the area for several hours.

The Closed sign was still hanging on the glass door pane of the tiny occult shop down the block from Rivera's Newsstand. But the place wasn't deserted.

The young man who had spent the last few hours sleeping on a woven mat in the cramped back storeroom emerged into the front of the store and walked over to the window.

He looked down the street and saw that two patrol cars were parked in front of Rivera's, their domed red lights spinning silently.

The sight didn't surprise him.

He had been awakened from a sound sleep by the sudden, certain knowledge that something had happened to Dalila Parker.

And he knew, just as clearly, that both Candra and Meg were still alive.

Oh, well.

There was still time. Still plenty of time.

Although, it was a pity that Dalila Parker wouldn't be able to tell him whatever it was that she'd been hiding from him. He'd sensed that she had some kind of secret when he'd first spoken to her. But the woman had insisted on keeping it to herself.

He'd figured he would force her, in time, to tell him whatever it was. Especially once he had her under his power.

He smiled, thinking about the monster he'd created in the middle-aged woman. Candra had thought she was so clever, casting that small spell on Dalila so that the woman would destroy Meg for her.

Little did the girl know that Dalila was under a much more powerful spell—or that someone else wanted Meg dead.

And he'd wanted Candra dead, too.

Now it appeared that he'd have to accomplish both deeds by himself. He hated to do it. Things could get messy that way.

He sighed and calmly ran his strong, ebony-skinned hands over his head to pat his close-cropped dark hair into place. He removed his long black coat from a hook, slipped into it, then unlocked the door and pushed it open.

The chill in the air took his breath away momentarily, accustomed as he was to the hot, balmy mornings back in Jamaica. But he plunged into the clammy weather anyway, striding along the sidewalk, focused on the building on the opposite corner.

A small crowd had gathered beside the patrol cars. He scanned it and noted that one could find two types of people out in this neighborhood at this early hour. One group consisted of the bleary-eyed barhoppers, drug users, and streetwalkers who prowled Elmont until the sun came up. The others were the poor-but-respectable men, women, and children who actually lived and worked here, most of them transplants from the Caribbean islands.

He crossed the street and sidled up to the fringes of the group that had gathered on the corner.

"What happened?" he asked the person directly to his right, a middle-aged black man who flashed a gold front tooth the moment he opened his mouth to answer.

"The woman who lived up there," the man said, and pointed to the row of windows above the newsstand. "Her name was Parker. They say she was killed last night, someplace out in the woods. Now the cops are searching her apartment."

"She was up to no good, that one," a dark-skinned woman commented, looking over her shoulder. She wore large gold hoop earrings and a bright pink turban. "I don't know what happened. Until a few days ago, she was okay. But I passed her on the street yesterday, and her eyes, *mon*—they were filled with—evil."

Gold-tooth nodded until the woman had faced the building again, then turned back to him and snickered. "Evil. Yeah, sure, evil. So, you know the Parker lady, kid?"

"No," he lied. "Just curious."

There was no way, right now, to get into the apartment and find what he needed.

He slipped out of the crowd and made his way along the street until he came to a storefront deli that was open. There, he bought the Spring City *Morning Herald* and a cup of coffee, knowing it would be disappointingly weak and bitter compared with the rich Blue Mountain blend he was used to. But he'd be back in Jamaica soon enough, he promised himself. Just as soon as he'd taken care of business.

As he headed back along Elmont toward the occult shop, he saw that the crowd had dispersed and that one

of the patrol cars had left. Inside the other, two officers sat filling out information on a clipboard.

They didn't notice him, but he kept his head down
just the same.

He was on the corner, about to cross back to his
block, when something soft bumped against his calves.

He looked down to see a sleek black cat staring up at
him. The animal's eyes were narrowed and it hissed
threateningly. It hadn't liked him from the start.

"Now, now, Erzulie," he said in his smooth, rich voice,
reaching down and scooping Dalila's pet into his arms.
He darted a glance at the cops to make sure they hadn't
noticed. "How did you get out? Did you sneak through
the door when they weren't looking?"

The animal squirmed in his grasp, but he easily bal-
anced his coffee and paper and held the cat firmly
against his chest. The light changed and he crossed the
street in a few quick strides.

"What's the matter? Don't you like me?" he murmured to the hissing, twitching cat, who was trying to
escape his grasp as he walked swiftly toward the shop.
"And why is that? You know I had nothing to do with
your mistress's unfortunate . . . demise. I am truly sorry
to hear about it."

And that, he acknowledged to himself with a cunning
smile, *is the truth.*

He would miss Dalila, if only because she would no
longer be available to help him with his little . . . mission. He had found her by chance, having followed
Candra to the woman's apartment one day. In no time,
he had Dalila Parker mesmerized and willing to do
whatever he asked.

Such a shame, he thought now, clucking his tongue

and shaking his head, that he could no longer rely on her.

A few moments later, he unlocked the door again and entered the occult shop. The cat squirmed in his arms as he turned the latch behind him, deposited the coffee and newspaper on the counter, and headed for the back room.

"What's the matter, Erzulie?" he asked, looking down at the animal with mock concern. "Are you frightened? Don't be. You see, I need you."

He walked over to the makeshift altar he'd arranged on top of some crates.

Then, still holding the cat firmly against his chest with one strong hand, he stroked the thick folds of fur beneath the cat's tense head with the other and crooned, "Are you ready to help me? Good. Just relax."

In one swift, violent motion, he clamped his fingers around the thin, bony feline neck and wrenched it. There was a high-pitched, staccato cry and then a pleasing snap before Erzulie went limp against him.

"See? That wasn't so bad, was it?" he asked in his thick Jamaican *patois*. "And now you can help me. You see, the ceremony I'm about to conduct calls for fresh blood. And yours will do perfectly."

With a chuckle, he laid the animal on the altar and removed a gleaming dagger from the folds of his long black coat.

Giselle McKenna Hudson was fully aware of the attention she was attracting from males and females alike as she moved through the waiting area at Los Angeles airport.

She was pleased, as always, to notice the envious

glares from the women, and the admiring stares from the men. She had been the target of those same reactions repeatedly over the years, in more places than she could recall.

In the South Pacific, where she had been until yesterday, her fair coloring had been a rarity, and some of the native men had practically treated her like a goddess.

Even here in L.A., where every other woman seemed to be as blond and willowy as she was, Giselle knew she stood out. She was wearing an expensive copper-colored sleeveless sheath that complimented her coloring. Her skin was honey-bronzed from the vacation in Fiji. Her long, light hair was worn loose and was more sunstreaked than ever.

As she approached the bank of pay telephones on the wall, she allowed her pale green eyes to meet and hold the appreciative gaze of a particularly good-looking blond man who was passing by. She realized that he was the star of last winter's biggest box office smash, a movie that had been shown on their flight out from New York last week.

He raised his eyebrow suggestively at her, and Giselle's delicate mouth curved into a knowing smile.

It was so tempting to simply stop and flirt with this man—to bask in the attention from one of the world's hottest sex symbols. She even allowed herself to imagine his strong hands roaming over her body as they had done to the actress in the movie during a steamy love scene. She would tilt her head back in ecstacy, and when she did, he would kiss the hollow of her throat, and . . .

Reality intruded.

Out of the corner of her eye, Giselle spotted Lester coming out of the men's room.

Reluctantly, she tore her eyes away from the movie

star and kept walking toward the telephones, pretending she didn't see her husband.

"Giselle," Lester said, catching up to her and grabbing her arm. "Who's watching the carry-on luggage?"

She shrugged. "I left it on the seat over there by the counter. It's fine."

A look of panic came over Lester's thin face, and his watery eyes widened behind their wire-framed glasses. Giselle stifled the urge to grin at his distress.

"You can't just leave brand new Vuitton luggage sitting in the middle of an airport!" he said frantically. "What's the matter with you, Giselle?"

She shrugged airily and pointed toward the phones. "I'm going to call the girls and tell them the flight was delayed because of the weather there."

Lester was already gone, scurrying through the boarding area to where she had left their bags. Actually, she *had* asked the middle-aged nun who was sitting beside her to watch them. But Giselle got such perverse pleasure out of watching Lester fret . . . why ruin the fun?

He's a weenie, she told herself as she covered the last few feet and picked up the receiver of a pay telephone. *You're married to a total weenie.*

How had it happened? She'd been so young when they met, so young and blind. Had she actually found Lester attractive? Now, with his limp reddish mustache and receding hairline, it was hard to believe.

But then, back then, she hadn't been all there. She was still too out of sorts, trying to forget what had happened in Jamaica, doing her best to raise Meg as a single mom.

And she'd been so young, really—so naive. Naive enough to be dazzled by the way Lester had treated her. The man had practically thrown himself at her feet and begged her to use him as a doormat. He had obviously worshiped everything about her, and Giselle had found herself addicted to his constant praise.

Unfortunately for him, her addiction hadn't lasted. And now that she could see things clearly, she couldn't imagine how she had stayed with him for so long.

Oh well, Giselle thought as she punched in the familiar number of the house back in Connecticut; she wouldn't be Mrs. Lester Hudson for long. She wanted a divorce—had wanted one for a long time now, in fact. But lately, she had decided the time had come to do something about it.

As the phone rang, she checked her Rolex and saw that it was ten o'clock back on the East Coast. She never bothered to change her watch to reflect the current time zone when she traveled. It was too complicated, and besides, Giselle wasn't one to worry about something as superfluous as time.

She wasn't one to call and check in on her daughters, either—she figured they were old enough to take care of themselves. At least, Meg was. And she looked out for Carrie, who was more trouble-prone. Besides, Giselle's mother lived nearby if anything went wrong.

Lord knew Hope McKenna worried enough for both of them. Giselle had vowed, growing up, that she would never be anything like her basket case of a mother, and thank God, she wasn't. No, she breezed through life with devil-may-care aplomb.

The only reason she was calling home now was to see what the story was with the weather. The airlines wouldn't give a straight answer—they'd just announced that the flight to New York was delayed indefinitely because of some storm.

Giselle had been counting on getting home in time for her standing manicure appointment later today.

As the phone continued to ring in her ear, she examined her nails and decided that she'd be in big trouble if she didn't make the appointment. The creamy coral polish was chipped and scarred in a number of places.

After four rings, the answering machine clicked on, and Giselle heard her own cheerful voice saying, "Hi! Lester, Giselle, Meg and Carrie can't come to the phone right now. Please leave a message, and we'll get back to you as soon as we can. Thanks!"

At the sound of the beep, she said, "Meg? Carrie? It's me, Mom. Are you guys there and screening calls? If you are, pick up. Come on, guys. . . . I'm on a pay phone at LAX." She waited another second or two, then sighed and said, "Okay, our flight is delayed and I don't know what time we're going to get home. We'll see you when we see you. Bye."

She hung up and frowned momentarily. Odd that no one would be home at this hour on a Saturday morning. Neither Meg nor Carrie was exactly an early riser—a trait they had undoubtedly inherited from her.

Giselle didn't allow herself to contemplate the situation for more than another second, though.

As she turned and made her way back to Lester and the luggage, she pushed the vague sense of curiosity out of her head. Life was too short to spend time wondering about such things.

Instead, she scanned the waiting area for another sign of that hunky movie star.

Eleven

Meg and Candra had been running through the dark, scary woods, fleeing from something dark and sinister that wasn't quite tangible. Just when they seemed to be hopelessly lost, they'd stumbled across a glass telephone booth.

For some reason, Meg wasn't surprised to see it there, in the middle of nowhere.

"Quick," Candra shouted, "let's call nine-one-one."

But when Meg lifted the receiver, she couldn't get a dial tone. Desperately, she kept putting it into the cradle and lifting it again, as Candra looked over her shoulder and pleaded, "Hurry . . . before it's too late. We have to get someone to help us. Hurry!"

Then, as Meg held the phone helplessly in her hand, it started to ring.

But it can't be ringing when it's off the hook, she thought dazedly in the dream.

It wasn't until she heard Candra's groggy moan beside her that she snapped out of it and realized where she was, and that the ringing phone was real.

But when she moved to get out of bed to answer the extension on her desk across the room, she found that her legs were too stiff and weak to function. She nearly fell, and had to sit quickly again on the edge of the mattress.

"Are you okay, Meg?" Candra asked.

She turned to see her twin lying beside her in the wide, queen-size bed, snuggled beneath the rose-patterned comforter. Candra's hair was tangled on the puffy goose-down pillow and her eyes were rimmed with dark circles.

"I'm just a little woozy, that's all," Meg said, and smiled. "It's so great waking up and seeing you here."

"You, too," Candra said, but she didn't smile back. Her dark eyes were solemn. "Was the phone ringing?"

"It was, but the machine must have picked it up downstairs. It's no big deal. They'll leave a message. Did you sleep all right?"

Candra nodded and yawned.

Meg thought about how the two of them had staggered up to bed as it was getting light out this morning, both utterly exhausted. Candra had wanted to sleep in the guest room, but Meg had begged her to stay here in her room.

Somehow, she'd been seized by the irrational fear that if she let her twin out of her sight for even an instant, she would vanish again—this time, for good.

"Maybe someone was calling with news about Mirabelle," Candra suggested.

Meg's stomach turned over with a sickening thud. Mirabelle. The helicopter accident. She'd forgotten all about it.

"I'm sorry I reminded you," Candra said quietly, as if she could read Meg's mind.

"It's okay."

"Was she . . . a good friend?"

Meg hesitated. "Well, I haven't known her for very long. But she was the kind of person who you have an instant connection with . . . you know what I mean?"

Candra nodded but said nothing.

"She's the one who told me I have . . ."

"What?"

"Powers," Meg said reluctantly, and waited for Candra's reaction.

Either she was going to think Meg was completely crazy, or she would understand . . . because she had powers, too.

But once again, Candra didn't reply, and it was impossible to read the closed-mouthed, veiled expression on her face.

Meg hastily said, "I guess 'powers' is a strong word for it."

Still, Candra was silent.

"It's just that sometimes," Meg went on cautiously, "I seem to . . . *know* things. Like, I'll be aware of something before it happens. Does that ever happen to you?"

After what seemed like a long time, Candra said slowly, "Yeah. It happens to me. And other stuff, too."

"Like what?"

"There have been times when I sense things about people . . . you know, things I couldn't possibly know because they're strangers, or whatever."

"Me, too," Meg said excitedly. "When did you realize you had the . . ."

"Powers?" Candra supplied with a tight-lipped smile.

"I guess it's as good a word as any, right? So when did you figure it out?"

"I've always known I had certain . . . capabilities. But I didn't really start to develop my skills until Rosamund—" She broke off, as though she'd caught herself saying something she shouldn't have said.

Meg saw the way her sister's expression clouded when she mentioned the name of the woman she'd believed was her grandmother.

"What did she do?" Meg asked gently when her sister remained silent.

Candra shrugged and turned her head on the pillow so that she was staring up at the ceiling.

And Meg knew the conversation was over.

When Candra came downstairs an hour later, her hair still damp from her shower, she found Meg in the enormous kitchen at the back of the house. She was dressed in jeans and a simple but expensive-looking navy sweater, sitting at the oak table eating a bowl of granola.

"Oh, good, you found the stuff I left out for you," she said, looking up when Candra walked in. "Does it fit okay?"

"Yeah, thanks," Candra said, feeling uncomfortable as Meg sized her up. She was wearing her sister's black leggings and a charcoal-colored top—one she'd already worn earlier this week when she was posing as Meg.

"God, it's so strange," Meg said, shaking her head. "You look exactly like me, especially dressed in my clothes."

"Any news about Mirabelle?" Candra asked abruptly, to change the subject.

"Not yet. It was my mother . . . I mean, Mom . . . who called before."

Candra flinched at the word *mom*. It implied a cozy intimacy that was the last thing she felt when she thought of Giselle—who was, after all, in addition to everything she'd done, a total stranger.

Meg apparently sensed her discomfort, because she quickly added, "She's not sure when she'll get home. She and Lester are stuck in L.A. because of the weather here."

Candra looked toward the double windows over the

sink. Outside, the world was still gray and dreary. Even the kitchen, with its pristine white walls and appliances and bright track lighting, looked somehow dark and dismal.

Suddenly, she heard an angry *meow*.

"Hey, C-A-T," Meg said sternly, "cut that out."

Candra stared at the familiar cat who had appeared in the doorway of the kitchen. The animal's green feline eyes were focused knowingly on hers.

"She's really a good kitty," Meg said, getting up and going over to scoop the cat into her arms. "It just takes her awhile to get used to strangers."

"Most cats are like that."

"Yeah, they are. You can pet her, though, and she'll warm right up to you."

"It's okay," Candra told her quickly when Meg came closer to her. "I'm allergic to cats anyway."

"You are? Oh, God, sorry. I'll let her outside for a while."

Candra didn't argue, just watched as Meg planted a kiss on the cat's furry head and carried her to the door.

"What other allergies do you have?" Meg asked, when she'd returned to the table.

"Hmm? Oh, none that I know of."

"God, I'm glad we're not *totally* alike. I'd hate to be allergic to cats. Sometimes I feel like C-A-T's the only one around here who understands me. . . . Want some?" she asked, holding up the cereal box and peering inside. "There's a little left."

"No, thanks."

"I'm starving." She refilled her bowl. "I feel like I haven't eaten in a week."

You haven't, Candra thought, as she glanced at the

light green ceramic tile counter and saw that there was a pot of coffee waiting.

"I don't usually drink coffee," Meg said, following her gaze, "but I feel so exhausted today that I figured I needed a shot of caffeine. Have some if you want . . . it's kind of strong, though. I didn't know how much to put in."

"I like strong coffee," Candra said, suddenly thinking of the all the warm, breezy mornings in Jamaica when she'd sipped her favorite Blue Mountain blend.

A wave of homesickness came over her, so acute that she had to turn away from Meg so that her sister wouldn't spot the sudden tears that filled her eyes.

Behind her, Meg said casually, "The mugs are up in that cupboard to your right."

Candra nodded and reached blindly for one.

She was seeing the glistening, translucent aqua waters of the Caribbean, and the waxy blue blossoms of the lignum-vitae trees in the garden of the Drayers' home in Ocho Rios, and the dazzling feathers of the exotic island birds: the Red-billed Streamertails and Jamaican Mangoes . . .

And Rosamund's lined chocolate-colored face, stern but so familiar that Candra was filled with an inexplicable ache to see the woman again.

Even though she had lied all those years, pretending to be someone she wasn't.

Why, Grandmother? Candra wondered, before catching herself.

Ironic, that she was no relation to Rosamund, yet still automatically referred to her as *Grandmother*. Meanwhile, Giselle was the woman who had given birth to her, and she couldn't bring herself to consider her as *Mom.*

Candra's hand shook as she reached for the pot and

poured steaming black liquid into her cup. She forced her thoughts away from Giselle, not wanting to arouse any more of the anger that had caused her to resent Meg so fiercely. That was behind her now.

So, for that matter, was Rosamund, but . . .

Why did you pose as my grandmother and raise me? What was your connection to Giselle?

She thought back to the day Dalila Parker had told her the truth. *Your whole life is a lie,* the woman had said. *You aren't who you think you are.*

Candra had been raised under the impression that her white mother had died in childbirth and her black father, supposedly Rosamund's son, had been killed shortly after. The moment Dalila told her that wasn't the case, she had been overcome by curiosity.

It came back at her full force now.

"It's time we figured out what happened in our past," Meg's voice interrupted her thoughts abruptly. "Don't you think?"

Startled, Candra wondered, not for the first time, if her twin could read her mind. Slowly, she turned, both hands wrapped around her mug.

"I mean, obviously something happened back in Jamaica when we were born—something that no one wanted us to know about," Meg said, and spooned more cereal into her mouth.

"Yeah, I know what happened." Candra sipped the acrid coffee, felt it burning her throat.

Meg put her spoon down. "You do? What?"

"She had two daughters, and gave one up. She chose to keep you and not me. *That's* what happened."

It was what Dalila had told her that day.

She didn't want to choose, but she had to—one for her, one for him . . .

But instinctively, Candra knew now that Dalila hadn't been telling her the whole truth. Giselle had chosen Meg, but Candra hadn't been given to her father. Somehow, she'd wound up with Rosamund.

And when she'd asked Dalila about her father, the woman had grown insistent that she couldn't reveal anything more.

Odd, Candra thought now, looking back, that Dalila had been so forthcoming about everything else in her past.

She glanced at Meg, who was staring off into space.

Candra went over to the table, pulled out a chair, and sat down heavily.

"She may not be a perfect mother." Meg's voice, when she spoke again, was reserved. "But believe it or not, she's not a terrible person, Candra. I don't think she *wanted* to keep just one of us. I think that for some reason, she had no choice. And that's what we need to find out."

"If you're so curious," Candra bit out, "why don't you just *ask* her?"

"Because she won't talk about it. I've asked her all my life about my past, and it's like it's this forbidden thing. No one talks about it. Even my grandfather, before he died, refused to tell me anything about how I got here. I used to think it was because my mother had been wild when she was a teenager, and everyone was ashamed when she got herself knocked up at sixteen. But that's not all there is to it . . . I'm positive of that."

It was Candra's turn to remain silent. She thought about the beautiful blond woman she'd only seen in the photographs that were scattered around this house.

And though she'd thought she could put her resentment behind her, it returned full force, more bitter than the muddy coffee Meg had made.

You gave me away, she accused the smiling, pretty face she could see clearly in her mind's eye. *How could you?*

"If you knew what she was like . . . She's weak, Candra," Meg said wistfully. "Weak and vain and self-centered and sometimes really . . . foolish."

"Sounds like the perfect mom," Candra replied on a caustic laugh.

"Who is?" Meg shot back. "Look, all I'm saying is that whatever she did, she obviously did for a reason. Maybe not the best of reasons, but we need to find out what it was. Something happened to her in Jamaica. She was just a kid, younger than we are now, and she got pregnant while she was there. I had always thought my real father was this guy, Stu Kingman, who lived here in Crawford Corners and was her high school boyfriend. But Dalila told me that wasn't true. She said the guy who got her pregnant was someone she met in Jamaica. And that wasn't all she told me."

"What else?" Candra prodded when Meg hesitated.

"She said that Mom got involved in something that was way over her head while she was down there. And she said 'she paid the price,' but she wouldn't tell me anything more than that. Something strange happened, Candra. I guess, deep down, I've always known it, too. Maybe that's why I never pressed her for the details. But now I have to know. Candra, we *have* to figure out what happened."

Candra looked into Meg's earnest almond-shaped eyes. Her sister was silently begging her to put aside her spite, at least until she understood what, exactly, had happened all those years ago.

Another little piece of Candra's hardened heart melted. She allowed more of her anger to dribble away.

After all, you owe her, she reminded herself sternly.

What you really owe her is a confession, but since you didn't go through with that, your cooperation and kindness would be a good substitute . . . for a start.

Besides, Meg was the one person in the world who shared her past . . . and who wanted to unlock the mystery.

"Don't you wonder about our father?" Meg went on. "Like, who he was? *Where* he is? Dalila wouldn't tell me. She got all silent and weird about it when I asked."

Candra thought about Dalila's similar reaction to her own questions about their father.

"And my grandmother acted funny about him, too. I mean, it isn't strange that she wouldn't want to admit that my mother got pregnant by some stranger who lived in another country, because she can be kind of . . . basically, she's a prude. But she got really upset when I kept pressing her for information about him."

An image of Hope McKenna, Meg's thin, perpetually nervous grandmother, popped into Candra's mind. Had it been only yesterday that Candra had ridden the train into Manhattan with her, to get the million-dollar check that had been left to Meg by her grandfather?

That money was supposed to give Candra a fresh start. At this moment, she and Landon were supposed to be on their way to a new life together.

Now it was sitting in Meg's bank account, where it rightfully belonged. And despite a flinch of regret that so much money had slipped through her fingers, Candra was relieved that it hadn't worked out that way . . . that Meg was still alive.

She focused her attention on her sister again.

"Isn't he just as much at fault as she is?" Meg was saying.

"Who?"

"Our father! After all, Mom at least raised *one* of us. I mean, where the hell is he?" Meg asked with uncharacteristic vehemence. "I think that our first step is to find out . . . and find him."

"You would think," Candra said slowly, after absorbing her sister's words, "that since we both have some kind of—you know, *powers*, as you put it . . . that one of us would be able to figure something out, here. You'd think that we have an edge over the average person."

"We do," Meg said excitedly. "Especially now that we're together. We can figure this out, Candra."

"How? It's not as though there's some trail of clues that's going to lead us right to the answers."

"No, but there's something. Last week, I found a box of my mother's things in my grandparents' attic. There was a sketchpad that had a picture of us, together when we were newborn babies—that was how I knew I had a twin. How . . . how did you find out?"

"Dalila told me," Candra said briefly. "What else was in the box, Meg?"

"Some other stuff, from the time when she spent in Jamaica. Weird stuff."

"Like what?" Candra reached for her coffee mug again, trying to act nonchalant.

"A little red drawstring bag," Meg said, frowning slightly.

Startled, Candra glanced up. "A conjure bag?"

"Mirabelle called it a *gris-gris* bag."

That was the voodoo version of the charm, Candra noted. "Same thing," she told Meg. "What was in it?"

"Some powdered herbs and baby hair."

"Baby hair?"

"I guess it was mine . . . or maybe yours. It was tied with a ribbon. Mirabelle told me that the bag was a charm and that my mother had probably made it to attract something."

Candra thought of the bag she had worn pinned over her heart, the one that had succeeded in winning Landon Keller's affection.

"Or," Meg continued hesitantly, "she said the charm could keep something away. Like evil spirits. And there was a blue candle in the box, too—Mirabelle said it symbolizes protection. And a doll."

"What kind of doll?"

"It was like . . . you know, a voodoo doll. Made out of clay, dressed in scraps of fabric that looked like they had been made from baby clothes. And there was more hair—dark hair, like ours—embedded in the head of the doll."

Candra's heart was pounding. "Where's this box you found?"

"In my room. I hid it in my closet."

Then why didn't I find it last week when I went through your stuff? Candra wondered, puzzled.

Aloud, she said, "Let's go get it. I want to see the stuff that's in it."

"Okay, come on." Meg pushed her chair back from the table and led the way upstairs.

A minute later, standing inside her closet, she turned and looked at Candra, her eyes wide with disbelief. "It's gone!"

"Are you sure?"

"I'm positive. It was right here. How could it just vanish?"

Candra thought about what had happened to her a few nights earlier, when she had been snooping through Lester Hudson's office down the hall. She'd found a file labeled *Merriweather,* and inside, a confidential report along with a scribbled phone number that had a Jamaican exchange. But before she could react, she'd had to leave the office for a few minutes. And when she'd returned, the file was gone.

"Someone must have taken the box," she told Meg now. "Do you have any idea who it could have been?"

Meg frowned. "No one even knew it was here. But I think there's some other stuff missing, too—my burgundy leather boots, and . . . my leather coat, and . . . who would snoop through my—Carrie!" she interrupted herself.

"What?" Candra asked, thinking of the missing clothing. She knew exactly where it was. Stashed in the trunk of the Honda, packed neatly into Meg's luggage. Meg, of course, had no idea the bags were there. Candra had been planning to take everything along when she started her new life with Landon.

"Carrie's my sister. *Half*-sister, actually. She's always doing something obnoxious. She probably came in here to borrow my clothes and boots, and found the box."

Candra contemplated that. She couldn't tell Meg, but she was sure Carrie hadn't been behind the theft of the box—or the file.

She was sure, because of what had happened the other night.

She recalled, with a chill, how she had entered Meg's bedroom after midnight, and had been instantly struck by the knowledge that someone else had been there. And she had been aware, in the way she had always *known* things, that it wasn't Carrie, or Sophie, the housekeeper. This was a dark, threatening presence.

She had felt it since that incident, too. The creepy feeling had descended over her again a few days ago, when she was on her way to Dalila's. She'd sensed someone watching her. The only person around had been a stranger . . . a young, dark-skinned guy dressed in black. He hadn't said anything, or done anything unusual, but something about him had made Candra uneasy.

She'd pushed that episode, and the others, out of her mind.

Now she wondered what it all meant—whether the sinister stranger had something to do with the missing box.

If so, how much did he know about Meg and Candra . . .

And why did he care?

Meg was about to ask Candra what she was thinking—she was wearing the oddest expression, and her dark eyes almost looked frightened—when the front door banged open downstairs.

They both jumped.

"Someone's here," Meg said, coming out of her closet and quickly closing the door behind her. Since it couldn't be her mom and Lester, and Sophie didn't work on Saturdays, there was only one possibility. "It must be Carrie."

Sure enough . . .

"Meg?" The familiar voice bellowed from downstairs.

"Up here," she called back, looking at Candra and rolling her eyes.

Then it struck her, as she heard Carrie's feet pounding up the stairs, that she had no idea whether her sister even knew about Candra's existence.

Had she told Carrie?

Had Carrie and Candra met?

Again, she felt the numbing chill that pervaded her

mind whenever she thought about the fact that she couldn't remember anything that had happened over the past week.

A moment later, Carrie was standing in the doorway of her room. Her sister's pale hair was unkempt and her face, with its delicate features that were so like Giselle's, seemed drawn and pasty. Baggy jeans and an enormous navy plaid flannel shirt hung on her tiny frame.

"Meg, I—"

Carrie stopped in midsentence and stood there, frozen, staring.

Well, there's your answer, Meg told herself, watching her sister's startled, light green eyes darting from her own face, to Candra's, and back again.

Until this moment, Carrie had obviously had no inkling that Candra existed.

"Carrie"—she said gently, and moved forward to put a steadying hand on her sister's bony wrist—"this is Candra. She's my twin."

Finally, Carrie blinked and made a sound—a faint gasp.

"I know it's a shock, Carrie," Meg told her. "Believe me, I was just as stunned as you are when I found out. I was thrilled, though." She looked at Candra and smiled.

Candra, however, was focused intently on Carrie.

Carrie opened her mouth, closed it again, then began, "Mom—"

"She doesn't know that Candra's back," Meg cut in quickly.

"Back from where?" Carrie's gaze darted to Candra again. "Where did she *come* from?"

"Jamaica," Candra said simply.

Carrie frowned.

Meg told her, "I was born there . . . you knew that,

right?" At Carrie's nod, she went on, "Obviously, Mom had two babies, and for some reason" —she looked at Candra, hoping she wouldn't interrupt, and continued— "she had to leave Candra behind. She never told me about Candra, and Candra never knew about me, either . . . until recently."

"This is totally unbelievable," Carrie said, shaking her head. "I mean . . . I just can't *believe* it. Does my dad know?"

"I have no idea," Meg told her shortly.

"If he doesn't, he's going to go nuts."

As far as Meg was concerned, who cared if Lester went nuts? Her stepfather doted on Carrie, his "real" daughter, but there was no love lost between him and Meg. Even Giselle seemed to have cooled toward her husband lately, which Meg took as a hopeful sign. Maybe her mom would wise up and dump the guy.

"So you just popped up recently, huh?" Carrie asked, and Meg saw that she was eyeing Candra shrewdly.

Candra nodded. "That's right."

"Interesting." Carrie looked thoughtful.

Meg cleared her throat. "Carrie," she said, "did you by any chance take some stuff out of my closet?"

"Like what?"

"My burgundy leather boots, for one thing. And . . . I had this metal box . . ."

"Meg, are you accusing me of stealing your stuff?"

"Not *stealing*. Borrowing. The way you borrowed my No Doubt CD and my Coach shoulder bag and my—"

"I haven't taken anything from your closet, Meg. Not your burgundy boots, and not some stupid box." Carrie lifted her chin, glanced at Candra, and asked Meg pointedly, "Are you sure you didn't pack them?"

"Huh?"

"You know. The other night, you were packing your bags for some trip to see a friend."

Startled, Meg said, "What friend?"

"You wouldn't tell me."

"Well, why would I?" Meg shot back, struggling not to let Carrie know she had no idea what she was talking about.

She snuck a glance at Candra, who seemed to be watching Carrie closely.

"Forget it, Meg." Carrie rolled her eyes. "I'm out of here."

"Fine. Go."

"I will. I just came home to change my clothes, anyway. When Mom and Dad get home, tell them I'm at Terry's. I won't be late, though. I need to talk to them."

"Mom called. She and Lester are stranded in L.A. and they don't know when they're coming home."

Carrie stopped in the doorway, and Meg saw her back stiffen. Slowly, she turned around. "You mean, they might not be back tonight?"

"I have no idea. Why? Hoping to get away with something else while they're still out of town?" Meg knew her sister had been running around with a wild crowd lately. Lord knew what Carrie had been up to ever since their parents had left for Fiji. Especially since Meg hadn't been able to keep an eye on her . . . or had she?

"No, it's not that . . ."

Surprised at Carrie's suddenly subdued tone, Meg looked closely at her. "What's wrong?"

"I just . . . something happened last night, that's all."

"What was it?" Meg walked over to her sister and put a hand on her bony wrist. She was shocked when she realized that Carrie was shaking. "Come on, Carrie, tell me—what happened?"

"Meg . . ."

"Tell me! I mean it!"

Carrie hesitated, her eyes sliding to Candra, whose expression remained veiled, and back to Meg again. "It's just . . . I mean, it's probably not—"

"Carrie!"

"Okay, I'll tell you. It was really late. I was here by myself, in bed—I couldn't sleep 'cause of the storm—when I heard something downstairs. I thought it was you. But then I remembered that you'd said you were going away overnight, so I snuck down . . . and I found someone creeping around the living room."

Meg felt sick. She glanced at Candra, and saw that she, too, was focused intently on what Carrie was saying.

"Someone had broken into the house?" Meg asked, and Carrie nodded. "Who was it?"

"I have no idea. He was a black guy, about your age, and he was dressed in dark clothes—he had on this creepy long coat, and he was just . . ." Carrie shook her head and shuddered. "When he saw me, he got this terrible look in his eyes, like he was going to hurt me."

"But he didn't, right?" Meg asked, suddenly feeling protective of poor frail, fragile Carrie. "He didn't do anything to you, did he?"

"No. He just *smiled.* It was so . . . eerie. I mean, the guy just smiled and looked at me in that terrible way, and then he turned around and disappeared."

"Did he, like, run out the front door, or out a window, or what?"

"No, Meg, I said he *disappeared!*" Carrie's voice rose shrilly. "As in, *poof,* he was gone!"

Meg stared at her, then sighed wearily. "What were you on last night, Carrie?"

"Nothing!"

"Yeah, right."

"I swear, Meg, I wasn't on anything. Okay, so I smoked a little dope and had a few beers at a party earlier, but I was fine when I got home. And it wasn't my imagination. This guy just vanished."

Meg hesitated.

Chances were that Carrie had been so stoned she'd been hallucinating.

But still, Meg couldn't help thinking about something Mirabelle had told her. About how people could use something called astral projection to experience out-of-body travel. Mirabelle said she'd done it herself.

Candra asked Carrie, "This guy didn't steal anything?"

Carrie shrugged. "Who knows? I didn't stick around to figure it out. I called Eddie, and he came and got me, and I spent the night with him."

Ordinarily, Meg would have been distressed to hear that her sister was still hanging around with a low-life dropout drug dealer like Eddie. But that was the least of her worries now.

Something told her that whoever had been in the house last night was no ordinary prowler.

She saw the contemplative look on Candra's face and sensed that her twin was thinking the same thing.

Twelve

"Any news?" Giselle asked Lester, as he plopped down in the seat next to her.

"Same story. There's a big storm on the East Coast, and everything's delayed. They have no idea how long. I demanded to speak with the supervisor, and that idiot behind the counter said she *is* the supervisor. I don't believe her."

Giselle rolled her eyes, feeling sorry for the girl behind the airline's boarding counter. Lester had been up there every fifteen minutes for the past two hours.

Giselle was half-embarrassed by the scenes he kept causing, and half-amused.

Lester was always demanding to see supervisors, wherever they went. If a waiter brought him something he didn't like, he demanded to speak with the supervisor. If a flight attendant told him that, unfortunately, all the pillows and blankets were being used, Lester demanded to speak with the supervisor.

It rarely got him anywhere, but he liked to think he could throw his weight around.

"Do you have any more Tums?" Lester asked her, moaning a little. "My ulcer's acting up again."

"You don't *have* an ulcer, Lester. Doctor Yoon said you're fine."

"What does he know? As soon as we get back home,

I'm going to make an appointment with a specialist. How about those Tums?"

"I'm all out," Giselle lied. "You'll have to go buy some. And while you're at it, see if they have the new *Vogue* yet."

Naturally, Lester wasn't thrilled about having to go "all the way back" to the main terminal.

Giselle watched him trudge away, relieved to be rid of him for even a short while.

As soon as we get home to Crawford Corners, she promised herself, *I'm going to make an appointment to see a lawyer.*

She leaned back against the seat and closed her eyes, thinking about how free she would feel the day she said good-bye, forever, to Lester.

Then she thought about Carrie. Her younger daughter wasn't going to take the divorce lightly, she knew. Carrie worshiped her father, and vice versa.

But Meg . . . Meg would be as thrilled as Giselle would be to see him go.

Giselle knew Lester considered himself a terrific stepfather. He was always telling people how he treated the girls equally—how whenever he bought something for Carrie, he bought something for Meg. How "the poor kid" was lucky to have a "caring" father figure in her life.

Whenever he brought that up, he would give Giselle a *look,* as if to remind her that it was her fault Meg didn't have a real father.

Until recently, Lester hadn't even known the whole story about Giselle's past. He'd believed what she'd told him when they first met over fifteen years ago . . . that she'd gotten pregnant after a one-night stand with an American tourist in Jamaica. That she hadn't even known his last name or bothered to try and track him down when she'd discovered she was expecting.

Giselle had never planned or wanted to tell Lester the terrible truth.

But she'd finally broken down this summer, when she'd started planning their annual trip to the South Pacific, and Lester had launched a campaign to go to the Caribbean instead. Several of his colleagues were planning to tour the islands for two weeks on someone's yacht, and Lester was determined to go.

"It'll be great for my career, babe," he'd told her. "These guys really look up to me. I can't let them down. I can get some great deals out of this trip."

Giselle knew he fancied himself a flourishing financier. The reality was that he was mediocre at best. In fact, he wouldn't even have a job if Giselle's father hadn't conceded to getting him the brokerage job back when she'd first started dating him.

Of course, Harry McKenna had first tried to convince Giselle that Lester was a gold-digging opportunist. But somehow, she had been caught up in his flat-out adulation of her to see him for what he really was. Being out-and-out worshiped wasn't such a bad thing.

Besides, she had seen bland, bespectacled Lester as *safe*. And after what she had been through in Jamaica, she wanted nothing more.

Jamaica.

Giselle had vowed, the day she left eighteen years ago, that she would never return.

So when Lester had repeatedly pestered her to make the trip with his colleagues, Giselle had steadfastly refused. And when he had badgered her for days, then ultimately demanded a rational explanation, what else could she do?

She had finally broken down and told him exactly why she didn't want to go.

Giselle knew the story was bizarre, and she hadn't entirely expected him to believe it.

But apparently, Lester had.

He had met her heart-wrenching confession with silence at first, and then with several questions—some she couldn't answer, and others she didn't want to consider.

And while he didn't seem sympathetic over what had happened to her during that terrible, long-ago year in Jamaica, he hadn't forced the issue of going to the Caribbean, either.

In fact, he hadn't mentioned it again.

But something told Giselle he hadn't forgotten what she'd told him.

Sometimes, in the past several weeks, she had caught him looking at her with a strange, thoughtful expression in his watery gray eyes.

Whenever that happened, she got the feeling that there was more to Lester than she'd ever suspected.

And that made her all the more eager to leave him.

She sighed and opened her eyes, looking around the crowded boarding area. No sign of him yet, but any minute now, she'd spot his familiar dull reddish hair and skinny frame making its way toward her.

Oh, well.

Soon, Giselle promised herself. *Soon, Lester Hudson will be history.*

He slipped through the misty rain to the back door of the Drayers' big white house and knocked. With cold, clammy hands, he wrapped his long black coat more tightly around him as he waited, cursing the nasty New England climate.

It would be good to get this prolonged mission over

with and get back home to Jamaica's blue skies and soothing sunshine.

After a few moments, the door opened and Rosamund stood there, holding a dish towel. "Yes?" she asked briefly, barely glancing at him as she dried her hands.

"Hello, Rosamund," he said evenly.

She gasped as soon as he spoke, and peered more closely at him, her eyes wide with disbelief. "What are *you* doing here?"

Taking pleasure from the flicker of fear in her expression, he said smoothly, "Oh, I think you know."

"I have no idea, *mon*."

"I have a little bone to pick with you," he said, stepping into the house and leaning against the wall. He folded his arms and looked at her, waiting.

"I don't know what you're talking about," she protested, retreating a few steps back, toward the kitchen.

He uttered a single word. "Meg."

At the mention of the name, Rosamund opened her mouth in surprise, then quickly closed it again.

"The baby you said was sacrificed? The way she was supposed to be?" he asked, enjoying the torment in her dark gaze.

The woman stiffened at his words, but said nothing.

"She's alive. Her mother brought her back to Connecticut. You lied to me, Rosamund. You said she was dead."

He watched her carefully. Her quivering lips were clamped shut.

"Meg's death in exchange for Candra. That was the deal you made. You were desperate to get your hands on that baby girl, weren't you, Rosamund? You had lost your own child, a little girl, too. Do you remember that awful day when you found her dead in her crib? No ex-

planation. Poor little baby . . . a victim of crib death."
He smiled. "Those things happen. But you always
wanted another baby. And finally, you got Candra. A
precious baby girl to raise as your own. It would be a
shame to lose her now."

Her black eyes were defiant, but a violent trembling
in her jaw betrayed her fear. "Candra isn't here. She ran
away."

It was the truth—he already knew it, of course. But
he feigned surprise. It was more fun that way. "Where
is she?"

"I don't know."

"You're lying again, Rosamund." He kept his voice
quiet and chillingly calm. "You know, you're not very
good at it."

"But I'm not lying. I haven't seen Candra since last
weekend. She's gone, and I don't think she's coming
back."

He smiled. Torturing her was even more entertaining
than he'd anticipated.

She took a step back. "You'll have to go now. Mrs.
Drayer doesn't like me to have visitors here."

"We both know Mrs. Drayer's not home. Nobody's
home except you."

"Well, I have someplace to go," she retorted, obviously trying not to seem fazed, but failing miserably.

His lips curved into a smile. "Oh? Where are you
going? To your sister's apartment on Elmont Avenue?"

"How did you know that?" she blurted.

"I know everything, Rosamund. I know that you and
Tish are in a coven, and that it meets on Saturday
nights. I know *where* it meets. And"—he paused and
looked her in the eye—"I know where Candra is."

Now her fright was plainly visible as she gazed at him.

Her voice shook as she said, "Get out of here. Go on, go away. You don't belong here."

"I think I do. You've kept the truth about Meg from me. And there's more, isn't there?"

"I don't know what you're talking about."

"I'm talking about your other secrets, Rosamund. Dalila Parker told me that you're hiding something else from me. She suspected that the secret could be found among Giselle's things. I sent her there just the other night, to Giselle's home, to see what she could find out. Unfortunately, whatever she came up with is unavailable to me at this time."

"What do you mean?"

"Dalila Parker is dead."

Rosamund gasped and brought a fist to her lips. "You killed her," she said in a whisper.

"No. It was an accident. Imagine that! Life is startlingly cruel at times. First, your baby daughter is stricken by crib death. Now Dalila Parker has an accident . . ." He chuckled softly, marveling at fate, then hardened his eyes. "Now, since I can't yet get into Dalila's apartment to see what she found, there's only one way for me to find out what it is that you're keeping from me."

He took a step closer and reached out for her.

Then froze.

They both heard it.

A door slamming somewhere in the front of the house. A moment later, a man's voice called, "Anybody home? Rosamund?"

After a moment's hesitation, she said, her voice high pitched and unnatural, "In here, Mr. Drayer."

As footsteps approached the kitchen, he moved swiftly away, through the door and back out into the rain. His long coat whipped around his legs in a sudden gust of wind.

He slipped across the landscaped yard and into the trees, then turned and looked over his shoulder.

Rosamund was just closing the back door.

And even from this distance, he could see the expression of terror on her face.

Good, he thought contentedly, as a smile played over his lips. *I've gotten to her.*

And though his objective had been interrupted this time, he knew there were other ways to get the information he wanted.

He always got what he wanted, sooner or later.

Thirteen

"She's still in critical condition," Meg reported to Candra, hanging up the cordless telephone and putting it on the polished coffee table. "They said there's been no change and she's still in a coma."

"That's too bad." Candra had been looking absently through the Irish lace curtained window, listening to Meg's conversation with the hospital. Now as she turned toward her sister, she kept her expression concerned and a little detached, the way anyone would be if something terrible happened to someone they didn't know.

It wasn't that she wanted Mirabelle to *die* . . .

Of course she didn't.

It was just that she knew that if Mirabelle *lived*, she could—and would—tell Meg what Candra had done.

If she even knows what you did, Candra reminded herself. She had no doubt that the girl had suspected she was impersonating Meg, but really, what proof did she have?

And even if she went to Meg with her suspicions, Candra could simply deny them. Meg would have to believe her over Mirabelle, wouldn't she?

Of course she would.

After all, we're flesh and blood, Candra reminded herself as her sister flopped down beside her on the floral chinz couch and sighed.

"So what do you think, Candra?" Meg asked in a sub-dued tone.

"About what?"

"About everything. Especially what Carrie told us about that intruder."

"I don't know what to think about that," Candra told her truthfully. "But the description of the guy sounds a lot like someone who was following me to Dalila's the other day."

Meg's eyes widened. "You're kidding."

"No. He was . . . bad," she said slowly, remembering. "I sensed that he was there, on the street, even before I turned around and saw him. He sent off dark, evil vibrations."

"Who was he?"

"I have no idea. I'd never seen him before in my life. But there's something else . . ."

"What?"

"Right before Dalila died, when I was struggling with her, she said that someone was after me—and you, too. That we were in danger. She said the person is more powerful than both of us."

"Do you think she was telling the truth? Maybe she was just desperate and . . . I don't know." Meg looked frightened. "Who could be after us?"

Candra shook her head. She was racking her brain, trying to come up with something . . . anything. But she kept drawing blanks.

"Why did Dalila try to kill me, Candra?" Meg asked suddenly.

"I . . . I have no idea, Meg."

"It just doesn't make sense. Nothing makes sense. How did you know where to find me last night?"

Candra paused for only the briefest moment before saying, "Instinct."

Meg nodded. "That's what I figured. You know, I've

read that the bond between twins is psychic, anyway. Since you and I seem to have stronger psychic abilities than most people, I guess it makes sense that we'd be able to find each other and help each other under dire circumstances. I feel safer, somehow, knowing that. Don't you?"

Candra merely nodded, then quickly changed the subject. "I wish we could find that metal box."

"I was thinking . . . maybe I'm the one who took it," Meg said. "After all, I can't remember anything about this past week. How do we know that I didn't just move the box and put it someplace else for safekeeping?"

"We don't *know* that," Candra said carefully, "but how likely is it?"

Meg shrugged. "We should probably search the entire house, just to make sure it isn't around someplace."

"You think so?" Candra asked, knowing it would be a waste of time. The box was gone. She was as certain about that as she was of the fact that the Merriweather Investigations file had disappeared the other night.

At the sudden sound of footsteps on the porch outside the living room window, she glanced at Meg.

"Someone's here," Meg said, a split second before the doorbell rang.

"Aren't you going to get it?" Candra asked, when her sister didn't move.

"I'm afraid."

"Oh, Meg, I'm sure that whoever's after us isn't going to come ringing the bell," Candra said, trying to make her voice light. But in reality, she wasn't so sure about that. She wasn't sure of anything anymore, and that bothered her. Candra liked to be in control.

"Will you get it?" Meg asked in a small voice.

Candra nodded, got off the couch, and went into the

foyer. She opened the door and found herself face to face with Shea Alcott.

"Meg!" he said, and immediately grabbed her into a bear hug. "Thank God you're okay. You have no idea how crazy I've been the last twenty-four hours."

Before Candra could reply, a voice behind her said, "Shea? That's my twin sister. *I'm* Meg."

He released Candra instantly, and she saw the displeasure in his eyes. She wondered what he was thinking. She'd forgotten all about the fact that he had been with Mirabelle, following Candra, the other day. Did he, too, have suspicions about what she had been up to?

The look on his face told her that he did, but he quickly looked past her to Meg. "I was so worried about you," he said, and moved toward her.

Candra watched as Shea pulled her twin into his arms. He held her tightly for a long time, and she saw Meg's hands wandering up around his neck, clinging there naturally as she rested her head on his shoulder.

It's so unfair, Candra found herself thinking. *Why can't someone care about me that much?*

Again, her thoughts flew to Landon Keller, but she forced herself to put him out of her mind. What he'd felt for her wasn't real. And it was over, anyway. She would never see him again.

"Shea, I want you to meet someone," Meg said, finally pulling back from him and glancing in Candra's direction. "This is Candra Bowen."

"I know. We've already met, haven't we, Candra?" Shea's eyes on her were cold. His hands were still possessively resting on Meg's waist.

Candra felt a little prickle of trepidation, but kept her face blank.

"You've met," Meg repeated, and looked upset. "God,

I didn't even remember. I can't take this. When am I going to get my memory back?"

"What are you talking about?" Shea asked, turning his attention back to her.

"It's the strangest thing. I have amnesia," Meg told him. "I can't remember anything that happened to me since Monday afternoon, when I met Candra for the first time. I guess the experience was so intense that some part of my mind totally shut down."

"Oh, Meg, get real," Shea said. "You know who's behind this, don't you?"

"Behind what?"

"This whole memory loss, or whatever it is that you think you have."

"What do you mean?"

"It's her," he said, pointing at Candra. "She did something to you."

Meg wrenched herself out of his grasp. "What are you talking about?"

"Candra has been posing as you, that's what I'm talking about. She's been wearing your clothes—"

"Oh, please," Meg interrupted. "I loaned her some stuff. Big deal. She's my sister."

"It's not just that, Meg. She's crazy."

"What are you talking about?" Meg looked over her shoulder at Candra, who made sure she wore a wounded expression. Meg saw it and said, "It's okay, Candra, don't—"

"Meg, are you crazy, too?" Shea demanded, waving a finger in her face. "She's no good. I swear, Meg. She even tried to kill you!"

"Shut up!" Meg shouted at him, shaking her head and stepping back from him, toward Candra, who remained silent. "You're the one who's crazy, Shea!

Candra didn't try to kill me—she saved me from Dalila Parker."

Shea shook his head. "You're wrong."

"No, *you're* wrong. She's my twin sister, for God's sake. Why would she try to kill me?"

"Ask her," Shea said, turning his gaze on Candra.

So did Meg.

Candra looked at her sister and shook her head. "Meg, I have no idea what he's talking about."

"Of course you don't, Candra. He and I haven't been getting along lately, and he can't stand the fact that I might be close to anyone other than him. Just ignore him."

"Jesus, Meg, you've got to be—"

"You know what, Shea?" she interrupted him. "Why don't you just get the hell out of here."

"But Meg—"

"I don't want to hear it," she said, holding up a hand and turning her back on him. "Your jealousy has totally ruined this relationship. First you accused me of going out with someone else behind your back, which was a total lie. And now you can't stand the fact that I have a sister who might take up some of my time, so you make up some crazy story about her. You want me all to yourself, and you're smothering me. I can't take it anymore. So just go."

Shea stared at Meg's back, and the look in his eyes filled Candra with guilt. He cared about her sister, she realized. A lot. He really, truly, loved Meg.

And Candra was the cause of the pain that was clearly eating away at him.

You should do it now, she told herself, as she looked from Shea to Meg. *Tell her the truth. Confess. Tell her that he's right.*

But again, somehow, she couldn't bring herself to do it.

Shea turned away from Meg and walked toward the door, passing Candra without meeting her eyes.

A moment later he was gone, closing the door quietly behind him.

"Slamming's not his style," Meg said in an odd, choked voice, and Candra looked up to see her looking at the door. "He's not the type to make a scene."

Candra didn't know what to say. Her sister's expression was a mirror of Shea's. She was in love with the guy, and he had broken her heart.

No.

Candra had. She was the one who was responsible for Meg's heartache.

Meg let out a shaky sigh, then said, "You know, I'm better off without him. We were too different anyway."

Candra wasn't fooled by her sister's attempt to shrug it off. "Maybe you'll get back together," she suggested, still unable to meet her sister's eyes for fear of what she would see there.

"No. No way. Not after what he said about you. And did you hear that crap about you posing as me? Obviously, since we're identical twins, people are going to mistake us for each other. That's how this whole thing started, you know, with Dalila. She thought I was you at the carnival that day. And then people started telling me they'd seen me in places where I hadn't been . . ."

"I know what you mean," Candra said, nodding. Relief was coursing through her. "It happened to me, too. Some of your friends thought I was you."

"Someday, we really should switch places," Meg said with a smile. "It would be fun."

"Yeah, sure, someday," Candra said, and looked away.

* * *

"This is crazy. I've been through this entire room before, and I never found anything unusual," Meg told Candra an hour later, as they slipped into the master bedroom.

Though her mother had been away for almost two weeks, the scent of her expensive perfume still hung in the air. The huge room looked like an ad out of a home decorating magazine, with its perfectly coordinated chintz bedspread, curtains, and wallpaper.

"Maybe you missed something," Candra said. "Besides, what other way is there to try and figure out what happened? We have to see if we can come up with something—anything at all."

Meg sighed. "You're right. You look in the closet, and I'll take her dresser drawers."

"What about Lester's dresser?"

"Oh, please. Who wants to touch all his underwear and socks and stuff like that?"

"I don't, especially, but we have to search everywhere," Candra said.

"Well, believe me, Lester's too boring to have anything interesting hidden in his dresser."

"Are you sure?"

Meg frowned at her sister. "What do you mean?"

"I mean, maybe he's not as boring as you think. Maybe he's got something to hide."

"Lester? The only thing he has to hide is the stupid bald spot on the top of his stupid head. It drives him crazy. He's always trying to comb his hair so it won't be so noticeable. He's such a dork."

Candra shrugged. "Maybe there's more to Lester than you think, Meg."

"I totally doubt it, but even if there is, he doesn't have anything to do with what happened to Mom in Jamaica," Meg said firmly, wondering why Candra seemed so insistent about Lester. It was almost as if she knew something about him . . .

"Candra," she said, "is there something you're not telling me? About Lester?"

"No. Well, not exactly."

I knew it, Meg thought. "What's up?" she asked aloud.

"I just have this feeling about him, that's all. A really strong feeling. I think he's up to something."

Meg stared at her. "Like what?"

"I have no idea."

"Why do you think so? What happened?"

"I told you. Nothing. It's just a feeling, Meg."

"Well, why don't I have the same feeling?" Meg asked, feeling irrational but unable to help herself. "After all, we both have powers. And I've lived with Lester practically my whole life. I never felt any odd vibes coming from him."

"Well, you might be immune where he's concerned, since you're used to having him around," Candra pointed out. "And," she added bluntly, "my powers are stronger than yours. I've been training myself to use them since I was a little girl."

"Maybe we should search Lester's study," Meg said slowly, after considering her sister's words.

Candra shrugged. "We can, but we might not find anything there."

"Yeah, but we might." Then Meg remembered something. "The only problem is, he keeps everything locked. His desk *and* the file cabinets."

"Locks," Candra said airily, heading for the door, "can be picked."

A few minutes later, Candra and Meg were on their knees in front of a file cabinet in Lester's office. Candra had inserted a bobby pin in the keyhole and was jiggling it around.

"Do you think it'll work?" Meg asked, even as Candra broke into a grin and said, "There it goes."

She pulled the drawer open and gestured. "Be my guest. You start looking through here, and I'll pick the lock on the other cabinet."

"What am I looking for, exactly?" Meg asked, staring at the row of manila file folders.

"I have no idea," Candra told her. "But you'll probably know if you find it."

Meg shook her head and lifted the first folder out. It was labeled AAA, and inside was a collection of canceled checks from Lester's membership fees for the American Automobile Association.

Meg sighed and jammed it back into the drawer.

Lester being involved in anything unusual, she thought, was about as likely as the notion of Candra plotting to kill her.

Still, she kept looking through the file cabinet.

Giselle closed her copy of *Vogue* and sighed moodily, tossing it into a trash can beside her seat.

"Now what?" Lester asked, looking up from the novel he was reading.

Or, Giselle thought, *pretending* to read. Lester, pretentious boor that he was, made a big show of reading the classics whenever anyone was around to see him, like here in the airport, or at the country club pool back in Connecticut. But Giselle knew he'd been on the same page—page thirty—of Tolstoy's *War and Peace* for several months now. And she'd seen the glazed look in his eyes as he stared at the book.

"Now what's the matter with you?" Lester repeated, closing the book over his index finger, to keep his place.

What a joke.

"What do you mean, what's the matter with me?" Giselle asked, frowning.

"You just sighed and tossed that thing like you're mad at the world."

"Don't be ridiculous, Lester," she said irritably. "I didn't toss it."

"Yes, you did. I saw you."

"How could you have seen me? I thought you were busy reading."

He reddened, and she smiled.

She was aware that the middle-aged woman on Lester's other side had looked up from her own magazine and was eavesdropping. So was the elderly couple sitting in the row of seats across from them. They were all poised for the next bit of dialogue, probably hoping for an out-and-out marital spat.

It figured. Everyone in the gate area was bored stiff. The last big event had been the gate attendant's announcement that although the flight was probably going to be delayed at least two more hours, they should all remain in the boarding area in case they suddenly got clearance to board the plane.

Giselle fixed the nosy couple across the way with a steely stare, and they quickly buried their noses in their newspapers again. The woman on Lester's other side got the hint and turned away.

"How much longer do you think it's going to be?" Giselle asked Lester, who had opened his book again.

"Hmmm?"

"Oh, as if," Giselle said, shaking her head.

"As if, what?"

"As if you're so busy reading that stupid book that you didn't hear what I said. Never mind." She stood and was about to walk away—not sure where she was going, only needing to escape Lester's mere presence for a while—when the gate attendant stepped in her path.

"Are you on the flight to New York, ma'am?" she chirped, her round face rosy above her crisp white blouse and the navy bow at her throat.

Giselle wanted to muster every ounce of sarcasm she possessed and say, *No. I'm just hanging around here because it's a fascinating way to spend a Saturday afternoon.*

But instead, she only nodded.

"Then I suggest you stay put for a few minutes. We might be able to board soon."

"Really?" Now *that* was a bit of good news. "How soon?"

The woman shrugged. "Could be only a few minutes, or . . ."

"Or . . . ?"

"Who knows? Why don't you have a seat again? We wouldn't want to lose you."

"No, we wouldn't," Giselle muttered, and went back to Lester.

He glanced up. "Where did you go?"

"Nowhere."

"Oh."

Giselle slumped in her seat and slipped her bare feet out of her copper-colored sandals. She studied her tanned toes, with their coat of coral polish, and thought that if she were any more bored, she'd be asleep.

Her mind drifted, meandering from how irritated she was with Lester, to why she'd married him in the first place. Mentally, she slipped back through the years to those dismal months when she was a stressed new mom being courted by a man who hung on her every word, who thought she was beautiful despite the ten extra pounds she hadn't yet lost from childbirth, despite the disgusting smell of faintly soured milk that seemed to cling to her in those early years of motherhood.

Then she went back further still, to Jamaica.

It wasn't a place she wanted to visit ever again, not even in her mind.

She usually tore her thoughts away whenever they started in that direction.

But somehow, she couldn't seem to help it today. There were no distractions here in the quiet, crowded airport waiting area.

Giselle closed her eyes and remembered what it had been like then . . . back when she was a seventeen-year-old American girl in Ocho Rios.

Paradise.

That had been her first impression of her new island home, with its backdrop of gentle breezes and perpetual sunshine, with its reggae beat and easygoing, black-skinned people who spoke in a lilting *patois*.

There, Giselle knew, her parents had hoped to isolate her from the fast crowd she'd been running with at her own school back in the States. They'd hoped that by taking her away from Stu Kingman, her devil-may-care boyfriend, they might make her into a chaste girl-next-door . . . something she had never been in the first place.

And, for the first week or so that she was a newcomer on the island, she had spent a lot of time hanging around their rented house in the hills above Ocho Rios.

She even, for lack of anything better to do, helped her mother and Letitia, the Jamaican housekeeper, get things unpacked and settled.

Giselle had to admit that the place was beautiful, all terra cotta and white stucco, with sweeping views from every window and from the sprawling open air poolside deck. There, a bikini-clad Giselle was able to perfect her tan while sketching the scene that lay before her. She thought she'd never tire of the scene below—the rolling green, flower-dotted foothills leading down to the picturesque, brightly colored buildings of Ocho Rios and the shimmering blue-green water of the Caribbean Sea.

Still, being Giselle, she soon started longing for some action. After all, she couldn't sun herself, sketch, and be a homebody forever. She needed *fun.*

One night, when her parents were at some welcome dinner for the SNE development executives who were temporarily relocating to Jamaica, she had snuck out of the house and borrowed the car her father had leased for her mother to drive. Not that Hope McKenna would have dared venture onto the winding, rutted island roads, particularly in a car where the steering wheel was on the wrong side. She'd already said so.

Giselle had a few close calls as she careened down to town, mostly when she forgot to drive on the left. Breathless and exhilerated from the adventure, she had parked on a narrow dirt street in front of the first nightclub she came to.

She knew it was a club because of the neon sign that read "Evil Annie's" out front and the reggae beat that throbbed into the street. But the building was little more than a low, pink-colored cinderblock shack, really . . . nothing like Studio 54 back in Manhattan, where

Giselle and her friends had gone disco dancing several times after seeing *Saturday Night Fever*.

She made her way into the dark, crowded interior of the club, mildly surprised at the familiar, sweet aroma that tinged the air. Ganga, they called it down here, didn't they? She had smoked it on several occasions with Stu and his friends—not that it ever did anything much for her.

Here, though, the stuff was probably a lot more potent. Feeling a little dizzy at the heady scent, Giselle pushed her way to the bar.

"What can I get you, milady?" the bartender asked in a singsong *patois*.

"Uh, I'll have a Sloe Gin Fizz." Giselle was new at this club stuff, though she and her friends had gone out a few times back home recently.

"Nah," he said. "Have a hummingbird."

"What's that?"

"You'll see. You'll like it."

She shrugged and watched him move over to a blender behind the bar. He hadn't bothered to ask her for ID, which was the first sign, to Giselle's way of thinking, that living in Jamaica for a while wouldn't be so bad. The fake Wyoming driver's license in her bag wasn't very convincing, and she'd rather not resort to using it if she didn't have to.

"You a tourist?" the bartender asked, setting a foamy, creamy pink drink in front of her. Sweat glistened on his dark skin; the place wasn't air-conditioned.

"No, a native," she'd retorted.

Looking surprised at her quip, he'd flashed a row of straight white teeth at her.

She'd grinned back, then asked, "So who's Evil Annie?"

"You never heard of the White Witch of Rose Hall?"

"The White Witch?" Giselle had repeated, after deciphering his rapid-fire island accent.

"Annie Palmer. She was a rich white lady who lived in a Great House down in Mo-Bay."

"Where?"

"Montego Bay," he clarified. "They say she murdered three of her husbands and tortured her slaves until they killed her during the uprising in 1833."

"Oh. It was a long time ago," Giselle said, losing interest. She wasn't crazy about history—in fact, she usually got Ds in it.

"Sure. But everyone who comes to Jamaica hears about the White Witch."

"She was a witch?" Giselle asked, her curiosity piqued again.

He nodded. "Black Magic. You know?"

She didn't. But she nodded anyway, wondering if Black Magic was a big thing here in Jamaica. She hadn't ever thought about witchcraft as being a real thing that people actually practiced. When someone said witch, she pictured the Halloween costume from Woolworth's that she'd worn in third grade—the pointy black hat and green mask with the long, wart-covered nose.

She wanted to ask the bartender more about it, but someone had called him down to the other end of the bar. It would have to wait.

Swaying slightly to the reggae beat, Giselle tasted her hummingbird. It was delicious, almost like a milk shake. She had only taken a few sips when she'd felt someone watching her.

Looking up, she'd locked eyes with him.

The first thing that struck her was his *darkness*. Virtually everything about him—skin, hair, eyes, even his

clothes—was blacker than an asphalt driveway on a swel-
tering July day. He sat at the far corner of the bar,
surrounded by a throng of people, a part of the crowd
and yet, somehow, not. His gaze was fixed intently on
Giselle.

She couldn't seem to tear her eyes away from his.

They'd watched each other for what felt like an endless interlude, and then the bartender had shattered
the spell, asking her if she wanted another drink. She
turned to say that she did, then looked back toward the
man in black.

He was gone, swallowed up, apparently, in the crowd.

Her hand gripping the icy, fresh drink the bartender
slid toward her, Giselle had scanned the smoky, jammed
room, looking for him with what felt almost like . . . desperation? But there was no sign of him, and she'd
finally left, feeling strangely hollow inside.

It was a full month before she saw him again, though
she hadn't forgotten him.

In the interim, she had become friendly with
Howard and Raymond, two teenage local boys who
tended to the lawn and garden at the house her parents were renting. They introduced her to the
pleasures of island rum and Bob Marley music and Ja-
maican-grown *ganga*. And one night just before dusk,
they drove her up into the mountains, speeding along
narrow, hairpin curves and swerving to avoid the
chickens and goats that wandered in the road. As they
drew farther from Ocho Rios, with its brand-new resort hotels and moored cruise ships, the scenery grew
more wildly beautiful and more desolate.

Here, a dense tangle of trees and vines shrouded the
road, dotted with fragrant blossoms and shielding the
birds whose startled, high-pitched calls were accompa-

nied by furiously beating wings as they were disturbed by the passing automobile.

"Where are we going?" Giselle had asked Howard, who was at the wheel.

He hadn't answered, merely looked over his shoulder at Raymond in the backseat. Giselle did the same.

"Ray?" she'd prodded, passing him the open bottle of Appleton's.

"You ever hear of *obeah*?" he'd asked in his thick Jamaican accent.

"Did I ever hear of *a beer*?" she'd repeated incredulously, after struggling to decipher his words.

"*Obeah*," Howard clarified. He was a little easier to understand, having spent several years of his childhood living with an American family his mother had worked for as a housekeeper.

"What's that?" Giselle accepted the bottle back from Ray and took a swig. The liquid sent a pleasant burning sensation down her throat.

"A religion," Ray told her; at the same time Howard said, "Witchcraft."

"Witchcraft?" Giselle echoed, lowering the bottle and staring at Howard. She thought about what the bartender at Evil Annie's had told her.

"In a way, yes. You're familiar with voodoo?"

"Sure. I mean, I'm not *familiar* with it, but a know what it is. Black Magic, right?"

"*Obeah* is like that," Raymond said from the backseat. "It's a religion. We worship—"

"What does that have to do with where we're going now?" Giselle had interrupted impatiently.

"There's a ceremony tonight," Howard told her. "We want to take you there."

"Why?" Giselle swiftly concluded she wasn't crazy

about the idea of going to any crazy religious ceremony. She didn't even go to church back home. And anyway, it was dark out here. And the middle of nowhere. Kind of . . . scary.

"We thought you would find it interesting," Ray said simply.

"I doubt it, guys."

Howard slowed the car and pulled off the road, and for a moment, Giselle thought he was going to turn around and take her back home. Instead, he stopped, turned off the motor, and announced, "We're here."

Giselle had looked around, seeing nothing but trees and shadows. Her heart was starting to beat a little frantically. She opened her mouth to demand that they take her home, but was stopped by the sound of thunder.

At least, she thought it was thunder at first.

Then she realized that it was drums.

They were off in the distance, beating a swift, steady rhythm that seemed to echo her own racing heart.

"Come on," Howard said, and he and Raymond climbed out of the car.

There was nothing for Giselle to do but follow suit, clutching the open bottle of rum in her hand.

"Leave that," Raymond told her. "You won't need it."

"What's that supposed to mean?" Giselle asked, but he didn't answer. Shrugging, she screwed the cap on and tossed the bottle back into the front seat through the open window.

Walking single file because the path was narrow, they made their way through the trees. The sound of the drums grew steadily louder and stronger, and Giselle could smell smoke. Not the ever-present marijuana haze that seemed to hover over Ocho Rios, but woodsmoke, reminding her of Girl Scout camp.

Finally, they reached a clearing that glowed from a small fire ringed by large stones. In the orangey light, Giselle could see several people milling around, many of them familiar from the bars in town.

And then she felt it again, for the first time in a month . . . the unsettling sensation that she was being watched. She knew before she turned her head and saw him that it would be the man she'd seen in the club that night—the one who had been cloaked in blackness.

He stood apart from the others in the clearing, watching her. And then Giselle thought—for no reason, really, it just popped into her head—that he'd been waiting for her.

Suddenly he smiled broadly as she stared at him, and his white teeth were a stark contrast to the rest of him.

Unnerved, Giselle clutched Howard's arm. "Who is that?"

"It's Manfred," he said, following her gaze. "He's the high priest."

Manfred.

Even now, years later and hundreds of miles from the mountains of Jamaica, the very name made Giselle shudder.

"It's no use," Meg said, rocking back on her heels and looking up at Candra.

"I know. I can't find anything either." She hated to give up, but there was nothing in this office that was going to incriminate Lester. She knew it.

Meg slid the bottom drawer closed and stood up. "What now?"

"I've been thinking," Candra said slowly, turning away from the file cabinet she'd just finished searching, and looking at her twin. "There's one person who probably knows what we want to find out."

"Who?"

"Rosamund," she said simply, trying to ignore the twinge of pain that jabbed her heart.

"Who?"

"My grandmother . . . I mean, she isn't really, but . . ."

"I know," Meg said, sympathy in her eyes.

And Candra thought again what a marvel it was that she actually had a sister. Someone who cared.

Someone who was there for her, despite what she'd done.

Not that Meg knew . . .

Stop it! she commanded her conscience.

"Anyway," Candra continued after a pause, looking away from Meg, "Rosamund has a . . . meeting every Saturday night. So I'd know where to find her."

"What kind of meeting?"

Again, Candra hesitated. Then she decided she might as well tell the truth. For a change. "It's a coven, actually," she told Meg frankly.

"A coven? You mean, she's a witch?"

"I guess you could say that."

Meg's eyes were big and fixed on Candra's face. And yet, there was something in them, some hint of acceptance, that told Candra her sister wasn't entirely surprised. After all, she had powers of her own, powers she had only recently discovered, and she knew Candra shared them. Was it so odd that Candra's would-be grandmother dabbled in Black Magic?

"So what do you want to do?" Meg asked. "Barge into this coven meeting and demand that Rosemary tell us the truth about our dad?"

"Rosamund," Candra corrected. "And no, we can't

just barge in. We have to be careful. This isn't something you mess around with. It might be dangerous."

"Okay," Meg said, looking a little spooked, but game. "Tell me what we do, then."

"We go to where the coven meets, and—"

"Wait," Meg interrupted, holding up a hand. "Why can't we just go to your grandmother's house? I mean, wherever it is that she's living now . . . with the Drayers, right?"

"Because I don't want to set foot there ever again!" Candra thought about the basement servant's quarters where she and her grandmother had lived, and about Craig Drayer and how he had always taunted her, and about Landon, who had kissed her in her room that day that seemed like years ago but had only been weeks.

"Okay, okay," Meg said, shaking her head. "We'll go to where the coven meets. Where is it?"

"Spring City."

Meg nodded. "Near where Dalila lives . . . lived?"

"Not far from there. It's off of Elmont Avenue."

"Okay. When do we go?"

"Tonight."

"Then I have time to go to the hospital," Meg said, looking distracted.

"I guess." Candra wondered about Mirabelle. What if she was awake? What if she told Meg the truth? It would ruin everything.

Well, chances were that she wasn't conscious, Candra comforted herself. Not yet, anyway.

But there's only one way to be sure Mirabelle will never tell Meg what I did, Candra thought, a desolate feeling settling over her.

"I'm going to get ready to go to the hospital," Meg said, and headed out of Lester's office.

Candra nodded absently and stayed there, sitting on the floor in front of the file cabinet, thinking disturbing thoughts that she couldn't seem to evade.

Fourteen

Meg hesitated in the corridor outside the sixth floor intensive care unit of Spring City General Hospital. Her legs felt wobbly, and she wanted to turn around and run in the opposite direction, back along the endless hallways to the main entrance, out into the blowing, icy rain she'd driven through to get here.

She had been here once before, when her grandfather was dying.

Harry McKenna—Harry of the twinkling eyes and easygoing laugh and fighting spirit—had lain in one of the beds beyond those doors. He had been hooked up to tubes and monitors, a pale apparition of the man he had once been. For weeks, he had drifted in and out of the twilight world that eventually claimed him. Even when he was awake, his eyes were often glassy and blank.

And yet, whenever Meg visited him, and he recognized who she was, he grew more lucid. He would beg her to grasp his hands in hers, claiming her touch worked magic, that it made his pain diminish. And after he'd lost his ability to speak, she had always known what he wanted, had always done it instinctively.

She would slip her strong, young hands into his weathered, pathetically thin ones, and she would stay there with him for as long as the nurse would let her. She would chatter to him about school and her cat and her friends, forcing herself to swallow her own sorrow over his condition and make bright conversation. The look that always lit her grandfather's eyes told her what he couldn't say—that having his Meggie there, feeling her touch, was more effective than any medicine the doctors could give him.

But in the end, that hadn't mattered.

Meg couldn't save him from the cancer that had ravaged his body, not any more than the doctors could.

Her beloved grandfather had slipped away, much too soon.

Now it was Meg's friend who lay there beyond the double doors.

And all because of her.

Meg took a deep breath and pushed through the doors, coming face to face with a haggard-looking dark-haired guy who was probably only a year or two older than she was.

"Sorry," they said in unison, and he offered her a brief, sad smile before walking past.

Meg walked the few steps to the desk. The nurse was someone she had never seen before, not one of the staff that had grown so familiar a few years ago when Harry was here.

The woman was looking up at her expectantly.

Meg shoved aside the memory of her grandfather once again and said, "I'm here to see Mirabelle Moreau."

"I'm sorry—she can't have any visitors unless . . . are you immediate family?"

"No."

"I'm sorry," the nurse said again, shaking her head. "It's ICU policy."

"I understand." She should have realized she wouldn't

be allowed in. Not when Mirabelle's condition was so critical.

Meg looked over her shoulder slowly, sensing that the guy who'd been on his way out of the ward had hesitated in the doorway behind her.

There he stood, watching her.

At the desk, the phone rang and the nurse picked it up, answering in a muted tone that was probably meant to offer comfort in case the caller had a loved one in the unit.

Meg waited, wanting to ask the nurse about Mirabelle, whether there had been any change—and wondering why the guy in the doorway was just standing there.

"You're Meg," he said flatly after a moment.

Startled, she said, "Do you . . . are you a friend of Mirabelle's?"

"I'm Ben." When she looked at him blankly, he gave a brief, bitter little laugh and said, "She never mentioned me, huh? I'm not surprised."

"I'm not sure . . . she may have," Meg told him truthfully, then wondered how she was going to explain her amnesia to this person.

She didn't have to bother. He didn't ask, only scuffed the toes of his sneakers along the white tile floor in a desolate gesture.

After a few moments, with the nurse involved in a hushed conversation on the phone, Meg said, "Are you and Mirabelle . . . ?" She trailed off, deciding to let him categorize their relationship.

"I don't know what we are, exactly," he said bleakly. "I know what *I* want us to be . . . but now, who knows? There's been no change in her condition."

"Still bad?" Meg asked softly.

He nodded.

"Have you been in to see her?" she asked when he didn't say anything more—probably because he couldn't. He appeared to be on the verge of tears. Clearly, Mirabelle meant an awful lot to him.

He shook his head, then found his voice. "I'm not immediate family, obviously. Just—a friend. Her parents are supposed to be flying in from New Orleans, but the airports are all closed because of the storm."

"I know. My mom . . ." Meg stopped herself again, realizing he wouldn't care that her mother was stranded in an airport somewhere, too. It was a trivial detail, meaningless small talk that had no place in this stark, somber place where lives hung precariously. Where *Mirabelle's* life hung precariously.

Meg and the stranger named Ben eyed each other uncomfortably until the nurse hung up the phone at the desk and cleared her throat.

Relieved, Meg turned back to her. "Can you tell me anything about her condition?" she asked, though it was a moot question now that she'd spoken to Ben.

"I'm sorry," the woman said, her tone kind but professional. "There's been no change. Her condition is critical, and she isn't conscious. Maybe," the nurse added, "the two of you should go down to the cafeteria on the basement level. The coffee isn't bad, and it's usually pretty empty on Saturday afternoons at this hour."

Meg looked back at Ben, wondering if the woman thought they already knew each other. She'd been busy on the phone, so she hadn't heard their conversation, had only seen them talking to each other. Maybe she expected them to cry on each other's shoulders over Mirabelle.

And maybe they should, Meg thought.

"Want to?" Ben asked with a shrug.

"Okay."

Together, they walked back through the double doors and along the hallway toward the elevator. Ben pushed the down button and they waited.

Meg was trying to think of something to say when he turned to her and said, "So you're all right, obviously."

Taken aback, she repeated, "All right? What do you mean?"

"I mean, she didn't get to you."

"Who? What are you talking about?"

"Your sister. Candra." The elevator doors slid open and he motioned for Meg to get on first.

She did, mechanically, positioning herself between two doctors who were having an animated conversation about one of their patients. The elevator was jammed, and Ben squeezed into the corner across from Meg.

As the doors closed and it lurched downward, she wondered what he was talking about. What did he know about Candra? And what did he mean about her getting to Meg?

Unfortunately, Meg thought as the elevator stopped at the fifth floor and two more people crammed their way on, her questions were going to have to wait.

He lay on the mattress of the musty back room of the occult shop on Elmont Avenue, mentally concentrating on Dalila Parker's apartment just a few blocks away.

There was only one way for him to get past the police who were still camped out in the apartment, conducting their investigation.

Closing his eyes, he imagined his astral self separating from his physical self. Years of practice enabled him to project in no time, and moments later he was rising above the body that lay prone on the mattress, gliding away from it and out through the back wall of the shop.

He passed swiftly over the rainy street, noting the squad cars that still sat in front of Rivera's Newsstand. Then, hoping that he could slip into her apartment unnoticed, he went through the outer wall and found himself in her closet, just as he had planned.

An overpowering hunch had drawn him to this very spot.

On the other side of the door, he could hear the television blaring what sounded like a football game from the living room. Two voices were carrying on a jocular conversation about something called the Fighting Irish.

Some investigation, he thought, and after listening to make sure he didn't hear anyone out in the bedroom, he cautiously opened the closet door a crack. Gauzy gray light filtered in and he was able to make out the row of dresses and blouses hanging behind him and the clutter of shoes on the floor.

Guardedly, he reached up and felt along the shelf above his head, beneath the stacks of sweaters and slacks that lined it. His fingers finally found something that didn't belong.

A triumphant smile curved his lips as he realized intuitively that this was the very thing he was looking for.

Ever so quietly, he pulled down the manila folder. In the dim light, he couldn't make out the label. Not that it mattered. This was it. He knew it. And there was more.

He reached up again and rooted among the clothes until his fingers brushed a cold, hard surface. He pulled and found himself holding a metal box.

Trembling with anticipation, he tucked it and the folder under his arm, and swept back through the wall.

The phone rang about a half hour after Meg had left. Candra, lying on her twin sister's bed and staring at the ceiling, was startled by it. She sat up and looked at the extension on Meg's desk, wondering who it could be.

If she didn't get it, the answering machine downstairs would pick it up and take a message.

But what if it was Meg?

What if something had happened to Mirabelle?

Impulsively, Candra reached out and picked up the receiver. "Hello?" she said tentatively, thinking that Meg wouldn't mind her taking the liberty of answering the phone. And anyone else would just assume she was Meg.

Except, she realized belatedly, one person . . .

"Candra? It's me, Landon."

For one wild, troubled moment, she contemplated hanging up on him. Then, if he called back, she could just let it ring.

But then the answering machine would pick up anyway.

And anyway, she had to face him sooner or later. It might as well be now.

"Oh, hi," she said in a detached tone. As if she were bored. As if her heart wasn't throbbing crazily at the mere sound of his voice. As if she weren't sobbing inside at the knowledge that all her dreams about Landon, everything she had imagined for the two of them, had dissolved.

"I was waiting for you to call me, but when you didn't,

I thought . . . I don't know, maybe you'd lost the number, or something."

"No," she said indifferently. "I have it."

"Oh . . . were you sleeping, then? I mean, you were probably exhausted after all that happened, and—"

"I've been up," she interrupted him. "I just didn't want to call."

"Why not?"

"Why would I?" she asked, forcing the chilly words past the lump that kept threatening to lodge in her throat.

There was silence on the other end of the line for a long moment.

Then Landon said slowly, "You obviously have no intention of . . . you know. Seeing me?"

"Obviously not."

Again, there was silence.

Candra wanted to sob into the phone, wanted to blurt out the whole sordid story, wanted to tell him that he didn't care about her, not really. He just thought he did, because she'd cast a spell on him.

But she didn't. She didn't say anything at all.

No, she just took the silent receiver away from her ear and replaced it carefully in its cradle. Just like that. Cut him off, and out of her life.

Then, swiping blindly at the tears that trickled down her cheeks, she locked the door. Thinking that there wasn't much time to waste before her sister came back home again, she went over to Meg's dresser and began to clear it off so she could use it, once more, as a makeshift altar.

It was time to remove the spell she had cast on Landon Keller.

Time to let go, once and for all, of the dream.

* * *

"Ooohh," Lester moaned, and Giselle glanced up at him. He had closed his book and was clutching his stomach, waiting for her to ask him what was wrong.

She closed her eyes again, not necessarily eager to go back to thinking about Manfred, but not wanting to give Lester the satisfaction of noticing his moan.

"Ooohh," he moaned again.

And again.

And louder.

Finally, Giselle looked at him. "What?" she asked, irritated and conscious that everyone around them was tuned in.

"My stomach. It's that damn ulcer acting up again."

"Take a Tums."

"I don't have any more."

"You just bought a roll."

"I finished it."

Giselle rolled her eyes. "So get another roll, then."

"I can't leave the boarding area now. What if we get clearance to go? Do you want me to get left behind in California?"

Giselle contemplated that briefly and decided to keep her answer to herself. She didn't want the eavesdroppers thinking she was a complete bitch.

"If they board the plane, I'll make sure they wait for you. And anyway, it'll take forever just to get everyone on. You have time to run to the gift shop and back. And this time, why don't you spring for a bottle instead of a roll? You go through those things like candy."

"Are you crazy?" he asked, standing and dumping *War and Peace* onto his seat without marking his place.

"Do you know what they charge for a bottle of Tums in this place?"

Giselle shrugged, thinking about the custom-made three-hundred-dollar shirts he claimed were necessary in his line of work, and the outrageously expensive single-malt-scotch he insisted on drinking after dinner in restaurants, though one glass of the stuff cost more than most entrées.

And just a few weeks ago, he'd charged nearly a thousand dollars' worth of clothes at Crawford Corners' finest men's shop just before leaving to go on a business trip. He'd told Giselle he needed a few new suits for a series of meetings in St. Louis, where he wanted to impress some important potential clients.

According to the Weather Channel, there had been so much rain in the Midwest on that particular week that the Mississippi had overrun its banks. When Lester had dutifully called home every night, she had asked him about the weather. He had always told her how lousy it was, how it had been pouring nonstop since he'd arrived, not that he cared since he was in meetings all day, every day.

But when he came home, his bulbous nose bore a telltale red tint. With his fair skin, Giselle knew, Lester never had been able to avoid a sunburn. Even with maximum sunscreen on, all he had to do was step outside for five minutes, and he was fried.

The sun hadn't shown in St. Louis in over a week.

So Old Lester was up to something.

Giselle had wondered who his mistress was, and why on earth she was with Lester. But then, even Giselle had been charmed by him all those years ago. She supposed that somewhere out there, some other woman might, in a weak moment, fall for her husband. Especially if he was whisking her off on tropical vacations under the guise of taking business trips.

And furthermore, Giselle didn't even care. The thought of her husband in another woman's arms left her utterly indifferent. Besides, the fact that Lester had a girlfriend would make it all the easier to dump him.

"I'll be right back, then. Make sure you keep an eye on the bags," Lester said, and walked away.

Giselle watched him. He was slightly doubled over as he left the gate area, but farther down the corridor, he straightened and his step became a purposeful stride.

"*Weenie,*" she muttered under her breath, and closed her eyes again.

Instantly, she was transported back to Jamaica, and Manfred.

She had little recollection of that first *obeah* ritual beyond the first moments, when she, flanked by Howard and Raymond, had been invited into the circle of participants. She remembered the constant drumbeat and the high-pitched chanting and Manfred's black eyes glittering in the firelight, always, it seemed, focused on her.

But then it became a blur, probably because of all the rum, she had always comforted herself. Because she didn't want to consider what else it could have been. Didn't want to elaborate on how she'd felt mesmerized by Manfred's gaze, how she'd been powerless to look away or run away, though somewhere in her mind, she heard a warning that this Black Magic stuff could be dangerous, that she might be in over her head.

The next thing she knew, after that first night, she was waking up in the front seat of Howard's car as they pulled up in front of her parents' rented house. And she was sore all over . . . sore in places where she had never ached before. Her upper thighs . . .

Now, she shuddered remembering how she'd tried to ignore the curious discomfort in muscles she'd never realized she had. Tried to ignore what that might mean.

Only later—more than a month later—was she forced to acknowledge what must have happened to her that night at the Black Magic ceremony.

Filled with dread, she realized, when she woke that terrible morning to an overwhelming sensation of nausea, what she'd been trying to deny: that her period was weeks overdue and she was, quite obviously, pregnant.

Meg waited until she and Ben were seated in the hospital cafeteria with two cups of coffee in front of them. The nurse upstairs had been right; the place was deserted except for the occasional orderly or nurse who sat gobbling lunch and constantly checking the large wall clock.

"Okay," Meg said, watching Ben dump three packets of sugar into his coffee, "what were you saying about Candra?"

For a moment, his bloodshot, shadow-rimmed dark eyes looked blank. Then he said, "You mean back upstairs? I said she obviously didn't hurt you."

"Why would she?"

He gave a bitter little laugh. "Oh, I don't know . . . because she's evil? At least, that was what Mirabelle thought. That was why she was trying to save you. That's why she went up in that damn helicopter in a storm."

"Mirabelle thought Candra was trying to hurt me?" Meg shook her head. "I can't believe she'd think that about my own sister."

"She thought Candra was trying to *kill* you, Meg. She and Shea were doing everything they could to—"

"Shea?" Meg blinked. "How does Mirabelle know Shea? I mean, they met at Zoe's party, but it's not like they pal around together . . . do they?" Suddenly, Meg wondered what had been going on while she—rather, her memory—was out of commission.

He shrugged. "I guess they were both concerned about you, and they said Candra was posing as you, and that she had you tucked away somewhere . . ."

"That's ridiculous!" Meg protested, despite a nagging voice in her mind. A voice that said, *But you have absolutely no recollection of the past week. Why not?* "Candra saved my life. Dalila Parker is the one who tried to kill me."

"Well, Mirabelle said that Candra and that woman were working together."

"They were not!"

"Calm down!" Ben said, looking around.

Meg saw two nurses at a nearby table glance up at them.

She lowered her voice to a fierce near-whisper. "I just don't understand where all this came from," she told Ben. "Why would Mirabelle be suspicious of Candra?"

"How well do you know Mirabelle?"

"Not very," Meg admitted, wanting desperately to believe that her friend might not be as sincere as Meg's instincts had told her she was. Maybe Mirabelle, with all her supposed powers, was just a big fake. But that was hard to believe. . . .

Suddenly, Meg was torn between wanting to believe in poor Mirabelle, who lay in a coma upstairs, and wanting to believe in her sister, her own flesh and blood. One of them, obviously, had been lying.

"Mirabelle *knows* things," Ben told her. "She has a . . . gift, she called it. She can—"

"I know all about her stupid powers," Meg cut in, shoving her untouched coffee away and pushing her chair back. "And as far as I'm concerned, it's all a bunch of bull."

Ben shrugged. "If that's what you want to believe, fine. But she risked her life for you."

"So did Candra," Meg bit out before jumping to her feet and fleeing the cafeteria, scurrying up the stairs and out into the driving rain, not caring when her hair and clothes were immediately soaked or when jagged lightning struck above her.

She's my sister, she kept thinking as she ran blindly through the parking lot toward her car.

She's my sister.

He settled onto the floor of the musty back room of the Elmont Avenue shop, easily wrapping his long dark limbs around each other and leaning back against the wall.

Then he reached for the metal box and the folder. It was labeled, he saw now, inspecting it, with a single word that meant nothing to him. *Merriweather.*

First, he would inspect the box, which wasn't locked. Not that that would have stopped him.

He lifted the lid and gave the contents a cursory glance before picking up the little red drawstring pouch. Instinctively, he knew that Giselle had made this conjure bag. Her very essence clung to it, and he closed his eyes, briefly, remembering what she'd looked like at seventeen. Winsome and sun-kissed, the very picture of wholesome innocence.

He loosened the drawstring, sniffed, and easily identified the powdered herbs inside by their smell. These particular herbs were used for protection.

A sinister smile curved his mouth as he lifted out the tuft of fine black baby hair. She was trying to protect her daughter . . . but which one? Meg? Or Candra?

He had no doubt *who* it was that Giselle feared.

Poor Giselle, he thought wickedly. *Worried that one of your children might be harmed by their very own daddy.*

Fifteen

Meg was pulling out of the hospital parking lot when she saw a familiar car approaching.

It's Zoe, she realized, and honked her horn as the car was about to pass her.

Obviously, her friend was on her way to visit Mirabelle. Meg wondered if a first cousin qualified as immediate family.

In response to the honking, Zoe's red Acura slowed alongside her.

The two cars were only a few feet apart, and despite the nasty weather, Meg saw Zoe's face clearly through the rain-splattered driver's side window.

She looked right at Meg, then turned away and kept driving, pulling away so quickly that her car hit a water-filled pothole with a scrape and a splash.

Meg knew how careful Zoe always was with her Acura these days. She'd already banged it up twice, and her parents had told her if she did it again, they'd take it away from her.

Obviously, her friend was in a big hurry to get away from her.

Meg's eyes narrowed as she looked back over her shoulder, watching Zoe's taillights disappear around a row of parked cars. What had she done to Zoe this past week?

Or . . .

No, she couldn't even think that what Ben had suggested was true.

But still . . .

What had Candra, if she really had been posing as Meg, done to Zoe?

Oblivious to the other passengers and the bustling activity of the airport boarding area, Giselle pressed her tanned, manicured, ring-covered fingers over her flat abdomen, just as she had done that long ago morning.

Of course, back then, a rush of bile had suddenly filled her mouth, and she had gone running for the bathroom. As she choked and spewed the bitter stuff into the toilet, she had wondered if it was mere morning sickness, or if the numbing horror of her realization had made her physically ill.

Even now, she felt a twinge of queasiness, just remembering that awful morning.

Not that she regretted having Meg. Her oldest daughter was dear to her, and as troubled as the circumstances of her birth had been, Giselle had never wished she had never been born. Only that things had been different.

She hadn't told a soul of her condition, but they knew. Everyone, she was convinced, but her parents, was aware that Giselle McKenna was pregnant. Howard and Raymond looked knowingly at her belly when they were around, and the housekeeper, Tish, caught her throwing up more than one morning. Even in town, Giselle was conscious of people staring at her and whispering behind her back.

And no matter how much she tried to convince herself that she was only imagining it, she knew that they knew. She didn't know how, but they did.

She half-dreaded, half-hoped, that she would stumble across *him* again. He consumed her every thought.

Manfred.

And one day, she found him. Rather, he found her.

It happened when she was walking down the winding road toward town about three months after she had discovered her condition; she was planning to buy some larger clothes. Her own waistbands were getting unbearably snug, though she knew she wasn't showing yet. Not in her baggy T-shirts and sundresses. And she had long since stopped wearing a bikini, upset at the mere sight of her own bare stomach, let alone the thought of someone else seeing it.

Her parents didn't suspect a thing, as far as she knew. Her father was too busy with his development project, and her mother was too busy being nervous and miserable about living so far from home.

As Giselle rounded a curve in the road, he suddenly stepped out in front of her, only a few yards away. She stopped and gave a startled little cry, and he simply stood there, looking at her. His black eyes bore into hers, then lowered to stare at her belly with an intensity that made her feel naked and completely vulnerable.

"I know," he said, and she had no doubt as to his meaning.

"Is it yours?"

He only nodded.

She found herself walking toward him as propelled by some force other than her own mind, covering the remaining distance swiftly and throwing herself on him, suddenly sobbing uncontrollably. He opened his arms and took her into his grasp, stroking her hair until she calmed, but still saying nothing.

Finally, she leaned back and looked up into his face. "Why did you rape me?"

"I didn't rape you, Giselle."

She marveled at the sound of her name on his lips, filled with wonder and pleasure that he knew it, that he knew who she was.

"I didn't rape you," he said again. "You were more than willing when I entered you."

Her insides stirred at his words, and she squirmed slightly at the image they created in her mind. "But . . . I can't remember any of it."

He shrugged. "Does it matter?"

"Was everyone there when we . . . did they see . . . ?"

"Of course. It was part of the ritual. And you enjoyed it, Giselle. You wanted me desperately, from the moment you saw me in the club that first night."

She nodded, knowing that what he said was true. She hadn't recognized her own heated desire for what it was. Now she knew that she had wanted him desperately, and she ached for him again.

Slowly, as if sensing what was going through her mind, he reached out and ran a long, tapered black finger down her bare throat. Then he dipped it between his own moist lips before slipping it, moistened with saliva, inside the open collar of her blouse. She trembled as he probed lower, as his cold, wet flesh found her right nipple and caressed it roughly. She felt herself grow painfully stiff beneath his touch, and her whole body tensed with longing.

"Please . . ." she whispered, sinking to her knees in the dusty road. "I want . . ."

"No."

The single word was tossed carelessly from his lips as

he withdrew his finger and looked down at her with contempt.

"Please, Manfred. I want you. Inside me. I want you now. Please . . ." She was begging and sobbing, suddenly crazed with need.

"Not now. You carry my child in your womb. You will have me . . . but only if you come to live with me."

Stunned, she whispered, "Live with you? Do you mean . . . you want me to leave my parents?"

He nodded.

"But what do I tell them?"

"What do I care what you tell them? You are going to bear my child. I want you with me."

Dazed, Giselle had watched as he started to walk away. Then, desperate at the thought of losing him, she called recklessly, "I'll do it, Manfred. I'll live with you."

He'd turned and nodded, his face stoic as ever. "I will send someone for you tomorrow at midnight. Be prepared."

From that moment on, Giselle had felt as though she were detached from her own body, watching what happened to herself over the next several months, but never participating.

She had fuzzy memories of a series of events that seemed surreal: stealthily slipping out of her parents' home in the dead of night without a backward glance, being driven by a silent Howard to Manfred's shack in the mountains high above Ocho Rios.

Manfred had been waiting for her, and after Howard left them alone, he had swiftly stripped her clothes off, and then his own, and made passionate love to her on the dirt floor. She was in utter ecstacy as he finally spilled warmly into her, his strong, lean body bucking above her in the dark.

And she thought, as she drifted off to sleep, that this was where she belonged.

The days all blurred together after that. Now, looking back, she semi-remembered the people who came and went, all of them treating Manfred with reverence; and she recalled the midwife, Rosamund, who occasionally came to Manfred's shack to examine her.

More vaguely, she remembered the ritualistic *obeah* ceremonies that took place in the woods under cover of darkness.

She never knew what had happened after they got under way; her mind always seemed to fog over once the drumbeats grew more frenzied and the chanting started.

Her belly protruded as time went on, growing impossibly enormous, and she wore very little clothing in the tropical heat. She didn't recall thinking once of the child she carried or of the parents she had left behind.

She lived only for Manfred, for the exquisite moments when he would grace her with his touch. She thought of nothing else during those hazy summer months. He consumed her very soul, even as his child squirmed and kicked within her.

"How did it go?" Candra asked Meg, hurrying down the stairs the moment she heard the front door open.

"All right." Meg, shrugging out of her navy Burberry trench coat, didn't look up.

Candra's pace slowed as she continued down the stairs, watching her sister.

Meg was at the closet, taking out a wooden hanger and carefully draping her coat over it. But her movements were stiff, and she seemed preoccupied.

"Meg?" Candra asked, frowning slightly. "Is Mirabelle . . . ?"

"There's no change."

"Oh." Candra tried to ignore the flicker of disappointment she felt at her sister's words.

Not that she wanted anything bad to happen to Mirabelle, she told herself. Of course she didn't.

"Well, did you get to see her?"

Meg turned from the closet, but didn't meet Candra's eyes. "No, she can't have visitors. Only immediate family."

Relief coursed over Candra. That meant Mirabelle couldn't have told Meg anything.

But then . . .

Was it her imagination, or did she see a trace of suspicion in her sister's eyes?

It was gone just as quickly as she'd glimpsed it, making her wonder if perhaps she'd been mistaken.

"What did you do while I was out?" Meg asked, sounding—and looking—like herself again.

"Nothing. I read a magazine—there was a copy of *Seventeen* on your nightstand and I figured you wouldn't mind if I borrowed it . . ." She waited for Meg to say no, of course she didn't mind. But Meg didn't say anything. Candra went on, keeping a calculating eye on her sister, ". . . and so I read the magazine and just, you know, hung around."

"Anyone call?" Meg asked, and Candra tensed, thinking of Landon.

"No, no one called," she said hastily.

"Oh. I thought maybe Mom would have. I wish she would get in touch."

"Why? I'm sure there's nothing to worry about. It's probably just the storm that's delaying everything."

"I know that. But I want to tell her about you."

"Why?" Candra asked again, feeling a prickle of alarm. Something in Meg's expression was making her nervous.

Her sister shrugged. "I just want her to know you're here, that's all. She's going to be thrilled."

"Why do you think that?" Candra asked darkly.

"Why wouldn't she be? After all, you're her daughter. Of course Mom's going to be glad you're here. Just like I am."

Those last words sounded hesitant, hollow. Again, Candra caught a fleeting expression of uncertainty in her sister's eyes.

For a moment, their gazes caught and held—Candra's probing, Meg's veiled.

The ringing telephone shattered the moment.

After only a moment's pause, Meg went for it in the next room.

"Hello? Oh, hi, Chasey," Candra heard her say.

Chasey Norman. Meg's nosy, redheaded chatterbox of a friend.

Candra sat absolutely still, straining to hear what she could of the conversation.

"What? When?" Meg asked. "Last night? Oh, right. I forgot all about making plans with you guys. Listen, is Zoe mad? . . . Of course I know how she is . . . I know, I'm sure she's very upset, but I couldn't help it. Something came up."

Suddenly, Candra remembered the plans she, posing as Meg, had made with Chasey and Zoe. They had wanted to take her out for her birthday, had said they would pick her up at eight.

"No, I can't tell you what it was. Not right now . . . Listen, Chasey," Meg was saying. "I don't care. I've had a crazy week, and I'm really not in the mood right now to deal with you and Zoe being annoyed with me for something that isn't even a big deal. . . . It is not. . . . Fine. If that's the way you guys want it."

She slammed down the receiver, and for a moment, there was only silence from the next room.

Then Candra heard it.

The muffled sound of sobbing.

She got up and went to the doorway. Meg sat there beside the telephone, her shoulders shaking and tears rolling down her cheeks. When she saw Candra, she wiped at them and looked away.

"What's wrong, Meg?" Candra asked quietly, taking a few tentative steps into the room.

"Nothing . . . Everything. I feel like I'm losing my mind. I can't remember anything that's happened to me, and my boyfriend and my friends are all upset with me, and I have no idea who to trust—" She broke off there and looked as though she'd said too much.

"You can trust me, Meg," Candra said after a moment, meaning it. "I'm your sister."

"I know. That's what I . . . I know."

"Do you trust me?"

Meg hesitated, and wiped at her eyes again.

Candra waited until her sister looked up at her, and when she did, Candra smiled. It was a sincere smile, one that held a multitude of promises.

Please, Meg, she begged silently. *Give me a chance. I'm your sister. You're mine . . . You're all I have.*

Meg sniffled and then her own mouth curved up. Only slightly, but it was a real smile. She nodded. "I do. I know I don't really know you, and I know you have plenty of reasons to hate me, but I don't think you do. And I trust you."

"I trust you, too," Candra said, and crossed the rest of the way to her sister. She paused awkwardly for a moment, then reached out and put her arm around Meg's shoulders.

"Thanks, Candra," Meg said gratefully, and Candra shoved aside another twinge of guilt.

Even when the sun was shining, there wasn't much light in the small room behind the occult shop. On a day like today, it was filled with shadows that made it difficult to see anything.

But he was young, and his vision was good. Even in the dim light, he could see the items he had found in the metal box.

And after glancing over them, he put them aside. They were interesting, but didn't reveal any secrets.

Like the conjure bag, the clay doll had obviously been fashioned for protection. The blue candle symbolized protection, too. Clearly, Giselle had felt threatened. The thought filled him with pleasure.

And as for the sketch pad—Giselle's, of course—it was filled with drawings of scenery, although there were one or two images that had captured his interest. One was an excellent likeness of himself, the simple line drawing radiating power and passion. The other was a careful depiction of two baby girls, newborn and identical, captured forever on paper by their mother's loving hand.

Meg and Candra.

He chuckled softly, thinking that all of Giselle's protective measures, and her ultimate attempt to flee, had been for nothing.

It was only a matter of time before her daughters met

their fate at his hands. And maybe Giselle would, too. It hadn't been his intention to harm her when he'd come here . . .

But then, sometimes impulsive pleasures were the best pleasures of all.

He turned his attention to the file folder.

The first thing he saw, upon opening it, was the pink invoice from Merriweather Investigative Services in Spring City, Connecticut. It bore Giselle's husband's name, and was stamped *Paid*.

Beneath it was a yellow sheet of legal paper on which was scribbled a phone number with an 809 area code.

His phone number.

Beneath that was a sheaf of bound papers that were labeled *Confidential*.

So. This was the report from that private detective Lester Hudson had hired.

Of course, it had been Lester who had stirred things up after so many years.

He thought back to the day, about a month ago, when his friend Reg, a native Jamaican who worked as a bartender at one of the new resorts in Ocho Rios, had come to tell him that someone had been asking questions.

Strange questions, about the past.

The nosy man was an American who looked like a tourist, according to Reg, but who was clearly in Jamaica for something other than sun and fun.

Hmm.

What was he up to?

It hadn't been too hard for Reg to get the American drunk the next night. After figuring the guy was a cheapskate, considering the meager tips he'd left, all Reg had to do was ply him with free drinks. Once he had grown slap-happy, bragging about his business and his travels, Reg had started asking questions. At first, the guy had been reticent about why he was sniffing around in Ocho Rios, claiming he was just there on vacation. But eventually, with his voice slurred and his eyes starting to look bleary, he'd started talking.

Afterward, when he was safely snoozing back in his room, Reg had driven up into the mountains to reveal what the American had told him.

The man's name was Lester Hudson, Reg reported, and he was from a little town in Connecticut. Crawford Corners.

So that was it. Giselle had been from Crawford Corners. This had something to do with her.

Sure enough, Reg went on to tell him that the man's wife's name was Giselle, and she had borne twin girls eighteen years ago, when she was a teenager living in Jamaica.

According to Lester's wife, one child, Candra, had stayed behind in Jamaica with the father, a local whose name was Manfred. For some reason, Giselle was under the impression that the child had died.

The other child, Meg, had gone back to America with Giselle.

The instant Reg told him that, shock and rage shot through him. He'd known where Candra was all along—that she was being raised by Rosamund, a local woman who had lost her own child in infancy.

But Meg . . .

Meg was supposed to be dead.

Rosamund had told him she was.

Rosamund had *promised* she was.

According to Reg, Lester wanted to talk to the twins' father, Manfred. He had found out, through the private detective he'd hired, that Candra hadn't died shortly after birth after all.

It seemed that Rosamund's sister, Tish, had a big mouth. She had been involved in the coverup, but had blabbed it to someone on the island. Pretty soon, it was common knowledge—although no one, in all these years, had dared to tell Manfred.

Lester had found out that Manfred had wanted Meg dead—and that he had no idea that she wasn't. He also knew that Manfred was quite wealthy.

What he didn't know, according to Reg, was that Manfred was a powerful high priest and that his wealth had come from spells he had cast.

Anyway, what Lester planned to do was blackmail Manfred—and Giselle.

He was going to tell Manfred that if he didn't come up with a considerable amount of money, Lester would tell his wife that her daughter Candra was still alive.

Meanwhile, he was going to tell Giselle that he had tracked down Meg's father, and that if she didn't pay him off, he would reveal to the man that Meg was still alive.

When Reg had asked him why he had to bother blackmailing his own wife, Lester had said, "Because I'm no fool. I know she wants to leave me. And if she does, I'll get nothing, thanks to a prenuptial agreement her father made me sign when I married her. My wife is loaded, and after all these years, I don't deserve to be left high and dry."

Furthermore, Lester had told Reg, he had found out something else. Something neither Giselle nor Manfred knew. And he was safeguarding that secret. Despite the haze of scotch, he had suddenly grown closemouthed. He wasn't going to reveal what he knew.

Poor Lester. The greedy fool had no idea he was dabbling in a dangerous place.

Now, he would find out just what it was that Lester had discovered about the past—the other thing Rosamund had been keeping from him.

He reached for the confidential report, opened it to the first page, and began to read.

And as he read, his eyes narrowed and darkened and his face contorted until he wore hideous mask of fury and hatred.

Now, at last, he knew the truth.

And now he would seek vengeance for this shocking deception.

Yes, all of them would pay for one woman's sins.

Rosamund Bowen would be the first to die.

Giselle would be the last.

"What took you so long?" Giselle asked, hearing Lester sit down in the seat beside her again. She opened her eyes and saw that he was unpeeling the foil end of a new roll of Tums.

He hesitated only a moment before saying, "I had to make a phone call."

Hmm. Why had he decided to be truthful for a change? Maybe he thought she had followed him and seen him. He wouldn't dream that she really could care less what he did.

"Who'd you call?" she asked, because he was obviously waiting for her to.

He popped a pastel green antacid tablet into his mouth. "My voice mail at the office. I needed to see if anyone was trying to reach me."

"On a Saturday?"

He scowled. "I'm a very important man, Giselle. Do you think my job ends at five o'clock on a Friday night? I need to be in contact every minute of every day in case one of my clients needs me."

"Lester, you've been in Fiji for the past week and a half."

"I know, and I've checked my voice mail several times every day."

Giselle wanted to say that he could stop playing at this silly charade, that she knew all about his mistress and that as far as she was concerned, Lester could just call her whenever he felt like it, in front of her. Hell, Giselle would even get on the line and say hello. She'd tell the pitiful woman, whoever she was, that she was more than welcome to Lester Hudson. She'd advise her to stock her medicine cabinet with Tums, and—

"What are you smiling at, Giselle?" Lester sounded irritated, and she shrugged. She noticed that his lips were coated with milky, pale green residue.

"Nothing. I'm not smiling at anything, Lester."

"Have they made any announcements about the flight?"

"Nope."

He sighed and checked his watch, then popped another Tums into his mouth.

Giselle closed her eyes again. Immediately, her thoughts went back to what had happened so long ago in Jamaica. After so many years of trying not to think of it, why was it on her mind so much today?

Because you have nothing else to do in this damn airport, she told herself. *And because yesterday was Meg's eighteenth birthday. Her twin sister would have been eighteen, too, now. What would it have been like if I had been able to bring her home with me, too?*

A lump rose in Giselle's throat, and she swallowed hard over it.

She remembered that terribly muggy September morning when her water had suddenly broken as she made Manfred's breakfast. She hadn't even known what it was, the sudden gush of warm liquid that trickled down her legs. Paralyzed with shame, thinking she had lost control of her bladder, she had given a little moan and stared down at the puddle on the floor.

Manfred had glanced up from his coffee, seen what had happened, and told her to lie down.

As she moved to obey him the first contraction had seized her, a breathtaking cramp that made her cry out and clutch her swollen abdomen.

"Help me, Manfred," she had gasped, suddenly terrified.

But he hadn't.

He had merely left the room, and sent one of the young men who were always hanging around the house to summon the midwife.

By the time Rosamund arrived, Giselle had been writhing on the bed, half-delirious in agony. She was alone in the house, Manfred had left her, saying that it wasn't his place to be here.

Giselle was vaguely aware that Rosamund had brought another woman with her—her sister, Letitia. The two women held a hushed conversation as they poked and prodded at Giselle, and she whimpered and screamed and implored them to make this stop. Her labor had progressed swiftly, and Giselle begged Rosamund to help her, to give her something for the pain.

"Yeah, *mon*, no problem," Rosamund had said, and moments later she was holding a damp, harsh-smelling cloth beneath Giselle's nose. She inhaled and was borne away on a wave of oblivion.

The next thing she remembered was sudden, unbearable pressure, and pushing and writhing, and bellowing at the top of her lungs.

And then, as if across a great distance, she heard a baby's angry cries.

Thank God it's over had been her only thought, as she drifted toward that blessed limbo again.

But there was more pressure, and Rosamund's hurried voice saying, "There's another one. Come on, my lady, push. Push . . ."

And for Giselle, too far gone to comprehend or care, the rest had been a blur. She had slipped in and out of consciousness, fighting the unbearable pain that tortured her body, shutting out the wailing baby, or babies . . .

She didn't care.

She didn't care about anything except ending this terrible suffering.

And Manfred . . .

Where was Manfred?

Why had he left her?

She needed him desperately . . .

And then that pungent cloth was pressed to her face again, and there was only darkness, and silence.

When she finally came to, Giselle saw that it was night. She was still lying in the bed, and the lamp was lit, and somewhere nearby she heard the faint whimpering of an infant.

She blinked and looked around, and her gaze came to rest on Rosamund, who sat in a rocking chair across the room crooning softly to the small bundle in her arms.

That's my child, Giselle had thought numbly, but she felt nothing. Nothing but relief . . . and confusion.

Where was Manfred?

And . . .

Hadn't there been two babies?

"Rosamund?" she croaked out. "Where's Manfred? And where's the other child?"

There was only silence for a long time.

Then the woman had stood and walked over to the bed. She had leaned over and deposited the baby in Giselle's arms.

"This is your daughter, my lady," she had said in her singsong Jamaican accent. "She is a beautiful, healthy child."

And in that first moment that she held her baby, Giselle was swamped in a rush of maternal love. This child, this tiny creature with a pinched red face and a headful of black hair, with those dark, solemn eyes that focused unwaveringly on her mother's face, was a part of Giselle . . . and the man she loved.

In wonder, Giselle reached out and caressed the baby's impossibly soft, smooth cheek with her fingertip, and was met with a hushed little coo.

"You're so beautiful," she whispered to her daughter. "I'm your mommy, and I'll always be there for you. Always."

And then, she had looked up at Rosamund, and the woman's eyes met hers with . . . was it guilt? The midwife broke the gaze hastily, looking away as she busied herself smoothing the blanket on the bed and plumping the pillows behind Giselle.

"Rosamund," Giselle said, fighting back an inexplicable rush of panic, "where's the other baby? There were two. I *know* there were two. I heard you say it. I remember . . ."

There was no reply.

Carefully, so she wouldn't jostle the baby in her arms, yet urgently, Giselle reached up and grabbed Rosamund's arm.

"Where is my baby? Tell me!"

"She is gone, my lady. But this child is here, and she is yours."

"She died?"

Again the slight hesitation, the evasive expression in Rosamund's gaze. "She did, yes."

A sob escaped Giselle's throat, and she was enveloped in grief for the daughter she had never even glimpsed. "Where's Manfred? Does he know?"

"He does."

"Where is he? Please, Rosamund," she said, crying now and clutching her baby to her breast, "please tell him I need him."

The woman had nodded and slipped away.

Giselle didn't know how long it was before Manfred came to her, only that it felt like hours, like days had passed as she sat in that bed rocking her daughter. The infant's eyes were closed and she slept soundly, her chest rising and falling in a rhythmic pattern. Giselle wanted to be reassured by those tiny breaths, by the child's warm body against her own, and yet . . .

"I can't lose you, too," she whispered to her daughter. "Please, my little love, please don't leave me, too."

Finally, she heard a sound and saw that Manfred was standing at the foot of her bed. He had always done that—slipped into and out of a room swiftly and silently, startling her with his comings and goings.

Now she burst into fresh tears at the sight of him.

"Oh, Manfred," she sobbed, yearning for him to come to her and comfort her, "we've lost our other daughter. She died, and—"

"She didn't die," he cut in.

His words stunned her, filled her with hope, and yet . . .

And yet, his tone was cold. And he hadn't moved to come near her, just stood there, watching her.

And that was when a chill came over her. She realized, in that moment, in a rush of stark revelation, that Manfred didn't love her . . .

And that she was afraid of him.

Deathly afraid.

"She's alive?" she asked hesitantly, watching him.

"No. But she did not 'die.' The other baby was killed, Giselle," Manfred said calmly.

"No . . ." Horrified, and numb with shock, Giselle had tightened her grasp on the baby in her arms, to protect her daughter from the man who had fathered her.

"Yes," Manfred said. "She was sacrificed."

"Oh, God, no . . . oh, please . . . why? Why?"

"Because when I was younger, I made a deal," he said matter-of-factly. "I was born with a gift . . . with power. But always, there was the potential for more . . . for obtaining a force beyond my wildest dreams. All I had to do was promise my firstborn child to the gods and I would rule all who encountered me."

"No . . . oh, Manfred," Giselle protested, unable to grasp what he was telling her. "Why. . . ? Why me?"

"The women here, the ones who partake in our ceremonies, have always been aware of my pledge. Who, of them, would bear my child, knowing its fate?"

The horror of what he was telling her, of what he had done to her, filled Giselle with rage. If not for the

helpless child in her arms, she would have lunged at
him, clawed at him, beaten him with her fists. But
all she could do was stare, and sob, and tremble
uncontrollably.

"The moment I saw you, I knew that you were the one
who would deliver me to my destiny," he mused. "It
wasn't difficult to place you under my spell . . . to make
you want me. Women have always wanted me. But you,
Giselle, you were the chosen one. You were perfect—an
outsider, reckless and vain and naive . . ."

"No, Manfred. Please don't talk this way . . ."

"I gave you a special potion at the ritual that first
night," he went on, oblivious to her torment, "the night
my children were conceived. A potion that was meant
to enhance fertility. It worked, of course, since you have
delivered not one, but *two* babies. Such a shame that
you won't be able to keep one for yourself."

She couldn't speak, could only cower against the pillows in dread, as he took a step toward her. And then
another.

He opened his hands. "Give me the baby."

"No!" she shrieked, clutching her crying daughter
against her. "You've already killed one child, Manfred . . . I won't let you have this one!"

"I'm not going to kill her," he said calmly. "I'm going
to give her to Rosamund. She wants a child, and I
promised to do that, in return for what she has done
for me."

"What? What did she do?"

"She disposed of the other one. She made the sacrifice for me."

"You . . . coward!" Giselle's voice was low with fury
and disbelief. "You couldn't do it yourself. You were too
weak, and—"

She was stopped short by a stinging slap across her cheek.

"*I* am not weak," he thundered. "*I* am not a coward."

In one flurry of movement, he descended on her and wrenched the now screaming baby out of her arms. Before she could react he was gone.

In a panic, Giselle scrambled out of the bed, but her legs seemed to dissolve the moment her feet hit the floor. Suddenly, the trauma of what she had been through, physically and emotionally, took its toll.

She was weak—and disoriented. Blindly, she took a step, and then another.

My baby . . .

I have to save my baby . . .

And then her legs had given out on her and she'd crumpled to the floor in a heap.

Sixteen

The violent storm had finally passed out of the New England region, leaving a surprisingly beautiful sunset in its wake.

Now the last pink-and-peach streaks had faded from the dusky September sky, and the deserted warehouse district in Spring City was cloaked in shadows.

"Are you sure this is the place?" Meg whispered dubiously as she and Candra picked their way across the muddy, shadowy, weed-and-debris-choked railyard.

"Of course I'm sure." Candra was several steps ahead of her, moving with purpose despite the obstacle course underfoot.

Meg scurried to keep up with her sister, trying not to think about snakes and rats and other creatures that might be lurking around them. Overhead, bats swooped across the twilight sky, and Meg kept a wary eye on them to make sure they kept their distance.

"No one's here," Candra called back to her, stopping abruptly a few yards ahead, beside a crumbling shack.

"What?" Meg came to a halt beside her sister and looked around. The shack was little more than a few vertical, rotted boards that had somehow managed to withstand the winds of today's storm.

"I said, they're not here. . . . Shhh." Candra frowned

and stood very still, her head cocked as though she were listening for something.

"Where do you think they are?" Meg asked after a moment of silence, knowing Candra was referring to the coven. Her sister only shrugged and didn't move.

Meg felt the hair on her arms prickling with goose bumps, and an eerie sensation was rapidly settling over her. Something was wrong here.

She could sense it.

Did Candra feel it, too?

"Did you hear that?" Candra asked.

"What?" Meg asked, even as a creepy sound reached her ears. It was a moan . . . or a wail. Something in between.

"That." Candra started in the direction from which the noise had come, in a wooded thicket off to the side, near the rusted, gravel-strewn track bed.

Meg hesitated, afraid to follow, afraid to ask Candra what she thought had made that sound. She thought it had come from an animal that had been wounded—or a person. A chill slid down her spine.

"Candra, wait," she called as her sister moved into the trees ahead.

She heard it again—a low-pitched whimper, followed by a gasp that had come from Candra.

"Oh, God, no! Grandmother!"

Meg broke into a run, and when she reached the spot where Candra had disappeared into the woods, she saw her sister crouched on the ground over something white.

A person, Meg realized as she drew closer. A dark-skinned person who was wearing something with a red-and-white pattern, a robe of some sort.

"Oh, Grandmother," Candra sobbed, and Meg

stopped just a few feet from them, realizing that the robe wasn't red and white patterned. It was white. The red was blood that seeped from the woman's stomach and shoulders and legs . . . she had been savagely butchered.

And she was still alive, moaning softly, staring up at Candra with wide brown eyes. She appeared startled—not just by what had happened to her, but also by the sight of Candra, here, hovering over her in this remote patch of trees.

"Who did this to you, Grandmother?" Candra asked, her voice choked with emotion, her face twisted in agony as she stared down at the woman who had raised her. Rosamund's head was cradled in her lap, and she stroked the woman's blood-spattered hair. "Who hurt you?"

Meg sank to her knees beside her sister and Rosamund, too shaken to utter a word. She touched Candra's arm in a feeble attempt to offer comfort, but her sister didn't seem to notice; she only went on running her fingers over Rosamund's head.

The woman started to speak, closed her eyes as if in pain, and then tried again.

"He's after you . . . too . . ." she said finally, and Meg saw that she was looking at both Candra and herself.

There was something about Rosamund that reached out to Meg, to some deep, forgotten place in her soul. It was almost as if Meg had known her, once, a long time ago . . . but then, that was impossible. There was only one time in her life when her path could ever have crossed Rosamund's, and she couldn't possibly remember anything that had happened when she was an infant in Jamaica.

And yet . . .

"Both of you," Rosamund went on, her words labored, "He's after you . . . and . . ."

"Who is, Grandmother?" Candra asked, her voice trembling with the barely controlled sorrow and rage that were etched across her face. "Who's after us? Who did this to you?"

Rosamund squeezed her eyes closed, then haltingly said, "After you . . . and your brother."

For a moment, the only sound was Rosamund's struggle to take another breath.

Meg felt as though she were hovering above this surreal scene, watching it happen to someone else.

The old woman's words echoed crazily in her mind.

Your brother . . .

Your brother . . .

Your brother . . .

Finally, Meg dared to tear her eyes away from Rosamund's pain-contorted face to focus on her sister. Candra's wide-eyed gaze met hers, and Meg saw the astonishment there.

Meg couldn't seem to find her voice.

But somehow, Candra found hers. She turned back to Rosamund, and, in a hushed tone, uttered the question that was in Meg's mind.

"Grandmother, are you saying that we have a brother?"

The old woman's head raised, then lowered in an almost imperceptible nod. "There . . . were . . . three babies," she whispered hoarsely. "The boy . . . was . . . first . . . firstborn . . ."

Somewhere, in the fog of confusion and dread that had overtaken Meg's mind, she realized that Rosamund knew she was dying; she was fighting to stay alive long enough to warn them, to tell them . . .

A brother, Meg thought incredulously. *We have a brother.*

"Three," Rosamund croaked again, her pain-racked gaze searching their faces as if for confirmation that they understood what she was saying.

"Three," Candra repeated softly, in wonder. "There were three babies. Me, and Meg, and a brother."

Again, the imperceptible nod. Rosamund closed her eyes as if the effort of even that slight movement had been too much for her.

For a moment, when she didn't move, Meg was seized by the horrible thought that she had died.

But then her eyelids fluttered again, and she opened her mouth to force more words past her parched lips. "Giselle . . . never . . . knew . . ."

"She never knew that there were three of us?" Meg asked, uncertain whether she was more stunned at the fact that she had a brother, or that her mother somehow hadn't realized she'd borne triplets.

But how could that be?

"Must . . . warn your brother."

"Where is he? Who is he?" Candra asked, clutching Rosamund's weathered hands. "Who is he, Grandmother? Please—"

"The one . . . with the . . . amulet."

"Amulet?" Meg repeated. "What do you mean?"

"For . . . protection." Her breaths were coming in short, shallow gasps now, and her expression had grown more tortured. "Sent it with him . . . before I . . . gave him away . . ."

"You gave him away, Grandmother?" Candra asked, leaning her head closer to the old woman's lips. "To who? Where is he?"

"Made of steel . . ." Rosamund said faintly.

"The amulet?" Meg asked, riveted, even as her mind screamed, *This isn't happening. This can't be happening.*

"Engraved . . . pentagram . . . powerful . . ."

"But where is he?" Candra asked urgently. "Where's our brother?"

The only answer was the most terrible thing Meg had ever heard—the gurgling, rasping sound of a human being's dire, futile effort to draw a last breath.

Meg watched in numb horror as Rosamund's eyes widened in frantic protest. The woman realized what was happening, and she was fighting it with everything she had.

"Candra . . . oh, God, do something," Meg sobbed in desperation, turning to her sister. "We have to help her."

But Candra, her face stricken and tears rolling down her cheeks, said nothing, did nothing—only stared in anguish at Rosamund.

And when Meg looked down at the woman again, she saw that her gaze had grown vacant, her battered, bloody body relaxed.

She was gone.

"This sandwich is disgusting," Lester announced, plunking it onto the plastic plate in front of him and making a face.

Giselle noticed that his pale red mustache was dotted with crumbs, and there was a slick of mustard in the corner of his mouth.

She looked away, down at the limp iceberg lettuce salad on her own plate, and poked at the sorry-looking greens with her fork.

"How's yours?" Lester asked, swiping a paper napkin

across his lips. He got the mustard, but most of the crumbs remained.

"Mine's fine," she lied.

"I should have ordered a salad. Or something hot."

"Go get something else."

"Are you kidding? Look at that line," he said, gesturing at the crowd of people just inside the cafeteria's doors. "And anyway, airport food costs a fortune. I should go back up to the gate and ask to speak to the supervisor. You know, I think I will. I'm going to demand that they give me another meal voucher."

Giselle rolled her eyes and put her fork down.

"And if they think I'm going to wait in that line again, they've got another thing coming. I'm going to go right to the front, and if they have a problem with that, I'll ask for the supervisor. And while I'm at it, I'm going to ask him why he thinks he can charge an arm and a leg for a sandwich."

"Oh, please, Lester, it's not as if you had to pay for it!"

"That's not the point. I'm going to ask him why, if a goddamn ham and cheese sandwich costs an arm and a leg, it tastes so lousy. How can anyone ruin a ham and cheese sandwich? And then I'm going to—"

"Oh, for God's sake, Lester, why don't you just shut up?" Giselle interrupted, shoving back her chair.

He looked startled.

So did the family of five seated at the next table. Even their toddler was watching Giselle with wide eyes.

She didn't care. Not about Lester, or the family, or what anyone else thought.

She got up and she ran, out of the restaurant and down the carpeted corridor to the ladies' room.

There was a line, she realized in dismay as she walked in the door. There was nothing to do but wait. And do her best not to think about the thing that had been on her mind all afternoon.

But it was no use.

Images kept bombarding her mind.

Manfred . . .

And Rosamund . . .

And the tiny, helpless baby who had died, Meg's identical twin . . .

Luckily, no one in line was paying any attention to her. No one seemed to notice the tears that kept slipping down her cheeks or the way she was trembling all over.

Finally, it was Giselle's turn to slip into one of the stalls.

She closed and locked the door behind her, then wiped at her eyes with a square of cheap, rough toilet paper, hoping that her mascara and eyeliner hadn't poured all over her face. She would check in the mirror before she returned to the gate area, but for now she just needed to be alone, to bury her face in her hands and mourn the baby she had lost so many years ago.

She rarely allowed herself to think of that horrible night; she seldom recollected the atrocious details of what Manfred had done.

Now, huddled in the corner of the tiny cubicle, she was barely aware of the running water and hand-dryers and chattering voices on the other side of the door. She was cut off from the rest of the world, wrapped in her bittersweet memories.

Bitter for the baby who had been murdered at Rosamund's hands.

Sweet for the one who had been saved . . . also at Rosamund's hands.

Giselle would never forget how, after fainting when

Manfred had stolen her second daughter, she had awakened to the sound of Rosamund's voice.

"It's all right, my lady," the woman had said, stroking her face with a damp, cool cloth. "He's gone. And I have your daughter."

Everything Manfred had said came rushing back at Giselle, and she'd sat up and lunged for the woman.

"You killed her," she screamed. "You killed her."

Rosamund gripped both her arms with surprising strength. "Yes, one of your children is gone," she told Giselle, "but the other is here. I've brought her back to you. Take her. And leave, now, quickly . . . before he discovers what I've done."

For the first time, Giselle noticed the wicker basket on the floor behind Rosamund, and heard the sweet sound of a baby's sweet gurgling.

"My baby," she cried out, and rushed to the basket. There, curled upon a nest of soft blankets, lay her daughter.

She scooped the infant into her arms and kissed her, over and over, kissed her warm little head and her fat silky cheeks, and even her petal-soft lips.

"Go," Rosamund urged her again, breaking the spell with her abrupt command. "Before he comes back."

"But where do I go?" Giselle had asked helplessly, confusion swirling through her mind. She could barely think, couldn't get past the overwhelming rush of relief that one of her precious children had been saved.

"Back to your parents," Rosamund said without hesitation, "and back home. To the States."

Giselle stared at her blankly, echoing her words. "Back home . . ."

"Listen to me," Rosamund said. "You must leave this island. You can't let anyone know about the child."

"He said he had promised her to you . . ." Giselle began.

"And he had. But I have given her back to you. You're her mother. I'll tell Manfred that she died. If he ever knew . . . if he finds out that you have her, he'll kill me . . . and both of you."

Chilled at her words, and not doubting that Rosamund spoke the truth, Giselle had nodded.

It had all happened so swiftly after that.

Making the endless, perilous, hurried journey down the dark mountain roads, with her newborn child snuggled against her breast . . .

Sneaking into the home she had fled eight months earlier . . .

Confronting the parents who had never stopped hoping for her return . . .

Seeing their tears of joy as they realized she was back, and their shock as they laid eyes on their tiny granddaughter . . .

She had told them the whole story, begging them all the while not to go to the police, not to confront Manfred.

And when she was finished, to her astonishment, her father told her that he would arrange for them to leave immediately—all of them. Not a word about the baby would be said to anyone.

Giselle had been stunned that Harry McKenna had believed what she'd told him.

Her father loved her fiercely, she knew, and would do anything for her. But she hadn't expected him to understand the urgency that was involved, or the danger.

It wasn't until later, much later, when they were safely home in Connecticut once again, that he told her why he had done what he had.

He knew all about Manfred, had ever since they'd arrived. The young man was legendary in Ocho Rios, for his ruthlessness and for his powers.

Harry had heard stories, terrible stories, about the Black Magic rituals over which Manfred presided. He had heard about how the locals feared him, though he was really little more than a boy. Manfred controlled the lives of those who were in his coven, yet he even dominated those who weren't. No one in Ocho Rios dared cross the powerful high priest.

And though Harry and Hope had assumed Giselle had gone back to the States when she'd run away, Harry had always feared, somewhere deep inside, that his daughter had been caught up in the dark side of life on the island. That somehow Manfred had gotten to her.

When she came safely back to him, all Harry could think was that he had to get her away from Manfred and his evil powers.

He had, and for eighteen years, Giselle had felt safe. Almost.

Giselle wasn't one to worry. She left that to her mother, who, she had always glibly said, worried enough for the entire population of Crawford Corners.

But somewhere, in the back of her mind, when Giselle was caught off guard by the intrusion of dark thoughts, she had sorrowfully remembered the daughter she had lost, the one who had been sacrificed in the name of her father's lust for power.

And she had carried the uneasy knowledge that someday Manfred might somehow find out that Meg was still alive.

If that ever happened . . .

Giselle shuddered to think of his reaction.

* * *

Only when she and Meg were safe inside the front door of 41 Meadowview Terrace did Candra give in to the desolate grief that had welled up inside her as they drove silently back from Spring City.

The moment the door clicked shut behind them, she burst into tears over the woman whose loss she felt so acutely that her heart literally ached.

Candra cried not just for Rosamund, for the way she had died, but for the wasted days Candra had spent since she'd left the Drayer house and the woman she'd thought was her grandmother. She cried for the pain she must have caused Rosamund when she'd abandoned her without explanation, and again for the bitterness she had felt over her discovery that Rosamund wasn't her grandmother after all.

Now she knew that no matter what the woman had done, no matter what she'd kept from Candra, she had loved her. Candra had seen it in the old woman's eyes as she lay dying. Rosamund may never have shown it, may not have been an affectionate woman who verbalized her emotions. But she had loved Candra. And she had, for whatever reason, taken in a baby who wasn't her flesh and blood, or her responsibility. And she had made sure Candra had food to eat and a bed to sleep in and clothes to wear . . .

She sniffled miserably, remembering the worn navy blue New York Yankee T-shirt that Rosamund had bought her for a dime, secondhand. The T-shirt Candra had loathed wearing, because it was so shabby compared with what the girls in Crawford Corners wore. The T-shirt she had traded for Meg's private school uniform, and a week of deception that had nearly ended in the death of her own sister.

And now, as she felt Meg's warm arms wrapping around her, steady and reassuring, she sobbed harder.

"It's all right, Candra," Meg murmured. "It's going to be okay."

Meg's hand stroked Candra's hair and her voice soothed her until Candra finally sniffled and pulled back, regaining some control.

"Are you all right?" Meg asked, concern in her eyes.

"I'm fine." She wasn't, but she couldn't fall apart again. She couldn't let her emotions rule her. She never had. And now she needed her wits about her more than ever.

"Meg"—she said, wiping at her wet cheeks—"we have to figure this out, and there's no time to waste."

"You mean about our brother . . ." Meg's voice still held a note of incredulity at the very notion.

Candra nodded. "Our brother, whoever he is . . . and the person who killed Rosamund. Whoever he is, he's after us, too. She warned us."

"I know, but who can it be? We have to get ahold of my mother. She might know something. I'll check the machine and see if she called while we were gone." Meg went into the other room, leaving Candra to search through her pocket for a tissue.

She found a crumpled one and blew her nose, and wiped her eyes dry. And by the time she was done removing traces of her grief, Meg was back.

"The only call was from my grandmother," she reported. "She wanted to see if Carrie and I were all right. Candra, we have to call the police."

Candra flinched inwardly at the mere word. "Why?"

"What do you mean, 'Why'? We can't just leave your

grandmother lying on the ground in the mud! We have to—"

"Meg, no." Candra cut her off, grabbing her arm and looking into her face. "We can't get the police involved."

"But why not? Someone murdered Rosamund, someone who wants to kill us . . . and this brother who—we didn't even know he existed! Now we have no idea who he is, or where he is. How are we supposed to warn him? And how can you even think of not doing anything about it? How can you just leave Rosamund there in the dark, all alone?"

"It's not Rosamund, Meg. She's gone, hopefully to a place where nothing matters anymore. That thing on the ground in the railyard is a shell. And someone will find her, sooner or later. We can't worry about that now. We have to find out who killed her."

"But how?"

"There's only one person I can think of who would know, besides . . . Mother." The word tasted strange on her tongue, less so than an affectionate *Mom* would have been, and yet not comfortable.

Not *right*.

"Who?" Meg asked. "Who's the other person?"

"Rosamund's sister . . . Aunt Tish. She might know something. She lives over on Elmont. We have to go back there."

Though it was relatively early on a Saturday evening—not quite nine—Elmont Avenue was in full swing, teeming with its usual illicit action.

The Alleycat Inn was a run-down tavern on the district's shabbiest block; it was a low, cement-block building with a neon sign that had seen brighter days.

As he walked through the door into the dim, smoky room, he saw that there were only a few customers slouched on stools along the scarred bar. They were pathetic specimens, every last one of them—barflies whose bleary eyes were focused on the grainy screen of the television above the row of bottles. There was no top-shelf liquor here, only the most basic stuff that would offer a reprieve from the disheartening world outside.

No matter. It would suit his purposes.

He was still trembling from the exertion of plunging that dagger, over and over, into Rosamund's resisting flesh. It wasn't that the attack hadn't given him pleasure, he told himself, because it had. Of course it had.

And yet . . .

She had stubbornly refused to give him the last piece of information he needed—the one thing he was desperate to know.

So she had deserved to die.

And yet . . .

Somewhere, deep in his hardened black heart, maybe . . . just maybe, he had felt a flicker of remorse as he killed her.

But he couldn't let that weakness take hold, couldn't let it grow so that he wouldn't be able to carry out the rest of his mission.

He needed a drink, to fortify his resolve, to quiet the trembling.

He walked swiftly across the sticky floor to the bar, and fixed the bartender with a stare. The man, a middle-aged Hispanic who wore a faded Red Dog T-shirt, looked up.

His eyebrows bobbed as he looked his new customer over. He rested his burning cigarette in an ashtray, then strolled over wearing an amused expression.

"Can I help you?" he asked, removing the rag that had been hooked at the waist of his cheap, stained jeans. He leisurely wiped up a ring of moisture left on the wooden surface.

"A shot of dark rum, straight up."

The bartender just looked at him, and he wondered, with a sudden stab of anxiety, if the man could smell the cloying scent of blood that clung to his clothes. He'd gone back to the room behind the shop to wash up, and he'd carefully blotted the few small dark stains on his black coat. But even now, he was aware of the telltale, vaguely metallic scent that lingered.

The bartender shook his head. "I can't serve you."

"What are you talking about?"

"You're underage. I can tell just by looking at you. You're a kid."

He stiffened, wrath darting through him. "I'm *not* a kid," he said icily.

"Oh, yeah? Prove it. Got some ID that says you're twenty-one?"

Of course he didn't.

His body tense with rage, he turned away from the bar and strode toward the door.

And as he went, he muttered under his breath.

A curse.

A curse on the man who had denied him the drink he needed, on the man who even now was exulting in how he had brandished his own miserable little allotment of power.

And, as he shoved the door open and swooped out into the night, he heard the groan that erupted suddenly behind him.

He didn't need to look back to know that the bartender had doubled over in pain.

Seventeen

Meg stood in the foyer with her coat on, fiddling with her keys while she waited for Candra, who was upstairs changing her clothes. She had told her sister to just borrow anything she wanted from her closet or drawers, and wondered if it was her imagination or if Candra had looked a little uncomfortable at the suggestion.

You have to stop questioning her, even just mentally, Meg warned herself. She had already chosen to believe Candra over everyone else: Shea and Mirabelle and Ben. And now that she had made that choice, she had better stick to it. Wholeheartedly.

A car door slammed out front.

It must be Carrie, Meg thought, turning to look out the window as another door slammed. *She must have someone with her . . . and it had better not be that dirtbag Eddie.*

She peered through the glass, and realized she didn't recognize the small, expensive compact car that sat on the driveway . . . or the two boys who were walking up the front steps.

Frowning, Meg walked to the door and opened it just as the taller boy was reaching for the bell. Startled, he glanced up at her. That was when she realized that she did know him, after all.

It was the boy who had been with the police last night, when they had found her and Candra at the park. He was broad shouldered and good-looking, with dark, wavy hair and a muscular build. He was looking Meg over intently with eyes that were an unusual, clear color—not quite blue and not entirely gray or green, either. The expression in them was bemused, and she realized that he was trying to figure out which sister she was.

"I'm Meg," she said, and offered a tentative smile.

She couldn't tell if he was relieved or disappointed as he smiled back. "Hi. I'm Landon Keller. We kind of met last night, but . . ." He trailed off and shrugged.

"Yeah," she said. "I know."

She looked over his shoulder, at the other boy. He had straight dark hair and tanned skin and intense dark eyes that caught and held hers.

Meg nodded slightly, wondering where she had seen him before.

"This is Jack," Landon said, motioning at him. "Is Candra around?" Landon asked, looking past Meg.

"She's upstairs, getting ready—"

"You're on your way out?" For the first time, Landon seemed to notice that she was wearing her coat and clutching her keys.

"Yeah, we have to go, um . . ." Meg hesitated, not sure what to tell him. Certainly not that they were headed over to Elmont Avenue in Spring City. Everyone knew that nice girls didn't venture into that neighborhood after dark.

Landon's expression clouded over, and Meg sensed what he was thinking. That Candra had a date. This guy was crazy about her sister. It was written all over his face.

"Meg?"

Behind her, she heard Candra's voice, calling as she walked down the stairs.

Meg turned and saw her sister at the exact moment her sister laid eyes on Landon. In the first fraction of a second, she seemed pleased . . . and then, immediately, she appeared indifferent.

"Candra?" Landon asked tentatively, stepping around Meg, into the foyer.

"What are you doing here?"

Meg watched as her sister calmly tossed her long, just-brushed hair over her shoulders. Candra was wearing Meg's black cashmere turtleneck tucked into a pair of snug black jeans. The outfit hugged her slender figure and made her appear to be about six feet tall and all legs.

For a moment, it seemed as though Landon was going to shrink back at Candra's haughty tone.

Don't, Meg wanted to tell him. *Don't let her push you away. She doesn't mean it. Can't you see that she's protecting herself from getting hurt?*

And even as that thought crossed her mind, she wondered how she knew that. Her twin was still a virtual stranger to her, and she had no idea what Candra's relationship with Landon Keller was all about. And yet, intuitively, she knew exactly what was going on here.

"Listen, Candra." Landon took a step closer to her, and his voice was filled with conviction. "I care about you, a lot, and I'm not going to let you shove me away as though you don't care about me, too. Because I know you do."

Way to go, Landon! Meg applauded mentally.

She glanced at Jack, to see if he was watching the little scene unfolding in the hall. He was, and he raised an eyebrow at Meg as if to say, *Do you know what's going on?*

She shrugged.

"You have no right to tell me who I care about," Candra was saying, and Meg turned back to see that her sister had planted her hands firmly on her hips and was standing her ground a foot or so away from Landon.

"And you might think you have feelings for me, but trust me, you don't."

"What the hell are you talking about, Candra? How do you know what I feel?"

"I just do."

Meg noted that Candra's voice had lost a little of its arrogant tone. And she had taken a step back, away from Landon. He was blocking Meg's view, so she couldn't see her sister's expression.

"Do you think that I would drive all the way over here from New London if I didn't have feelings for you?" Landon asked.

"You didn't drive. Jack did," Candra observed, glancing for the first time at the other boy, who was standing beside Meg in the doorway. "Right?"

"What does that have to do with anything?" Landon asked incredulously.

"I don't know," Candra said, suddenly sounding deflated and weary.

"Listen to me, Candra." Landon put his hands on her upper arms and bent forward so that his face was on her level, only inches from hers. "I've never felt like this about anyone before. I'm crazy about you. Last night when I thought you were out there in the woods somewhere, in that storm . . . you don't know how worried I was. Don't play games with me now. Tell me what's going on."

"I can't . . ."

"Why can't you?"

"Because it's none of your business."

"I want it to be my business. I want *you* to be my business, Candra."

"Well, I'm not. I think you should leave."

"This is ridiculous," Landon said. "What's with you? Why are you doing this to me?"

Candra shrugged and leaned to the side, looking at Meg. "Will you please tell these two to get out of your house so we can leave, Meg?" Her prickly tone was back, but Meg detected a wistful note there, too.

"We do have to go," Meg said, semi-apologetically.

"Where?" Landon asked again.

Candra bristled. "I told you—"

"It's none of my business. I know." Landon spun and stalked away from her, to the door.

Meg stepped aside to let him pass, and she and Jack exchanged a glance before Jack followed Landon down the steps.

"Nice meeting you," Meg called after them, knowing that the words sounded ludicrous, but feeling as though she had to say something.

Landon didn't reply, but Jack responded, "You, too," before getting into the driver's seat of the car.

Only when they had driven away did Meg turn to her sister, who stood motionless in the foyer behind her.

"Do you want to tell me about him?" she asked Candra.

"No. I don't ever want to talk about him, or see him, again."

Meg knew better than to push. Her sister was obviously not the type to go around spilling details about her private life under normal circumstances. Tonight, with everything that had happened, Meg would have been astonished if Candra actually did elaborate on her relationship with Landon Keller.

There was nothing to do but wonder . . .

And head for Elmont Avenue to confront Candra's Aunt Tish.

* * *

"Would you like another glass of champagne?" the pretty first-class flight attendant asked pleasantly.

"I will," Lester said, before Giselle could open her eyes to respond. "But shhh . . . my wife is sleeping."

Giselle kept her eyes closed, listening.

"Do you think she'd like a pillow?" the woman whispered.

"Nah, she's fine. What did you say your name was?"

"I didn't," the flight attendant said, sounding a little less jaunty than before, "but it's Missy."

"Missy? As in Melissa? Nice name," Lester said. "Listen, Missy, will you do me a favor?"

"If I can," she said, sounding leery.

"My wife and I are celebrating our wedding anniversary tomorrow—"

"Oh, congratulations," Missy said, obviously relieved that he wasn't hitting on her, which was probably what she'd been expecting.

It was what Giselle had been expecting, too. Now she wondered what he was up to, since their anniversary wasn't actually until November.

"Thank you," Lester said politely. "Anyway, because of all these flight delays, by the time we land in Connecticut, it will be the middle of the night. I'd been planning to surprise my wife with a home-cooked, candlelight dinner and a bottle of good champagne for dinner tomorrow night, but you can't buy liquor in Connecticut on a Sunday. So I was wondering . . . you wouldn't have an extra bottle of this delicious bubbly back there, would you?"

"Oh, I—I just . . . I'm not sure I can—"

"I understand, of course, Missy, if you can't let me have one. It's just that my wife and I toasted with this particular champagne on our wedding night, and it would mean so much to her if—well, you know."

"Let me just see what I can do," Missy said, and Giselle heard her walking away.

"You," Giselle said, opening her eyes and looking directly at Lester, "are the biggest cheapskate I've ever known in my life."

He looked startled, and dismayed. "What are you talking about?"

"I heard what just went on. You just lied to that poor girl about our anniversary, just so you can get a free bottle of champagne."

"Would you keep your voice down?" he hissed, glancing about at the other first-class passengers, none of whom appeared to be paying attention. "Maybe I lied about our anniversary, but I really was going to surprise you with a candlelight dinner and—"

"Bull," Giselle snapped. "You were not. You're cheap, Lester, and that's all there is to it."

"Oh, get off your high horse, Giselle," he shot right back in a low voice. "A crummy bottle of booze is the very least this stupid airline can give us after stranding us in L.A. for hours on end."

"The storm wasn't their fault, Lester. And I don't see anyone else around here trying to scam free goodies to take home. I've really had it with you."

"What's that supposed to mean?"

"It means I want a divorce."

The words had tumbled out of her mouth before she could stop them. She hadn't meant to tell him this way—impulsively, in the heat of anger.

And yet, now that it was out, she felt relieved . . .

And pleased by the bright red flush that rushed over

his face, and by the shock and fury etched in his watery light blue eyes.

"What are you talking about?" he asked in a barely controlled whisper.

"I want a divorce," she repeated almost glibly, and settled back in her seat to glance out the window. They must be somewhere over the heartland now, she thought, seeing only a vast patch of darkness below, marred only by an occasional cluster of small-town lights.

"Well, *I* don't want a divorce," Lester said, touching her arm. "Giselle, look at me. Would you look at me, for God's sake?"

"No," she told him. "I'm tired of looking at you. I've been looking at you for the past fifteen years, and frankly, I wouldn't care if I never laid eyes on you again."

There was silence while Lester apparently contemplated that insult.

Then he said, sounding surprisingly composed, "You won't divorce me."

Caught off guard by his tone, Giselle turned to him. "Oh, I won't? Why not?"

"Trust me. You just won't. I'm not going to go into it here," he said, glancing again at the other passengers, all of whom remained carefully detached.

But Giselle knew they were probably listening, most of them caught up in the domestic drama being played out in seats 3A and 3B.

She shrugged and tried not to let Lester know that she was curious about why he thought she wouldn't divorce him.

Much as Giselle wanted to think he was simply being his usual irritating, argumentative self, she couldn't help wondering at the smug little grin that sat below his pale red mustache.

It was almost as if . . .

As if Lester were up to something. Something other than an affair.

Hmm.

"Here we are, Mr. Hudson. . . . One glass of champagne." Missy reappeared in the aisle, wearing a conspiratory smile, and lowered her voice to a whisper, "And one bottle to go."

All troubling thoughts of Landon Keller vanished from Candra's mind the moment she and Meg arrived in the familiar third-floor hallway of the shabby apartment building where her aunt lived.

She fought back a lump in her throat as she recalled how many Saturday afternoons she and Rosamund had visited Aunt Tish here. Always, they were greeted by the smell of ammonia—though she worked full-time as a maid, Aunt Tish kept her own home meticulous, too, and was always in the middle of scrubbing something, usually with the television blaring in the background. Her aunt was crazy about American TV—she'd watch anything that was on, even those crazy infomercial shows that Rosamund had always scoffed at.

But tonight, there was no smell of ammonia and no sound of the television. Only silence from beyond the door to apartment 3B, with its peeling olive-colored paint.

"Aren't you going to knock?" Meg whispered.

Candra hesitated. "She can't be home."

"How do you know?"

Because nothing smells or sounds right, Candra wanted to

tell her. And yet, she knew, somehow, that despite the silence, her aunt was there. She could feel Tish's presence, as tangible as Rosamund's had been earlier in the railyard.

Then, Candra had let her instincts take over, leading her to where her grandmother lay in the bushes.

Now, she did the same, and knocked tentatively on the door.

There was no sound from behind it, and yet Candra knew her aunt was there, poised, listening . . . and frightened. The vibration of fear reached out from behind the door, grabbed Candra, and made her tense all over.

She turned to Meg, wondering if her sister felt it, too.

Meg's eyes were wide, and she caught her lower lip in her top teeth. She nodded slightly, as if to tell Candra that she knew what she was thinking.

"Aunt Tish?" Candra called softly. "It's me. Candra."

No answer.

"Aunt Tish, please. I have to talk to you . . . it's about Grandmother."

At that, there was the sound of bolts and chains being undone on the other side of the door. Startled, Candra realized that her aunt had been hovering right there all along.

The door opened a mere crack, then wider, and Tish said in a hushed voice, "Okay, come in. But hurry—"

She stopped short as she caught sight of Meg. Her jaw literally dropped and she stared from one sister to the other.

"This is my twin, Meg," Candra told her.

Aunt Tish snapped out of it, nodded, and hurried them both inside. Then she closed the door behind them and triple locked it again.

Candra faced her aunt, and again was seized by a twinge of grief. The image of her sister Rosamund, Tish had finely wrinkled dark skin and short, curly, salt-and-pepper hair. But unlike her sister, who still wore bright island clothing reminiscent of her native Jamaica, Tish's overweight figure was clad in an outfit that was distinctly American: blue jeans, white sneakers, and a red sweatshirt that read WAINWRIGHT COLLEGE in navy blue letters.

"Aunt Tish, we have to—where are you going?" Candra interrupted herself, catching sight of the two bulging duffel bags sitting just inside the door.

Her aunt hesitated, then said, "I have to leave." Her gaze was still resting on Meg, as though she couldn't quite believe what she was seeing.

"Leave? Where are you going?"

Tish shrugged and wearing a closed expression turned back to Candra. "What are you doing here? What do you have to tell me about Rosamund?"

"She . . ." Candra paused, stricken with a sudden rush of sorrow, not sure if she could bring herself to say the words aloud. She cleared her throat, and saw that Meg was watching her sympathetically.

"Aunt Tish," she began again, determined not to lose control of her emotions, "my grandmother—Rosamund—is dead."

"*What?*" The woman clasped her hands to her lips and let out a tortured sob. She managed to utter one more word—"How?"—before breaking down into tears. She sank into a chair, her body trembling all over.

Candra felt her own mouth quivering.

"She was murdered," Meg said, after glancing at Candra, who stood unable to speak. "We found her, just before she died, in the railyard near here."

"No . . . no . . ." Tish wailed, rocking back and forth.

For a long time, there was only the sound of her bitter sobbing. Candra laid a hand stiffly on her aunt's shoulder, wanting to comfort her but not knowing how.

It was Meg who, when Tish had calmed herself, went on, "Before she died, Rosamund told us that whoever attacked her was after us. She also said we have a brother somewhere, but she died before she could tell us who he is, or how to find him."

Candra watched her aunt carefully. She had stiffened at Meg's words, and now her dark eyes were darting from Meg to Candra and back again. There was a hint of questioning in them, as though she wondered whether they knew anything more.

"Do you know, Aunt Tish?" Candra asked.

"About your brother? No," she said, standing up, and Candra knew she was lying. "Please, I have to go . . ."

"Where?"

"Away. Just . . . away."

"Why didn't the coven meet in the railyard tonight? Why was my grandmother the only one there?"

"Because of what happened to Dalila," Tish said, looking only momentarily surprised that Candra knew about the coven. "We called off our regular meeting. I told Rosamund, but she said she wanted to go to the spot anyway. It's consecrated, you know. There was something she wanted to do there." She checked her watch and looked at the door. "Candra, please . . ."

"You're involved in this somehow." Candra stepped between her aunt and the two bags she was eyeing.

She realized that while Tish's reaction to the news of her sister's death had been authentically sorrowful, she hadn't seemed shocked. It was almost as though she had . . . expected it?

"You spoke to my grandmother about more than Dalila's death today, didn't you?" Candra accused, pointing a finger in her aunt's face. "You knew she was in danger. She told you. And you're involved, too. You're in danger, too. She warned you. That's why you're leaving."

"No . . ."

"Yes."

"Candra, please," Tish said, her voice a pathetic wail. "I have to go. Before he gets to me, too. He's coming. I know he is."

"Can't you just tell us who?" Meg asked.

But Tish's only response was a quick movement as she sidestepped Candra and swooped down over the two bags beside the door. She grabbed them and scurried out into the hall almost before they realized what was happening.

"Aunt Tish!" Candra hollered, starting to go after her.

"I'm so sorry. Be careful, Candra," her aunt called back, already halfway down to the second floor. "You, too, Meg. Don't let him get you."

And then she was gone, and Meg and Candra were left to stare at each other. Candra knew that the apprehension and terror she saw in her sister's eyes were mirrored in her own.

Somewhere out there was a young man who was their brother . . .

And a ruthless man who wanted him—and them—dead.

"Let's get out of here," Meg said, nudging Candra.

"Wait . . . maybe we should snoop around."

"Why?"

"In case we can find a clue," Candra said, but she suddenly had lost any desire to remain in Tish's apartment.

The back of her neck was prickling and an uneasy feeling was slipping over her.

"I want to leave," Meg said, her voice rising a little in urgency. "Please, Candra. I'm afraid."

"Okay." Candra couldn't admit to her sister that she, too, was frightened.

One of us has to be strong, she told herself as she followed Meg out into the hall, pulling the door closed behind her.

And yet, as she and Meg hurried down the stairs and out into the seedy, neon-lit avenue, her legs felt wobbly with anxiety and she had to fight the urge to break into a run—almost as though the devil himself was at their heels.

He halted in front of the shabby apartment building and narrowed his eyes, scanning the sidewalk. There was nothing to see but the usual Saturday night crowd of drunks and drug dealers and streetwalkers and junkies.

And yet . . .

He frowned.

Someone was nearby, he realized.

Was it Candra, or Meg, or . . .

Both?

That would explain the overpowering perception of the presence. And of course, after last night, the two sisters would probably stick close together.

He watched the street for a moment, half-expecting them to appear, and wondering what he would do when they did. He certainly couldn't grab them, both of them, out here in front of hundreds of witnesses.

And there was no need to do that, really. He would

get to them when the time came. There was no doubt about that. They couldn't hide—not from him.

So, really, he would simply bide his time and wait, even if he did happen to collide with them here, on the street.

Life is full of little surprises, he thought to himself, chuckling under his breath at the coincidence.

But after a few moments, he realized that the presence had grown weaker, not stronger.

That could only mean that they were going in the opposite direction.

He wondered, as he turned and briskly entered the dingy building, what they had been doing here in the first place. Had they spoken with Tish? Had she given them the information that *he* was seeking?

No matter. She would tell him, too. He would see to that . . . and then he would kill her.

But as he approached the door marked 3B, he knew instinctively that it was already too late.

That didn't stop him from knocking on the door, and then, when there was no response, heaving his muscular shoulder against it. All it took was once, and the door burst inward.

He stepped over the threshold, his dark coat flapping around his ankles, and looked around.

Tish was gone. He didn't know where, but there was a sense of finality about the apartment's emptiness.

But she had left something behind, he realized as he walked through the tiny rooms to her bedroom. His gaze fell on the battered desk beneath the window.

In it, he knew, would be the missing piece to the puzzle he was desperate to solve.

* * *

Meg sat up in her darkened bedroom with a gasp and uttered her sister's name.

Beside her, Candra stirred, made an incoherent murmuring, groaning noise.

"Candra," Meg repeated, reaching toward the huddled form beneath the down comforter and shaking her sister's shoulder. "Wake up."

"What? What time is it?" Candra asked groggily.

Meg looked at the glowing digital numbers on the clock on her nightstand. "Almost midnight."

"Midnight?" Candra yawned and rolled over, murmuring, "We went to bed less than an hour ago."

It was true. When they'd returned from Elmont, they had realized they were both utterly exhausted. Though Meg had been afraid to sleep, even after making sure the doors and windows were all locked, she must have drifted off anyway.

Now, though, she was wide awake.

"Wait," she told Candra, "don't go back to sleep. I just had this dream." She shivered and pulled her knees up to her chin, wrapping her arms around them. "About our brother."

She heard a rustling as her sister sat up in bed. "What about him?"

"Rosamund was there," Meg remembered, squeezing her eyes closed, chasing the fragmented images of the dream before they could escape her. Already, the details were starting to grow fuzzy.

"What was she doing?" Candra asked breathlessly.

"She was just sitting there, talking to me. To us, actually . . . you were there, too. She was telling us that we had to be careful, that someone was after us."

Candra made a scoffing sound. "That's just what she said today, Meg. That wasn't a dream."

"No, there was more. I asked her who our brother was, and she—Candra, I swear, she told me his name."

There was silence for a moment. Meg turned, and in the shadowy room, saw the silhouette of her sister. She was stiff, tense, and yet when she spoke, her tone was impassive.

"So? It was just a dream. It doesn't mean anything."

"No, Candra, I can feel it. This is real. Rosamund was sending us a message."

"Then why wouldn't she send it through *me*? I'm the one she raised, the one she was supposedly related to, remember? You meant nothing to her."

Hurt by her sister's scornful words, Meg tried to tell herself that Candra was just defensive, that was all. She was that way by nature, and competitive, too. Meg couldn't hold it against her.

"I don't know why she wouldn't go through you," Meg said gently. "Maybe because you *were* closer to her. Maybe she couldn't get past the grief you're suffering over her death."

"So what's his name?" Candra asked, after a moment.

"I don't have the first. Just the last."

"How come?"

Meg shrugged. "That's all I remember, I guess . . ."

"Well? What is it?"

"It's someone that we know," Meg said, suddenly leery of revealing it to her sister. How was Candra going to react?

"Who?"

Meg took a deep breath. "Our brother's last name," she said slowly, "is Keller."

* * *

His hands shook with anticipation as he lifted the paper-clipped document he'd found buried beneath piles of other papers—old leases and bills and letters—in the bottom desk drawer.

This was what he had been looking for. The moment his fingers had touched it, he had known.

He carried it over to the window and held it up to the streetlight that filtered between the starched white curtains. Though the typed page was partly hidden in shadow, he could make out the words.

It was a contract, dated eighteen years ago this week.

Letitia Harrison, it seemed, had played a pivotal role in an illegal adoption.

At the time, she had been employed on the household staff of an American family that was living in Ocho Rios for a year. She had placed a newborn baby boy with them, a mulatto child whose parents were unmarried. The mother was an American and the father was a native Jamaican.

Neither of them was named, but he knew, without a doubt, who they were.

He knew that the child was the missing brother of Meg and Candra.

In addition to being paid handsomely for her services, Tish was promised a position as the baby's nanny, and would return to the United States with them when their time on the island was up.

The adoptive father was a contractor with SNE Development, which was based in Crawford Corners, Connecticut.

And the family's last name was Keller.

Eighteen

"Good morning, The Lawson School," said a male voice with a British accent.

"Yes, hello . . . may I please speak to Landon Keller?" Candra asked, clutching the telephone receiver so hard that her hand hurt.

Meg stood beside her, chewing her lower lip and fiddling with the belt on her bathrobe.

"It's rather early to be calling a student," came the crisp response on the other end of the line.

Candra cleared her throat and glanced at the clock on Meg's nightstand. It was just past six. She and Meg had spent the last several hours trying unsuccessfully to sleep. Finally, they had gotten out of bed and talked, endlessly going over the details of what had happened, trying to unravel the mystery of their birth and Rosamund's death, and coming up with nothing.

Nothing but the realization that Landon Keller was somehow their long-lost brother, and that they had to get ahold of him, to break the startling news . . .

And to warn him that someone wanted him—all three of them—dead.

"I realize that it's early," Candra said into the phone, "and I do apologize, but this is a family emergency." She had tried this family emergency tact to get to Landon once before, and it had worked, although it had been someone else, a female, who had answered the phone that day.

The voice became slightly less frosty. "I see. I'll ring his room."

Candra nodded, so nervous at the prospect of speaking to Landon that she couldn't reply.

"What's happening?" Meg asked after a few moments.

"Nothing."

"What do you mean, nothing?"

"I'm on hold. They're ringing his room," Candra snapped. Then she quickly added, in a softened tone, "Sorry. I didn't mean to bark at you."

Her sister didn't seem fazed. "It's okay. I know how you must feel. If I ever found out that Shea might be my brother, I don't know—"

Candra cut her off with an abrupt "Shhh!" as she heard a click in her ear.

"Hello, ma'am?"

It was the Brit again, sounding a little distressed.

"Yes?" Candra asked, and held her breath, not sure whether she felt relief or disappointment over not hearing Landon's voice.

"I'm afraid Mr. Keller is not available."

"Excuse me?"

"Oh, dear . . ." The man cleared his throat. "Apparently, Mr. Keller is not in his room. In fact, his roommate has informed me that he left last evening and never came back. As you may be aware, Mr. Keller has been restricted to his room ever since he violated curfew on Friday evening."

Candra hadn't been aware of that. Friday was the night she and Landon had been planning to run off together. The night she'd abandoned him at that gas station near the state park. It must have been almost dawn by the time he'd been driven back to school by the police. She should have realized that he would be punished.

"It's all right," Candra cut in, as the man on the phone babbled on about how this type of thing rarely happened at a fine institute of learning like The Lawson School, how they prided themselves in discipline.

"May I deliver a message when I do locate Mr. Keller?"

"No, it's okay," Candra said curtly. "Thanks anyway. Good-bye."

With that, she hung up the phone and met her sister's anxious gaze.

"He's gone?" Meg asked.

Candra nodded. "He never went back last night. He and Jack must have—"

She broke off in midsentence and stood there motionless, stunned.

"What?" Meg asked urgently. "Candra, what's wrong?"

"I just remembered something. Oh, God, I can't believe I managed to overlook it . . ."

"What?"

"Jack," she said, feeling an overwhelming surge of relief. "He's Landon's cousin. They told me that when I met them, and I must have forgotten . . ."

"So what does that— oh!" As though she'd just figured out what Candra was getting at, Meg clapped a hand to her chin. "You mean, Jack's last name is Keller, too?"

Candra nodded.

"So Jack might be our brother, instead of Landon?" Meg asked, in disbelief. "But he doesn't look like us."

"Neither does Landon."

"No . . ." Meg said slowly, pondering that. "But just because we're identical doesn't mean our brother looks like us. Does it?"

Candra shrugged and said, "I don't know."

"They both have dark coloring," Meg observed. "You know? Dark hair and dark eyes. And Jack's skin is pretty dark, too. Darker than Landon's. Although it could just be a tan from the summer. Still . . . I don't know. Do you think it's Jack?"

"I'm not sure." Candra shook her head, trying to calm the flutter of excitement that hovered in the vicinity of her heart. "Not that it matters, anyway. Landon and I aren't . . . involved. Not anymore."

"But you do care about him, Candra. I know you do. And he cares about you. It was obvious."

Irritation mingled with pleasure at her sister's words. Still, Candra scowled and said, "The only thing that's obvious is that one of those two guys might be our brother. Which means that he's in terrible danger. And if we don't find him, and warn him—"

"But how can we possibly find him?"

"I don't know. Both Landon and Jack are from an island. No," she corrected herself, remembering, "they're from a state with island in the name."

"Rhode Island," Meg said. "That's just east of Connecticut, less than two hours from here. But even if they are in Rhode Island, we have no idea where they might be."

"No," Candra mused, "but there is a way to try and locate them . . ."

Meg looked incredulous. "How?"

"I know a spell," Candra said, mentally conjuring a list of the items she would need in order to cast it.

* * *

"Welcome to JFK International Airport, ladies and gentlemen. We'll be arriving at the gate shortly. Thank you for flying with us, and have a safe and pleasant stay in the New York area."

The Captain's voice over the loudspeaker and a bumping sound as the plane taxied to a stop intruded upon Giselle's deep, dreamless sleep.

Yawning, she opened her eyes, glanced out the window, and saw the milky gray light of dawn illuminating the airport runway. Beside her, Lester was stirring, and she turned to see him fumbling for his glasses, which he had placed in the seat pocket in front of him.

Considering, and promptly discarding, the notion of helping him, Giselle finger-fluffed her hair, which must be a wreck. She reached beneath her seat for her bag and took out a compact and a tube of lipstick.

"Ladies and gentlemen, please remain seated until we have come to a full complete stop at the gate and sounded the three-bell signal," announced Missy, the flight attendant. She was walking down the aisle toward coach.

Lester, who had found his glasses at last, put them on and checked his watch.

"What time is it?" Giselle asked, yawning.

"Where's *your* watch?" was his reply.

"I took it off before I went to sleep. It's somewhere in the bottom of my bag."

He raised an eyebrow, and she knew he would never be so careless with his own Rolex. He rarely took it off—and especially not when they were sitting in first class. Giselle was fully aware that he wanted everyone to know that he had money—that he had paid full price for his seat.

He had even commented, on the trip out, that these

days, too many frequent fliers were using their mileage points to get bumped up from coach.

"It isn't fair"—he'd told Giselle, glancing about the first-class cabin with a wrinkled nose—"that just *anyone* can sit up here these days."

Apparently, Lester didn't consider himself to be "just anyone." At the time, Giselle had chuckled to herself, thinking that after she divorced him, he would be riding in coach for the rest of his life . . . *if* he could even afford to fly.

But now, remembering that cryptic statement he'd made last night—"You *won't* divorce me"—Giselle couldn't help feeling a little unsettled.

"Please, Lester . . . what time is it?" she asked again, smiling sweetly at him though she wanted to gag.

He sighed, though he looked pleased, and said, "It's six-eleven."

He always did that—gave the exact time, instead of a rough estimate, like *It's ten after six.* It was one of the countless things that irked her about him.

But this time, she didn't automatically think that she wouldn't have to deal with his stupid idiosyncrasies for much longer. This time, she thought, *What if he really does have a way to make me stay with him? What if I'm trapped in this hellish marriage forever?*

She thanked Lester stiffly and went back to applying her makeup in the compact mirror. But as she glided the copper-colored tube over her full lips, she couldn't help wondering, again, what Lester thought he was up to.

What could he possibly be planning to do to her if she left him?

There was nothing he could do that would make her stay . . .

Giselle tried to ignore a vague sense of unrest as she

recalled the secret she had shared with Lester not so long ago. About Meg's birth. And Manfred.

She frowned, remembering that it hadn't been long afterward that Lester had started acting secretive. Holding whispered phone conversations in his study. And taking that supposed business trip to St. Louis.

Giselle glanced at him.

He was removing the sleep from the corners of his eyes, rubbing it onto the back of the seat in front of him.

Nah, Giselle told herself. *The only thing he's up to—if he's up to anything at all—is an affair with some pathetic bimbo.*

Nothing more than that.

Giselle snapped her compact closed decisively and tossed it back into her bag.

Meg's bedroom was as dark as Candra could get it, now that the sun was up. She'd drawn the shades and the floral-patterned drapes, and turned off the lamps.

Now the only light in the room came from Meg's dresser, where a solitary candle flickered. Its wax was a light shade of purple, which, according to Candra, symbolized psychic power. It had taken some searching for Meg to locate the right color. Luckily, her mother was crazy about votive candles—she liked the way they smelled—and Meg had finally located a lilac-scented one sitting inside a glass globe on the sink in the guest bathroom.

Now, Meg stood back trying not to get the creeps as Candra presided over the makeshift altar she'd created on the bureau. She sprinkled some kind of oil, which she'd mixed herself after fifteen minutes of rummaging through the cabinets in the kitchen, over the candle, then chanted some kind of gibberish under her breath as she waved her arms around.

Finally, she closed her eyes, raised her hands high above her head, and said clearly,

> *Spirits of the dawn,*
> *Now fill my mind*
> *With visions of the one*
> *I need to find.*

She bowed her head and stood for a long time, motionless.

Meg watched her from across the room, where she perched on the edge of her bed, waiting for something to happen. It was impossible to believe that this stuff she had found around the house—a candle and some herbs and oil—could possibly help them find their missing brother.

Besides, they were basing this whole thing on a mere dream. The more time that had gone by since Meg had awakened this morning, the more she was beginning to doubt that her vision of Rosamund meant anything. It certainly wasn't proof that their brother's name was Keller, though Candra seemed to believe that it was.

And yet, now, as she watched her sister, who appeared to be slipping into a daze, Meg was filled with a tingling awareness, as though something were about to happen.

But nothing did.

At least, not before the shrill ringing of the telephone on the desk broke the mood.

Candra jumped at the sound, looking around in confusion, as though she were disoriented.

"I'll get it," Meg told her, already halfway to the desk. "It might be Mom. Hello?" she said, snatching up the receiver.

"Meg?" The voice was masculine, and unfamiliar.

"Yes?"

"I'm sorry to call you so early. This is Ben Schacter— we met at the hospital the other day?"

"Right, I remember . . ." Her heart sunk, and she wondered if Mirabelle's condition had worsened, if she had—

"Mirabelle regained consciousness a little while ago," Ben said, and Meg's knees turned to liquid.

"Thank God," she breathed, sinking into her desk chair. "How is she now?"

"She seems okay, but they're keeping a close eye on her. She has broken bones and bruises from the crash, but they don't think there's any internal damage. And Meg, she's begging to see you."

"She is?" Meg glanced at her sister.

Candra still stood by the dresser, as if frozen. She seemed lost in her own little world, staring off into space.

"If you could come down here to the hospital right away, it would be a good idea," Ben said. "She's been through a lot, and they don't want her to get all worked up. And besides, she's exhausted, and I don't know how long she's going to be able to stay awake. She said she wants to tell you something."

"I . . . okay. I'll get there as fast as I can," Meg agreed, putting aside her protests. She wasn't sure she wanted to hear what Mirabelle wanted to say to her—not if it was about Candra. Not if Mirabelle wanted her to believe that her sister was up to no good.

No matter what, Meg knew now that her sister cared

about her. Candra had had a rough life, and she wasn't the most easygoing person Meg had ever met. But she certainly wasn't dangerous. And Meg refused to believe otherwise.

"She's in a private room now," Ben was saying. "On the fourth floor. Just tell the nurse who you are when you get here."

"Okay. I'm on my way." Meg hung up the phone and turned back to her sister. "Candra. . . ?" she asked tentatively.

Candra looked startled, and her eyes flew to Meg's face. "What?" she asked in a faraway voice.

"That was Mirabelle's—boyfriend, I guess. Ben. I have to go to the hospital now. She's awake."

"Okay." Candra's expression was slightly glassy, and she spoke in a faraway voice, as though she were in a trance.

Was she? Meg studied her sister carefully, frowning. Candra appeared to be concentrating on something, and her eyes were drifting closed again.

"Is it okay if I leave you like this?" Meg asked hesitantly.

"Please," Candra said. "Leave me alone."

Meg shrugged and headed for the door.

As she walked down the stairs and grabbed her coat and car keys, she realized that she suddenly felt overwhelmed. It was all too much—finding Candra, and Rosamund's death, and knowing she and Candra had a brother out there somewhere, and that all three of them were in danger—and now Mirabelle . . .

One thing at a time, she told herself, taking a deep breath and going out the front door into the sunny Sunday morning. *That's all you can handle. Just take it one thing at a time.*

* * *

The purple wax was dripping steadily onto the crate as the wick burned lower, but he barely noticed.

All was silent in the back room of the occult shop; El-mont Avenue, outside, was at its quietest in the early morning hours of a Sunday.

The young, dark-skinned man stood beside the improvised altar, his eyes closed tightly in concentration.

Somewhere out there was the missing triplet, the child who should never have been allowed to live.

And as long as that boy remained alive, Manfred would never achieve the greatest power of all . . . the power he had mistakenly believed was already his.

But there was no need for panic.

Where are you, young Mr. Keller? he asked mentally, waiting for a vision.

Where are you?

The spell had to work.

It had to.

And yet, he felt nothing—not the usual electricity that darted through him whenever he chanted the spell that would draw psychic awareness.

Today, his mind remained a blank screen.

And the more he struggled to concentrate, the more his frustration grew—making concentration all the more difficult.

It was a vicious circle, and now anger was beginning to eat away at him, destroying what was left of his powers to focus.

Finally, incensed, he slammed his fists down on the crates and screamed, long and loud and primal.

But it had released only a tiny portion of his pent-up fury.

Seething, he bent and abruptly blew out the candle's flame. Then he stalked to the door, threw it open, and headed out to avenge his wrath.

Giselle settled back against the leather seat as the limo pulled out onto the Van Wyck Expressway. It was inexplicably jammed for this hour of a Sunday morning, and she scowled out at the traffic, thinking of how much she hated the city.

It wasn't as though she came here a lot, but Crawford Corners was too close for comfort, in her opinion. Maybe, after the divorce, she and the girls would move someplace where there was more . . . space. Where no one could find them.

Where had that thought come from? she wondered, puzzled. She must have been thinking of Lester—but then, escaping him for the rest of her life was too much to hope for. There was Carrie to consider, after all. Lester was her father; he would have to have visitation rights.

No, maybe it hadn't been Lester she was thinking of, after all.

Maybe it was Manfred.

The mere thought of his name sent a chill through Giselle, despite the warm sun that beamed through the tinted windows.

Why, after all these years, are you suddenly thinking of Manfred again?

She tried to force her thoughts away.

Think of something pleasant . . . like the divorce.

Which reminded her . . .

"Lester?" she said, turning to him. She saw that he had opened the business section of the Sunday *Times* he'd bought in the airport after they landed. He always made a big show of reading the financial pages, throwing out little comments about the stock tables as if to prove he knew that he was a big financier.

"Hmm?" he murmured, his eyes focused on the paper.

But Giselle could tell that he wasn't reading it. His whole body was tense, as though he was just waiting for her to bring up the divorce.

Which she did, promptly.

"I want to talk about our so-called marriage," she told him, glancing at the driver and seeing that he was looking at the road, out of earshot behind the privacy panel of glass. "I'm planning to see a lawyer tomorrow."

"I wouldn't recommend that," he said, turning the page of the paper with an un-Lester-like aplomb that contradicted the tension that still emanated from him.

"Oh, you wouldn't? Why wouldn't you, Lester?"

There was a pause, and she thought he wasn't going to answer her at all.

Finally, he set down the paper and said, in a perfectly unruffled voice, "I told you. You won't divorce me."

"Oh, but I will. I have every intention of doing it."

"After I tell you what I have to tell you, I'm sure you'll change your mind."

"Lester, this is ridiculous." She looked out the window, fighting to keep her emotions under control. The last thing she wanted was to give him the satisfaction of playing his stupid game. He probably wanted her to get all worked up, wanted her to beg him to tell her his little secret.

Giselle refused to play into his hands.

After a few moments, he said, "When we get home,

I'll be happy to tell you what I have to tell you, Giselle. All right?"

She shrugged, not turning back to him, not wanting to see the self-satisfied look on his insipid, sunburnt face.

"Oh, I think it's something you'll want to know, Giselle," he said, chuckling softly. "I hadn't planned to tell you . . . not until I had exhausted my other options. But since you've forced my hand by bringing up this preposterous suggestion that we split up . . . well, I'll have to let you in on it."

Fed up, she twisted in her seat and saw that he was picking up the *Times* again. He pretended to ignore her pointed stare, but she was satisfied to see that his hands trembled as he unfolded the newspaper.

Giselle smiled to herself despite her sense of apprehension. Lester might think he was capable of controlling her, but when it came right down to it, the man was a weenie, just as she'd always suspected.

With a sigh, she turned back to the window and stared out at the crawling traffic.

In Meg's darkened bedroom, Candra centered every ounce of her being on a single thought . . .

Where are you, Landon—and Jack?

Her entire body tingled with the energy that coursed through her, the energy she'd conjured with her spell.

It was working . . .

She knew that it was. She had felt a surge of power the moment she'd finished the chant.

All she had to do was focus . . .

Focus . . .

Where are you?

Where are you?

Somewhere outside, a dog was barking . . .

No distractions. She couldn't let anything divert her attention.

She was sinking deeper into the pool of concentration, approaching a remote, tranquil place where nothing could reach her.

Nothing but that which she sought.

Where are you? she beseeched her unknown brother, as her rhythmic breathing carried her further into the trance.

Where are you?

Nineteen

Meg hesitated in the doorway of the hospital room, seeing that Mirabelle wasn't alone.

An attractive, worried-looking middle-aged couple sat beside her bed. Meg knew they had to be Mirabelle's parents. The woman was the complete opposite of Mirabelle—a powder-puff blonde, with thick makeup and teased hair and long, brightly polished nails that she kept running over her daughter's arm. The man was tall and distinguished looking, and Meg saw, in the instant that he turned and noticed her standing in the doorway, that Mirabelle was the image of him.

"You must be Meg—we've been waitin' for you," he said, in an accent that sounded like Kevin Costner's in the movie *The Big Easy*. "I'm Michael Moreau, and this is my wife, Jeanette."

"Hi," Meg said, nodding first at Mirabelle's father, and then at her mother.

Her friend Zoe had often scoffed about her Aunt Jeanette. Tara Cunningham's older sister was a former Miss Connecticut, and Zoe often said that she was as brassy as Tara was elegant. Now Meg noticed the large gold hoop earrings that brushed against Jeanette's brightly rouged cheeks, and saw that her tanned wrists were stacked with flashy gold bracelets.

"Hello, Meg, honey," Jeanette drawled, and Meg remembered that Zoe had said her aunt had an exaggerated Southern accent despite having grown up in Connecticut. "Mirabelle has been waitin' for y'all, haven't you, sweetheart?"

There was a murmur from the bed. Meg's eyes fell on Mirabelle, who lay beneath several blankets, her head propped on a pillow.

"Come in, Meg," Mirabelle said, her voice sounding hoarse.

Meg stepped into the room. Only then did she see Ben, who stood just inside the door, leaning against the wall. He had changed his clothes. Now he wore a pair of pressed khaki pants and a dusty blue sweater, and his dark hair appeared to have been combed carefully. He glanced at Meg, and then his eyes, which were filled with concern, slid back to Mirabelle.

"Why don't we go downstairs to see if we can make a hotel reservation for you, Mr. and Mrs. Moreau?" he suggested.

When Jeanette started to protest, her husband said, "Come on, Jeanette. Let's leave Mirabelle alone to talk to Meg."

As soon as the three of them had left, Meg perched awkwardly in the chair Mr. Moreau had vacated, and looked at her friend.

"Hi," Mirabelle said weakly, offering a faint smile.

"How do you feel?" Meg asked, barraged by a sudden attack of guilt. If it weren't for her, Mirabelle wouldn't be lying here, battered, in the hospital.

"Way too hot," Mirabelle said.

"Excuse me?"

"You asked how I feel, and I feel way too hot," Mirabelle told her. "Would you mind taking a few of these blankets off of me? My mother insisted on burying me in them, even though this room is about ninety degrees."

Feeling comforted by Mirabelle's grin, Meg stood and peeled off several layers of wool, folding the blankets carefully and stacking them at the foot of the bed.

Then, reluctantly, she returned to her seat and met Mirabelle's direct gaze.

"You're in danger, Meg," her friend said bluntly.

"Mirabelle, I know what you think about Candra, but she—"

"It's not Candra," Mirabelle cut her off, and Meg raised her eyebrows. "I thought it was, but . . . I don't know, maybe I was wrong. I'm not feeling animosity from her—at least, not now. It's someone else. Someone far more powerful than your sister."

"I know," Meg said, and it was Mirabelle's turn to look surprised.

"How do you know?"

"Candra's grandmother warned us that someone is after us," she said. "And then she died. He—whoever he is—had attacked her. Look, I know this sounds crazy," she said, seeing Mirabelle's wide-eyed reaction to her words, "but strange things have been happening to me ever since the last time I saw you. I have no memory of what happened to me last week—"

"That's because you were under a spell," Mirabelle said.

Meg's mouth dropped open. "*What?*"

"Dalila Parker cast it on you, and I have no idea why. All I know is that you were in her apartment, unconscious, and Candra was posing as you."

Meg's thoughts were reeling. Shea had told her the same thing. But he had also said Candra had tried to kill her. And Meg couldn't—wouldn't—believe that.

"How do you know about this?" she asked Mirabelle when she could find her voice again.

"I saw you," Mirabelle said simply. "I used astral projection to get into Dalila Parker's apartment, and I saw you there."

"How do you know it was me? How do you know it wasn't Candra?"

"Meg, you have to trust me."

"Candra is my sister, Mirabelle," she said, fighting to keep her voice from rising.

"And I'm your friend. I risked my life for you, Meg."

Those words hung in the air, instantly filling Meg with remorse.

"Look, Meg," Mirabelle said more gently, after a moment, "I'm not trying to make you feel guilty for what happened to me. I only want you to understand that something very serious . . . very deadly . . . is going on. Regardless of what you want to believe about what your sister did or didn't do. You're in danger. Both of you . . . and your brother."

She said those last words tentatively, slowly, as though she wasn't sure how Meg would react.

"I know about him, too," she told Mirabelle. "Candra's grandmother, Rosamund, told us. She said he has some kind of amulet, something that's supposed to protect him. But she didn't say from who."

"I don't know who he is, either, Meg," Mirabelle said, and her words were becoming more urgent, even as exhaustion stole over her face. "But he's pure evil. I'm getting the darkest, most frightening vibes from him."

"When?" Meg asked. "When did you sense all of this?"

"While I was out. It was as though I was trapped in some other world, trying to fight my way back, and I kept getting images. About you, and about Candra, and your brother. And this dark man was always there . . ."

Meg shivered despite the steam heat blasting from the register by the window. "Are you sure you don't know who he is, Mirabelle?"

"I'm sure. But I know who your brother is."

Meg's heart skipped a beat. "Who?" she asked breathlessly.

"I don't know his first name," Mirabelle said, "but he was adopted by a couple whose last name is Keller. Does the name ring a bell?"

That was it, Meg realized. That was the proof she'd been looking for, the proof that her dream really *had* been a vision—a message from Rosamund. Mirabelle's coming up with the same name was too much of a coincidence.

Their missing brother was definitely a Keller—but which one?

Landon . . . or Jack?

Giselle unlocked the front door as Lester paid the limo driver, signing off on their joint credit card.

That was the first thing she'd do, Giselle promised herself as she stepped over the threshold—cancel all their credit cards. Lester would be lost without his plastic.

"Hello?" she called as she walked briskly into the foyer, glancing around to make sure everything was just as she had left it. Sometimes, Sophie liked to move things around when she cleaned, even though Giselle was always telling her not to rearrange anything.

Everything was silent. Meg's car wasn't in its usual spot outside, and Giselle wondered where she could be so early on a Sunday morning.

But Carrie must be home. The house didn't feel empty.

Anxious to greet her daughter, Giselle hurried upstairs and opened Carrie's bedroom door. "Carrie? We're home."

But the room was deserted.

That was odd.

Giselle felt a vague uneasiness. Something didn't seem quite right.

She turned and glanced at the closed door to Meg's room. Maybe Carrie was in there, for some reason. She knew her younger daughter had, on occasion, snuck in to borrow her sister's clothes. Giselle suspected Carrie mostly did it to pester Meg, since the two girls had vastly different taste in wardrobes.

Sighing, Giselle started toward Meg's room, planning to burst in and catch Carrie red-handed.

"Giselle?" Downstairs, the front door slammed shut, and Lester's footsteps headed for the stairs. "Are the girls here?"

"No," she said, turning away from Meg's door. If Carrie was in there, she would come running as soon as she heard her father's voice. She adored her daddy. Giselle knew why. Lester doted on his "real" daughter.

"Where are they?" he asked, arriving in the hallway.

"Do I look like Kreskin?" Giselle headed for the master bedroom, kicking off her pumps as she walked. Her feet were killing her, and she couldn't wait to get into the shower. She'd been wearing the same clothes for far too long, and her hair felt disgusting.

"Where are you going?" Lester asked, following her.

"To take a shower."

"I think we should talk *now*, before the girls come home. I don't want them involved in this."

"Involved in what?" Giselle opened the door to their bedroom.

He was right at her heels. "I don't think you'd want Meg to know what I found out," he said pointedly.

Giselle stopped and turned slowly, standing in the middle of the room. "What are you talking about, Lester?" she asked, as a wave of panic rose in her gut.

"I happen to know that Meg's real father—*Manfred*—is a powerful voodoo priest in Jamaica. And that you had—*two* babies. One was sacrificed—right, Giselle? And Manfred never knew that you took the other back to the States with you. She was supposed to stay there, with some old woman, as a reward to her for destroying the other child. But the old woman felt sorry for you. And Manfred was told that she died, too."

Reeling in shock, Giselle fumbled her way to the bed and sank onto the mattress. How could Lester know about Manfred?

"Who told you that?" she asked weakly, hating him, hating the way he stood there, watching her through those watery blue eyes behind his glasses.

"Does it matter?"

"Yes."

"Well, I can't give you that information," he said, taking his glasses off and breathing onto the left lens. He busied himself polishing it on his shirt.

Giselle felt sick inside. She had triggered this herself. After all these years, why had she ever told Lester anything about Meg's birth?

Because he kept badgering you about going to the Caribbean.

Now, remembering the trip Lester had supposedly taken to St. Louis, when he had come back sunburnt, she wondered if he had actually gone to Jamaica. Had he poked around until he discovered the truth about her past?

Had he . . .

Had he spoken to Manfred?

Manfred would be in his late thirties now, a decade younger than Lester, but, Giselle knew, infinitely more powerful. A man like Manfred would *shred* a man like Lester.

The thought was comforting . . . and yet, not.

Giselle didn't want to think about what a man like Manfred would do to her, or to Meg, if he found out she was still alive.

"Lester," she said, panic edging up inside of her, "he doesn't know, does he?"

"Who?" he asked blandly, putting his glasses back on. "Who doesn't know what?"

"You know damn well what I'm talking about! Manfred doesn't know that I brought Meg back with me . . . that she's still alive?"

"No, he doesn't know. Not yet."

She wanted to kill him. She wanted to throw herself on him, and claw at him, and screech at him that he had no right to do this to her . . . or to Meg.

Somehow, she managed to keep her emotions under control. She cleared her throat, asked Lester, "What do you want from me, Lester?"

"It's simple. I want you to stay married to me."

She expelled a heavy sigh, buried her face in her hands for a moment, then looked up at him. "Why? We don't love each other."

"No," he agreed. "We don't. But I'm comfortable, Giselle. And I have no intention of giving up my lifestyle now. This is where I belong—with you. I took care of you and Meg when you had no one else. Now it's your turn to take care of me."

"Lester, I will. I'll make sure you have everything you need if we split up," she promised blindly. "Whatever you want."

"No, you won't," he said. "We signed a prenuptial agreement, courtesy of your dear daddy, remember?"

She hated him for the sarcastic tone he used when he spoke of her father.

And Harry McKenna had never liked Lester, either. He had warned her not to marry him, warned her that he was a gold-digger, warned her not to trust him.

But you were weak, Giselle cursed herself. *And a fool. You couldn't see past Lester's all-out adoration of you, past the constant compliments he gave you.*

And after Manfred, he was so . . . safe.

"Lester," she said, pulling herself together for Meg's sake. "Listen to me. You cannot go to Manfred. If you do, he'll kill me, and he'll kill Meg."

"I'd hate to have that happen, Giselle."

You bastard, she thought, keeping her expression neutral.

"I promise that if we split, you can have as much money as you need. You can have your car . . . and the house," she added desperately.

"What about my daughter?"

Her stomach churned. "You can spend as much time with her as you want," she assured him.

"But I wouldn't be able to live with her, is that it? I would have the house, but I wouldn't have my family here where they belong? What good is that?"

"You just said that you don't love me!" she protested, her voice rising. "And I sure as hell know you don't love Meg."

"I never said that."

"You didn't have to! The only person in this house that you care about is yourself."

"And Carrie," he added. "And I won't let you have my daughter. I won't let you take away my lifestyle. It's that simple. I like our social life, Giselle. Playing golf and having dinner at the 4C . . ."

4C was the local slang for Crawford Corners Country Club, and Giselle knew his membership would be revoked the moment she divorced him. They had strict policies at the club. Giselle's father had been a member, and his father before him. She, and not Lester, had the membership legacy.

"And I like our travels, and our friends."

My friends, she corrected mentally. She knew they only tolerated him. Without her, he'd be cast out of their elite circle, and he knew it.

"I like my job," he added.

And she knew what he was thinking. That without her, he wouldn't have a job. When Giselle had insisted on marrying Lester, Harry McKenna had fought to get one of his friends to offer Lester a position as a financial consultant. Giselle knew they just kept him on out of respect for Harry and Giselle. Lester knew it, too. If she ever dumped him, he'd be fired in two seconds flat.

"I can make sure you keep your job," she lied, desperate to appease him.

"No, you can't," he said. "The only way I get to keep everything I want is if I keep *you*, Giselle. I'm no fool. I won't pretend that I control my lifestyle. But I can control *you* . . . thanks to what I've discovered."

She couldn't argue with him. He had her right where he wanted her, and they both knew it.

She watched desolately as he disappeared into the alcove off their bedroom, the small space he insisted on calling his dressing room. A few minutes later, he emerged wearing lime and tangerine plaid pants and a matching golf shirt.

"Don't look so unhappy, Giselle," he said, glancing over at the bed. "Just think, it wouldn't be easy to be single again at your age. I don't know very many men who would want a woman who's approaching middle age when they could find someone young—someone who isn't saddled with two kids and a rather . . . demanding ex-husband."

His words stung, and they were meant to. *Middle age.* She cringed at the knowledge that there was truth in his words. She was getting older. Years of worshiping the sun seemed to have caught up with her all of a sudden. Her skin grew more wrinkled by the day. And her once firm figure seemed a little soft lately.

Panic-stricken, she saw Lester sizing her up. He nodded, and she knew he had concluded that he was right. She wouldn't leave him.

"I'm going over to the club to play a few holes," he told her, heading for the door. "I'll be back later. Think about what I've said. Although I'm sure your decision has already been made."

She was silent as he left.

Then she gave a little moan, thinking that her whole world had come crashing in on her. Tears started trickling down her cheeks, and she didn't try to stop them.

She was about to fling herself into her pillow and sob her heart out when something stopped her.

A thumping sound.

And it had come from Meg's bedroom.

* * *

He had decided to pay a *real* visit to Meadowview Terrace, rather than project himself there. He needed the full force of his power with him, and there were times, when he used astral projection, that he wondered if his strength wasn't slightly diminished that way.

He would need every ounce of power he possessed to accomplish the tasks that lay ahead of him.

Getting from Spring City to Crawford Corners meant taking a bus. As he disembarked at the busy intersection of Broad Street and Highland Boulevard, the Episcopalian Church services were just letting out.

The streets were crowded with residents who were dressed in their expensive Sunday best. He was fully aware of their suspicious glances as they passed him on the sidewalk.

He knew these well-to-do suburbanites were wondering what an outsider—a young, black teenager—was doing here among them. And he knew what they were thinking—that he was up to no good.

Well, they were right, he thought to himself, amused. But imagine if they knew what he was really involved in.

At the edge of town, he turned toward Long Neck Road, the broad expanse that led out to winding, tree-lined Soundview Drive. Giselle's home was in that exclusive neighborhood of quiet mansions and sweeping lawns overlooking the water.

As he walked, he felt a twinge of trepidation stealing over him. He recalled how he had attempted to locate the missing boy through a spell—and failed.

No, he warned himself. *You must never doubt your powers.*

He set his mouth grimly and turned onto Soundview Drive just as a familiar black Honda drove by, splashing him with water from a deep puddle in the road.

Megan McKenna, he thought, watching as the car disappeared around the bend, heading in the direction of Meadowview Terrace.

He wiped the muddy droplets from his long black coat and narrowed his eyes.

Candra removed a pen and a scrap of paper from the desk drawer, then started writing without bothering to close it. She couldn't waste any time. She had snapped out of her trance only moments before, and she had to jot down everything she remembered of her vision before the details started fading.

It had come to her slowly, yet so vividly that she knew it had to be real.

Landon and Jack were together, in some kind of cabin or lodge. It was located in a place called Hillside Haven or Hillside Heaven. There was a road nearby, a highway that bore the number 44. And the cabin sat on a rise above a creek or stream.

Candra swiftly got everything on paper, then started toward Meg's bookshelf, to see if she had an atlas.

Something stopped her in her tracks.

Footsteps just outside the door.

She frowned, thinking that Meg must be home—she had been so far gone that she hadn't even heard her come in downstairs.

And then there was a knock, and the bedroom door was opening, and a voice was calling, "Meg? Carrie?"

A voice Candra had never heard before . . .

Or at least, not since the very first moments after her birth.

The sound slammed into her, stole her breath away, sent a rush of emotion coursing through her.

She stood there, rooted, as the door opened all the way and she found herself face to face with Giselle McKenna Hudson.

Her mother.

"You *are* home," Giselle said, moving toward her. "I didn't see your car, so I thought you were out."

Candra allowed herself to be pulled into her mother's arms, to be squeezed tightly and kissed on the head. She was enveloped in warmth, in the scent of expensive perfume, in the musical voice that was saying something about how long it had taken to get home, and how exhausted she was, and . . .

"Meg," her mother said, pulling back abruptly and looking at her. "Did you . . . did you hear us talking just now? Lester and me? In our bedroom?"

Candra could only shake her head, too overwhelmed to even attempt to find her voice. Her lips were quivering and she felt as though if she moved any other part of her body, she would absolutely fall apart. She would start sobbing and fling herself into this beautiful blond woman's arms, and she would call her *Mom* and tell her how she had been longing for this moment all her life.

But she didn't move; she didn't do any of those things.

She only stared at Giselle.

Her mother.

The photographs Candra had seen had captured Giselle's flaxen-haired beauty and youth, and the impish sparkle in her light green eyes. But in person, she looked slightly different. A fine network of wrinkles wove around her eyes, and instead of reflecting frothy light-heartedness, they showed . . .

Exhaustion?

Concern?

"Meg," Giselle repeated, "I can tell by looking at you that something's wrong. You heard us, didn't you?"

Again Candra shook her head, unable to wrench her gaze away from her mother's face. She had waited so long, so impossibly long, to see her. There was so much to take in—the deep tan that made her cheeks glow and the long, sun-streaked tresses that looked soft and naturally wavy. Candra wanted to reach out and touch that hair, wanted to catch and clasp the manicured hand that fluttered nervously to smooth it.

"Meg," her mother started again, and then stopped short.

Candra had heard it, too. A car door slamming someplace nearby.

And now the front door was opening, and footsteps were pounding up the stairs.

Giselle looked toward the door expectantly. "Carrie must be—"

The rest of her words were lost to a high-pitched gasp the instant Meg appeared in the hallway.

"Mirabelle?"

She looked up sleepily and saw Ben standing at the foot of her bed.

"Hi," she murmured.

"Hi." He came closer, slid into the chair Meg had vacated, and took her hand gently. "Did you tell Meg?"

She yawned and nodded. "I did. She already knew."

"About having a brother?"

"Mmm hmm. And that someone is after her."

"Does she know who it is?"

"No. But, Ben, I'm worried." She felt him squeeze her

fingers and realized that his grasp made her feel safe. What had she done without him in her life?

"You need to get some rest," he said softly, and reached up to push a strand of hair back from her face.

"I'm not tired," she lied, and fought back another yawn. "I have to make sure that Meg—"

"You've done everything you can do for Meg, Mirabelle," Ben said. "Now you have to concentrate on getting better. For me."

She raised an eyebrow. "For you?"

"Yup." He smiled at her, a smile that told her exactly how he felt. And she realized that she had always known, anyway. From the moment their eyes had first met several weeks ago in Philosophy class.

The odd thing was, it no longer bothered her.

Ben wasn't Alex. He wasn't going to hurt her the way Alex had. Ben was someone she could count on.

"Where are my parents?" she asked, suddenly remembering.

"In the lobby, arguing."

"About what?"

"Your mother wants to stay at her sister's. Your father wants to get a hotel."

"That's because Aunt Tara drives him crazy. She freaks out if there's a crumb in her kitchen." She paused to yawn. "And she doesn't let anyone in the house with their shoes on. He says he always feels like he's going to be scolded when he's there."

Ben smiled. "That's what he told me. He's a nice guy. And your mom's all right, too."

"Yeah," Mirabelle agreed, and felt her eyelids trying to flutter closed.

"They were so worried about you," Ben told her. "They were upset they couldn't get here right away yesterday. But I told them that I was taking care of you, even though the nurse wouldn't let me into the ICU unit."

"Why wouldn't she?" Mirabelle mumbled, as sleep struggled to claim her.

"Because we're not related."

"Mmm."

"She wanted to know who I was. I told her I was your boyfriend."

"Mmm."

"Am I?" she heard Ben ask.

She smiled. "Mmm hmm," she said, and then drifted away toward pleasant dreams.

Twenty

Meg looked from her mother to Candra, even as Giselle's astonished gaze darted rapidly between Candra and herself.

For a moment, no one spoke.

Then her mother clapped a hand to her mouth and weakly said, "Oh my God," as Meg burst out, "Mom, this is Candra!"

Giselle just shook her head in disbelief.

"My twin sister, Mom," Meg went on gently, laying a hand on her mother's arm. She could feel Giselle trembling violently beneath her touch, and she propelled her a few feet to the rose-colored chair beside the bookcase.

Her mother sank into the cushions, still looking dazed and staring at Candra.

Meg glanced at her sister and saw that she hadn't moved. She was riveted on Giselle, and Meg realized, with a start, that Candra's eyes were shiny. Her sister blinked, and teardrops escaped her lashes, plopping onto her high cheekbones and glistening there. Candra didn't seem to notice. Joy radiated from her face—pure joy, as she looked at their mother—and Meg had to swallow hard over a lump in her own throat.

"Mom," she said thickly, her voice choked with emotion, "Candra has been waiting a long, long time to meet you."

"My God," Giselle breathed at last. "My other baby. I never knew you were still alive."

She stood and moved toward Candra, gathering her into her arms with a sob. The moment she felt her mother's touch, Candra seemed to crumple, collapsing against Giselle and weeping herself.

Meg smiled as she watched them, her mother and her sister, squeezing each other and crying and laughing in sheer joy and relief.

Finally, Giselle held Candra back slightly and said, "Let me see you. You're beautiful. You look exactly like Meg."

Candra smiled and nodded. "I know . . ."

"I can't believe this," Giselle said, and then repeated it. "How did this happen? Where did you come from? Where have you been all these years?"

"With Rosamund Bowen, in Ocho Rios," Candra said, her expression growing somber. "She raised me."

Giselle nodded. "He—your father—he had promised that she would get one of you. But I thought— Rosamund said she was giving you to me, and that she was going to tell him you had died."

A chill shot through Meg. "She was going to tell our father that Candra had *died?* But why?"

"Candra," Giselle repeated in a far-off voice, ignoring Meg's question. "So that's your name. I like it."

"Rosamund must have given it to me, if you didn't," Candra said, almost seeming shy. "She always said it meant 'white fire.'"

"White fire . . ." Giselle echoed.

"Like the moon."

Her mother nodded. "It suits you."

"Mom," Meg cut in, "Why would Rosamund have told

our father that Candra was dead? And you said *you* thought she was dead."

Giselle's jaw stiffened grimly. "Your father," she said hesitantly, "wasn't . . . he wasn't . . ."

She trailed off, and Meg waited, breathlessly, for her to go on. All her life, she had wondered about her father. Now, at last, she was about to hear the truth. And she had a feeling, from the look on her mother's face, that the truth was far from pleasant.

"Manfred was his name," Giselle told them after a long pause.

Candra gave a little gasp, and Meg saw recognition in her sister's eyes.

"He was Jamaican, the high priest of a Black Magic coven. He was probably around my age, but he was respected and feared by everyone he encountered. He was very powerful."

Feared, Meg thought, and the back of her neck prickled.

"I never knew that Manfred had made a pact with . . . *his gods* . . . to sacrifice his firstborn child in exchange for more power," Giselle went on in a faraway voice.

Her chilling words caught Meg off guard. Shocked, she glanced at Candra. Her sister met her gaze, mirroring Meg's horror.

"The birth was very difficult," Giselle was saying. "Rosamund and her sister were there with me, but I have very little memory of the experience. When I came to, I held one of you. I have no idea which one. Then you were taken away from me. I later discovered that you had supposedly been . . . killed. By Rosamund. On Manfred's behalf."

"Oh, my God," Meg whispered, stunned.

"But apparently, she lied to me *and* to him. I thought

she had carried out his orders and killed one of you. I thought that the baby she gave me was the one she was supposed to keep for herself. Now I realize what she did. She kept one of you and gave the other to me."

"You mean," Candra said, seeming to find her voice at last, "that my father was *Manfred*? Oh, God."

"You know who he is," Giselle said.

"Everyone knows who he is. But no one has ever really seen him. He lives in the mountains above town, and people tell stories about him. They say—that he's evil . . ." Candra's voice trailed off.

"He is." Giselle nodded, and her voice shook. "If he knew that Meg was still alive—that I had her—"

"Mom," Meg interrupted, "he *does* know. He's after us. It has to be him," she told Candra, her voice rising as the horrible reality sunk in.

The dark person Rosamund and Mirabelle had warned them about, the one who was trying to kill her and Candra . . .

He was their own father.

Hot tears spilled out of Meg's eyes and a wave of nausea rose in her throat.

"What do you mean?" Giselle asked, her eyes wide and her tone high pitched. "What do you mean he's after you?"

"He killed Rosamund," Candra said, and Giselle flinched. "And before she died, she told us that someone was out to get us. And . . ."

"And our brother," Meg finished when Candra hesitated, watching Giselle intently.

Her mother frowned. "Who?" she asked, staring hard at Meg, as though she sensed what was coming next . . . as though she feared it.

"There were three of us, Mom," Meg said quietly. "Not twins. Triplets."

The look of shock on her mother's face was even more intense than when Meg had first come into the room. "*What* did you say, Meg?"

"You had triplets. We have a brother. And he was born first."

"I never knew . . ." She shook her head, and clutched the arm of the chair as if to steady herself. Then she took a deep breath and asked faintly, "Does Manfred know?"

"We think he just found out."

Giselle closed her eyes, as if to shield herself from pain. "Where is he? Your . . . brother, I mean."

"He was adopted—we think, by an American family. And we think we know who he is," Meg said slowly. "The name is Keller."

"Keller," Giselle repeated, opening her eyes abruptly.

"Is it familiar to you?"

"I think there was a family named Keller in Jamaica back when we were there. Yes, there was. A couple, and they were a lot younger than my parents. The man was with SNE, too, working on the resort project with my father. But after we got back to the States, I never heard anything more about them. I don't know if they lived here in Crawford Corners, but I doubt it."

"You told me that both Landon and Jack are from Rhode Island," Meg reminded her sister.

"Landon and Jack?" Giselle asked.

"Friends of Candra's—both of them are named Keller. They're cousins. We think one of them is our brother."

Giselle's hand flew up to her face, and she ran her

fingers through her hair, looking distraught. "This is . . . I can't . . ."

"Mom," Meg said, quickly putting a hand under her elbow. "You need to lie down."

"And we need to get to Landon and Jack," Candra said. "I know where they are."

"You do?" Startled, Meg looked at her sister, who nodded.

"Did you ever hear of a place called Hillside Haven? Or Hillside Heaven?"

"No."

"How about a road called Forty-four?"

"Route Forty-four? It runs across the top of Connecticut, from Rhode Island all the way to New York, I think. They could be in any of the three states."

"They're in a cabin off that road," Candra told her. "And it's in Connecticut."

"Are you sure?"

Her sister raised a brow as if to say, *Of course I'm sure.*

"Let's go," Meg said, looking down at her mother. "Mom, we have to go there."

Giselle nodded, still looking numb.

"But where are we going?" Candra asked. "You said the road cuts across the whole state."

"Well, it would make sense that this cabin's toward the eastern side, closer to the Rhode Island border, since Jack and Landon are from there, right?"

"I have no idea," Candra said.

"Well, whose cabin is it?"

"It belongs to Jack's parents, I think."

"We have to find this Hillside place." Meg started for the door. "Lester has all kinds of atlases and tour books. You help Mom to bed while I look it up."

Candra nodded and took their mother's arm as Meg,

her heart pounding, hurried down the hall to Lester's study.

The black Honda again, he thought, slipping into a clump of trees at the edge of the road as the car went barreling down Meadowview Terrace toward Soundview.

He glimpsed two heads inside. Meg . . . and Candra? Where were they going?

Torn, he looked from the car back to the stately brick home marked number 41.

Giselle is there, he thought, sensing her presence, and his mind was made up.

It was time he confronted her.

Swiftly, moving with deadly purpose, he covered the remaining quarter of a mile to the Hudson home. He moved stealthily across the expansive lawn, slipping to the bushes that bordered the front of the house. And he saw, as he crept toward the front door, that it was standing partly open, almost as though it were an invitation for him to enter.

Meg and Candra must not have closed it all the way in their haste to get to wherever they were going. He frowned, and again looked down the street in the direction where the car had disappeared.

Then he glanced back at the door, and once again made up his mind.

This time, it would be Giselle.

He was inside the house moments later, standing in the foyer and listening.

There was only silence, and he decided she was home alone. He didn't feel another presence. Of course, if he was wrong . . . if that fool Lester was here, too—or

Giselle's younger daughter, the blonde who looked just like her . . .

Well, he would just have to take care of them, too.

As he moved up the stairs, he looked around, remembering how it had been dark when he was here on those other occasions. He had crept in to snoop around, to see if he could discover Lester's secret. Once, he had bumped into Meg's sister, the little blonde, and she had been terrified.

He'd entertained the notion of killing her, but he'd seen a spark of defiance in her frightened light green eyes, and it had filled him with admiration. She was no pushover, Giselle's younger daughter. She had a steely core of inner strength, and a dark side that Giselle and Meg lacked.

So he hadn't bothered to harm her. Instead, he'd simply vanished, projecting himself back along the astral plane to his body, no doubt leaving the young blonde rubbing her eyes in astonishment.

At the top of the stairs, he turned toward the master bedroom, and his heart beat faster as he approached the door. Behind it, he knew, was the woman who had fallen under his spell once before.

The woman who had borne his children . . . and then betrayed him.

"What if this Hilltop Haven isn't it?" Meg asked, looking over her shoulder as she merged onto Interstate 95 headed north.

"It is," Candra said, studying the map in the seat beside her. From what she could see, they had to follow 95 to Route 91, which led from New Haven up to Hartford.

From there, they would pick up 84, and then 44. It seemed complicated.

"Are you *sure*?" Meg asked for what seemed like the thousandth time.

Candra sighed and felt in her pocket for the scrap of paper where she'd scribbled the notes about her vision. It wasn't there. She must have left it back in Meg's room . . . though she was pretty positive she'd brought it with her.

"Candra?"

"Yes, I'm sure, Meg," she said, feeling slightly exasperated.

"But at first you said it was called Hillside something," Meg reminded her. "You said Hillside Heaven, didn't you?"

"I saw a sign," Candra said. "I couldn't read it exactly, and I thought it said Hillside, and not Hilltop."

"Where?" Meg's head swung around, searching the side of the road. "What sign?"

"In my vision," Candra said impatiently. "When I cast the spell."

"Oh."

Candra searched her other pocket and came up empty. She must have left the paper behind.

"I can't believe how lucky we are that Lester is so anal when it comes to his travel books," Meg was saying. "He must have more geographic information than some libraries do."

Candra nodded. They had found a listing for Hilltop Haven in a book called *New England Resorts: Something for Everyone*. It was a rural summer community in eastern Connecticut off Route 44, and according to the book's description, a "babbling brook, perfect for trout fishing" ran right through it.

"Lester thinks he's such a world traveler," Meg said derisively, changing lanes to pass a slow-moving pickup truck. "He's always planning these trips for him and my mom—I mean, *Mom*"—she amended, glancing at Candra, then she went on—"to take with her money. He always wants to go off to these spas and ski chalets, you know?"

Candra nodded, suspecting that Meg was keeping up a steady stream of chatter so they wouldn't be able to discuss what was really on both their minds.

The fact that they had an evil murderer for a father.

That right this very minute, he might be closing in on their unsuspecting brother. His firstborn.

"Listen," Candra interrupted, looking at the map again, "how long does it take to get to New Haven?"

"Less than an hour if I speed," Meg said.

"Then speed."

"Giselle . . . wake up, Giselle."

The voice traveled to her as if across a great distance, shattering the tranquil twilight world where she had retreated as soon as Candra had left her in her bed.

"Giselle . . ."

I'm not waking up, she thought, confused. *I'm sleeping. This is a nightmare.*

Only in a nightmare would she hear that voice.

Unless . . .

Her eyes snapped open and she gasped.

"Hello, Giselle."

Manfred.

He stood over her, smiling down at her, his white teeth gleaming in that dark, dark face.

But it couldn't be, she realized a split second later. It

couldn't be Manfred, because he looked exactly the same as he had eighteen years ago. The man standing above her wasn't yet twenty.

But . . .

"Confused, my dear?" he asked, and his voice was Manfred's voice. And his eyes—those hard, bottomless, probing black eyes—they, too, belonged to Manfred.

But this couldn't be the man she had known almost twenty years ago. Manfred would be around her age now. This was someone who looked and sounded just like him. Someone who, like Manfred, was pure evil.

It radiated from the man standing over her bed, like a heavy shroud that threatened to descend and smother her.

There was only one person, Giselle thought, searching her mind frantically and hating the knowledge she retrieved, only one person who would look and sound like Manfred, who would have inherited his dark powers.

Manfred's son.

Could this person—this boy who was watching her with such venom in his gaze—actually be her child, too?

Please, no, she begged silently, and yet she knew it had to be the truth. He looked nothing like her, and his skin was dark—far darker than Meg's, and darker than Candra's, too. But if he had grown up in the islands . . .

"Who are you?" she whispered, and waited in dread for his answer.

Meg looked over at Candra, wondering if she was asleep. She hadn't spoken in several minutes.

But she was awake, Meg saw, and staring bleakly through the windshield at the road ahead.

"What are you thinking about?" Meg asked.

"Him."

"Our father?"

"In a way, but mostly about . . ."

"Our brother."

Candra nodded.

"Do you think it's Landon or Jack?" Meg asked her sister, focusing her eyes on the road again as she passed a large Stop & Shop truck.

"I don't know," Candra replied. "I spent some time talking to Jack the night we met, and I remember him telling me about his background, and Landon's, too. I wish I'd paid more attention. At the time, I was only interested in keeping an eye on Landon. We were at a party out at some park—"

"Moseby!" Meg interrupted, as something clicked in her mind. "On a Friday night, right?"

When Candra nodded, Meg went on, "A lot of my friends were there, too. People saw you with someone, and assumed it was me. They told Shea that I was cheating on him."

"I'm sorry," Candra said quietly, and it was so out of character that Meg looked at her in surprise. "I'm afraid I've caused you a lot of trouble, Meg."

"What do you mean?" Something told Meg that her sister was talking about more than just that night at Moseby.

Candra took a deep breath. "There's something I have to confess."

"There is?" Meg held her breath, not daring to remove her eyes from the road as they rounded a curve going nearly eighty miles an hour, but longing to look at her sister. Then she realized that it was probably easier for Candra not to meet her gaze as she spilled whatever secret she was about to reveal.

"You know how you can't remember anything that happened to you all week?" Candra asked, and Meg nodded. "Well, you don't have amnesia. I mean, you *do* . . . but it's because of a spell. Dalila cast it on you—because I asked her to." Those last words tumbled out in a rush, as though Candra had forced herself to expel them.

"What kind of spell?" Meg asked slowly, struggling to focus on the road.

"Nothing dangerous," Candra told her quickly. "Just . . . I wanted to get you out of the way for a little while. I wanted to see what it was like to be you, instead of me. I wanted . . . to meet Mom."

Meg thought back to the scene in her bedroom, remembered how her sister had clung to their mother, how her eyes had been filled with tears of joy. She wondered what it would have been like if *she* had been the one left behind in Jamaica, left to a lonely life of poverty, raised by an older woman who didn't know how to show affection . . . a woman who had kept the truth from her.

And she understood.

If she had been in Candra's shoes, she might have done the same thing.

"It's okay," she said after a long time, and she heard Candra let out a deep sigh, as though she'd been holding her breath.

"I didn't mean to hurt you, Meg," her sister said.

Meg looked at her, and saw that Candra was crying. Her dark eyes were begging Meg's forgiveness.

"Hey, it's okay," Meg reminded her, wanting nothing more than to pull over to the side of the road and hug her sister, to reassure her and comfort her. But there wasn't a minute to spare. She had to keep driving.

"You didn't hurt me," she told Candra as she glanced back at the road. "Not really."

"But I almost did. I wanted to."

Meg's hands stiffened on the steering wheel. "What do you mean?"

"I told Dalila . . ." Candra paused, then took a deep breath. "I told Dalila to kill you."

"Who am I?" he echoed, and chuckled softly, watching the woman on the bed carefully. "But I thought you knew."

"I don't." Her voice came out in a near-whimper, and the pathetic sound filled him with pleasure.

"Think carefully, Giselle. Who am I?"

"I . . . don't . . . know." She was crying now, her large green eyes riveted on his face.

"Of course you do. I'm Manfred."

She seemed to stiffen at the sound of his name. Then she shook her head.

"No," she whispered. "You can't be him."

"Oh? Why can't I be?" He was enjoying this, far more than he had ever anticipated.

"Because you . . . you can't even be twenty years old. Manfred was my age."

He shrugged. "Age is a number."

"What do you mean?"

"First, Giselle, are you convinced that I am who I say I am?"

"No." Her chin lifted stubbornly. "Of course I'm not. You're too young to be Manfred."

"I'll prove to you that I am."

"How?"

"Like this." Slowly, he bent over her, lowering his face until his lips brushed against hers. She tasted as sweet as he remembered, and he deepened the kiss, probing into her mouth with his insistent tongue and tangling his fingers in her silky blond hair. She moaned and sighed, and opened herself up to him—helpless, he knew, to resist him.

Even now.

Even after all these years, after what he had done to her.

Heady with his own power, he broke the kiss and pulled away.

Her eyelashes fluttered and she stared up at him in disbelief.

"It is you," she said in a hushed voice. A wanton expression had replaced the dread that had been in her eyes only moments before. Now she looked at him in awe . . . and blatant yearning.

He smiled. "I told you."

"But how can you look the way you do?"

"I'm powerful, Giselle, more powerful than any man you have ever known or will ever know. Even now, I have you slipping under my control."

She shook her head, as if to deny it. But he was well aware that she was falling under in his spell, just as she had been eighteen years ago. He had always been able to charm women this way, had always had the ability to captivate them before they knew what hit them.

With Giselle, it had been even easier than with the rest. She was so weak, so frivolous, so ready to be overpowered.

"My powers led me to a secret. A way to maintain my physical youth, even as my mind obtains the wisdom and potency that comes with age. My body will remain nineteen forever. I will live for eternity."

"How?" she breathed, wide-eyed, and he knew he had her.

"A spell," he said, thinking back to the glorious day when he had stumbled upon the magical incantation and realized that it meant immortality.

"A spell?" Giselle echoed. "Cast it on me."

He laughed aloud at her petulant tone, then firmly said, "No."

"Please, Manfred . . ." Her voice was filled with urgency, and her eyes were wild with need.

He wanted to laugh again, this time at how very simple it was. He should have realized . . . He should never have doubted that he could win her.

He had always known that Giselle's greatest weakness was her vanity. She was a creature of pride, a woman who had always based her entire sense of self-worth on her appearance. To her—and to most people—beauty meant youth.

He looked more closely at her face, noting the wrinkles that lined her lovely seafoam-colored eyes. "You're aging, my dear," he said, and she winced.

"Please, Manfred," she begged again, this time more fervently. "Please share your potion and your spell with me."

He watched her closely.

She was running her fingers over her face, tracing the web of fine lines that betrayed her age. "Please, Manfred . . . can't you erase these wrinkles?"

"Of course I can. I can restore the face you had eighteen years ago."

Her eyes widened. "Oh, Manfred, please . . . I'll do anything."

His gaze narrowed and he shrewdly repeated, "Anything?"

"Anything."

"All right," he agreed, nodding. "I want to know where Meg and Candra have gone . . . and where I can find our son."

Candra wanted, more than anything, to be able to take back the words she had uttered—the words that had clearly stung her sister harder than if Candra had slapped her.

She wanted to be able to tell Meg that it wasn't true, that she was just joking, that of course she hadn't tried to kill her.

But it was time that the truth came out. She would never be able to live with it bottled up inside of her.

For a long time, there was silence in the car, the only sound coming from the air rushing through the vent on the dashboard. Then Meg inhaled, exhaled, and, still looking straight ahead through the windshield, uttered a single word.

"Why?"

And so Candra tried to tell her. How she had been caught up in greed, and in her own fury over how Giselle had abandoned her, and how she'd chosen Meg over Candra. Now that she knew it hadn't happened that way, she felt sick over how much energy had been wasted, channeled into a negative cause.

She sounded pathetic to her own ears, but Meg listened intently. At least, she seemed to be listening. She nodded thoughtfully when Candra was through.

And she said nothing.

Not for a long time.

Candra sat there, alternately watching the highway and her sister, fighting back the tears that were so ready to spill over again. In her whole life, she hadn't cried as much as she had in the last twenty-four hours. She had always thought tears were a sign of weakness. Rosamund had told her that.

But now Candra knew that emotions weren't always easily controlled. That sometimes, you had to let go. Sometimes, you had to give in.

Finally, Meg spoke.

"I understand," she said simply, "and I forgive you."

"You do?" Candra stared at her sister in disbelief.

"I have to," Meg said, nodding. "You're my sister. And I know you did what you did because you had to. I know—don't ask me how, I just do—that you'll never do anything to hurt me again. I trust you."

Meg had said it once before, just yesterday, but it seemed like years ago. Then, Candra had been racked with guilt when her sister said those words. Now, she was elated. Meg trusted her. Meg had forgiven her!

"All my life," Meg was saying, "I felt as though something was missing. I felt as though some part of me was incomplete. When I found you, I knew that we belonged together, Candra. We were together before we were born, and we'll be together from now on."

Candra wiped at her eyes again. This was one of those times when you had to give in to emotion. "Thank you, Meg," she said, and her heart overflowed with love of her sister.

"Now we have to find him," Meg said, looking at the road again.

"Our brother." Candra wondered again if it was Landon or Jack.

"He's a part of us, just like we're a part of each other. He belongs with us too, Candra."

She nodded, not wanting to voice the words Meg had left unsaid.

If only we can get to him in time.

Twenty-one

Hilltop Haven.

"Is that the sign you saw in your vision?" Meg asked Candra as she turned the Honda onto the narrow road leading upward, around a bend.

"Yes," Candra said, sitting forward in her seat and drumming her fingertips on the dashboard.

Ever since they'd left the Interstate behind a short time ago, Candra had been fidgety.

Meanwhile, Meg had fought the urge to step even harder on the gas, knowing it would be dangerous to go much above sixty on the rural two-lane highway 44. It was dotted with farmhouses and produce stands and antique stores, and it seemed to have taken forever to reach the resort community, which was tucked into a wooded hillside.

Now, as they followed the road upward, deer darted into the underbrush and birds chirped from the boughs of ancient trees that towered above. They passed cottages and cabins where families barbecued and children splashed in kiddie pools.

"Maybe we should stop and ask someone if they've heard of the Kellers," Meg suggested after a few minutes of driving.

"No, keep going. It's up there," Candra said, her eyes on the grassy, tree-dotted slope ahead. "We can't be more than a few minutes away."

Meg's heart was pounding so loudly that she was sure Candra could hear it. "What are we going to do when we get there?" she asked, chewing on her lower lip and feeling uncertain.

But Candra would know, of course. Candra always seemed to know.

Not this time, Meg realized in dismay.

"I have no idea," Candra said, shrugging.

"I mean, do we just burst in and tell Landon and Jack that we think one of them is our brother?"

"I don't know," Candra said again. "What do you— there it is!" she interrupted herself, pointing at a cabin nestled on the hillside ahead.

Meg's stomach flip-flopped.

"Are you sure that's it?"

"I'm positive. I saw it in my vision. That's the place. There's the stream," she said, and Meg saw a groove carved out of the hillside, lined with tall grasses and dense undergrowth that marked the water's path.

The cabin itself was isolated from the rest of the resort, perched in its own little world, looking like part of the land that surrounded it. It had been built of dark rough-hewn logs, with a massive stone chimney going up one side. It was two stories tall, with lots of windows and red-painted shutters, the kind that actually closed.

"How close should we get?" Meg whispered, as if the boys could somehow overhear them. Which was, of course, impossible, since they were in the car with the windows rolled up and there didn't seem to be a soul hanging around outside the cabin, anyway.

"I don't know. I guess you should pull up right outside the door." Candra's voice was a whisper, too, and Meg felt slightly less foolish.

Moments later, as she put the car into Park and

turned the key in the ignition, the cabin door was suddenly thrown open.

Candra let out a little gasp, and Meg looked up to see Landon Keller standing in the threshold. He wore navy sweatpants and a matching sweatshirt, and his feet were bare. His hair was disheveled, as though he'd been sleeping.

He looked startled, and his hand shielded his eyes from the sun as he peered through the windshield at them.

"Candra?"

Meg easily read his lips, and even from several yards away, she could see the elation in his eyes at the sight of her sister. With all her heart, she hoped that Landon wasn't their brother.

"Let's go," she told Candra, and saw that her sister was staring at him, as if frozen in her seat.

"I can't . . . you do it," Candra said in a small, frightened voice that didn't sound at all like her.

"Candra, you have to face him," Meg said gently. "Come on. It might not be him. It might be Jack."

"That's not what I'm afraid of," Candra protested, and Meg knew she was lying.

Candra was terrified that Landon Keller was their brother because she was in love with him. Meg could see it on her face.

And she suddenly thought wistfully of Shea. She had been head over heels with him . . .

I still am, she realized.

He'd been right about Candra. She *had* been trying to harm Meg. He had been trying to save her, trying to do what he thought was right. He couldn't know what Meg knew about her sister.

Would he ever be able to understand?

You have to give him a chance, Meg told herself, putting her hand on the car door handle. *The first thing you have to do when this is over is explain everything to Shea. Maybe it's not too late to salvage what you had together.*

"Meg?" Candra said.

"Yeah?"

"Come on." As though she'd suddenly been infused with strength, Candra opened her car door and stepped out to face Landon.

"How did you find me?" he asked, taking the few steps down to the dirt driveway and coming face to face with her.

Meg got out and joined them, but hung back a little. This was Candra's territory.

"It's not important how we found you," Candra said.

There was a sound beyond them, and Meg looked up to see that Jack had come out of the cabin. He was rubbing his eyes as though he'd just woken up, and he, too, wore sweatpants. But his chest was bare.

Meg was about to call to Jack, to tell him they all needed to talk, when suddenly two things caught her eye.

One was a five-pointed pendant on a chain around Jack's neck, glinting in the sun.

Rosamund's words echoed through Meg's mind.

". . . *he has an amulet . . . made of steel . . . a pentagram . . .*"

And the other thing . . .

The other thing she noticed was the tall dark shadow that suddenly loomed in the doorway behind Jack.

The boy had no idea he was there, Manfred realized, and a delicious shiver slithered down his spine.

But Meg knew. He saw the way her eyes widened in

disbelief. And now Candra had seen him, too. And the other kid—Landon.

All three of them were staring, motionless, as though they were paralyzed with fear.

Only the boy was oblivious.

Jack.

His son.

"What are you guys doing here?" Jack called to the girls, taking a step out onto the cabin's small porch.

None of them dared reply.

"What's going on?" Jack asked.

Manfred couldn't see his face, of course. But he could imagine the bafflement that would be in Jack's eyes. He would be wondering what his friends were looking at . . .

And now he would be realizing that whatever it was, was behind him.

And now he would look over his shoulder.

The moment his son turned and locked eyes with him, Manfred felt a surge, as though he'd been zapped with an electrical current.

This was the moment he had been waiting for. He had been so filled with anticipation as he tried to project himself across the astral plane to the cabin, in fact, that it had taken him longer than usual to leave his physical self behind.

That unprecedented difficulty had ignited a tiny flicker of doubt—doubt in his powers. Now that he knew he hadn't held up his end of the bargain with the gods, he couldn't help but wonder if he was as strong and capable as he'd always assumed.

Now, as Jack gasped in surprise, there was no more room for doubt. The moment of reckoning had arrived. Manfred summoned all of his power, reached out and closed his massive black hands around the boy's shoulders.

For a second, the two stared—*glared*—at each other.

And Manfred saw that the boy resembled his sisters more than was immediately obvious. Though his features were larger, more masculine, his dark eyes had the same exotic slant as Meg and Candra's . . . and the same depth, as though they were full of mystery and secrets and an inner fortitude unusual for someone so young.

"Who are you?" Jack asked finally, squirming beneath the iron grip that held him.

But his tone wasn't plaintive, as Manfred would have expected. He sounded curious . . . yet not afraid.

Why wasn't he afraid?

Thrown, Manfred loosened his hands for the merest moment.

That was all it took.

Jack wriggled out of his grasp and darted down the steps onto the ground, instantly positioning himself between the other three and the cabin. As though he could protect his sisters and Landon, Manfred thought, bemused—yet still unsettled by the boy's startlingly unruffled, assertive reaction.

When he turned to face Manfred again, Jack's expression was one of defiance.

"Come back here and face your fate," Manfred said, struggling against a tiny shred of misgiving that had somehow flitted through his mind.

"And what would that be?" Jack asked, a gleam in his dark eyes, as though he was daring Manfred to say it.

"Death," he spat out promptly, ominously. "You were my firstborn, a son. Death is your destiny . . . has always been your destiny, before you were ever conceived."

"So you're my father," Jack said, nodding. "Lately, I've

had visions of you—of a man with evil eyes, stalking me. I suspected who you might be, but I never wanted to believe it."

Visions? Manfred thought. *So he has inherited my powers. Not surprising. But . . . to what extent?*

"Until recently, I never knew *you* existed," Manfred told Jack, trying to quell the questions that thrust at his consciousness. "But I'm going to make up for those lost years. I made a pact to sacrifice my firstborn child to the gods, in exchange for supreme power. Now it's time to honor that deal."

He took a step toward the boy, who stood his ground.

Manfred felt an absurd, unwanted prickle of admiration.

He's my son, he told himself, with a curious sense of pride. *Of course he's no coward.*

And though he knew what he had to do, someplace deep inside of him, in a place he hadn't even known existed, he wavered.

Only for an instant, but it was enough to fill him with apprehension.

You cannot bend now, he told himself. *You must remain strong enough to do what is expected of you.*

"It's time for you to pay for my great gift," he thundered at the boy who stood before him. "To pay with your life. And you, too, must pay," he said, looking past Jack to the two girls who stood watching him in dread.

Jack's gaze narrowed. "What are you talking about? Why would you want to hurt them? They're nothing to you."

"Nothing to me?" Manfred's lips spread into a smile. "They haven't told you yet?"

"Told me what?" For the first time, Jack looked uncertain.

Pleased, Manfred took strength from that uncertainty, regained a sense of his own dominance.

"They haven't told you who they are," he crooned to Jack. "That they're your sisters."

Pure astonishment spread over Jack's face.

The boy turned to look at Meg and Candra, and Manfred seized his chance.

As he charged forward, he reached inside his long coat for the dagger that he knew was there.

This isn't how it's supposed to happen, he thought, even as he brandished the weapon for the attack. *The sacrifice was supposed to be part of a ritual . . . not an impulsive act of . . .*

Self-defense?

The notion confused him. Defense against what? He himself was the almighty. No mere mortal could depose him of his power.

In the instant before he leapt at Jack, Manfred saw something that changed everything.

An amulet . . .

The amulet.

Sunlight bounced off its polished steel surface, searing into Manfred like a ray of fire.

Stunned, he stopped in his tracks and stared.

"Where did you get that?" he rasped, looking from the pentagram to his son's icy eyes.

"I've had it all my life," Jack said, and as he spoke, he reached for Meg's hand with his left, and Candra's with his right.

Manfred felt his insides quivering. An unfamiliar sensation was stealing over his body.

He didn't have to look closely at the amulet to know that it was etched with symbols—Black Magic symbols that, combined, represented supreme protection and strength. Even from a few feet away, its energy radiated at him.

On a normal human, a person without the mystical powers that can only be passed down through the generations, the amulet would be a mere ornament. But its significance was profoundly enhanced when the charm was worn by one who possessed inner forces that greatly surpassed a mere mortal's.

And there was only one way for the legendary amulet to come into a person's possession: it had to be bestowed by the gods at birth. Manfred had heard tales of this happening—it was part of island lore. But never, in all his life, had he encountered someone who actually possessed the mystical charm.

"That should have been mine!" he boomed, reaching out to wrench the amulet off his son's neck.

Instantly, his arm was charged with excruciating pain. He whimpered and stepped back.

He dropped the dagger, clutched his arm, and looked up at the triplets.

Their hands were linked to form a stalwart chain of defiance. Three identical sets of ebony eyes bore into him with an intensity that unnerved him. He was forced to look away, to avoid the hatred that hurtled at him like a thousand daggers—and the intimidating might they had inherited from Manfred himself.

He again became aware of the foreign feeling that made his heart pound rapidly and his legs feel like liquid.

Fear.

It came upon him swiftly—the realization that he, Manfred, was afraid . . .

Afraid of mere children.

But they were *his* children.

And together, they represented a force that could never be crushed.

With that shattering knowledge came the ultimate enemy to a person who has astrally projected himself across a great distance.

Panic.

It descended upon him in a sudden, lethal torrent, and Manfred began to thrash about wildly, helplessly, desperate to save himself.

He howled, a primal sound that beckoned the forces of evil that had always given him sustenance.

For the first time in his life, there was no reply.

Frantic, Manfred clawed for the silver cord that connected his astral self to his physical self, which lay inert, miles away.

And then the horror of his plight struck him in a devastating final blow.

It was already too late.

The cord had been severed.

Back at 41 Meadowview Terrace, Giselle slowly opened her eyes and looked around, dazed.

She saw the familiar floral decorator wallpaper and drapes and knew that she was in her bedroom . . . lying on her bed.

Sun streamed in the window, and the clock on the nightstand announced that it was just past noon.

Noon?

She stretched, yawned, and got up, wondering what she was doing asleep so late in the day.

Halfway to the door she froze, struck by the sudden, terrible memory of what had happened.

Manfred.

He had been here.

It all came back to her in a rush, and she remembered that he had demanded that she tell him where Meg and Candra were . . . where he could find their brother.

He had promised to cast a spell on her, a spell that would guarantee her eternal youth.

All she had to do was tell him where the children were.

Giselle gasped and clapped a hand to her lips.

"Oh, no," she whispered, shaking her head. "Oh, please, no . . ."

In a panic, she rushed out into the hall and down the stairs, running blindly, wanting only to escape the chilling reality of what she had done.

How could you have sacrificed your own children? Oh, God, you're no better than he is . . .

And then, at the bottom of the stairs, on the floor of the foyer, she saw him.

Manfred.

He lay still, on his back, his black coat spread around him on the polished hardwood floor.

Summoning every ounce of courage she possessed, Giselle took a hesitant step toward him.

And then another.

And then, cautiously, she bent over him.

His face looked stiff, as though it had been carved of wax. His eyes were open and unblinking. She looked into those cold black depths, searching for a glimmer of the evil that had always been rooted there.

But she saw only emptiness, and realized that this wasn't Manfred. Not anymore.

It was only a shell.

He was gone.

Relief coursed over her in a great wave, only to be followed by despair.

Her children . . .

Where were her children?

What have you done?

Giselle straightened and spun around in a near panic.

And as she did, she caught sight of a movement across the room.

She gasped, then saw that it was her own reflection in the enormous mirror that hung opposite the front door.

Slowly, her breath suspended in dread, Giselle moved toward it.

She squeezed her eyes closed as she arrived in front of it, terrified of what she would see.

Then she forced herself to open them, prepared to confront her own face—and her own unspeakable sin.

The first thing Giselle saw was the anxiety that pooled in her light green eyes.

And then she saw the wrinkles—the network of fine lines that traveled over her face.

I'm middle aged, she realized, and the knowledge brought the most overwhelming flood of joy she had ever experienced.

With it came the deep-seated certainty that her children were safe. Somehow, she knew they were all right: Meg, and Candra, and the son she had yet to meet. She hadn't betrayed them to Manfred.

And now, as she turned back to his body, she remembered what had happened.

She had wavered on the verge of accepting his dazzling offer to restore her youth and beauty, tantalized at the prospect of the most miraculous gift she could imagine . . .

Or was it?

Slowly, the memory of another gift . . . a far greater miracle . . . had stolen into her heart and her mind.

She had been carried back to that long-ago day in Jamaica, to the moment when she had cradled her new-born child in her arms.

Now she had no idea which one it had been: Meg, or Candra, or perhaps even her son.

But Giselle remembered the words she had whis-pered to her baby. "I'm your mommy, and I'll always be there for you. Always."

It had been a promise . . .

A promise she would never break.

"No," she had told Manfred, lifting her chin in defi-ance, fortified by a sudden sense of love and responsibility, understanding for the first time what it meant to be a parent. "I won't betray my children."

Shock and rage had filled his black eyes. "You'll be sorry," he had spat out at her.

And then he had raised his arms and begun to chant. As he uttered a chain of commands, Giselle had been engulfed by a shadowy tide that bore her away into silent, smothering darkness.

The spell he had cast must have been broken when he died, she realized now.

But what had happened to him?

Again she stepped over to his body. This time, she saw something clutched in his fingers. Bending, she re-trieved it and saw that it was a scrap of paper. On it was jotted the information about where Meg and Candra had gone. They must have dropped it on their way out the door.

And Manfred obviously had found it.

Giselle felt a twinge of fear and uncertainty . . . just as the phone rang, piercing the stillness.

Hurrying into the next room, she snatched up the receiver. "Hello?" she asked, her heart pounding in sudden apprehension.

"Mom?"

"Oh, Meg . . ." Giselle's voice was so choked with emotion that she could barely speak. "Are you all right?"

"I'm fine," her daughter said breathlessly. "We all are. And Mom, we're on our way home . . . all three of us. Everything's okay now."

Yes, Giselle thought as she hung up the phone and wiped away the tears of joy that trickled down her cheeks. *Everything really is okay . . . at last.*

More Thrilling Suspense From
Wendy Corsi Staub